Book Four

By Evangeline Parsons Yazzie

Designed by Corey Begay

ISBN 978-1-893354-32-6
First Edition, Second Printing
Printed in the United States of America

Salina Bookshelf, Inc.
Flagstaff, Arizona 86001
www.salinabookshelf.com
www.facebook.com/salinabookshelf

Dedication

First and foremost, to my Lord and Savior Christ Jesus through Whom all things are possible. At a time when I needed strength, the Lord reminded me of my father's and my maternal grandmother's stories and guided me through the writing process to complete these novels.

To my beautiful son Daniel Parsons, son, brother, uncle, brother-in-law, friend, and most talented chef. Your gentleness reflected that of your maternal grandfather.

To my mother and my father, the late Etta and Rev. Bruce Yazzie, Sr. who told me my first stories and taught me the value of storytelling.

To my four wonderful children, Daniel, Melody, Naomi, and Bruce who were my first audience. They heard my stories and listened anxiously. In listening to my stories, my children kept the stories alive within me. I love sharing my stories with my precious granddaughter April. Her beautiful presence and thoughts of her inspire me in my writing. The thoughts of my children and my granddaughter present me with a sense of urgency to continue writing about the history of our Navajo people.

To my maternal grandmother, the one who safely deposited the stories of the Navajo Long Walk in my mind and in my heart by saying, "Kwe'é shíighahgi dah nídah, shitsóí yázhí, nił hashne'. Hwééldi... Sit right here next to me, my little granddaughter, let me tell you a story. At Fort Sumner...

To my precious Naabeehó elders who have proven that oral history is trustworthy, alive, reliable, and true. Many elders reminded me of my father's stories when they said, "Nizhé'é 'éí kót'éego yaa halne' łeh nít'ę́ę́'... Your father used to tell it this way...

To Naabeehó women and girls who continue to be the strength of the matriarchal society of the Navajo people.

Map

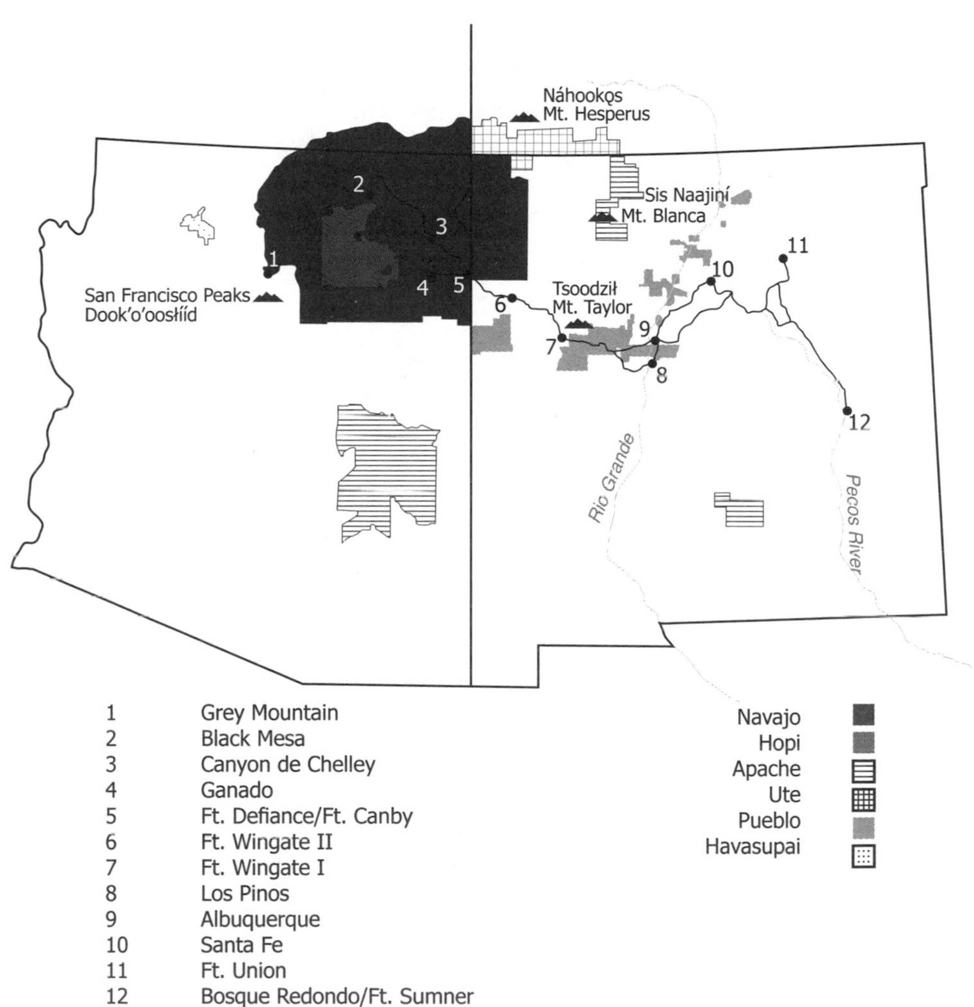
Náhookǫs
Mt. Hesperus
Sis Naajiní
Mt. Blanca
San Francisco Peaks
Dook'o'oosłííd
Tsoodził
Mt. Taylor
Rio Grande
Pecos River
1
2
3
4
5
6
7
8
9
10
11
12
1 Grey Mountain
2 Black Mesa
3 Canyon de Chelley
4 Ganado
5 Ft. Defiance/Ft. Canby
6 Ft. Wingate II
7 Ft. Wingate I
8 Los Pinos
9 Albuquerque
10 Santa Fe
11 Ft. Union
12 Bosque Redondo/Ft. Sumner
Navajo
Hopi
Apache
Ute
Pueblo
Havasupai

Table of Contents

Chapter One

Hopes, Dreams, and Concerns...

Hashké Yił Naabaah and his people were glad the late winter weather was becoming slightly warmer. The people got up earlier in the morning because the sun was rising earlier and they stayed up later in the evening to take advantage of the daylight. The elder Naabeehó people encouraged their people to get up before sunrise and to remain busy throughout the day.

"T'áá nihikéyah bikáa'gi 'ádeiit'į́ nahalingo nidaołnish. T'áadoo ni'jį' dah daohtłishí. Bee nídanohjahí hasht'e daohłe'. T'áadoo t'óó ni'góó naazkaadí. Daohhxáád. Ch'osh da ła' bíijée'go 'át'ée łeh. Yéego daohhxáád. Bíni'dii biih nídaach'iih. Ałhą́ąh daohłe'. Nídanohjahgóó nidahohshooh. Hosh béédahadzidii łą́ągo dahólǫ́. Danihimá bíká'anídaohjah." *Work as if we were still on our own land. Don't keep wanting to lie back down. Fix your bedding. Shake them out. Bugs may have run into your bedding. Shake them hard. Air them out. Fold them. Sweep the places where you sleep. There are many dangerous thorns (mesquite thorns) and cactus needles. Help your mothers.* The people were intently listening to the elders when soldiers arrived on horseback. Following on their horses were three interpreters. In one swift movement, the girls and the young women disappeared under their rug blankets to hide.

"There is going to be a large meeting at the parade grounds. We have our orders to count all the Navajo prisoners. Bring everyone there!" a stout soldier yelled. In response to the interpreter's message, the people slowly gathered in one area. Looking from one person to another the stout soldier shouted,

"Where are the young women? There have to be more. Bring them all out!" the stout soldier demanded. Once the interpreter relayed the message, Dzáníbaa', Dédii and Tsék'iz Naazbaa' slowly got up from their hiding place and stood with their people.

"Where are the children? Bring out the children too. Quickly! Bring the children!" The impatience in the voice of the stout soldier brought the children out, one by one. Dzáníbaa''s son slowly stepped forward and stood by his mother. The soldiers used a thick pencil to point at the people as they counted each one.

To protect her people, Nínááníbaa' told the women,

"Nihada'áłchíní bich'ą́ąh nisoozį́." *Stand in front of your children.* She was nervous about the soldier counting her people. Many of her people had died each time the people had been counted. She knew her husband could not bear losing any more of his people.

The soldiers reported to the stout soldier that a young boy with light colored skin was not among the children counted.

"He would be around three or four years old," was the answer of the stout soldier.

"Lt. Col. Folton will be disappointed. We have our orders," the stout soldier said as he shook his head, turned and left with the soldiers as quickly as they had arrived.

****

A week later, an Apache interpreter arrived at their camp and announced to Hashké Yił Naabaah and his people they were to gather at the parade grounds on a specified day. He further announced that all men as well as women and children and old people were to appear at the parade grounds.

"Nihizáanii dóó niha'áłchíní bił nihí'dóoltah, jiní." *You along with your wives and children will be counted, it is said,* he reported. The Naabeehó people were immediately filled with fear. The women refused to go to the parade grounds. The Naabeehó men became afraid for their wives and their children because the soldiers were always angry with the people. With one voice they expressed their fear.

"Hatxíhíláane'ęę'! Aak'eedą́ą́' t'áá'ániiltso danihídéelta', éí bikéédóó kodi nániikaigo nihidine'é díkwííshį́į́ be'iina' baa náádadiilyá. Hatxíhíláane'ęę'. Dooda, nihí 'éí dooda. 'Ákó náánodoo'nííł, dooda!" *So scary. Last fall after we were all counted, we came back here and many of our people had their lives taken from them. Scary. No, we will not go. The same thing will happen again, no.*

It took a lot of convincing on the part of the leaders but on the specified day, Hashké Yił Naabaah and his family and his people began their walk to the parade grounds. The men were used to walking to the parade grounds once or twice a week but the women and children were not. The walk to the parade grounds was a two-day walk for the men. Hashké Yił Naabaah worried about the women, children and elders walking so far and so quickly. Nínáánibaa' complained to her husband but he said they had to comply with the orders of their enemy.

Nínáánibaa' was comforted by the swift flowing waters of the Pecos River as the soldiers and the Naabeehó men led them along the river. She murmured words of gratitude to the river for bringing her children back to her each time their path led away from the river and then rejoined the river once again. Nínáánibaa' and her daughters could not believe the number of Naabeehó people who lived along the path. They could hear cries of hunger and pain from the children and cries of pain and loneliness from the elders who all tried in vain to find comfort but could not find it among their people because everyone was miserable, lonely and in pain.

The row of picket forts along their path brought fear and anger to the women and children as they hurried along. They were followed by soldiers who were assigned to the picket forts. The soldiers ahead of the procession let the horses set the pace for the people

As a distraction, Nínáánibaa' listened to her daughters describe the place where Dzáníbaa' and her husband lived among the Naashgálí dine'é *Mescalero Apache people*. The two sisters kept their eyes on the landscape across the river. They were surprised to find Naabeehó settlements on the lands the Naashgálí dine'é *Mescalero Apache people* had cleared for their own settlements. Still hopeful, Dzáníbaa' kept looking for the many wickiups *brush shelters* that hugged the ground when she lived among the Naashgálí dine'é. She was disappointed to find the wickiups absent. The landscape did not look the same without them. Nínááníbaa' interrupted her thoughts when she asked,

"Naabeehó dine'é tsé'naají 'adabidi'neeskaad lá. Háádę́ę́' da shą' ch'ídabidi'neeskaad? Hait'éego da shą' atsį' díílדzidígií bich'į' ch'ídadit'ááh?" *Some Navajo people have been chased to the area across the river. I wonder from what place (on Navajo lands) they were chased out of? How are they given their ration of rotten meat?* Dzáníbaa' explained to their mother about the long logs the soldiers placed across the river to create a log bridge over which the young Naashgálí men walked on their way to construct the buildings of the fort. In unison, the three women searched the area for long logs. They saw some logs on the ground near a picket fort and wondered if those were the logs that were placed across the river to carry rations to the Naabeehó people who lived on the opposite side of the river.

Dzáníbaa' told her mother of the sweet water that ran into the river from the eastern side of the river, saying,

"Díí tó nílínígíí tsé'naadęę' tó biih nílínígíí 'ayóo łikango 'át'é." *The water that runs into the river from the other side is actually really sweet.*

"T'áá nihí nihikéyahdi, Dziłíjiindi, tó hadaazlínígíí shįį́gi 'áhálniih, ya'?" *It probably tastes like the water that runs out of the springs that are upon our own lands at Black Mesa, right?* Nínáánîbaa' asked. Dédii added,

"Kodęę'go tó biih nílínígíí ts'ídá doo łikan da. 'Ayóo dích'íí'." *The water that runs into the river from this side does not taste good at all. It is very bitter.*

"Díí tóhígíí ts'ídá doo shił łikan da. Tó łikanígíí ts'ídá k'adni' ła' yishdlą́," *I do not like this water at all. I am so anxious to drink some water that is sweet,* answered Nínáánîbaa'. Walking along the river and talking and greeting the water made the ground move faster under their feet. Fear rose in the hearts of the people who arrived at the fort.

Nínáánîbaa' saw many Naabeehó people walking to the parade grounds with gray colored blankets wrapped around them. Hashké Yił Naabaah winced at seeing other Naabeehó leaders walking to the meeting wearing the blankets. "They need to be wearing their own rug blankets, not the blanket of the enemy. If we wear our enemy's blanket, it will confuse our thoughts," he reasoned. He complained to Nínáánîbaa' and his sons regarding his disappointment in the actions of other leaders.

After they left Nínáánîbaa' and her daughters and their children near the parade grounds, it was with great apprehension that Hashké Yił Naabaah and his sons and Kiizhóní turned toward the issue house. Hashké Yił Naabaah kept looking back to see if his Nínáánībaa' and their daughters and grandchildren were safe. Hashké Yił Naabaah and his sons patiently waited in line for their rations. The Naabeehó men were worried for their families.

The women were ordered to stand and wait in the large parade grounds. As they slowly walked, the women felt unprotected and vulnerable because their enemies with white skin were so near and watched them intently with greedy eyes. Nínáánībaa' looked back to search for the maroon fabric attached to her husband's leadership stick. Just the sight of the maroon fabric softly blowing in the breeze brought her strength.

As soon as Hashké Yił Naabaah and his sons and Kiizhóní received their ration of rancid bacon, buggy flour, and hard coffee beans, they hurried to the parade grounds where many Naabeehó people had already gathered.

Making their way through the crowds of people, they witnessed young Naabeehó women being harassed by dirty soldiers. A soldier was standing between Nínáánībaa' and her daughters and her grandchildren.

An interpreter was rushed toward the tall gray-haired one who had entered the parade grounds. Hashké Yił Naabaah and his sons followed the interpreter, quickly greeting the Naabeehó leaders who held out their hands to greet Hashké Yił Naabaah and his sons.

According to the interpreter, the tall gray-haired one was demanding the Navajo leaders identify themselves.

When Hashké Yił Naabaah held up his leadership stick with its maroon piece of fabric fluttering in the wind, the tall gray-haired one wanted to know why the men who stood with him were not covered with the gray blankets they were given. Hashké Yił Naabaah let the interpreter know that at leadership meetings, the leaders were to have the appearance of a Naabeehó leader and that their dress was not to resemble that of the enemy. Once the message was relayed to the tall gray-haired one in English, a tall skinny soldier yelled at the interpreter saying,

"These ungrateful savages!" The interpreter shook his head and told Hashké Yił Naabaah the tall skinny soldier was crazy. The people watched the tall gray-haired one lean heavily on his cane to walk toward the perimeter of the parade grounds. Every once in a while, he hobbled onto a short tree stump and looked among the Naabeehó people as if he was looking for a certain person.

"We have to invite another group of Navajo leaders and their people to the parade grounds tomorrow. I know the leaders are not bringing all the people for whom they are responsible. I thought the blankets would bring them in, but they are not all wearing the blankets." The tall gray-haired one became weary looking for his beautiful Sunflower but he kept the reason for his search to himself. He was searching for Dédii, Hashké Yił Naabaah's daughter, the woman he fell in love with and married at Fort Canby (Fort Defiance).

"I will not give up until I find my beautiful Sunflower and the young Navajo boy!" he whispered gruffly.

Turning to see if anyone was near, the tall gray-haired one lowered his head and quietly said,

"Where are you, my beautiful Sunflower? Your memory kept me alive in the south when I fought in the Civil War, a devastating war. I was determined to return to you because of your love. Your love kept me alive. I can't stand seeing you with a little boy whose father is one of our soldiers. I wanted you to have *my* baby, not someone else's! I rescued you! You are my wife! You belong to me! I didn't rescue you so another man could have you! My darling, come back to me. I know you are here. I will not stop looking for you until I find you. I will have to figure out what to do with your son. I do not want to raise another man's son. He is not a part of me or my plan for us."

Discouraged, the tall gray-haired one entered a building. He repositioned the patch over his eye, shook his injured leg, straightened his back and walked to the window and squinted as he searched the faces of the many young Naabeehó women who were walking by to gather at the parade grounds. It was no use, he could not see clearly. Once again, he repositioned the patch over his eye and squinted to look for his Sunflower. He cussed, and in whispers he said,

"My beautiful Sunflower, where are you? I will bring all the Navajo groups here to the parade grounds under the guise of counting your people in my attempts to find you. If I can get back here to the west under very difficult circumstances, I can find you. I saw you once before but the young boy you held in your arms distracted me. I wanted to push him away and take you in my arms and hold you, blisters and all on your face."

Still peering into each face, he swallowed a sob before continuing his thoughts,

"Next week, the soldiers will be kept extremely busy ordering different groups of leaders to bring their people to the parade grounds for the purpose of counting them. To make sure all the people are counted, I will command soldiers who were assigned to the picket forts to accompany each group to the parade grounds," the tall gray-haired one thought as he set plans forward to find his beautiful Sunflower.

"She has to be here!" he said, shaking his fist. Realizing he was not alone, he turned to his assistant and said,

"We have our orders to give the Washington delegation the number of Navajo people held here at Fort Sumner. When you bring in the men, bring all the women and children too. We will perform our duty. Make sure the interpreters are available when each group comes in. We cannot neglect our duty," he snapped.

Dédii's fear was alleviated slightly in seeing her father and Kiizhóní reappear. She had been especially fearful of the tall gray-haired one seeing her. She agonized over the fact that she had married an enemy, especially one who was responsible for her people's torture and suffering. The women held their breath when they saw the tall gray-haired one exit one of the large stone buildings.

He used his cane to steady himself as he walked down some steps. The women who were under Hashké Yił Naabaah's leadership gathered around Dédii to protect her and her little one from the angry soldiers and the tall gray-haired soldier. They had seen the older one searching for someone.

Nínáánísbaa' was so proud of the women. She vowed to ask her oldest son to obtain some fresh mutton for the women who protected her family. She looked for her husband and saw him standing straight and tall as he held his leadership stick with the maroon material attached to it. She whispered,

"Shinaat'áanii. Doo lá dó' naadzólníi da. Nizhónígo nihá nahó'áago kǫ́ǫ́ hoolzhish." *My leader, you are so handsome. You have been a good leader for us.*

The women whispered to one another, encouraging one another to protect their leader's daughter and her little one who was born for the white enemy. Hearing the whispers, Naabeehó 'Ashkii *Navajo Boy,* Dédii's son whom she adopted at Fort Canby, pushed through the crowd of women and children unnoticed and stood at the front of the crowd and stared at the tall gray-haired soldier. With admiration in his eyes he hoarsely whispered,

"Folton! Folton!" A soldier who was standing nearby heard the young boy whispering Lt. Col. Folton's name and bolted forward, grabbing the young boy by one arm then yanked him away from the crowd of women. In loud voices, the Naabeehó women yelled at the young boy, telling him to get away from the mean soldier. Instead, the young boy yelled out,

"Folton! Folton, help! Folton, help!" The tall gray-haired officer turned toward the voice of the young boy calling him. The mean soldier shoved the young boy toward the building and yelled,

"Sir, here is the dirty savage calling your name in a disrespectful manner! What do you want me to do with him? We need a young boy to tend to the horses. Will he do?"

"Bring him to me," the tall gray-haired one ordered. The mean soldier yanked the young Naabeehó 'Ashkii *Navajo Boy* further away from the women and toward the officer who stood on the steps. Naabeehó 'Ashkii yelled back,

"Shimá, kodi! Ha'át'ííshą' bidishní?" *My mother! What shall I tell him?* Horrified and embarrassed, Dédii watched the tall gray-haired one take her son by the shoulders. Using the young boy's shoulders as support, the tall gray-haired one hobbled back up the steps and led her son into the building as the women scolded the young boy, demanding that he escape from the gray-haired man.

"Doo lá dó' dooda da!" *What a horrible thing to have happened!* Nínáánísbaa' lamented. Dédii spoke up quietly to alleviate her mother's fear, saying,

"Shimá, she'awéé' ei hastiin yáshchíín." *My mother, my baby is born for that man.* Nínáánísbaa' spun around to face her daughter and demanded in a whisper,

"Da' ei shaadaaní nilį?" *You mean that one is my son-in-law?* Not waiting for an answer, she continued, "Yáadish óolyé, shiyázhí. Shąhanii t'ah ániid naagháhígíí shaadaaní nilįį lá ni!" *What a thing to say, my little one. I thought a younger man was my son-in-law!*

"T'ahdoo hazhó'ó bił ná'ahiistséhí k'ad daats'í dįį' náhááh, 'áyaaní da shiyáázh táá' bináháai. Dííghaaí dįį' binídoohah," *It has been four years since I last visited with him. That is evident because my son is three years old. This coming winter he will turn four,* Dédii explained.

"Yáa, shiyázhí. Haashą' jiidzaago nazh'niłhod? Bináá' dó' t'óó bik'é'ástxi'. Bináá' daats'í díínii'go t'óó bik'é'ástxi'. Hanáák'is daats'í. Háida daats'í hanáá' hayíí'ą?" *What a thing, my little one. What happened to cause him to limp? He also has a patch over his eye. Maybe his eye has been hurting and that is why he has a patch over his eye? Maybe he only has one seeing eye? Maybe someone took out his eye?*

Dédii remained thoughtful before she answered her mother. She thought about the time when she and the tall gray-haired one had become acquainted with one another. At the time she had never thought to question him as to the reason he limped. She thought back to the time two years ago when she saw him again at the parade grounds, when the mean Naabeehó woman tried to take her son away from her once the woman realized her son was born for a member of the enemy with white skin. At the time, Dédii noticed his limp was even more pronounced and she had to admit she was shocked to see he had a patch over his eye. She had not noticed his left arm was paralyzed until her son, Naabeehó 'Ashkii told her Folton had to reach over with his right hand and move his left arm into place.

A little piece of Dédii's heart felt sorry for the tall gray-haired one but the rest of her heart could not overlook the fact that he left her nearly four years ago without a word, without telling her where he was going. Further, he left her with a child for whom she was grateful to the tall gray-haired man. Her child was a testament of her love for the tall gray-haired one and the love he once had for her. She reached down and patted the top of her son's head and whispered,

"Shiyázhí." *My little one.* She felt her son lean into her touch.

Thinking about the man she loved years before brought great sadness to her heart. She wanted him to communicate to her the reason he abandoned her and left her to fend for herself. If it was not for her younger brother, she and her little one would have not survived being held prisoner at Fort Canby, neither would they have survived the severity of the many days of walking to this place of great sadness.

Dédii worried the tall gray-haired one would seek her out. She did not want to speak with him in the presence of her people. Sensing her apprehension, the women stepped closer to surround her and her family. Dzáníbaa' stared at Dédii and snickered at the appearance of her face. To distract her sister, Dzáníbaa' whispered to Dédii,

"T'óó naa'ih." *You are ugly.* Dédii snickered and answered,

"Ni dó', t'óó naa'ih," *You too, you are ugly,* to which they giggled while holding their little ones tightly.

Their mother frowned at them, bringing her daughters' giggles to a stop. After her sister's silly comment, Dédii was confident the tall gray-haired one would not recognize her with mud and crushed leaves plastered on her face.

Their fears were lessened a bit when the interpreter announced the adult Naabeehó men and women would be given gray blankets and a round disk-like container of water. Further, the women would be given a few yards of calico fabric along with a little sewing kit. The interpreter told the women they were to use the fabric and the sewing kit to make clothes for themselves and their children. Without receiving these items, Hashké Yił Naabaah and his people were hurried from the parade grounds and ordered to walk by the Commissary to pick up a pair of shoes for themselves and their children.

The people wondered what brought about a sense of kindness among the soldiers. Many of their Naabeehó people had been without shoes for nearly four years. They were grateful for the shoes knowing the elders and children had been especially susceptible to the devastation of gangrene when their feet became frostbitten from the cold. Leaders lamented they had no pinon tree pitch or herbs with which to treat the wounds of their people.

Nínáánínbaa' heard her people ask,

"Ha'át'íísha̜' biniinaa k'ad índa ké nihá shódajoost'e'? Ałk'idą́ą́' yee' nihinaat'áanii ch'ééh ké nihá yókeedgo nahashzhiizh. Wónáasii' t'áá bí nihikélchí bitł'áahgi nidoolkałígíí nihá nishóyoołt'eehgo hoolzhish."

Why are they just now providing shoes for us? A long time ago our leaders tried asking for shoes to no avail, instead our leaders made soles for our moccasins. The leaders braided yucca leaves to place in the moccasins or tied the braided leaves to the soles of the people's feet to serve as shoes.

First, the men and boys were given work boots then ordered back to the parade grounds. The women and girls were given high-heeled boots, boots that were foreign to them. The boots given to the women and girls were very narrow and came to a sharp point at the toe. In their attempts to hurry the people along, the soldiers guessed at the size of shoe each Naabeehó person wore. The soldiers demanded for the people to be happy and contented with the pair of shoes he or she was given.

Anxiously Dédii looked toward the group of Naabeehó men who were kept in an enclosed area and who were under the watchful eye of the soldiers on horseback. Each soldier had his rifle drawn and pointed toward the Naabeehó men. She was grateful her father was not aware her son had been taken into a building and had not been released by the tall gray-haired one. Her brothers and Kiizhóní were standing near her father.

Her eye caught a glimpse of Kiizhóní. Her mind felt a subtle lightness as she watched him talking to her brothers. His shoulders were wide and strong. His frame was lean, and his hips were narrow, and his legs were long. Kindness was written on his face and on his hands.

Her mind played with the idea of love with Kiizhóní as her heart questioned her loyalty to the tall gray-haired one. Her heart was torn. The tall gray-haired one did not greet his little one when he met him at the parade grounds two years ago. Instead, it was Kiizhóní who greeted her little one and cared for him as if he were his own. He also cared for her adopted sons as if they were his own. He further cared for the old man she called shicheii *my maternal grandfather* as if he was his father.

Dédii shocked herself when she whispered,

"T'óó la' jízhóní. Kiizhóní joolyéego 'ayóo hweełt'é." *He is so beautiful. The name Beautiful Boy matches him.* She looked around and noticed her mother was watching her. Her mother leaned over, pointed her lips at Kiizhóní and whispered,

"Ei shaadaaní nilį́įgo beełt'é. Bił da'ahidiits'a' dóó doo bąąh dah haz'ą́ą da dóó nihe'í'óol'įįł yii' neeyą́. Nihe'anaa'í, shaadaaní nilínígíí, doo bił da'ahidiits'a' da dóó bizaak'ehgo txi'dahwii'níih. Txi'nihiyoołnííh." *It would make more sense if he was my son-in-law. We understand him, he is healthy, and he grew up in our culture. We do not understand my son-in-law who is our enemy and it is according to his word that we are suffering. He is making us suffer.* Dédii responded in a whisper,

"Shimá, kéédahwiit'į́įdi nániikaigo shí dóó shiyázhí bii' tádiit'ázhígíí hazhó'ó bee nił hodeeshnih." *My mother, when we return to our camping area, I will tell you what my little one and I went through.*

"Ts'ídá ha'át'íishį́į́ bii' tádííníyáhígíí, bii' nishoo'ázhígíí, ni dóó niyázhí bił, doo ts'íí'át'éégóó baa shíni'. Éí shá niniih dooleeł, shiyázhí." *I am very sorry for what you endured, what you and your little one endured. I want you to know that, my little one.* Their conversation was forgotten when the door of the large building opened and the young Naabeehó 'Ashkii and Lt. Col. Folton exited the building. Dédii held herself back. She wanted to bolt forward and grab her son and take him back to their camping area.

Still holding onto the young boy's shoulders for strength, the tall gray-haired one slowly walked down the steps. Dédii noticed he winced as he slowly walked down the steps. A soldier followed, carrying his officer's cane. Dédii heard her mother mumble,

"Yíiyá! Hastiin chą́ą́hdógeeh lágo. T'óó la' baa hastxi'. Aláhída léi' bináák'is ałdó'. Haadaaní hólǫ́ǫgóósh t'éí." *Yikes! The man better not fall. He is so fragile. In addition, he can see only out of one eye. What a way to have a son-in-law.*

Watching the tall gray-haired one, Dédii held her breath. She felt compassion for the tall gray-haired one, but when she watched him step off the last step she felt an unfamiliar emotion surface. As much as she tried denying her feelings, she felt the absence of love for the tall gray-haired one. She sadly admitted that her love for him had remained unclaimed for the past four years. During that time, she lovingly nurtured the memory of the last few weeks she spent with him before he abandoned her.

The man she was now watching was not the same man who passionately and gently made love to her. His gentle facial expression that won her over was missing from his face. "Where did he go after he left me? It must have been a terrible place for him to leave his kindness behind," she wondered.

Instead of releasing her son to return to her, the tall gray-haired one guided Naabeehó 'Ashkii to the area where the Naabeehó men were gathered.

Dzáníbaa' interrupted Dédii's thoughts when she asked,

"Hastiin sání shą' niyáázh háágóó yoolóós? Hatxíhíláane'ęę'!" *Where is the old man leading your son? What a terrible happening!* Dédii stood on tiptoe to watch for her son. She held her breath when she saw the tall gray-haired man lead him toward the soldiers who had their rifles aimed at the group of Naabeehó men.

The young Naabeehó 'Ashkii *Navajo Boy* left the side of the tall gray-haired man and ran toward the crowd of Naabehó men. Without hesitation, he ran to his grandfather Hashké Yił Naabaah and led him to face the tall gray-haired man. Two interpreters stood behind the officer ready to relay messages between the two men.

With anxious dreadful thoughts crashing into one another in her mind, Dédii watched her son and her father face the tall gray-haired man. Her father proudly held his leadership stick high in the air. The maroon piece of material fluttered in the brisk wind that blew from the north. She noticed her father's rug blanket did not hide how thin he appeared. Her father was dangerously thin, which was made obvious as he stood before the well-fed interpreter and the tall gray-haired man. Dédii wondered what her father thought of the tall gray-haired man. She wanted to be standing at the side of her father to listen to their conversation. She noticed he listened intently to the interpreter. She was so proud of her father.

Instantly, Dédii felt resentment building up within her for the tall gray-haired one. "How could he allow his little one and the Naabeehó people suffer for the past three and a half years?" she asked herself. She could not remember a time when she ate a full meal, not even when she was held at Fort Canby against her will. She knew her mother was suffering even more because she could not provide for her family by offering a sheep or a goat for her family to butcher, cook, and eat. Her memory teased her mind with the strong scent of mutton cooking over the hot coals. Her nostrils flared at the memory. Soon, saliva laden with the memory of the taste of a tender piece of lamb cooked over the hot coals collected in her mouth. Dédii lifted the tattered end of her rug blanket to wipe her mouth to erase the stubborn memory from her mind. For now, "I will have to get full on my saliva," she thought. Still thinking of a savory strip of mutton she resentfully said,

"T'óó la' nihizhéé' bee nínádaniicha'. Hó 'éiyá t'áá hó dazhnízinjį' nída'jidį́į́h. Yáadilá bíká kwe'é 'ąąhéeshjéé' ádanihijiilaa? Háishą' bee da'neet'į́į'go?" *We get full by swallowing our saliva (because we are thinking of the food that we deem delicious). They eat all they want and at any time they want. Why are they holding us as prisoners here? Who did we steal from?* Dédii felt a sharp pain of anger shoot into her abdomen.

"Hó yee' shimá bidibé bee dazhneez'į́į' dóó shizhé'é bilį́į' bee dazhneez'į́į'. Hó yee' da'ni'įįhii dajílį́. Nihí 'éí dooda. Shiyázhí t'áadoo nidi 'aneez'įį' da, t'áadoo hwee 'aneez'įį' da, 'áko nidi 'atah kwe'é bi'dótą'go t'óó baa hojoobá'ígo 'atah txi'hooníih." *They (the soldiers) are the ones who stole my mother's sheep and my father's horses. My little one did not steal, he did not steal from them, but yet he is being held here and it is sad that he is suffering right alongside the others.* Her thoughts continued to plague her. "My sister and I were kidnapped, and the enemy were not punished the way we are being punished now! Worse yet, the same soldiers who accused my people of stealing were the ones who held me against my will at the fort! The tall gray-haired one held me against my will! He did not try to help me find my mother or my father or my family! He is truly my enemy!" she breathed in anger.

Dédii shook her head to rid her mind of thoughts of the tall gray-haired one, but her heart was cruel in that it reminded her of the last days and nights she spent with him before he abandoned her. Her little one is a testimony of their love. Her anger escalated with her thoughts. "He did not love me!" To rid her mind of her thoughts, she returned her gaze to her thin father who was still talking with the tall gray-haired one. The sight caused her anger to return. Dédii shook her shoulders and stomped her feet on the ground.

Noticing her daughter shaking her shoulders and stomping her feet, Nínááníbaa' asked in a concerned voice,

"Ha'át'íishą' náníiga'?" *What caused you to shudder?*

"Shiyázhí bizhé'é yee baa nitsídiiskosgo, t'óó shánáháchįįh. T'áá 'óolyéego nihik'izhníícháą́'. Tsídii nidi biyázhí t'áá yik'i déez'į́į' łeh. Ei éí doo jída da!" *When I start thinking about my little one's father, I get really mad. There is no question that he abandoned us. Even birds care for their little ones! He is no good!*

Nínááníbaa' felt so much compassion and sympathy for her oldest daughter. She admired her Dédii for being loyal to a member of the enemy who never cared for her. There was no doubt in Nínáánbaa''s mind that Kiizhóní loved her daughter. She knew it was because of her teachings that her daughter was so loyal. She wiped away hot tears that slid down her face.

Nínááníbaa' and Dédii released a sigh of relief when Hashké Yił Naabaah reached out to the young Naabeehó 'Ashkii and pulled him close to him. Soon after, he turned and walked back to rejoin his sons and Kiizhóní.

The women patiently waited for the interpreter to shout the orders of the soldiers, but they were never voiced. The tall gray-haired one looked among the Naabeehó women as he slowly made his way back to the large building. He asked the soldiers to accompany the Navajo prisoners back to their respective camps and return to their station at the picket forts. After giving his orders, he looked among the Naabeehó people and disappeared inside the building.

Chapter Two

The Scent of Rain is in the Air

After much confusion, Hashké Yił Naabaah and his people were ordered to return to their camp. The women began their long walk back to their camp under the warm afternoon sun.

Nínáánííbaa' looked up and noticed thin little clouds scurrying across the sky. After having walked several miles, she noticed the entire sky was covered with thin clouds. Toward the south, she saw thick clouds beginning to pile up on top of one another. She thought back to the night they saw the beautiful sliver of the new moon as it boldly placed itself in the night sky to tell her people the coming month would bring moisture.

"Dah yiitánéedą́ą́' bidee' deez'áa ne'," When *the sliver of the new moon appeared, it's horns were pointing up,* she breathed as she noticed more clouds in the south forming to produce the moisture the moon predicted. When the light from the sun disappeared over the horizon, she hurried her grandchildren along, saying,

"Tsxį́įłgo 'akéé' deiyínółyeed. T'áá deiyíníiltł'éełgo 'i'íí'ą́. Wónáasii' chahóółhéelgo doo hoot'į́į da doo. Nízaadi kéédahwiit'į́. Tsíłkéí dóó ch'ikéí danohłínígíí 'áłchíní yázhí deiyínółjiid. Deiyínółtł'éełgo nida'doh'a', áko tsxį́įłgo nihich'į' nahaldoh doo." *Hurry and run along after us. The sun has set while we are still running along. Soon it will become dark and we will not be able to see anything. We live a long way away. Those of you who are teenage boys and teenage girls, carry the little children on your backs. Sing while you run along, in that way you will cover more ground.*

She looked up into the northeastern sky and saw the faded image of stars faintly flickering in the sky. The southern sky was dark. "The constellations in the south are hidden by thick clouds that would soon multiply and fill the eastern and western skies, then hide the stars flickering in the northern sky," she thought. She sniffed the air to detect the scent of níłtsą *rain*, but the air was heavy with the sense of weariness.

The many flickering fires from the camps of the Naabeehó people and the lights pouring out of the picket forts outlined the path Hashké Yił Naabaah and his people followed. Naabeehó men were asked to walk ahead, beside and behind the women and children as they made a long procession in an eastern direction. The night air was still as the people picked their way through the darkness.

The people heard two distinct sounds. On their right, they heard the echoing cries of despair coming from the mouths of their fellow Naabeehó prisoners. On their left, they heard the soothing sound of the flowing waters of the Pecos River. The men wondered if the usually noisy, rowdy soldiers in the picket forts were asleep.

To drown out the cries of despair and to keep the children from becoming disheartened and fatigued, Hashké Yił Naabaah started singing a song for the children to keep them focused on their walk. When the song ended, another man started singing another song to carry the people along. In between the songs, the men heard their kind leader say,

"T'áadoo nihada'áłchíní daachaaí. Dichin yik'ee t'áá łáhígi 'át'éego nihikéé' deiyílyeed. Deiyínółjiid. Azhą́ shį́į́ 'ayóo dadilwo' dóó dadijáad nidi, chahałheeł bii' kónízáajį' 'adi'doodáłígíí doo yídaneesdin da dóó ła' shį́į́ doo yídaneel'ą́ą da. Baa dahojoobá'íyee'. Kéédahwiit'į́įdi nániikaigo, 'ałk'íniilgizh hasht'e' nidanii'nilęę bá doolt'is. T'óó yisdlįhígo bitaa daashgizhgo nidi yikiin t'áá kóníshgháníjį' da'iidoołhosh." *Don't let your children cry. Although they are hungry, they are maintaining the pace as they follow us. Carry them on your backs. Although they have stamina while running and they can run fast, they are not used to traveling this far on foot in the dark and some are not able to. Have sympathy for them. When we get back to our camp we will cook the jerky we set aside for them. We can cut the jerky into little pieces, so they can have just enough to get a taste then they can at least go to sleep for a little while.*

To encourage the women, Nínááníbaa' said,

"Áłchíní saad bee ha'ahónínígíí bee bich'į'

háádaohdzih. Nihizaad yee 'ak'ídahałta' doo. Nihí dó' saad bee ha'ahónínígíí bee 'ałch'į' háádaohdzih. Saad bee ha'ahónínígíí nídadiits'ííhgo doo ts'íí'át'éégóó bee háá'iidááh. Bí dó' ákódaat'é." *Speak words of encouragement to the children. They will be able to comfort themselves with your words. You too, speak words of encouragement to one another. When we hear words of encouragement, we are greatly uplifted. They are like that too.*

Nínááníbaa' spoke directly to the children saying,

"Tsxíįłgo, sha'áłchíní. Nihikéé' deiyínółyeedgo sin bee nida'doh'a' áko tsíįłgo nihich'į' nahaldoh dooleeł. Háshinee' dó' ádaoht'į, sha'áłchíní." *Hurry, my children. As you run along after us, sing a song, that way you will walk faster. Dear ones, my children.* Nínááníbaa' heard the little ones respond to her words by speeding up their footsteps. Touched with emotion, she wanted to cry. All she had to offer the little children were words of encouragement.

"Háshinee'," *Dear ones,* she breathed as she quickly walked along in the dark.

The light that hugged the horizon in the east provided a faint light for Hashké Yił Naabaah and his people. Near their path they could hear the sound of many Naabeehó people mourning the arrival of another day of suffering. The sound echoed in the faint light of dawn as the people began to stir from their troubled slumber. People who were camped close to the well-worn path peered at Hashké Yił Naabaah's parade of people walking eastward. The gaunt faces and concave abdomens of the young and old Naabeehó people staring at them were evidence of their malnourished bodies. A brisk breeze stirred the stagnant air that hovered around the many camps of the Naabeehó people.

The dew that settled on the heads and shoulders of Hashké Yił Naabaah's people intensified the cold brisk breeze that blew from the south. Thankful for the breeze that stirred the air that was stagnant with the smell of human waste and acrid smoke from small fires, Hashké Yił Naabaah lifted his face to the faint eastern light and breathed in deeply. Behind him he heard his people breathe a deep collective breath. With tears making a path down his thin face, he smiled and said,

"Ahéhee', shiTaa', shidine'é t'ah shił dahóló̜. Yéego txi'dahooníih nidi t'áá̜łáhígi 'át'éego shikéé' adahidíízį́. Shá baa 'áhólyą́." *Thank you, my Spiritual Father, my people are still with me. Although they are enduring great suffering they still faithfully stand behind me. Take care of them for me.*

Speaking to his people who were humming a familiar tune, he said

"Háláane'ę́ę́', shidine'é." *Dear ones, my people.* He knew his promise of cooking and feeding them little pieces of jerky kept his people placing one foot in front of the other. In addition to his promise, he knew the men placed one foot in front of the other as an example for their families. The women placed one foot in front of the other to keep from falling from fatigue and hunger. The children placed one foot in front of the other so as to not fall behind. The words of their elders lured the people onward.

In their haste, the people kept their eyes on the ground to keep themselves and one another from tripping. They had not noticed the stars were hidden by a thick blanket of clouds. Hashké Yił Naabaah broke the silence by shouting,

"Níłtsą́ la' halchin!" *It smells like rain!* The people could not see the thick clouds pregnant with moisture. With hope in their hearts, they lifted their faces and breathed in the scent of níłtsą́.

The white light of dawn stretching it's rays from the eastern horizon illuminated the familiar bend in the river which prompted the men to walk faster in spite of hearing complaints from the women and children. Once the people walked further they saw the familiar sights of their camping area. Before them lay the clean landscape free of human waste. The people were pulled forward by the sight of the welcoming fires maintained by the young Mescalero Apache man for the elders who were too frail or too weak to make the trek to the parade grounds.

The people rushed to their camps and collectively plopped themselves down on the ground to rest. Children softly cried. Women quietly comforted their little ones. The elders who remained at the camp cried tears of relief at seeing the return of their loved ones. The young Mescalero Apache man had several small fires burning to warm the women and children who were damp from their long walk back to the camp from the parade grounds.

Hashké Yił Naabaah and his sons skewered ałk'íniilgizh *jerky* to prepare it for cooking.

"Shaadaaní tsíid nihá 'ahaaniiníziid. Doo hodidoonaał da. Díí tsį́įłgo doot'is." *My son-in-law raked the coals in one place for us. This won't take long. It will cook quickly.* The men gathered around the fire, each one held two skewers loaded with long strips of jerky. The cold brisk wind picked up the scent of meat cooking over the hot coals and carried it into the nostrils of the people who sat nearby. The pesky wind teased the starving people as it carried the scent further into the air.

"Áłchíní 'áłtsé bada'diiltsoł. Baa dahojoobá'í. Ch'ééh hada'oolniih. T'áadoo nidi saad dahółóní nihikéé' nidaastł'áh. Ałk'íniilgizh kónìshéhígo bitaadaas'nii'go nidi yikiin da'iidoołhosh." *Let's feed the children first. They need our sympathy. They are trying to be strong. They did not complain as they ran after us. Even if they are given a small piece of jerky, they will be able to go to sleep on the taste.* Hashké Yił Naabaah turned away from the sight of the children patiently waiting with open hands to receive their little pieces of roasted jerky. He heard his Dédii telling her children,

"Áłtsé t'óó daohts'ǫǫs. Doo halniih da silį́į'jį' índa dadoh'ał." *Just suck on it first. When it does not have a taste anymore then you can chew it.* Hashké Yił Naabaah caught a sob just before it escaped his throat when he witnessed Dédii's youngest adopted son tear his little piece of jerky in half then gave the piece he tore off to his mother. Dédii pretended she tasted the jerky and said,

"Doo lá dó' ayóó 'áhálniih da, shiyázhí. Hazhóó'ígo nits'ǫǫs. Ahéhee' sha'íínííłtsood, shiyázhí." *It is so tasty, my little one. Suck on it slowly. Thank you for sharing your food with me, my little one.* Looking at her children she said,

"Nihicheii dóó nihimá sání 'Ahéhee' niha'nołtsood' dabididohniił, sha'áłchíní. 'Ałk'íniilgizh yee nihaajoozba'. Nihicheii dóó nihimá sání 'ayóó'ánihó'ní." *Tell your maternal grandfather and your maternal grandmother 'Thank you for giving us some food'. They were kind to give you jerky. Your maternal grandfather and your maternal grandmother love you.* Naabeehó 'Ashkii *Navajo Boy* responded for his siblings, saying,

"Aoo', éí nihił béédahózin, shimá. Nihí dó' nihicheii dóó nihimá sání 'ayóó'ádeiiyíníi'ní." *Yes, we know that, my mother. We also love our maternal grandfather and our maternal grandmother.*

"Nizhónígi 'át'éego háínídzíí', shiyázhí. Shí dó' t'áá'ánóht'é 'ayóó'ádanihíínísh'ní, sha'áłchíní." *You spoke well, my little one. I also love all of you, my children.* Kiizhóní stood nearby with the old man whom Dédii adopted as her maternal grandfather. With a big grin on his face, Kiizhóní asked,

"Nihí shą'?" *What about us?* Dédii wrinkled her face and said with a laugh,

"Nihí shį́į́ 'ałdó'." *You probably as well too.* Kiizhóní still wearing a grin on his face quickly responded with the question,

"Nihí dó', ha'át'íí?" *Us too, what?* Dédii acted impatient when she said,

"Yáadilá diníí dó'. T'áadoo ne'ádíláhí! 'Ałk'íniilgizh didííłiił. Baa 'áhólyą́. *What a thing to say. Don't be silly. You might burn the jerky. Be careful.*

"Da' baa 'áháshyą́? *I'm to take care of it?* he asked, smiling.

"Aoo', yáadilá," *Yes,* Dédii responded impatiently.

"Hágoshį́į́. Díí 'ayóo t'áá'áshi'di'nínígi 'ánísht'é." *Alright. I do everything I'm told to do.* With those words, the men started laughing at the flirty banter between Kiizhóní and their kind leader's oldest daughter.

Hashké Yił Naabaah announced the next batch of roasted jerky was for the women. Reluctantly, the women approached the men who were roasting the meat and took a piece. Nínáánībaa' knew the women were thinking of their children whose hunger was not satisfied by the small piece of jerky, but they huddled in a group and slowly ate their piece of roasted meat. The men and Hashké Yił Naabaah and his sons and son-in-law fed themselves last. The few pieces of jerky that were left were given to Nínáánībaa' to distribute to the women who were nursing their little ones. Nínáánībaa' claimed the nursing mothers were feeding two people. No one complained. Miraculously everyone was given a piece of jerky. Hashké Yił Naabaah hugged his Nínáánībaa' and asked her if she was still hungry. She confidently answered,

"Nidashołzhee'go shį́į́ náádada'diilghał. Ahéhee' nihidine'é bik'ijiisíníba'. Atsį' la' nídasiidlįh." *When you go hunting is when we will have meat again. Thank you for the kindness you placed upon our people. We tasted meat once again.* Hashké Yił Naabaah hugged his beautiful Nínáánííbaa' and promised her,

"T'áá nihí nihikéyahdi nániikaigo nihá nideeshzhah. T'áá ni nínízinjį' adíílghał, shiyázhí. Nihitsóóké da'doolghał. Niha'áłchíní 'ałdó' da'doolghał. Áda'azįįdgo haz'ą́ą dooleeł." *When we return to our own land I will hunt for you. You can eat all the meat you want, my little one. Our grandchildren will eat meat. Our children will also eat meat. There will be a feast.* Hashké Yił Naabaah kissed Nínáánííbaa' to comfort her.

When Nínáánííbaa' felt her husband move slightly away from her, she turned toward him and fell against him, burying her face in his chest. She could smell the smoke that saturated his thin shirt. She knew the meat he ordered to have cooked for his people was supposed to have been saved for the next day but in his compassion for his people and the long distance his people walked during the day and throughout the night, he sacrificed the meat to feed his people who did not complain the entire time they walked to the parade grounds and back to their camp. It was his way of thanking his people for the effort they put forth although they were weak, hungry, exhausted, and weary.

She felt her husband hugging her close and felt his tears moisten her cheek as she hugged him back. She sobbed quietly when she heard him hoarsely whisper,

"Shiyázhí, 'ahéhee', sha'áłchíní shá shíníłchį, biniiłt'aa shicheii yázhíké hólǫ. Ninahjį' azhé'é séłįį' dóó 'acheii séłįį'. Éí 'ayóó'át'éego shił nilį. Háshinee', shiyázhí." *My little one, thank you for bearing my children. It is because of you that I have become a father and a maternal grandfather. I am very respectful of that. Dear one, my little one.*

Quickly, Hashké Yił Naabaah tore himself away from his beautiful Nínáánítbaa' and walked into the middle of his people who had crowded together to listen to their leaders. He walked to the far side of the crowd to stand near his elder Peace Leader.

When Hashké Yił Naabaah approached the elder Peace Leader, the first thunder of the spring season was heard. Excitedly the people looked up into the sky at the sound of the thunder. Without hesitation, Hashké Yił Naabaah shook the elder leader's hand and placed his left hand on the old man's shoulder then prayed a prayer of protection for the new leader and for his people. When his voice trailed off into the sound of more thunder, he nodded to the elder Peace Leader who stood straight and tall and stood shoulder to shoulder with the men. Hashké Yił Naabaah retrieved his leadership stick and smoothed the elongated piece of fabric that was attached to it then reverently placed it in the hands of the elder Peace Leader. Turning to his people, he said,

"Shidine'é, ahéhee', nihinaat'áanii nishłįįgo, nihá nahash'áago 'aak'eedą́ą' hahoolzhiizh. Ániid da'di'níigo diists'ą́ą'. K'ad dąąjį' anáhoolzhiizhígíí yaa halne'.
K'ad éí nihahastói kodóó náasjį' nihá naha'áa dooleeł.

Baa 'ádahołyą́ą́ dóó bikéé' nisoozį́. Bá sodadołzin dóó saad bee ha'ahónínígíí bee bich'į' háádaodzih." *My people, thank you, I have been your leader, planning for you since the fall season began. And now the first thunder of the spring season was heard a little bit ago. It tells us that the spring season has come upon us. Now, our elder will be leading us from here on. Take care of him and support him. Pray for him and speak words of encouragement to him.* Turning to the elder leader, Hashké Yił Naabaah said,

"Shinaat'áanii, nizhónígo 'éí nihidine'é bá ninááhó'áa dooleeł." *My leader, you will be effective in leading and planning for our people.*

****

After witnessing the change of leadership from their War Leader to their Peace Leader, the men immediately went to work cutting apart the high-heeled boots which were given to the women and girls.

Dzáníbaa' and Dédii put their feet into their boots and tried walking but kept falling and dropped into a laughing heap which kept their exhausted people laughing for quite some time. The shoes were too narrow, crushed their toes, and the leather was harsh and cut into their tender skin on their feet and ankles. The two sisters found stepping on the soft sand nearly impossible where the heels of their boots sunk into the sand. On the areas where the ground was hard, they had to extend their arms to keep their balance as they walked awkwardly. Dzáníbaa' heard her sister say,

"Hazhóó'ígo," *Slowly,* an amused elder said,

"Háíshą' bąąh nidooh'nah? Ayóó 'íits'a'go la' ninááhidoołtaał. Ei ké bikétal nineez, éí shįį biniinaa ayóó 'íits'a'go ninááhidoołtaał. Nihikélchí bii' soo'eezgo 'éí doo 'íits'a'ígóó ninááhidoołtaał dooleeł." *Who can you sneak up on? When you take steps, it makes a lot of noise. Those shoes have a tall heel, that is probably why it makes a lot of noise when you take steps. When you wear your moccasins, you take steps that cannot be heard.*

Dzáníbaa' told her mother of the shoes she was forced to wear when she was sold to the kind old Mexican man who lived in the beautiful white house. In telling of the shoes she was forced to wear, Dzáníbaa' said,

"Íídą́ą́' doo chohoo'į́įgóó naanáhonoogah ne'.
Áko 'éí kéhígíí bitł'áahgi sitánígíí 'áłt'ą́ą́'íyee' ne'.
Shá bíighah séí bik'i'diidíingo, ayóo bits'áníłdoi łeh ne',
áko bikáá' ninááhidishtaałgo kéhígíí bitł'ááhdę́ę́' ayóo biníkáníłdoi ne'. Éí kéhígíí di'įdígo 'ádaalyaa lá, t'óó niizį́į'." *At that time, I remember it was really hot. Those shoes had been made with a sole that was very thin. When the sun shone on the sand, the sand became really hot and when I stepped on the sand, the heat came through the bottom of the shoes. I thought those shoes were not made to hold up.*

Dédii also told her mother and her sister of the time the soldiers at the small fort (Fort Defiance) forced her to wear boots that looked a lot like the ones given to the Naabeehó men and boys.

"Éí kéhígíí 'ayóo nidaazgo bénáshniih. Íídą́ą́' ayóó 'íits'a'go nináhidishtaał łeh ne'. Bee na'adá ts'ídá doo yá'áshǫ́ǫ da ne'." *I remember those shoes were very heavy. Whenever I took a step they made a lot of noise. It was very difficult to walk in them.*

The Naabeehó men used sharp flat flint stones to slice through the upper parts of the boots which were made of leather. The women and children were asked to step on the soft sand to leave an imprint of their feet in the sand. The soles of the moccasins were cut according to the imprint made by their feet in the soft sand. Additional wide leather strips were sliced off, cut, then shaped and crudely sewn to the soles to create moccasins. The sole and heel of each boot were set aside for fuel to keep small fires lit. For several days the men were kept busy making moccasins for the women and children. For the women and children whose moccasins remained functional, the men created a sole from the leather and crudely sewed it onto the bottom of their old moccasins.

Nínáánábaa' looked at the moccasins her husband created and was surprised at his handiwork although he had limited tools with which to work. She was amazed at how thin he sliced strips of leather which he used to sew the sole of the moccasins to the top portion. Nínáánábaa' smiled when she saw the women and girls wearing their "new" moccasins. She knew they were grateful for their moccasins.

At night the people heard the elders tell their grandchildren to place their moccasins in a safe place.

Hashké Yił Naabaah wondered why after nearly four years the soldiers had given his Naabeehó people shoes for their feet. He was grateful his Nínááníbaa"s and his children's moccasins had held up for nearly four years. His father-in-law was a master craftsman of sturdy comfortable moccasins.

He looked up into the sky and softly said,

"Baadaaní nishłínígií nihá bił honílǫ́ǫ le'. Nihí dó' nihił honílǫ́. T'áá nihí nihikéyah biih nídiikah. Éí baa nánooshkąąh, shiTaa'. Ahéhee', nihaa 'áhólyą́ągo kǫ́ǫ́ hoolzhiish." *Be with my father-in-law. Be with us as well. I plead with You, my Spiritual Father, that we will walk back into our own land. Thank you for taking care of us.* Nínááníbaa' heard her husband's prayer and moved closer to him to let him know she appreciated his thoughtfulness.

"Ayóó'ánííníish'ní, shiyázhí," *I love you, my little one,* she whispered. Her husband giggled and poked his finger through a hole in her tattered rug dress and tickled her.

"Noozhníí' yilzhóólíyee'," *The side of your abdomen is soft,* he whispered as he kissed her ear and breathed softly into her ear,

"Hágo, 'ádíniistsóód. Íłhosh. Háánílyį́įh." *Come here. Let me hold you close. Go to sleep. Get some rest.* At her husband's words, Nínááníbaa' sighed a contented sigh and snuggled even closer into the arms of her beautiful man. She fell asleep to the sound of her husband's sleepy breathing and her people talking softly, or sleeping soundly.

****

An Apache interpreter arrived at Hashké Yił Naabaah's camp followed by a group of soldiers. A tall soldier surveyed the scene before them. He shook his head and asked the interpreter to find out what the Navajos had done with the woolen blankets and yards of fabric that were given to all the Navajo prisoners. Hashké Yił Naabaah told the interpreter his people had never received any woolen blankets except for the thin fabric that was similar to the thin fabric the soldier's shirt was made from. Once again, the tall soldier shook his head. He shouted to his soldiers, telling them to bring the wagon with the woolen blankets.

"We need it now!" he shouted. The elder Peace Leader asked the interpreter,

"Ha'át'íí lá biniinaa binaabaahii yich'į' dilwosh? Shidine'é t'áadoo beeldléí 'aghaa' bee 'ádaalyaaígíí bitaadaas'nii' da. Niha'áłchíní nihitxa' naazhjée'go nídanihiilkááh. Nihee daazdogo nídabiilkááh. Nihí dó' bee dasiidogo nídanihiilkááh. Díí diyogí hooghandę́ę́' bee niikai yę́ę t'ah nihik'i naazhjoolgo bee neiikai." *Why is he yelling at his warriors? My people were never given blankets made of woolen fabric. Our children sleep between us. We keep them warm at night. They also keep us warm throughout the night. These rug blankets that we brought from home are the only ones we have covering us.*

The interpreter turned toward Hashké Yił Naabaah and told him,

Nihí beeldléí t'áadoo nihitaadaas'nii' daígíí bee bił hweeshne' nít'ę́ę́' yiniinaa binaabaahii yich'ahóóshkeed.

Beeldléí yaa halne'ígíí 'éí tsinaabąąs bee ła' nihąąh nidoogééł, ní." *I told him you never received blankets and that was the reason he was yelling at his soldiers. The blankets I was talking about will be brought to you by wagon, he said.* Then the tall soldier ordered his soldiers toward other Navajo camps.

The two leaders knew their people had suffered through three very cold winters. Every day their people found more holes appearing in their rug blankets and rug dresses. The weather and constant use of their rug blankets and dresses caused the wool fibers to become brittle and break.

Hashké Yił Naabaah loved his rug blanket which he wore proudly every day because his beautiful Nínááníbaa' had woven it for him when they still lived at the base of Dziłíjiin *Black Mesa.* He looked at Nínááníbaa''s biil éé' *rug dress* she was wearing. He remembered he had tickled her on several occasions by gently poking his finger through the little holes that had appeared. Looking at her rug dress, he noticed the holes had become much larger and more had appeared, and yet his Nínááníbaa' never complained. She wore her biil éé' proudly.

His thoughts flew back to the time when they were still on their land at the base of Dziłíjiin *Black Mesa.* Nínááníbaa' had woven rug dresses for her daughters in anticipation and in the hope of seeing them again. She also wove for their daughter-in-law and their adopted children a rug dress or a rug blanket. She had woven rug blankets for her sons and a beautiful leadership blanket for him, but his Nínáánibaa' had not woven a beautiful rug dress for herself. Tears welled up in his eyes. He wondered how many Naabeehó women forgot to weave a biil éé' *rug dress* for themselves because they were busy weaving for their daughters and for their sons and their husbands.

****

The Peace Leader and his people intently watched the northwestern horizon when they heard the sound of horses approaching. A wagon pulled by four horses appeared. The people stared at the contents of the wagon. A long wide roll of some kind of thick material was in the bed of the wagon. After the wagon entered their camping area, two soldiers pulled long pieces of thick fabric off of the roll. Without the interpreters, the soldiers tried to order the women to get in line to receive a six-foot long piece of fabric that would serve as a blanket. The men stood close by, watching the women reluctantly form a line to receive their blankets. The women hurriedly snatched their blanket and disappeared behind the men, afraid the soldiers would try to chase them down to hurt them.

Although happy with their new blankets, Nínáánibaa' along with her daughters could not forgo an expert weaver's inspection of the thick gray blankets they were given. The blankets were woven but woven very loosely and the wool that was used was not spun very tightly.

"Díí 'aghaa' náánásdizgo nizhóní doo. Doo 'áłts'óózígo yisdiz da háálá t'áadoo hazhó'ó deisdiz da. Díí beeldléí yistł'ǫǫgi nidi t'áá bita' adahoosdzą́ągo yistł'ǫ́. Deistł'ónígíí daats'í bee 'adzooí bee 'ádaadingo biniinaa," *It would be good if this wool was respun. It was not spun very well and was not spun into tight thin yarns. Even in the weaving, this blanket has been woven where there are big spaces between the yarns. Maybe the weaver did not have weaving combs,* Nínáánîbaa' said. Still, she was very happy she and her daughters and all the women received a blanket. It would help to keep them warm on the cold spring nights. Nínáánîbaa' vowed to unravel the blanket, spin the wool to produce thinner yarns then use the yarns to weave a thicker blanket that would keep them warm. Nínáánîbaa' and her daughters tucked their blankets in the midst of their meager belongings.

****

While resting his chin on Nínáánîbaa''s head, Hashké Yił Naabaah took his mind off of the welfare of his people and allowed his thoughts to roam through memories of his beautiful wife. The scent of yucca was absent from her hair. He felt guilty. He knew she loved washing her hair with the root of the yucca plant. Her hair had lost its sheen long ago and had thinned. Her beautiful tsiiyéél *hair bun* was not thick like he remembered. Pangs of guilt stabbed at his heart when he saw that her hairline above her forehead had thinned so much that it left a small oval-shaped bald spot where her hair no longer grew. He knew it was because of the extreme conditions they were thrust into. The tsiitł'óół *hair tie* with which she tied her hair into a bun was frayed and of a grey color instead of its vibrant white color. Hot tears slid down Hashké Yił Naabaah's face and landed in his beautiful

Nínááníbaa"s hair. She turned toward him and buried her face in her husband's chest.

"Shí 'ádíshníigo biniinaa kodi 'atah ąąhéeshjéé' dasiidlįį́'. Shich'é'éké hadínéeshtaał dishníigo biniinaa kwe'é danihi'dótą'. Doo 'éí t'áá sáhí shi'íínílnii' da. 'Txį', nihiyázhí t'áá 'áłah hadíníitaał,' shidíníniid. Áádóó nihidine'é binaat'áanii nílínígíí biniinaa nihidine'é nihikéé' dah diiná. 'Ayóó'áshi'dó'níí lá nisin łeh. Ayóó'ánihi'dó'níigo 'át'é. Nihidine'é 'ayóó'ádanó'ní. 'Éí baa nitsídiiskosgo 'ayóo na'iiłnáago 'át'é. T'áadoo shąąh níni'í. Ts'ídá t'áadoo shik'i nííníchą́ą' da, nidine'é t'áadoo bik'i nííníchą́ą' da. Honíyóí, shicheii. Háshinee' dó' íinidzaa. Niniiłt'aa kwe'é nihe'awéé' bik'íniit'áázh. Bíhásáahgo biniinaa shijéí k'asídą́ą' yíníił yik'ee niiltłah." *It was because of my words that we have become prisoners here. I wanted to look for my daughters and that is why we are being held here. You didn't allow me to go alone, instead you said to me, 'Come on, let's go look for both of our daughters'. And because you are the leader of our people, our people followed us. I often think I am loved so much. We are dearly loved. Our people love you so much. Whenever I think about that, I become very emotional. Don't feel sorry for me. You never forsook me, you never forsook your people. You are an excellent worker, my maternal grandfather. What a wonderful thing to do. It was because of you, we found our daughters. My heart almost stopped because I missed them so much.*

Hashké Yił Naabaah pulled his beautiful Nínááníbaa' close and wrapped his rug blanket around them and felt his tears leave his eyes in a continuous flow. With much emotion in his voice, he said,

"Saad bee shich'į' háínídzí'ígíí doodagóó bee chánah ánáshiinidlaa. 'Ahéhee', shiyázhí. 'Aoo', ayóó'áni'dó'níigo 'át'é. Ni yee' nihidine'é 'íiyisíí 'ayóó'ádanó'ní. Shí dó' ayóó'áníínísh'níí dóó niha'áłchíní dóó nihitsóóké 'ayóó'ádanó'ní. Niniiłt'aa shitah yá'áhoot'éehgo 'át'é, shiyázhí. Nits'ą́ąjį' dah nídiishdáahgo 'ayóo nídin náshdleeh. Azhą́ shį́į́ yéego txi'hwii'níih nidi 'ałhaa 'áhwiilyą́ągo t'áá nihí nihikéyah bii' náhwiidiiltséél dóó t'áá nihí nihikéyah biih néiikaigo nihighan biih nídii'nééł. Nilį́į́', dibé dóó tł'ízí, nee náähódlǫ́ǫ dooleeł áádóó t'áá nihí niidzinjį' níná'iil'ah doo. 'Átsą́ą' ak'ah łání bik'ésti'go tsíídkáá' ádá néiilt'is doo. 'Átsą́ą' éí bínáádiit'ą́ąh dooleeł áádóó 'ak'ah łání 'éí 'ayóó 'áhálniihgo yiilchozh doo." *You greatly comforted me with the words you spoke to me. Thank you, my little one. Yes, you are loved. You are the one who is loved by our people. I love you too, and our children and our grandchildren love you. It is because of you that I am healthy. Whenever I leave your side, I miss you greatly. Although we are really suffering, if we take care of one another we will be able to see inside our land again. Once we return to our own land we will move back into our own home. You will have your livestock again, you will have your herds of sheep and goats again and we will butcher anytime we want. We will cook ribs with a layer of fat on it over the hot coals. With our teeth we will pull the meat off of the rib and we will chew the delicious fat.*
Nínááníbaa' interrupted him saying,

"Nidá'ák'eh t'óó bik'eh haz'ánée hózhǫ́ nitsaago 'áhodíílíiłii' bii' níná'níłt'į́įh doo. Naadą́ą' łeeyi' shibézhíígíí doolgą́ąłii' neeshjį́zhii bee 'ádoolnííł. Neeshjį́zhiigíí 'atoo' biih náshjihgo neeshjį́zhii yiit'aał dooleeł. Áádóó 'abííníg tóshchíín nihá 'ánéiish'įįhgo tóshchíín yiilts'éeh doo." *You can enlarge the area where you once had your cornfield and reap a bountiful harvest. The corn that is baked in the ground will be dried. I will place the dried corn in a stew and we will chew the stewed corn. And in the early morning, I will make blue corn mush and we will eat the blue corn mush.* Hashké Yił Naabaah pulled Nínááníbaa' even closer and said in a low voice,

"Deesk'aaz náhádleehgo 'éí dah yistin nihá 'ánéinil'įįhgo yiidą́ą dooleeł. Dah yistinígíí taaskáál bik'éshjaa'go 'éí taaskálígíí bąąh yishnaad doo." *When it gets really cold, you will freeze blue corn mush and we will eat it. Baked ground corn will be placed on the frozen blue corn mush and I will lick the baked ground corn off of the frozen blue corn mush.* Before he could say anything else, Nínááníbaa' added,

"Atsį' dóó ts'inígíí 'atoo' bee 'ánéiish'įįhgo t'áá nihí niidzinjį' iilghał dooleeł áádóó ni 'éí ts'inígíí 'awol bii'dę́ę́' hanáníłt'o'go 'ahíłt'ood dooleeł. Áádóó shí 'éiyá bááh dootł'izhí nihá 'ánéiish'įįhgo bihidiitííhgo yiidą́ą doo. Shí 'éí bááh dootł'izhí tł'ízí bibe' sidooígíí bínásh'áahgo bił náshdį́įh doo. Mmmm, ayóó 'áhálniih łeh." *I will make stew with the meat and the bones and we will eat as much meat as we want, and you can suck the marrow out of the bones and eat the marrow. And I will make blue bread from blue corn flour and we will break off pieces of the bread and eat it. I will take the blue corn bread and dip it in hot goats milk and eat it.* Hashké Yił Naabaah chuckled and added,

"Shí 'éí 'atoo'ígíí yishch'al dooleeł. Ayóó 'áhálniihgo yishch'al doo," *I will lap up the soup. I will lap up the delicious soup,* he said as he poked his finger into a hole he found in Nínáánībaa''s dress and tickled her to hear her giggle. Not wanting to abandon their imaginary feast, Nínáánībaa' continued,

"Naayízí łeeh shibézhígíí dóó dibé bitsį' ałk'íniilgizhgo tsíídkáá' sit'éego 'ayóó 'áhálniih łeh. Naayízí dóó 'ałk'íniilgizh tsíídkáá' bááh bee bił ałch'į' át'éego 'ayóó 'áhálniih łeh. Éí doodai' da, naayízí łeeh shibézhígíí t'áá nímazgo yiilkeed dooleeł." *To wrap a whole squash that is cooked in the ground and pieces of mutton jerky in a tortilla that is cooked over the hot coals is so delicious. Or else, we could eat a whole squash that is baked in the ground.*

Hashké Yił Naabaah did not mean to spit in Nínáánībaa''s hair when he said,

"Shizhéé' la' deesdááz." *My saliva just burst forth.* After a short silence, he said,

"Aak'eejį' ahoolzhiizhgo 'éí neeshch'íí' náheedla'ígíí 'e'e'áahgo néiilt'isgo yiilts'il doo 'áádóó yiit'aał doo. T'ahdoo ná'iilwoshjį' ahalzhíishgóó 'éí tsin bijeeh yiit'aał doo." *When it has come to the fall season, we can cook pinon nuts and break the shell and eat them. Before it becomes time for us to go to bed, we will chew the pitch of the pinon tree.* Nínáánībaa' poked her husband in the ribs with her elbow and said chidingly,

"Yáadilá dii'níí dó', t'óó 'ayóo ch'iiyáán baa yéiilti'! Díí yee' doo ts'íí'át'éégóó hodíichįįd léi'gi 'ąąhéeshjéé' daniidlį́įgo 'ádanihi'diilyaa. Shizhéé' bee nániichaad."

What are we saying as we talk about food! We have been placed here as prisoners of war in a place where there is an extreme shortage of food. I have become full on my saliva.

When they had thoroughly discussed their dreams of the feasts they would eat when they arrived in their own land, Hashké Yił Naabaah lifted his head and noticed all of his people were gathered around their elder Peace Leader, listening to him telling stories.

Chapter Three
The Sheep Bring Healing

Nínáánííbaa' woke to the sound of sheep bleating in the distance. Sitting up, she steadied herself by reaching out and placing her hands on the red sandy ground. Afraid it was a dream, she asked herself,

"Háíshą' bidibé 'aadę́ę́' yikah yiits'a'?
Baa neiiyéyeelísh?" *Whose sheep are coming this way? Did I dream it?* She closed her eyes to bring her dream back to her mind. "In my sleep, I heard the sound of many sheep in the distance," she thought. The sound carried Nínáánííbaa' back home to Dziłíjiin *Black Mesa*.

Looking around her she saw her people hugging themselves to keep their tattered rug blankets from being blown off of them by the angry wind gusts that ran in circles, taunting them. Her daughters and her daughter-in-law were cooking long thin strips of mutton jerky on wooden skewers over the hot coals. Her sons and her son-in-law and Kiizhóní were testing their skills with their slingshots shooting at a lone mouse that ran into their camping area. She could hear Hashké Yił Naabaah's voice, but she did not see him anywhere.

To keep herself occupied, Nínááníbaa' looked up into the sky and watched the clouds change shapes as they were chased about by the cold, wild wind gusts of early spring.

"Shash yáázh la' bijaa' deez'á... Gídí yázhí léi' sidá... Dibé neesk'ah léi' hanályįįhgo ni'góó sitį... 'Ásaa' hashtł'ish bee 'ályaaígíí ła' niilts'id..." *A bear with extended ears... A little kitten is sitting... A fat sheep is lying down resting... A pot made of pottery appeared...* Viewing the last shape, Nínááníbaa' grabbed her rug blanket, pulled it close, and hugged her empty stomach even tighter. She thought back to the time when her family had a full meal.

More soldiers were sent to Fort Sumner to live in the newly built picket forts close to Hashké Yił Naabaah's camping area, which was an unfortunate happening for Nínááníbaa''s group of people in that the men who used to provide fresh meat and sweet tasting water for her people were wary of being discovered by the soldiers. Her sons and Kiizhóní had to venture farther out from their camping area to meet the men who had obtained meat and water for their people. They were cooking the last of the mutton that had been cut and made into jerky strips. Nínááníbaa' knew everyone would be given a small piece of meat, just enough to taste because of the size of the meat that was brought to them.

She glanced at her brave little grandsons who were napping near her. Reaching out she patted them on the head and said,

"Háshinee', shitsóí yázhí, nihiniiłt'aa nihikáa'jį' hodooleeł. Háshinee', shinaabaahii yázhí nohłíinii." *Dear ones, my little grandsons, it will be because of you that we will be spared. Dear ones, my little warriors.* Craving warmth, Nínáánibaa' moved closer to her grandsons. Cold, tired and drowsy, Nínáánibaa' toppled to one side near her young grandsons and rested her mind and her body. The closing of her heavy eyelids carried her home to the base of Dziłíjiin *Black Mesa* once again. With the beautiful sounds of home, Nínáánibaa' drifted back into a deep sleep. She was gently nudged awake by her husband. In a sleepy voice she said,

"T'áá shich'į' yáníłti'go ch'éédeesdził." *Talk to me while I wake up.*

"Shiyázhí, ch'éénídzíid. Nihe'anaa'í ła' aadę́ę́' yikah. Dibé ła' deinoołkał. Háágóóshį́į́ deidínéeskaad, sha'shin, hóla. Shíla' yiiłtsóód, nídiidááh." *My little one, wake up. Some of our enemies are coming near. They are herding sheep this way. It is uncertain which direction they are herding the sheep. I don't know. Take a hold of my hand, get up.*

Nínáánibaa' clearly heard the sound of the bleating of sheep again. She sat up without the help of her husband's extended hand. "I am not dreaming!" she thought, as she stood up, then stood on tiptoe to search for the herd of sheep. She had yearned to hear the sound of sheep. She looked around her. The people in their camping area were already up and were shaking out their tattered pieces of bedding.

"Ałk'idą́ą́' yee' ch'ééshidíísił nít'ę́ę́' lá," *You should have awakened me a long time ago,* Nínáánibaa' scolded in an embarrassed tone of voice. "Diné 'ałk'idą́ą́' nídiijée'go t'óó'ayóo doo hodítxééhgóó 'ashhosh. Yáadilá bizhąą'ą́ąd t'éí 'akót'įį́ dó'?" *The people got up a long time ago and here I am, still sleeping. Whose daughter-in-law does that?* Nínáánibaa' said in a self-effacing manner.

"Nizhónígo 'íłhoshgo biniinaa t'áadoo ch'ééninísid da," *You were sleeping so nicely and that is why I did not want to wake you,* her husband answered with a smile. Hashké Yił Naabaah knew how much his wife needed her rest.

Nínáánibaa' had been very worried that the tall gray-haired one knew where their daughter Dédii and their grandson lived. She lived with the constant fear that the tall gray-haired one would come back and kidnap their daughter and her son. Just knowing of his status as a soldier brought fear to her heart. She could not bear to lose either one of her daughters again. She fought to stay alive just so she could see her daughters again, and now that she was reunited with them, she could not live without them.

The worried look and the frown on Nínáánibaa''s face mellowed when her mind returned to the sound of the sheep bleating in the distance.

"Háíshą' bidibégo 'aadę́ę́' yikah yiits'a'. Be'iinéé' t'óó nizhónígo diits'a'. T'áá shiidą́ą'dii doo 'akót'éego dibé 'ádaaníigo diist'įįh da nít'ę́ę́'. Bidi'noolkałísh?" *Whose sheep are coming this way? The sound of their bleating is so beautiful. I have not heard the sound of sheep bleating like that in so long.*

The people under Hashké Yił Naabaah's leadership were standing and looking in the direction of the sound of the sheep. Soon a herd of sheep came into view. Nínááníbaa' stood on tiptoe to see the sheep that were herded by soldiers! Excitement and fear gripped her heart. She could not believe her eyes! She was afraid to blink, afraid that if she blinked, the sheep would disappear. Quickly she counted.

"T'áałá'í, naaki, táá', dį́į́', ashdla', hastą́ą́, tsosts'id, tseebíí, náhást'éí, neeznáá..." *One, two, three, four, five, six, seven, eight, nine, ten...* Twenty-five sheep in all.

"Háágóóshą' dibé deinoołkał?" *Where are they herding the sheep to?* she asked. The question echoed throughout their camp.

Lifting her hand to smooth away stray strands of hair that a cold, gentle breeze lifted out of place, she pointed toward the herd of sheep, as she whispered,

"K'ad dibé tádadigéeshjį' hoolzhish. Dąąjį' hoolzhish." *The time to shear the sheep is approaching. The Spring season is approaching.* Hashké Yił Naabaah placed his arm around his Nínááníbaa' and hugged her close.

"Dibé binahjį' tł'óo'di łahgo 'ánáhoo'níłígíí hazhó'ó 'ałkéé' ninádínóodah. Nihinaagóó daan náhodoodleeł. Hak'az nihik'i hoole'go t'óó nihikáa'gi niiltee'. Dibé hak'az yóó 'adeidínóołchééł. K'ad lá 'índa dibé biniiłt'aa nída'iidiidził nih." *The presence of the sheep will restore the alignment of the seasons again. It will be Spring around us again. The sheep will chase away the cold that has stubbornly settled upon us. Now, we will finally get warm again.*

As if the scene before them was not enough excitement, three wagons, each drawn by two horses appeared next. The wagons were hauling logs. All the logs had been cut the same length. The Naabeehó people held their collective breath.

When the soldiers on horseback and the soldiers driving the wagons came closer, the elder Peace Leader and Hashké Yił Naabaah walked to stand between their people and the soldiers. Wrapped around Hashké Yił Naabaah was a faded rug blanket with several holes. He stood with his back straight. Beside him stood the elder Peace Leader bravely holding his leadership stick with the maroon strip of material attached to it. He raised the stick when the soldiers reached his people's camping area.

A young soldier shouted,

"Sir, there is a man with a maroon flag identifying him as a leader, shall I shoot him?" he said with a laugh. The young soldier's smile disappeared when one of the soldiers who rode on a horse shouted the order for the soldiers to keep on going.

Nínáánábaa' and the Naabeehó people were still very excited, but their excitement turned to disappointment. The soldiers obeyed the orders to ride past the crowd of Naabeehó and to continue herding the sheep toward the eastern direction. The procession of wagons followed in the same direction.

Nínáánábaa' looked around her. Her daughters and her daughter-in-law were not anywhere near her! Neither were her grandsons! She frantically searched for their faces among the crowd whose gaze followed the procession of sheep, horses, and wagons. She saw her sons standing in front of a large bundle. She rushed to her sons to ask them about her daughters and her daughter-in-law. Turning their heads toward the side, her sons pointed with their pursed lips to where her daughters and her two grandsons and her daughter-in-law and her adopted children were hiding under some old rug blankets. When she realized her daughters and her grandchildren were safe, Nínááníbaa' turned toward the east to listen for the bleating of the sheep. Mesmerized by the sound, she stood and stared after the sheep. She wanted so much to rush after the sheep just to hold one close but she had to stay and protect her children.

"Yáadilá! 'Áhodiilzééh!" *(A term of frustration) Stop it!* she said, perturbed at a strong breeze that carried away the sounds of the bleating of the sheep. She closed her eyes real tight so she could hear the sounds but they were gone. She was relieved the sheep led the soldiers eastward, farther away from her family and her people.

Feeling a strong sense of strength flow into her body, Nínááníbaa' lifted her arms and whispered,

"Ahéhee'." *Thank you.* She thought, "I have not been so close to sheep in three years and a few months. I want to be near my own sheep. Although the sheep that passed by were not my sheep, they still strengthened and comforted me." She missed her sheep. She wrapped her arms around herself, imagining she was holding a lamb in her arms. The scent of a newborn lamb drifted into her nostrils and remained there for a few more soft breaths.

"Mmmmm, háshinee', shiłįį'. Shik'i dashiisohdli'. Ahéhee'. Sha'áłchíní danohłį nahalingo nihaa nitséskees łeh nít'ę́ę́'. Háshinee'." *Mmmmm, dear ones, my sheep and goats. You have blessed me. Thank you. I used to think of you as if you were my children. Dear ones.* To end her expression of gratitude, she voiced,

"Mééeeee', mééeeee', mééeeee', mééeeee'..." Tears mingled with her voice as she mimicked the sound the sheep make. She wondered whether her own herd of sheep had survived the past few years. Tears slipped from her eyes at the thought.

Nínáánībaa' shivered when she remembered the day when soldiers forced them to walk over the rise that led into Fort Sumner. She remembered seeing so many of their people suffering from the cold, hunger, and various illnesses. That was the day the soldiers carelessly took her herd of sheep and goats out of her sight. She never saw her sheep and her goats again. She yearned for the taste of Dziłíjiin *Black Mesa* grown mutton cooked over the hot coals. The yearning made her stomach hurt. Nínáánībaa' shook her head to force the memory of fresh mutton from her mind. The thoughts reminded her of just how desperately hungry she was.

She had to admit to herself that they were better off than many Naabeehó who were imprisoned at the fort just like she and her family were. Her oldest son continued to receive little bundles of meat from his friends he used to work with at the Mexican man's ranch. Lately, the meat was venison, antelope meat, or beef. Nínáánībaa' wanted mutton, or better yet, lamb.

Her gaze followed the path the sheep followed,

"Ha'át'ííshą' biniiyé nihich'į' nidahojiyiiłná?" *Why are they making it so difficult for us?* she asked in a demanding tone. One tear... Two tears... Three tears... Pretty soon, a flow of tears ran down her face. As the tears dropped off of her face and onto her hands, Nínáánîbaa' felt the moist paths the tears left as they were cooled by the cold early spring air. Her little grandsons and her young adopted children gathered around her and held her. Her oldest son, Nahat'á Yił Naabaah promised his mother he would let his friends know they needed to bring some fresh lamb for their mother and fresh mutton for their father's people.

Nínáánîbaa' was crying because she wanted to feel the soft wool of the sheep and goats. She wanted to bury her face in the wool and take the deepest breaths her lungs would allow her to take. She wanted to feel the soothing lanolin that would gently lubricate her hands after rubbing the soft wool between her fingers and her hands.

Her daughters and her daughter-in-law were crying right alongside her. They were crying for a different reason. They were worried about their mother, worried she would become very sick again. Her daughters had been told about her illness when she and her people were forced to walk to Fort Sumner in search of her daughters.

Her daughters had to admit they also cried because they were hungry for prairie dog meat. They were getting tired of the potatoes and onions they had been cooking in the hot coals and eating with a thin short strip of jerky for the past few weeks.

Nínáánbaa' and her daughters were startled by the sound of horses' hooves pounding on the sandy reddish ground. They held their breath. They had not heard this many horses coming to their camping area before. The horses and their riders came into view, led by the tall gray-haired one. In a sling that was attached to the horse's bridle was the cane the soldier used to walk steadily.

Nínáánbaa''s heart filled with fear. She knew he would come back! She quickly pulled her daughter Dédii down with her as she sat down on the ground while a little group of Naabeehó women surrounded them. Dédii's young son cried out of fear because his mother's protective arms were crushing him.

The toddler's cries got the attention of the soldiers who slowed their horses and brought them to a stop. The tall gray-haired one looked among the Naabeehó people and recognized Hashké Yił Naabaah. He called for the interpreter who was sent with the soldiers who took the sheep eastward.

"Where are the sheep? They were to herd them to this leader's camp!" the tall gray-haired one yelled.

Nínáánbaa' noticed a skinny soldier who sat on a horse near the back of the procession of soldiers on horseback. The skinny soldier stared at the Naabeehó women who stood in little groups. She watched his eyes dart from one woman's face to another. He smiled a crooked smile that revealed his large crooked teeth and spaces where his teeth were missing. When the skinny soldier noticed he had the attention of a woman, young or old, he smiled his crooked smile then quickly looked away, rolled his eyes back, then looked back and smiled an even wider smile, exposing his large crooked teeth again. The longer the skinny soldier sat on his horse, the more daring he became in his antics. He boldly stared at the women, smiled, rolled his eyes back, glanced back at the women, winked at them, turned his face away and laughed a hoarse sounding laugh. The Naabeehó women became uncomfortable with the skinny soldier's stares and wild glances. The women communicated in whispers, saying,

"Yáadishą' eidí, t'óó baa'ihígi 'áát'įįł." *Disgusting, he is acting awful.* An older woman scolded and told the young women and girls,

"T'áadoo danółʼíní. Tsík'eh hanii 'ájít'é. T'óó nichǫ'ígi 'áát'įįł. Diigis shįį nilį. T'áadoo danółʼíní. Yíiyá!" *Don't look at him. He is not great. His actions are disgusting. He is probably crazy. Scary!* The women threw their tattered rug blankets over the girls and covered themselves as well.

The tall gray-haired one politely stared at the elder Peace Leader in silence while he waited for the interpreter to come and help them communicate with one another. Hashké Yił Naabaah silently stood by his elder leader's side. After an agonizing amount of time passed, the interpreter was brought back to join the soldiers.

"Tell these people they have orders to take care of the small herd of sheep that we bought from some New Mexican ranchers. Tell them the land on the rest of the military reservation has been picked over by their people and there is no vegetation for the sheep to subsist upon so we are bringing the sheep here. This is the far eastern section of the Indian Reservation. Very few Navajos live east of this settlement. Some of the sheep will be having lambs so they will need to care for them. Tell them that. Those are my orders." The tall gray-haired one waited for the interpreter to inform the Navajo people of his orders. Nínááníbaa' listened to the interpreter slowly interpret the message. She could not believe her ears! She was dizzy with happiness!

"Ata' halne'é daats'í t'áá'aaníígóó nihił halne?" *Is the interpreter really telling us the truth?* she asked. Without waiting for an answer, she stood up and asked,

"Dibé shą' háájí 'adeineeskaad?" As if the tall gray-haired one understood her, he demanded in a loud voice,

"Where are the sheep? I told my soldiers to herd them to this camp! I don't see any sheep on the premises? Who did not follow my orders? Where are the wagons? Where are the logs for the sheep corral?" The interpreter told the tall gray-haired one his soldiers took the sheep to the lands in the distance so the Navajos would not eat them. The tall gray-haired one took out a metal spyglass, looked into one end of it, and cursed. He looked around him and ordered four soldiers to bring the sheep back.

"The sheep are to be kept near this leader's settlement! Tell those illiterate idiots to look for the Navajo leader who carries the leader stick with a maroon piece of material attached to it. Don't those idiots know the color of maroon? They were given specific instructions!" he yelled.

While the tall gray-haired one gave additional orders, the skinny soldier returned to his antics, attempting to get the attention of Navajo women and girls. The skinny soldier took off his hat to scratch his head. In doing so, he exposed a bald head and a few dirty orange-colored strands of hair that looked as dry as the straw that was left for the horses. In unison, the Navajo women reacted with disgust, saying,

"We'! We'! We'! Wéée'!" *Yuck! Yuck! Yuck! Yuck!* as they shuddered in disgust. The skinny soldier was delighted he had the attention of the women and girls. He smiled his disgusting crooked smile, then winked at someone and rubbed his bony chest through his woolen coat. He stopped smiling when he noticed the women had turned their backs to the soldiers. The young girls were warned by their mothers never to go outside of the camping area because of dangerous soldiers like the skinny soldier.

"Yíiyá! Bááhádzid! Doo 'áhályą́ą da!" *Scary! He is to be feared! He is crazy!*

Through the interpreter, the elder Peace Leader and Hashké Yił Naabaah learned the tall gray-haired one also wanted to talk about a sheep corral. The interpreter explained that a sheep corral was to be built and that the soldiers were to build the corral. The elder Peace Leader asked if his men could build the corral. He further communicated to the tall gray-haired one how a proper corral was to be built, but the tall gray-haired one was adamant that his soldiers would do a better job since they had all the supplies on hand. The Naabeehó men shook their heads as they listened to the interpreter relay the message to the people. The elder Peace Leader once again asked if his men could build the corral.

"Nihinaanish ádin. Doo nihilák'ee siláhí da. T'áá shǫǫ dibé bighan binideiilnishgo binahjį' ak'ídahwiilta' dooleeł. Dinééh dóó 'ashiiké dibé bighan yinidaalnishgo yaa bił dahózhǫ́ǫ doo. Tsxįįłgo nidaalnish dóó binaanish dahólǫ́ǫgo bił yá'ádaat'ééh dóó yídaneedlį́. T'áadoo hooyání dibé bighan nidoolts'ił. Haa'íyee', naanish nihaa diní'aah." *We do not have any work. There is nothing in our hands. We can keep ourselves busy building the sheep corral. The young men and the boys will be happy to work on the sheep corral. They work fast and they like to work and they enjoy it. The sheep corral will fall into place real fast. Give us the opportunity.* The tall gray-haired one thought for a while, then asked his soldiers to bring the logs back to the tall leader's camp where the corral would be built.

"They want to build their own corral. We will allow them to build it," he announced with authority. A messenger was sent to the soldiers who hauled the logs past Hashké Yił Naabaah's camp. The Naabeehó people watched the messenger leave and watched until he could not be seen any longer.

"Shooh! Łeezh yadiit'i'!" *Look! There is a cloud of dust going up in the air!* Hashké Yił Naabaah's youngest son excitedly reported. In unison, the people turned their heads toward the east and watched in anticipation as the cloud of dust grew.

"Tsin naalbąąsí táa'go 'ałkéé' yijahgo da'íyeeh," *There are three wagons following one another, carrying cargo,* he reported. Soon, the people could hear the sound of wagon wheels turning. The soldiers whistled at their horses to pick up speed and urged their horses forward as the sound of whips landing on the backs of the horses was clearly heard. The logs were hauled back and without another word the confused soldiers threw the logs on the ground and quickly left with their empty wagons.

Throughout the rest of the day, plans for the sheep corral were discussed among the older Naabeehó men and shared with the young men and boys. The corral's opening faced the eastern direction, according to the plans.
The next day, work began on the sheep corral. The young men used flat rocks to dig holes for the logs that made the structural foundation for the corral. The young men and boys closely followed the instructions of the older men. By sundown of the second day, the sheep corral was completed. The elder men walked around the corral to inspect the work of their young warriors. The men pushed and pulled at the logs that sturdily remained in place, then proudly nodded their heads. The elder Peace Leader and Hashké Yił Naabaah turned their heads toward their brave warriors. The Peace Leader said,

"Díí łáą. Díí lá dibé bighan wolyée ni. Nizhónígo la' nidanoo'ą́. T'áá nihí nihikéyah biih néiikaigo, t'áá nihí nihizáanii bidibé bighan bá nidanoo'ą́ągo bídayínóhah. Ahéhee', tsxį́įłgo dóó nizhónígo nidashołnish. Asdzání hwee haleehgo díigi 'át'éego bá nishó'jiyoołt'eeh łeh dóó bá hájít'įį łeh." *This is it. This is called a sheep corral. You set it in place nicely. When we reenter our own land, you will be able to build a sheep corral for your wife. Thank you, you worked well and worked fast. When you are given a wife, it is in this way that you obtain what you need and do what you need to do for her.* The elder Peace Leader and Hashké Yił Naabaah led a procession of elder men who shook hands with the young warriors and complimented them on their work. Nínáánîbaa"s sons and Kiizhóní stood proudly as they humbly accepted the praise of their leader and their elders. Hashké Yił Naabaah was touched and smiled proudly when the elder men shook the hand of the young Mescalero Apache man who smiled a bright wide smile with each handshake.

Hashké Yił Naabaah knew the real test was yet to come. He smiled at the young men whose faces immediately took on worried looks when he said,

"Sáanii hágo dabidohní. 'Íishjáąshįį́ 'éí ha'át'íí daaníi dooleeł. Jó bí 'éí dibé nanilkaad dóó dibé baa 'áháyą́ągi bee bídahólníih." *Tell the women to come. Let's see what they will say. You see, they are the ones who are in charge of herding the sheep and caring for their sheep.*

Nahat'á Yinaabaah raced toward his mother and his wife, and Tł'ée'go Naabaah excitedly raced toward his sisters and pulled them to their feet and led them back to the new sheep corral they helped build. The young men waited with anxious anticipation as their mothers, sisters, aunts, and grandmothers inspected the new sheep corral. The women spoke quietly to one another without showing a hint of how impressed they were of the young men's work. Nínááníbaa' was the first to speak. The men and boys were anxious to know the reaction of the women.

"Dibé shą'?" *Where are the sheep?* Nínááníbaa' asked. She was notified of the agreement between their leaders and the tall gray-haired one. The women snickered as the young men looked around and pointed in different directions. The elder men started laughing, but Nínááníbaa' maintained her questioning stance without smiling.

Careful not to alert the soldiers who watched over them from the picket forts, the young men nonchalantly walked toward the eastern direction in search of the herd of sheep that disappeared in that direction earlier in the week.

By sundown the sheep were herded back to Hashké Yił Naabaah's camp by the young Naabeehó men and boys who found the sheep standing in an open field. Tears made marks on the faces of all the Naabeehó women who watched the sheep enter the sheep corral. Nínááníbaa' listened to her people counting the sheep as each sheep entered their corral.

"T'áálá'í, naaki, t'áá', dį́į́', ashdla', hastą́ą́, tsosts'id, tseebíí, náhást'éí, neeznáá, ła'ts'áadah, naakits'áadah, táá'ts'áadah, dį́į́'ts'áadah, ashdla'áadah, hastą́'áadah, tsosts'idts'áadah, tseebííts'áadah, náhást'éíts'áadah, naadiin, naadiin ła', naadiin naaki, naadiin táá', naadiin dį́į́', naadiin ashdla'." *One, two, three, four, five, six, seven, eight, nine, ten, eleven, twelve, thirteen, fourteen, fifteen, sixteen, seventeen, eighteen, nineteen, twenty,*

twenty-one, twenty-two, twenty-three, twenty-four, twenty-five. When her people spoke the number twenty-five, Nínááníbaa' heard her people take deep, deep breaths. They were breathing in the scent of the sheep. The women were shaking from excitement and the children shook from starvation, where the sight of the sheep multiplied their hunger pangs.

When the sheep settled down in their corral, the young men searched the women's faces, still waiting to know what the women thought of their workmanship. A collective nod and a collective voice said,

"Nizhónígo 'áda'ohłaa. Nizhónígi 'ádanihoohłaa. Dibé nihiná naakai dooleeł biniiyé nídanihiilkáhígi dibé bighan nidanoo'ą́. Nihik'idahojisdli' la'. T'áá 'óolyéego nihik'idahojisdli'." *You did nice work. You have done something wonderful for us. You made a sheep corral near the place where we sleep so the sheep will be near us. We have been blessed. We truly have been blessed.*

Nínááníbaa' spoke and said,

"T'áá'aaníí 'ahéhee'gi 'ádanihoohłaa. Nizhónígo binidashołnish. Dibé bighan ayóó'ánoolningo nidanoo'ą́. Nízaadgóó choo'įį dooleeł. T'áá nihí nihikéyah biih néiikaigo nidi, díí dibé bighan t'ah si'ą́ą dooleeł dóó nízaadgóó nihe'anaa'í chodayooł'įį doo." *We are truly grateful for what you have done for us. You have worked well. You have set a beautiful sheep corral in place. It will be used for a long time. Even when we reenter our own land, this sheep corral will still be standing and our enemies will use it for a long time.*

Two days later, the tall gray-haired one returned with an interpreter. With difficulty and with the help of two young soldiers, the tall gray-haired one got off of his horse and walked slowly toward the sheep corral.

"Ask them who helped them build this corral? We were just here two days ago and brought them the supplies, but we had to wait for the nine-inch nails and ropes that would be used to bind the logs together, but look at this corral! It is perfectly symmetrical! It's surprisingly sturdy! Did these men work on the construction of the buildings at the fort? No matter how hard I shake the logs, they don't give. What did they use to attach the logs together to make each log so perfectly aligned with the one next to it? They may have learned a few things from the local builders. Just look at the handiwork! Ask them who helped them."

The interpreter turned to the elder Peace Leader and Hashké Yił Naabaah and asked resentfully,

"Háísh nihiká'ííjée'go dibé bighan ádaohłaa? ní. Háísh nanihinitingo 'ádaohłaa?" *Who helped you build the sheep corral? Who taught you as you built it?* the interpreter asked. With all eyes on the elder Peace Leader, he said,

"Dinééh danilínígíí dóó 'ashiiké yinidaashnish. Hastói danilínígíí bizaa k'ehgo 'ályaa. Doo 'éiyá nááná ła' da yínanihineeztą́ą' da. Díí t'áá nihí nihikéyah bikáa'gi kót'éego dibé bighan ninádeiit'ááh." *The young men and the boys are the ones who worked on the sheep corral. It was constructed according to the instructions of the men. No one else taught us. We build our sheep corrals just like this on our own land.*

The interpreter turned toward the tall gray-haired one and said,

"No one teach. Just them. Boys and little men." The tall gray-haired one walked around the corral again, whistling at the quality of work.

"Amazing!" was all he could say.

The interpreter turned toward the Naabeehó people and told them they were to care for the sheep and that the animals were not to be butchered for meat.

"Díí dibé baa 'ádahołyą́ą dooleeł, ní. Doo 'éí ná'ah biniiyé da. Wááshindoon bá nida'nołkaad dooleeł. Haashílá dibé ła' nídajił'ah," *You are to care for the sheep. They are not for butchering. You will be herding sheep for the federal government. Don't you dare butcher one of them,* the interpreter said as he drew a line across his neck with his index finger.

The people still could not believe their ears. The sheep were to stay near them. The tall gray-haired one told the interpreter to tell the two leaders twenty-four sheep had been placed in their care. Hashké Yił Naabaah stopped the interpreter by saying,

"Áłtsé. Doo 'ákót'ée da. Dibé naadiin ashdla'go yee' yah adeineeskaad. Naadiin dį́į' éí dooda. Nihá bee bił hólne'." *Wait. That is not right. Twenty-five sheep were herded in. Not twenty-four. Tell him for us.*

The tall gray-haired one and the interpreter discussed the number of sheep. The tall gray-haired one insisted the number of sheep was twenty-four, then told the interpreter his services were needed at the fort and waited for the interpreter to disappear over the shallow hill before he called for the young Naabeehó 'Ashkii *Navajo Boy.*

Naabeehó 'Ashkii stood bravely before the tall gray-haired one. The tall gray-haired one reached out and placed his hands on Naabeehó 'Ashkii's shoulders and looked directly in the face of the young boy and spoke slowly saying,

"Please tell your leader twenty-four sheep were placed in his care." Naabeehó 'Ashkii straightened his shoulders, in spite of having the heavy hands of the tall gray-haired one on his shoulders, he responded, saying,

"No, naadiin ashdla' yee'." *No, it is actually twenty-five.* Seeing the confused expression on the tall gray-haired one's face, the boy held up his hands and counted his fingers in Navajo to demonstrate to the tall gray-haired one that twenty-five sheep had been placed in the sheep corral. The tall gray-haired one sighed loudly and said,

"I am saying twenty-four sheep have been placed in the corral and that is final. No more discussion. Do you understand? Look at me and answer me," he demanded.

"Yes," the young boy said. The tall gray-haired one turned and walked toward his horse and waited for his soldiers to place a step stool near his horse so he could get on the horse. The young Naabeehó 'Ashkii told the elder Peace Leader and Hashké Yił Naabaah what the tall gray-haired one said. The two leaders looked at each other. Hashké Yił Naabaah sighed and said,

"Jó 'ákót'éé lá." *Well, it is that way.* The number of sheep in the corral was never discussed again by the two leaders.

****

Hashké Yił Naabaah noticed the effect the bleating of the sheep had on his people. As he and Nínáánîbaa' settled down for the night, they listened. Something was strange. Smiling, Hashké Yił Naabaah said,

"Doo la' íits'a'í da. 'Áłchíní la' doo nídaachah yęęgi 'át'éego daacha da. T'óó la' hodéezyéél." *There is no sound. The children are not crying like they used to. It is peacefully quiet.*

Nínáánîbaa' held her breath. She had not heard such peaceful silence in the past three years. Her people were always in pain. Their continual cries were testimony of that. The children and the elders were usually heard crying out in pain, fear, hunger, destitution, loneliness due to the death of a loved one or loneliness because the elders missed their land between the four sacred mountains. It seemed as if her people were collectively holding their breath so they could hear the sounds of the sheep. All she could hear were the muffled sounds of the sheep bleating.

Hashké Yił Naabaah hugged his beautiful Nínáánîbaa' as they lay side by side looking into the dark sky. They could hear the sounds of the sheep moving around in the corral. He smiled, then kissed his beautiful wife softly on the lips. Nínáánîbaa' kissed her husband back, reassured in knowing the seasons would return to her people. It was their livestock that initiated the entrance and observance of each season.

"K'ad łą́ą, dibé biniiłt'aa dą́ą nihee náhodoodleeł," *Now, because of the sheep we will have the spring season again,* she said quietly. She turned toward her husband and kissed him deeply and felt his wanting of her. They were content to lie side by side, holding hands, and kissing.

Nínáánibaa' held her beautiful Hashké Yił Naabaah as she listened to the silence. Soon, she heard the even breaths of his slumber. She watched the stars march across the sky. Near her, she could also hear the sound of her grandchildren and her children and her adopted children as they slept.

She kissed her husband's shoulder through his worn leather shirt. Nínáánibaa' wished she could feel his breath on her hair as she lay close to him. For now, she would accept the beautiful sound of her husband sleeping. For now, he was able to set his burden of leadership down as he slept.

Chapter Four
The Sheep Evoke Mixed Emotions

When the tall gray-haired one placed a large herd of sheep in the care of Hashké Yił Naabaah and the elder Peace Leader, Hashké Yił Naabaah was well aware of the cultural protocol that dictated the women as the owners and caretakers of sheep and goats, but he assigned the care of the soldiers' sheep to the young men and boys because it was not safe for the women and girls to herd the sheep to the pasture land that lay west of and parallel to the Pecos River. Although the plants did not grow in abundance, there was plenty of land where the men and boys could herd the sheep to find grass.

The first day when the young men and boys prepared themselves to take the sheep to the nearby pasture, the women anxiously leaned forward as they watched them release the sheep from the corral. They could hear the men whistling at the herd of skinny sheep.

"Yáadishą' eidí, nihe'anaa'í bidibé yéego dabííts'iiní. Yáadilá, t'áá hadibéjį' nidi k'adni' dichin yik'ee naa'ahinidééh. Dibé nizhónígo baa 'ádahojilyą́ągo 'ayóo haa dajooba' łeh. Yáadilá, nihe'anaa'í ts'ídá doo 'ádahalyą́ą da! Doo hanii dibé tł'oh ła' bá ninádajiłjoł da? T'áá nihí, sáanii daniidlínígíí dibé baa 'ádahwiilyą́ą dooleeł nít'ę́ę́', t'áá shǫǫh dibé nidaniilkaadgo bee 'ak'ídahwiilta'go binahjį' yá'át'ééh nídadiidleeł nít'ę́ę́'. Ei 'ashiiké nida'niłkaadgo, dibé tsį́į́ł ádeił'į́igo dibé hózhǫ́ dabíítsʼiiní dadooleeł. Yáadilá, 'ałdó'." *Look at them, our enemy's sheep are really skinny. Even their sheep are ready to fall over from starvation. When you take good care of sheep, they are kind to you. Our enemies are not smart at all! Why didn't they put out hay for the sheep? We, women, should have been the ones to care for the sheep. In caring for the sheep, we could have at least comforted ourselves and would have been made well. When the boys start herding sheep, they will hurry them and when they do, the sheep will become even more skinny. How frustrating!* Although the care of the sheep was not left in the hands of the women, the women were excited about being near a herd of sheep once again. The women told each other stories of the times when they personally owned a large herd of sheep.

At night, Hashké Yił Naabaah noticed his family and his people slept better because they could hear the sound of the sheep softly bleating.

Several mornings after the sheep were placed in their father's care, Dédii woke Dzáníbaa' saying,

"Shideezhí, ch'éénídzíid. K'adę́ę ha'a'aah. Níléí dibé shijé'ígóó diit'ash. Áadi siil dibé bikáa'gi naanáaldohígíí hádídíít'įįł. Siil níil'įį'go bee nihee ninháháltįįh doo. Shą́ą́' nihizhé'é 'ákónihiłníí łeh ne'?" *My younger sister, wake up. The sun is going to rise soon. Let's go where the sheep are kept. We will look for the steam that forms above the sheep. When we see the steam hovering above the sheep, it will begin to rain on us more often. Remember, our father used to tell us that?* Dzáníbaa' sleepily asked,

"Deesk'aazísh?" *Is it cold?*

"Doo 'ayóo deesk'aaz da," *No, it's not very cold,* Dédii impatiently answered. "Hooghandi kohgo nahalzhiishgo 'ayóo deesk'aaz łeh áádóó t'ah nádzas łeh ne'. Kodi 'éí jįįgo honeezílí łeh dóó t'óó níyol łeh. Níyol k'os níłtsą́ yił nidaaldohígíí doo nihik'ijį' kwííł'įį da. T'óó ni'góó náhooltsei nít'ę́ę́', shą́ą́' t'áá shǫǫh nihee nahóółtą́. Doo nahałtingóó díkwííshįį́ nídeezid. Txį', shideezhí, siil hádídíít'įįł." *At home during this time of the year, it is really cold and it still snows. Here, it is warm during the day and the wind blows. The wind does not bring the clouds that carry moisture. The ground was dry but it finally rained after it had not rained for several months. Let's go, my younger sister, let's go look for the steam.*

Dzáníbaa' lazily answered, saying,

"Shádí, shił hóyéé' dóó shi'niidlí." *My older sister, I am lazy and I am cold.* After much coaxing, Dzáníbaa' got up and followed Dédii as they walked toward the sheep corral. Dzáníbaa' gasped and nearly screamed when she stepped on something soft. Peering down at the ground in the dim light from the eastern horizon, she froze when she realized she stepped on someone's hand. She jumped away and heard a sleepy voice say,

"Ha'át'íí lá?" *What is it?* The two sisters grabbed one another when they saw several men sleeping on the ground. Their fear was alleviated a little when they heard the person speaking Naabeehó.

"Háish ání?" *Who is talking?* Dédii whispered. Wild thoughts were rushing through her mind. "Could it be an enemy who learned their language and was looking for a woman or child to kidnap? Was it an enemy who came to kill members of her father's people?" she wondered. She grabbed her sister and pulled her away from the sleeping bodies. The man who spoke was not in a hurry to rush after the two sisters. Dédii was sick to her stomach. They had been in this situation before when their evil enemies came to their home at the base of Dziłíjiin *Black Mesa* and kidnapped her and her sister.

One by one, the sleepy bodies pulled themselves up off of the ground and stood menacingly close to Dédii and her sister. Dédii's mind was not put at ease when she heard someone hoarsely whisper her name.

"Dédii." "How does the person know my name? Did he hear Dzáníbaa' speak my name?" she wondered in fear. A different voice whispered,

"Dzáníbaa', niísh ánít'į́? *Dzáníbaa', is it you?* The two sisters grabbed one another's hands, and with their free hands, they pulled their rug dresses up above their knees and ran as fast as their legs could carry them. The light from the rising sun was not bright enough to illuminate their surroundings so the two sisters had to depend on their sense of hearing to survive. They heard water running nearby. They also heard footsteps behind them. Their thoughts became frantic when they could hear heavy footsteps. Someone was chasing them!

A hand slipped around Dédii's waist and lifted her off of her feet. Kicking and hitting, she frantically fought the one holding her. Dzáníbaa' found her voice and screamed,

"Shizhé'é, kodi! Shizhé'é!" *My father, over here! My father!*

Dédii heard more footsteps chasing them. A man said in a low voice,

"Dédii, shí 'ásht'į́. K'adí 'áhodiilzééh! Ayá! T'áadoo náshiníłts'iní. K'adí nidishní! 'Áhodiilzééh! Aajigo tó néigeeh. Nahodits'ǫ' léi'jigo 'ahi'noołchééł. Nahodits'ǫ' biih dínóohdah! Ayá! T'áadoo náshinítałí! Ayá!" *Dédii, it is me. Now stop! Ow! Stop hitting me! I said stop! Settle down! Water settles in one place there. You are both running toward quicksand! You might fall into quicksand. Ouch! Don't kick me! Ouch!* Dédii kept fighting, hitting the hands that held her tight and kicking the legs that were planted on the ground. She could hear her sister's name called by one of their assailants. In all the confusion, Dédii saw her sister break free from the man holding her, and ran away from him toward the same direction they had been running.

Dedii heard the comforting sound of her father's voice breaking through the silence of the early dawn.

"Haash hóót'įįd? Haash hóót'įįd? Dédii! Dzáníbaa'!" *What happened? What happened? Dédii! Dzáníbaa'!* Dzáníbaa' crashed into her father's thin frame. Hashké Yił Naabaah grabbed his youngest daughter and held her close, whispering,

"Shiyázhí, 'áhodiilzééh, niyol nii' hadoolwoł. Áhodiilzééh." *My little one, settle down, your breath will leave your body. Settle down.* Dzáníbaa' was hyperventilating. She was taking quick deep breaths and could not stop the loud gasping sound she made in the still early dawn air. When Dédii heard her father's voice she sobbed in a weak voice,

"Shizhé'é! Shizhé'é! Haíshįį́ t'ą́ą́' shótą'!" *My father! My father! Someone is holding me back!* Her father gently picked up Dzáníbaa' and rushed her to where Dédii was standing. Still being held back by the strong hands, Dédii turned toward her father's voice. In his soothing voice he said,

"Hágo, shiyázhí, hágo. T'áadoo nichaaí, shiyázhí. K'adí. Nitah hoditsxiz la'. Doo háida 'atxínidoolíił da, shiyázhí. Shinahjį' sínítį." *Come here, my little one, come here. Don't cry, my little one. That's enough. You are shaking. No one will hurt you, my little one. Lean against me.* Dédii reached out toward the sound of her father's gentle strong voice and collapsed into his arms. Sobs exited her body in high-pitched sounds. Strong hands reached up to keep her from falling. Father and daughters collapsed down on the ground in one heap.

Dédii heard the sounds of many footsteps approaching. She was too weak to lift her head. She was afraid it was the soldiers approaching her father's warriors. The footsteps were menacingly close. In spite of her weakness, Dédii forced herself to lift her head and in the dim light that pierced the eastern darkness, she saw her mother and several Naabeehó women marching toward them. Each woman carried rocks in one hand and a stick in the other hand. Nínááníbaa' was loudly scolding her daughters' attackers. The army of Naabeehó women were ready to attack the ones who assaulted their kind leader's daughters.

Without questioning, a tall Naabeehó woman with a booming voice grabbed the opposite corners of her gray blanket and twisted her blanket to form a thick rope of woolen material. Still holding both ends of the blanket in each hand, she swung the blanket in large circles above her head and let one end go. Without unwrapping, one end of the blanket flew out and wrapped around Kiizhóní's ankles. The woman hollered loudly and jerked the end of the blanket, sending Kiizhóní sprawling on the ground. Nínááníbaa' heard a woman say,

"Ei 'asdząą bilahkéí t'éí yił biyaa hoo'a'. T'ah awéé' nilínéedą́ą́' bimá bits'ą́ą́' ádin. Bizhé'é dóó bilahkéí dabineesą. Ts'ídá doo nidilna' da, 'ei 'asdząą. Hastóí nidi 'ayóo béédaaldzid. Báhojiłchįįhgo ts'ídá doo ts'íí'át'ée da, 'ei 'asdząą." *That woman was raised with brothers. When she was still a baby, her mother died. Her father and her brothers raised her. She is very quick to act, that woman.*

Even men are afraid of her. When you make her mad, that woman is very difficult. "If I didn't know the woman, I would be afraid of her and say, 'Yíiyá! *Scary!*' but she is very strong and extremely kind. She even used the blanket as a weapon and brought one of our strongest young men to the ground," Nínáánídbaa' thought with pride for her Naabeehó women.

When Nínáánídbaa' saw that her daughters were in the protective hands of her husband, she dropped to the ground near her daughters and hugged them closely. She lifted her head and demanded of the young men,

"Haash hóót'įįd?" *What happened?* After recovering from his humiliating fall at the hands of a woman, Kiizhóní stepped forward to face the women. He told them he and several young men were sleeping near the sheep corral to protect the sheep when Dédii and Dzáníbaa' approached the corral. He explained he and the young men were just as surprised to find Dédii and Dzáníbaa' at the corral. He reported he was startled when one of the sisters stepped on his hand. He stated he was just as surprised as the two women. He said he jumped up to obtain their identity when Dédii and Dzáníbaa' started running in the direction of the river. He further reported,

"Nahodits'ǫ' náhádleehjigo dah ahi'dí'níilchą́ą'go biniinaa bikéé' dah yiishtxe'. 'Shí 'ásht'į́,' ch'ééh bidishníigo, t'óó yówohgo da shits'ą́ąjigo 'ahi'noolchééł. Dédii sésił áádóó dinééh ła' Dzáníbaa' yisił nít'ę́ę' ch'ééh nihilák'ee ha'ahi'nilchéehgo biniinaa boozhníí' gónaa yíníitą' nít'ę́ę' nich'é'éké t'óó bił yéé' hazlį́į'. T'óó t'ą́ą' yíníitą'go t'óó yówehgo da bił yéé' hazlį́į́'. Shinaat'áanii nihaiyílwodgo 'índa Dédii dóó Dzáníbaa' áhodiilzee'. T'áadoo siilziłgóó shį́į́ 'éí nahodits'ǫ' yiih níídee' doo ni'. Ei nahodits'ǫ' bááhádzidgo 'át'é. T'óó bik'ee shił yéé' hazlį́į́'." *They ran in the direction of the quicksand and that is why I ran after them. I tried telling them it was me but they ran away from me. I grabbed Dédii and another young man grabbed Dzáníbaa' and they tried in vain to escape the hold we had of them and that is why we held them by their waists. They were filled with fear when we held them back. It wasn't until my leader came running that Dédii and Dzáníbaa' stopped. If we had not grabbed hold of them, they would have fallen into the quicksand. That quicksand is very dangerous. I became fearful of it too.* Nínááníbaa' turned toward her daughters and asked in a quiet voice,

"Ha'át'íishą' haoh'aash nít'ę́ę́'? Háágóóshą' woh'ash nít'ę́ę́'?" *What was your purpose for being there? Where were you going?* Still wailing, Dédii told her mother,

"Siil dibé bikáa'gi naanáaldoh łehígíí yidiiltséél niidzingo biniiyé dibé bighangóó yiit'ash nít'ę́ę́'. Dibé bighan binaagi nídahwiilkáhígíí 'éí doo nihił bééhozingóó. Doo chohoo'į́į́góó nihiyaa dahozdeeshxiz. Dzáníbaa' háíshį́į́ bíla' yik'idiiltáalgo yiyaa hodeeshxiz lá. Hó 'ádajit'ínígíí 'éí doo nihił bééhozingóó t'óó hats'ą́ą́' dah ahi'dí'níilchą́ą́'. Nahodits'ǫ' náhádleehígíí doo shił bééhozingóó, Dzáníbaa' bíla' sésił dóó t'óó 'áajigo biłą́ąjį' yaashtáál."

Nínááníbaa' turned toward the men and said,

"Háágóó da nídadohkahgo t'áá shǫǫh bee nihił nídahołnihgo nizhóní doo nít'ę́ę́'. K'asídą́ą́' yee' doodahígi 'áhoodzaa! K'asídą́ą́' yee' ałk'iijéé'! *Whenever you are going somewhere, it would be good if you would tell us. Something terrible almost took place! We almost got into a big fight!*

The women dropped the rocks they held in their hands and started giggling. One woman said,

"Nihí shį́į́ hak'eh dadeedlį́į' doo ni'." *We probably would have defeated them.* The men knew not to respond, because they knew their Naabeehó women were very strong. The people surrounded their kind leader's family and spoke encouraging words to their War Leader's daughters. The entire group left the dangerous place where the ground was soft near where the quicksand deepened.

Kiizhóní and the young warrior were praised by their kind leader.

"K'asídą́ą́' shį́į́ doo dahígi 'áhoodzaa. 'Ahéhee'. Sha'ałchíní t'ą́ą́' yínóhtą'go bee t'áadoo nahodits'ǫ' yiih níídee' da." *Something terrible nearly happened. Thank you. By holding my children back, they did not fall into the quicksand.*

Dédii and Dzáníbaa' were surrounded by the Naabeehó women as they silently followed their mother back to their camp and to their sleeping little ones. The two sisters collapsed on their mother's rug blanket and welcomed their mother and father's gentle hugs and kisses and their comforting words.

Kiizhóní watched Dédii from a distance. He wanted to be the one to comfort her and kiss her and hold her.

He was thankful he was able to catch up with her before she fell into the dangerous quicksand. He was thankful he was able to hold her even though she fiercely fought him. He vowed to hold her once again at a time when she welcomed his arms. He yearned to hold her close. He loved Dédii.

****

Every morning, the men walked to the bank of the river where the bank widely sloped down to the river. Thin strips of grass grew in patches where the evidence of the deadly alkaline was absent from the soil. When the white line of alkaline became evident along the waterline, the men knew they would have to build a new ditch through which fresh water could flow to the trough they built for the sheep. The men knew they had to protect the sheep at all cost. Their mothers', sisters', aunts', and grandmothers' well-being was dependent upon the survival of a healthy herd of sheep.

The men walked in various directions to observe the activities of the soldiers who lived in the picket forts. In the afternoon, they led the sheep to a different area, and sat nearby while the sheep grazed. In the late afternoon, the sheep were herded to the riverbank again. The men watched the activities around their camp and watched for the safety of the ones who were out with the sheep.

After many meetings with the elder Peace Leader, the men decided the women would care for the sheep just as they had done at their home at the base of

Dziłíjiin *Black Mesa.* It was also agreed upon that a few Naabeehó warriors would have to stand guard over the women to ensure their safety.

To further ensure protection of the young women and girls, the men and boys were asked by the leaders to,

"T'áadoo t'áá kǫ́ǫ́ nihinaagóó nida'nołkaadí. T'áá nízaadi dibé 'ałnáádanołka'. Ch'ikéí dóó sáanii, 'asdzání danilínígíí, dibé nideiniłkaadgo 'éí nihinaagóó t'éiyá nida'niłkaadgo 'ádeiíníilzingo yá'át'ééh. T'áá kǫ́ǫ́ nihinaagóó nida'niłkaadgo 'éí nihe'anaa'í doo baa tįįh nákah da doo. Nihí 'éí naabaahii danohłį́. Nihe'anaa'í bitsį' daashtłizhígíí t'áá nihich'į' daastxi'. Sáanii dóó ch'ikéí 'éí doo yich'į' daastxi' da. 'Éí biniinaa doo nízaadgóó 'ałnááda'niłka' da doo. T'áá kodóó bik'i dadíníit'įį' dooleeł." *Don't herd the sheep nearby. Take the sheep out farther. When the teenage girls and the young women herd the sheep, they will herd sheep near us so our enemies will not bother the girls and women. You are warriors. Our enemies who have dark skin (Indians) are careful not to come close to you, but they are not afraid to come close to the young women and the teenage girls, that is the reason they need to herd sheep only in nearby places where we can keep an eye on them.*

Nínááníbaa' remembered back to when the men and boys were the only ones allowed to herd the sheep. She thought back to when the women sadly watched the men disappear over the shallow hill. She knew the sheep kept the womens' thoughts clear of the destitute conditions in which they were forced to survive.

Nááníbaa' thought of the deep collective sigh that could be heard every morning and afternoon when the women and girls watched the last sheep disappear over the hill with the men following. The women and girls would walk slowly back to their camping areas and wait for the sheep to return. When they heard the familiar whistle of the young men as they followed the sheep back to the corral in the late morning, the young women and girls left what they were doing and walked quickly toward the sheep corral to meet the sheep. The form of their bodies as they hurried to meet the sheep would make a person believe the young women and girls were tied to a rope and were being drawn forward by the rope.

The men could not help noticing the growing excitement that enveloped the women and girls as they watched the sheep enter the corral. The sheep disbursed in different directions and ran up to the women and girls who stood on the outside of the corral. Each day, the women and girls giggled and some cried when the sheep nuzzled against the palms of their open hands. The men found their wives, mothers, daughters, sisters, and aunts a bit more content, although they were faced with dire circumstances.

The Naabeehó men were wary of and did not trust the man the Naabeehó women called "diigisii" *Crazy One*. They knew Diigisii was capable of harming their women, daughters, sisters, mothers, grandmothers and aunts. Diigisii had hair like straw and was the color of the straw that was strewn across the parade ground.

At the time when the Naabeehó people were first placed into prisoner of war status at Fort Canby or Fort Fauntleroy, the men were required to surrender their weapons. NínáánÍbaa' remembered seeing bows, arrows, lances, shields, and spears placed on the ground to form a large heap. The soldiers set fire to the weapons. The Naabeehó men watched in horror as their weapons were reduced to ashes, the weapons they considered sacred. At the time, Nínáánibaa' was keenly aware of the fact that the minds of the Naabeehó men were bruised when they saw their weapons burning.

At Fort Sumner, the Naabeehó men only had one weapon, which was a braided strip made of yucca leaves or a short strip of thick cowhide. The braided strip of yucca leaves had a piece of leather attached to one end, into which they placed a smooth pebble. As a weapon, the braided strip was wrapped around the pebble several times and released when a target was identified. The pebble was propelled through the air by the snapping of the braided strip at an incredible speed. When the pebble hit its intended target, the small animal was stunned and incapacitated for a time which made the animal easy to kill.

Hashké Yił Naabaah and his warriors met with the elder Peace Leader to obtain his permission to teach the women to use this weapon. The young boys collected many small round pebbles to be used for practice. In the darkness and in the still of night, Hashké Yił Naabaah's warriors took their time demonstrating to the women the most effective way of using the weapon. Targets were set up when the moon was bright. The women practiced until the men were comfortable the women were hitting their target.

Nínáánébaa' and her daughters and her daughter-in-law also learned to use the weapon. Although she knew the reason for their need to learn to protect themselves, Nínáánébaa' said,

"Yáadilá baa neiikai dó'?" *What are we doing?* After a moment of silence she said,

"Bee danihi'dójíhígíí, danihízhi', "baa' " bee nihool'á. 'Éísh doo naabaahii 'óolyée da. T'áá shįį 'áko." *Our names end with the word "the one who went to war and came back". Isn't that what you call a warrior? It is probably alright that women learn to use a weapon to protect themselves.*

****

The next project for the men was to dig a shallow trough, which they lined with the logs that were left over from the sheep corral. The trough was built to provide water for the sheep so the women would not have to herd the sheep very far from their camp. Using clay bowls and pots, the men and boys spent many hours filling the trough with water they obtained from the Pecos River that ran nearby. Instead of using clay pots and bowls to fill the trough, the older men decided it would be better to build a shallow ditch through which the water could flow from the river to the trough.

While creating the trough and hollowing out the ditch, the men found the ground very hard and full of thorns that had dropped from the mesquite trees that used to dot the landscape when Hashké Yił Naabaah and his people first arrived at Fort Sumner.

"Díí nahasdzáán nidi nihijoołá. Ts'ídá doo nihíłdin da. Doo nihaajooba da," *Even the earth hates us. It cannot stand us. It is not kind to us,* the elder Peace Leader told the men. Hashké Yił Naabaah's youngest son worked alongside the elder Peace Leader and enthusiastically dug the sand out with his bare hands. After a day of digging, the men returned to their camps with their hands swollen from having been pricked by mesquite thorns. Many men found infection settling in their hands.

Hashké Yił Naabaah spent the night melting hardened tsin bijeeh *pinion tree pitch* he obtained from the pinon trees that lined the path when they were chased though the mountain pass on their forced walk to Fort Sumner over three years earlier. When the melted tsin bijeeh cooled down, he placed the pitch on a strip of calico fabric then placed the tsin bijeeh on the infected area and wrapped the infected area with the loose ends of the cloth to hold the pitch in place next to the wound. Within days, the tsin bijeeh drew out the thorn and the infection and the wound was completely healed. Naabeehó people who did not have tsin bijeeh became very afraid of the mesquite thorns. The thorns were scattered all over the ground, left behind by the men who cut the trees down for firewood to use for warmth or cooking purposes.

Many Naabeehó people believed the thorns were carried by the fierce winds to further torture them. Many times, Hashké Yił Naabaah voiced a prayer to thank the Creator for providing the pitch from the pinon trees. He still had an ample supply of pitch which he carefully and sparingly gave to those who needed it.

Nínááníbaa' knew their people had great respect for her husband. Many times, the people expressed gratitude to her husband for his knowledge of remedies and his consistency in being thoughtful of his people. "He is a good leader because he cares for his people in the same way he cares for his own family," she thought.

Many Naabeehó people died from their infected wounds, which usually escalated to blood poisoning because the wound was uncared for. The Fort Sumner Indian Reservation was a place that was void of herbs, herbs that would bring quick healing.

After many days of digging with their bare hands and using hollowed out pieces of logs to remove dirt, pebbles, rocks, sand, and mesquite thorns, the irrigation ditch was opened to divert water to the watering trough. At first a shallow stream, the water made its way to the watering trough. The men made clicking sounds when the water began to flow.

****

Nínááníbaa''s youngest son, Tł'ée'go Naabaah, was helping with the digging of the ditch when a sliver from the log he was using as a make-shift shovel entered his skin and lodged itself deep in the flesh of the palm of his hand. Thinking of the safety of his mother and his sisters and his sister-in-law, he continued to work throughout the day. Immediately, the infection settled in the palm of his right hand. After close inspection of his son's wound, Hashké Yił Naabaah noticed a mesquite thorn was also embedded in the wound. Hashké Yił Naabaah and Nínááníbaa' knew the wound was extremely serious because the poison from the mesquite thorn increased the gravity of the situation.

As their son lay listless and in great pain, Hashké Yił Naabaah set a shallow pot of water over the small fire and boiled herbs in addition to warming the tsin bijeeh. He washed the infected area with the herbal solution then applied a generous amount of tsin bijeeh to the wound and wrapped his son's hand. Nínááníbaa' used a shallow gourd to offer her son a small amount of the herbal solution to drink while his sisters held a small, wet piece of their calico fabric to their younger brother's head to cool his forehead which was hot to the touch and to keep the warm sun off of his face.

For four days, the family watched Tł'ée'go Naabaah drift in and out of consciousness. Family members gave him the herbal medicine to drink and they kept the wound wrapped. They trusted the tsin bijeeh *pinion pitch* along with the herb they brought with them from their land at the base of Dziłíjiin *Black Mesa* to heal their son and brother.

A young woman named Akéé' Naazbaa', who was the granddaughter of the elder Peace Leader became friends with Dzáníbaa' and Dédii. Without asking for permission, she sat with the two sisters to help keep watch over their brother. She first introduced herself to Dzáníbaa' and Dédii when she brought blue corn crepes and water to keep them nourished. Nínááníbaa' knew the young woman and her family had sacrificed their precious supply of blue corn flour and cedar ashes to help her family. Silent tears flowed from Nínááníbaa''s eyes knowing her people wanted her son to survive even if it meant they, themselves, would be left with less food to eat.

Nínááníbaa' and Dzáníbaa' and Dédii noticed the special care the young woman named Akéé' Naazbaa' provided to their family and Tł'ée'go Naabaah. At first, they thought it was because she was a newly gained friend but their thoughts changed when they saw the look in the young woman's eyes when she gazed upon Tł'ée'go Naabaah.

After four days, Tł'ée'go Naabaah regained consciousness. Akéé' Naazbaa' let Nínááníbaa' know her son was fully awake and was asking for his mother.

"Niyáázh ch'énádzid. Nína'ídíłkid." *Your son woke up. He is asking for you.* Nínááníbaa' was by her son's side within a few steps. She fell to her knees at his side and asked,

"Nitah lá haa hoot'é? T'ah nidiísh yéego nił hodiniih?" *How are you feeling? Are you still in great pain?* Before he could answer his mother, Akéé' Naazbaa' looked into his eyes and asked in a soft voice,

"Nitahísh yá'áhoot'ééh k'ad?" *Are you alright now?* With a confused look on his face, Tł'ée'go Naabaah looked into the face of the young woman. Without waiting, she asked again,

"Nitahísh yá'áhoot'ééh k'ad?" *Are you alright now?* Tł'ée'go Naabaah looked past the young woman and searched for his mother and father. The rest of the family rushed to his side and voiced prayers of gratitude to the Creator for sparing their son and brother and helping him survive a grave illness that killed many Naabeehó people.

Nínáánībaa' watched her youngest son closely. He seemed perturbed that he woke to find a stranger sitting close to him, instead of a member of his family. Nínáánībaa' waited until her daughters gave their brother some herbal medicine before she told her son of the four days he was gravely ill.

"Shiyázhí, yéego txi'hwiisíníníi'. Nílátł'ááh baa 'i'íízhoozh dóó hosh nílátł'áh baa 'eelwod. Éí bits'ą́ądóó doochohoo'íįgóó nitah honiigai. Nizhé'é tsin bijeeh níla' yąąh ánáyiil'įįhgo t'áá shǫǫh hosh dóó hxis hayíídzíįz. Éí bee níla' nádziih k'ad. T'ah nidiiísh yéego nił honeezgai, shiyázhí?" *My little one, you really suffered. A sliver and a thorn lodged in the palm of your hand. You became extremely sick from that. Your father placed pinon pitch on your hand and it pulled out the thorn and the infection. Now, your hand has started to heal. Are you still in a lot of pain, my little one?* Weakly, her son answered,

"Aoo', shimá, shílátł'ááh doochohoo'íįgóó neezgai," *Yes, the palm of my hand really hurts,* Tł'ée'go Naabaah weakly responded, then asked,

"Níléí 'asdzání shą' háí 'át'į, shimá?" *Who is that young woman, my mother?* he asked.

"Ei 'Akéé' Naazbaa' wolyé. Nitah honiigaigo t'óó kwe'é nésdáá nít'ę́ę́'. Bité'ázíní yił díkwíidishį́į́ abe' bee neezmasí nihá 'ádayiilaa dóó 'azee' ła' nihá deishbéezhii' nihaa deizką́. 'Abe' bee neezmasí t'éí bikiin kǫ́ǫ́ nínahísíiltą́ą́ nít'ę́ę́'." *Her name is One Who Came Home After Following in Warfare. When you were very sick, she came and sat with us. She, along with her relatives, prepared blue corn crepes for us several times and they provided us some herbal medicine. The crepes were all we ate while we sat near you.*

"Ei 'asdzání, 'Akéé' Naazbaa' wolyéhígíí, nihaa nádáahgo nihik'ihałta'go kwe'é bił nahísíitą́ą́ nít'ę́ę́'. Ayóo bá hózhǫ́. Nihinaat'áanii k'ad nihá hoo'áłígíí bitsóí nilį́." *The young woman called, One Who Came Home After Following in Warfare would come here and sit with us. She is very friendly. She is the granddaughter of our Peace Leader.*

"Háíshį́į́ hataałgo nídiist'į́į́h nít'ę́ę́'. Éí shą' háí hataał nít'ę́ę́'?" *Every once in a while, I heard someone singing. Who was the one singing?* asked Tł'ée'go Naabaah.

"Ei 'asdzání, baa hashne'ígíí, t'óó nésdáago hataał nít'ę́ę́'. *It was the young woman I talked about who sat near you and sang.*

"Nihí shą' háadi naohkaigo?" *What about you, where were all of you?* he asked his mother.

"Nihí 'éí kǫ́ǫ́ nínahísíiltą́ą́ nít'ę́ę́' ałdó'," *We were also sitting here near you,* Nínááníbaa' answered.

Tł'ée'go Naabaah weakly attempted to lift his head so he could look over his mother's shoulder to see if he could get a glimpse of the young woman. Nínáánībaa' moved to the side of her son so he could see the young woman. She was pleased to see that her son was much better, and better yet, he was possibly interested in this particular young woman.

Later that evening, as they were putting out their tattered rug blankets on which to sleep, Nínáánībaa' mentioned her son's possible interest in the young woman named Akéé' Naazbaa'. She wanted to know what her husband thought of the young woman and her family. Hashké Yił Naabaah told her in gentle words that they could not allow their son and the young woman to get any closer. To explain further, he said,

"Kwe'é nihidine'é t'óó'ahayóí daniné. Níléí t'áá nihí nihikéyah biih néiikaigo 'índa nabik'íyádeiilti'go beełt'ée dooleeł. K'ad éí dooda, shiyázhí. Nihe'awéé' bee bich'į' hadeesdzih. *This is a place where many of our people are dying every day. It would be more appropriate if we discussed this once we have returned to our own land. Not now, my little one. I will speak to our baby about it.*

Hashké Yił Naabaah was true to his word. He spoke to his son about the young woman. He also spoke to the young woman's family and found her parents also noticed the attraction their daughter had for Hashké Yił Naabaah's son. The young woman's parents agreed to wait until they left the land of torture and had reentered their own land before they allowed their daughter to be within the same vicinity of Tł'ée'go Naabaah.

When Nínáánîbaa' heard about the discussion, she felt a sense of peace about the young woman's attraction to her son. It is the place of the father and the grandfather of the young man to ask for the hand of a woman in marriage. "The youth are losing an important part of our culture in this horrible place," she thought. Nínáánîbaa' was relieved to notice that the young woman did not come to their camping area as often. She vowed to thank the young woman and her family for helping care for her son. She told Hashké Yił Naabaah that as parents of their son, they needed to reciprocate by doing something nice for the young woman and her family.

Once Nínáánîbaa' knew her youngest son was feeling better, she sat down on the ground near her husband and sighed softly. She untied her loose tsiiyééł *hair bun* and with her fingers, smoothed the loose strands of hair into place. Hashké Yił Naabaah smoothed the loose strands of hair and tucked them behind her ears then reached out and took her long hair that was still unfurling from being held in place by her tsiitł'óół *hair tie* and held it up and watched it fall into place on his lap. He took her hair and lifted it to his face and gently rubbed his face in the soft, curled pile of Nínáánîbaa''s hair. He lifted his face and looked into Nínáánîbaa''s face and told her,

"Nitsii' t'óó shił nizhóníyee'. Łah da tł'ée'go nitsii' t'áá k'íhineestahgo ná'iilwoshgo nitsii' shiyid bikáá' dah náshjoł. Áko doo ts'íí'át'éégóó ná'iishwosh dóó bik'e'ahwiihgo hanínáshyįh. T'áá nitsii'jį' nidi shaa jooba', shiyázhí." *Your hair is beautiful to me. Sometimes at night when you go to sleep with your hair left untied, I place your hair on my chest. When I do, I fall into a deep sleep and I experience a restful sleep. Even your hair is kind to me, my little one.* Nínááníbaa' interrupted him with her soft giggles and said,

"Áyaaní da, łahda shitsii' nik'ídeesdiz łeh éí doodai' bik'i sínítį́į́ łeh. Ni dó' nitsii' t'áá k'íhineestahgo yiistséehgo t'óó shił nizhóní łeh. Nidejį' éé' t'áágééd naninááago, nikágí yishtłizhgo shił nizhónígó nésh'į́į́ łeh. Áádóó nitsii' t'áá k'íhineestahgo nikágí bik'ésti'go, t'óó shił nizhóníyee' łeh ałdó'. Ayóo dó' naadzólní..." *No wonder, sometimes my hair would be wrapped around you or you would be sleeping on my hair. You too, I love to see your hair untied. When you walk around without your shirt, I love to see your beautifully browned skin. And I love to see your hair draped over your skin. You are so handsome...*

"Yáadilá 'óolyé, shiyázhí. Ni yee' ayóó'ánííníłnin. Nik'i náshgałgo shijéí t'óó dah naaltal łeh. Nániistséehgo 'ayóo nashiiłná. Doo ts'íí'át'éégóó naa 'ahééh nisin, shiyázhí. Háshinee', t'ah shíighah sínízį́." *What a thing to say, my little one. You are the one who is beautiful. When I glance upon you, my heart beats more heartily. I am moved with emotion when I see you. I am extremely thankful for you, my little one. Dear one, you are still standing by me with your support.* With those words, Nínááníbaa' saw a couple of tears drop onto the strands of hair her husband was holding in his hands. Breathless, she responded,

"Jó ni dó', hastiin ílíinii dóó hastiin yá'át'éehii nílįįgo kónízah iiná 'ahił íilyaa. Ayóó'áshííní'níí dóó niha'áłchíní 'ałdó' ayóó'ííní'níigo nizhónígo biyaa hwiinił'a'. Éí doo ts'íí'át'éégóó nich'į' baa 'ahééh nisin. Shich'į' ná 'í'déékid dóó bee lą́ 'azlį́į' yęędą́ą' t'áá'óolyéego 'iiná 'ílíinii nihílák'eelyáá lá nisin łeh. Ayóo shaa jiiníba', éí 'éí nich'į' baa 'ahééh nisin, sha'áłchíní bizhé'é nílíinii." *Well, you too, you are a highly valued man and you have been a good man as we have made our lives together. You love me and you also love our children and you have raised our children in a wonderful way. I am so very thankful to you for that. When you asked for me in marriage and when your request was agreed to, I believe a life of great value was placed in our hands. You are so kind to me, for which I am so thankful to you, you who are the father of my children.* Hashké Yił Naabaah dropped a few more tears on Nínáánībaa"s hair that lay in his outstretched hands. After a long silence, while remembering what his wife told him, he reached out and placed his arm around her to hold her close. He leaned down and placed his mouth next to her ear and whispered,

"Mmmmmmm, ahéhee'go 'áshiinilaa,
shił nahosínílne'ígíí. 'Ayóo nidáahjį' nishłį́, shiyázhí.
Shíí'ii nílį́. Nits'ą́ąjį' dah nídiishdáahgo 'ayóo nídin náshdleeh." *Mmmmmmm, in speaking with me, you have done something I am so grateful for. I yearn for you, my little one. You are mine. I miss you greatly whenever I leave you behind.* Nínáánībaa' looked up toward the clear blue skies and whispered,

"Ahéhee', shiTaa'. T'áá'óolyéego nihaa jiisíníba'. Nich'į' ahééh nisin. Sha'áłchíní bizh'é'é shá baa 'áhólyą. Sha'áłchíní dóó shitsóóké shá baa 'áhólyą 'ałdó'."
Thank you, my Spiritual Father. I am thankful to You. Take care of my children's father for me. Take care of my children and my grandsons for me as well.

****

The sound of the sheep brought Nínáánibaa' a great sense of calm in a menacing place. She was silently thankful to the tall gray-haired one who claimed to be her son-in-law for bringing the sheep for them to care for. She was so proud of her sons and the men who put many long hours working hard to provide water for the few sheep that were placed in their care. She was also thankful to the men who worked hard teaching the women to use the weapon to protect themselves when they took the sheep out to the nearby hills that were sparsely dotted with bushes and skinny plants of grass. Although she was grateful to the tall gray-haired one, her mind was more at ease lately because he had not come back in a few days.

When Nínáánibaa' shared her thoughts with Hashké Yił Naabaah, he claimed he was also grateful to the tall gray-haired one. Hashké Yił Naabaah had observed a slight sense of contentment he had not witnessed in three years among the women, which relieved the ache he had in his heart for his people. Instead of sitting around the small fires discussing their extreme hunger, their shortage of clothes and shoes, and their indescribable intense loneliness for their land, the women were getting up early in the morning to greet the dawn and stand at the entrance of the sheep corral to watch the sheep.

Hashké Yił Naabaah promised Nínáánibaa' that he would boldly ask the tall gray-haired one if his people could have two female goats that had little kid goats so the children in his camp could have warm milk to drink. Nínáánibaa' answered with a soft,

"Mmmmmm, k'adę́ę tł'ízí bibe' shibézhígíí ła' yishdlą́."
Mmmmmm, I want to drink some goat's milk that has been boiled.

"Ni lá ná 'ałdó' ni," *For you too,* her husband said, holding her close.

*****

The men smiled when they saw more young women arrive at the sheep corral ready to herd sheep. There were more women than the number of sheep. Nínáánibaa' and her daughters and her daughter-in-law were ready to help. The men warned the women of the dangers that abounded nearby. Hashké Yił Naabaah voiced the wishes of all the men when he said,

"Ádaa 'ádahołyą́. 'Ádaa 'ádahołchį́įh. Nihinaagóó doo 'ééhózin da. Nihe'anaa'í nihinaagóó nidaakai. Nihe'anaa'í nihą́ąh nidaa'na'go 'át'é. Baa 'ádahołchį́įh. T'áadoo nízaadgóó 'ałnánída'nołka'í. T'áá kǫ́ǫ t'éí." *Take care of yourselves. Be aware. There is uncertainty around you. Our enemies are around us. Our enemies may sneak up on you. Be aware of that. Don't take the sheep out too far.* Hashké Yił Naabaah told his young warriors to accompany the women and girls when they took the sheep out of the corral. He did not trust the soldiers and he did not trust their enemies who were known to cross the Pecos River to steal a Naabeehó woman or girl.

The sheep were taken out to graze in the open areas. Nínáánібaa"s daughters searched the weeds for little tufts of wool that were left behind by the sheep when the sheep brushed against the weeds. The little tufts of wool were collected for their mother. They remembered their mother kept the little tufts of wool in a pouch she brought from her home.

In the evenings, their mother would take out the little tufts of wool, sniff them, roll them between her hands to allow the lanolin to seep into the dried parts of the palms of her hands, then she would pull the fibers apart to realign them, an action that took the place of carding the wool. The two sisters watched as their mother placed the aligned fibers between her hands and rubbed her hands together to twist the aligned wool fibers which took the place of spinning the wool. Her daughters and her daughter-in-law felt a sense of pride in caring for their mother by providing her with a steady supply of little tufts of wool. Soon, a group of women were bringing their own little supply of tufts of wool to ceremoniously card and spin the wool in preparation of weaving an imaginary rug.

Chapter Five

A War Leader or a Peace Leader

As the faint light burst forth on the eastern horizon to announce a new day, Hashké Yił Naabaah lay quietly near his beautiful Nínáánísbaa'. He was very worried about his people, the ones they would be leaving behind as he, his oldest son, Kiizhóní, and his men were preparing their minds to be absent from their families. Prayers were spoken and gratitude was vocalized to the Creator. He and the elder Peace Leader decided to leave the women and children behind although the orders were for all the Navajo people to arrive at the parade grounds.

As most of the men were leaving on their two-day walk to and from the parade grounds, Hashké Yił Naabaah worried about his Nínáánísbaa', his daughters, his youngest son, grandsons, and his people. He wondered if the women were prepared to fight an enemy, keep a wild soldier at a distance, or stun a dangerous animal that might try to get one of the sheep. Many dangerous scenarios marched through his worried mind. He had to trust the women and the few warriors and his Mescalero son-in-law to protect one another. He took solace in the fact that his beautiful Nínáánímbaa' would not be going out with the young women when they took out the sheep because he knew she would be caring for their youngest son who was still weak from his recent illness.

The young Naabeehó women could not be stopped from going out after the sheep. He could hear Nínáánímbaa''s soothing voice when she warned her daughters and the young women to be cautious of dangers that loomed close. He closed his eyes, lifted his face to the dark sky and softly spoke a prayer to the Creator.

Nínáánímbaa' watched her daughters prepare themselves to follow the sheep to a nearby hill where the sheep loved to graze. She warned her daughters of the crazy soldier and the enemies that might be lurking just beyond the fast running river. Her daughters sat down in front of her waiting for their mother to tie their hair in a tsiiyéél *Navajo bun.* Amidst friendly chatter, she told her daughters and her daughter-in-law that she was going to tie their hair a bit tighter than usual so they would be mindful of their dangerous plight, that of being away from the camp with most of the men gone. Nínáánímbaa' did not want her daughters to become complacent during the day. She wanted them to be constantly aware of their surroundings. With their hair tied tight in a tsiiyéél, she knew her daughters would be alert.

"Nihitsii' yéego be'ashtł'ó. Nánohkaigo 'índa beda'doh'ał. K'ad éí bíni'dii yéego be'astł'ǫ́. 'Ííshją́ą́h, hada'ohsíid doo. Nihe'anaa'í t'óó diigis yę́ę t'áadoo baa 'ádahołchįįhí nihąąh noo'nééh lágo. 'Áádóó nihe'anaa'í t'ah nidii nihinaagóó nidanit'in." *I am going to tie your hair real tight. When you come back, you can loosen your hair. For now, leave it tied real tight. You must be observant. Don't allow the crazy soldier to sneak up on you without notice. Our enemies are still lurking around you.*

Nínááníbaa' watched the young women silently prepare to leave. The procession of women quietly moved as one as they walked toward the sheep corral. She watched her daughters disappear among the many women. She noticed they quietly talked to one another. She wished she was among the group but reminded herself of her son's grave condition.

"T'áá kwe'é sédáago shá yá'át'ééh," *It is better that I stay here,* she told herself.

Early morning was her favorite time of the day. Nínááníbaa' closed her eyes to bring back to her memory the daily activity of taking out the sheep to graze and drink water at her home on Dziłíjiin *Black Mesa.* She remembered that as she walked toward the dibé bighan *sheep corral* in the cold dawn air, she would have been looking at the air just above the place where the sheep huddled together as they waited patiently for her to let them out of the corral. She would see steam that hung thickly in the air that was generated from the breath of the sheep. She caught herself smiling.

All of a sudden, Nínáánībaa' caught her breath! She did not want to scare her son so she turned away from him to hide her face. Her mind flew back several years, back to her home, to the morning when she tied her daughters' hair real tight just before she sent her daughters and her sons out after the sheep. It was later that day her daughters were kidnapped!

Today, like the day in the past when her daughters were kidnapped, she had tied her daughters' hair real tight to make sure they remained alert. Her heart beat loudly in her chest. She could feel her emotions getting the best of her. She frantically looked around her, hoping to see the procession of women walking, but the form of the procession was absent from her view. Covering her mouth, she quietly chided herself, saying,

"Ha'át'íí lá biniiyé shich'é'éké 'atah t'óó bi'níłnii'?" *Why did I let my daughters go along?* Her mind would not settle down! In desperation, she reached for the pouch in which she kept her prized possessions. She shoved her hand into the soft worn bag. The first thing her hand touched was the soft tufts of wool her daughters had gathered for her. She pulled out several tufts and lifted them to her nose to fill her lungs with the calming scent of the wool. Lovingly, she rubbed the tufts in between her hands and felt the lanolin seep into her hands. A slight sense of calm entered her body through her hands.

Sitting on the ground, Nínáánībaa' rocked herself while she held the tufts of wool in her hands. She looked up to check the position of the sun. It was not moving across the cloudy sky. She looked at the clouds and scolded,

"Tsxį́įłgo jóhonaa'éí 'e'e'aahjigo nihaiyilwoł!" Bidadohchííd!" *Hurry and chase the sun toward the west! Release your hold on it!* All she could think about was how desperately she wanted to see her daughters. "At the time my daughters were kidnapped, their father was away at a War Leadership meeting, and now he is away meeting with the enemy." Her thoughts were getting the best of her once again so she squeezed the tufts of wool tightly, hoping her action would squeeze her morose thoughts out of her mind.

She was relieved when her son stirred from his fitful sleep. She turned toward him and offered him a bowlful of broth. He looked at her and asked,

"Shimá, shizhé'é shą'?" *My mother, where is my father?*

"Nihe'anaa'í hágo dabiłníigo, hastóí 'ákǫ́ǫ́ yił 'eekai. 'Áłah adooleeł ha'níigo. Háánílyį́į́h, shiyázhí." *Our enemies told them to come and so he left with the men to go there. They said there is to be a meeting. Rest, my little one.* Her son, Tł'ée'go Naabaah looked around nervously before he said,

"Kwe'é t'áá sáhí siikéhígíí shił yá'át'ééh," *It is good that we are sitting here alone,* her son said unexpectedly.

"Ha'át'íí lá, shiyázhí?" *What is it, my little one?* Nínááníbaa' answered quietly, with a sense of concern in her voice. Her youngest son had always been a quiet and reserved baby, toddler, child, boy, and now as a young man, he was still always quiet. Her son looked deep into her eyes and with difficulty spoke, saying,

"Yéego shitah honeezgaigo doo 'éí t'óó 'ashhoshgo kwe'é sétįį da nít'ę́ę́'. T'áadoo le'é yee' baa nitséskeesgo t'óó yíníshch'ilgo sétį́į́ nít'ę́ę́'. Haaléit'éego lá shizhé'é bił..." *When I was very sick, I was not fully asleep. I lay here and kept my eyes closed because I was thinking about something. I wondered how, my father...* Already anxious from her earlier thoughts, Nínááníbaa' interrupted her son and asked,

"Ha'át'íísh ą' baa yáníłti', shiyázhí?" *What are you talking about, my little one?* she quietly asked.

"Éí yee' shizhé'é nahalingo naat'áanii deeshłeeł nisin, áko nidi doo naabaahii binaat'áanii deeshłeeł da. Shínaaí t'áá'íídą́ą́' áájí naat'áanii nilįį dooleeł yiniiyé nihizhé'é yits'ą́ą́dóó 'íhooł'aah. Shí 'éí 'ił hodéezyéelgo naat'áanii nilínígíí nishłį́į dooleeł nisin. Na'abaahjí 'éí doo bidínéeshnáa da. Naat'áanii dąągo dóó shįįgo bidine'é yá nidaha'áhígíí 'atah nishłį́į doo nisin. Éí biniiyé kodóó dóó náasjį' éí baa 'íhoosh'aah dooleeł nisingo yee' baa nitséskees." *I want to become a leader just like my father, but I do not want to become a War Leader. My older brother is already training to become such a leader as he is training and learning from our father. It is my desire to become a leader in times of peace. I want to become one who leads in the spring and summer seasons. My thoughts are not compatible to the thoughts of war. For that reason, from here on, I want to learn from someone who leads during times of peace.*

"Dá'ák'eh baa 'áháyą́ągi shinaanish naat'i' dooleeł nisin. Áko nidi, nihe'anaa'í nihik'ijį' nídadibahgo 'éí shizhé'é dóó shínaaí t'áá bíighah naashbaah dooleeł. Haaléit'éego lá shizhé'é bee bił hodeeshnih nisingo yee' ch'ééh baa nitséskees. Shizhé'é bee bił hweeshne'go daats'í t'óó bąąh nahodookał nisingo biniinaa t'ahdoo baa hashne' da nít'ęę́. K'ad índa baa hashne'. T'áá ni t'éiyá niniih, shimá. Nił lá hait'é, shimá? Hait'éego lá baa nitsíníkees?" *I want to make the care of the cornfield my main area of work. When our enemies make war against us, I will fight right alongside my father and my older brother, but I will not make that my life's work. I keep thinking about the best way to tell my father. If I tell my father, he may be real disappointed and that is why I have not said anything about it. I am just now telling about it. You are the only one who knows, my mother. How do you feel about it, my mother? What do you think about it?* her usually quiet son asked, searching her face for an answer. Stunned by the many words her son spoke at one time, Nínáánibaa' searched her son's face to give herself time to contemplate on how best to answer him. Several times she opened her mouth to respond then closed it to think a little longer. Finally, she said,

"Jó naat'áanii 'ídlįįgi yéego baa nitsísíníkéez gi'át'é. Doo 'éí t'óó honoochééł nahalingo baa 'ádíínít'ą́ą da. T'áá'áníidlah shįį́ nizhé'é bee bich'į' hadiidzih. Íishją́ąshįį́ ha'át'íí níi dooleeł. Doo 'éí t'áá sáhí bił ahił nahodíilnih da. T'áá níighah sézįį dooleeł, shiyázhí," *It seems the matter of becoming a Peace Leader is one that you have thought over very well. You did not hurriedly make your decision. We will both speak with your father about it. We'll see what he says. You will not have to face him alone. I will stand right beside you,* his mother assured him. With a look of relief that was long searched and wished for, Tł'ée'go Naabaah lay back down to rest his tired body. His mother was his ally. He opened his eyes and looked at his mother with admiration in his eyes.

Just when Nínáánībaa' had finished speaking with her son, she heard a commotion coming from the direction of the sheep corral. Feeling sick to her stomach, she held her breath. Several women and girls were talking loudly, almost yelling at one another. Nínáánībaa' lifted the tufts of wool and held them tightly against her heart as she fought the wild thoughts that were assaulting her mind. She was slightly relieved to see her daughters and her daughter-in-law hurrying up the hill toward her. Dzánībaa' reached her mother first and words spilled out,

"Shimá, hastiin diigisii nilínée t'óó béédasiildzííd. Nihąąh nii'na' dóó bik'ijį' bidejį' éé' haidiigį́. T'óó 'ayóo biyid di'ilgo yídílnih. Hááhgóóshįį́ binii' nihich'į' yiyoołdlohgo yéego hodíína'. Bibe'aldǫǫh nihich'į' dah yootį́įłgo, t'óó baa'iihígi 'áát'įįłgo ná'ahóónáád. Dibé tsxį́įłgo 'aadę́ę́' nihaa dah nídiijéé'." *My mother, we got scared of the man who is crazy. He came sneaking up on us and took off his upper garment (shirt). He was rubbing his hairy chest and smiling at us. He pointed his gun at us and kept doing awful things in front of us. We brought the sheep back here in a hurry.* Dzánībaa' stopped speaking to shake her entire body as if she was trying to shed her thoughts of the crazy soldier, after which she continued,

"Hastiin diigisii nihich'į' t'óó baa'iihígi 'áát'įįłgo bik'ídasiigal. Nihizhé'é dóó nihilah dóó Kiizhóní shą'? T'ahdoósh nákáah da?" *We looked up and saw the crazy man doing awful things. Where is our father and our brother and Kiizhóní? Have they come back yet?* Dédii interrupted her sister and asked,

"ShiKiizhóní shą'?" *Where is my Kiizhóní?* Her mother and her sister turned toward her and stared at her. Dédii had never shown a sign of affection toward Kiizhóní in the presence of her family. Noticing their surprise, Dédii asked,

"Háísh dó' bíí'ii jílį?" *Who else does he belong to?* Nínááníbaa' gasped. Her daughter surprised her with her flippant question. Her heart was so sad for her daughter who fell in love with a member of their enemy and who continued to love him through his long absence and now gave a hint of her affection for another man, a man who met with Hashké Yił Naabaah's approval as well as her own. Nínááníbaa' wanted to see her daughter happy and loved. Her Dédii deserved happiness. Dzáníbaa' interrupted her mother's thoughts when she said to Dédii,

"Na'áłchíní Kiizhóní 'ayóó'ádayó'ní. Bí dó', na'áłchíní bił ayóó'át'é, shádí. 'Éí bił nani'aashgo shą'?" *Your children love Kiizhóní. He also thinks your children are wonderful, my older sister. What if you settle down with him?*

"Ákǫ́ǫ́ 'éí doo nitséskees da, háálá shiyáázh bizhé'é hólǫ. 'Áko nidi Kiizhóní 'éí 'áłchíní nahalingo 'ayóo be'ádílááh. Bich'į' hanii' bijiyoołdlohgo t'éí bił hózhǫ́ǫ łeh." *I do not think that way because my son has a father. Kiizhóní is so silly, just like a child. He is happy only when you are smiling at him.* Nínáánîbaa' knew her entire family would be so pleased if Dédii and Kiizhóní were married. Speaking her thoughts Nínáánîbaa' said,

"Azhą́ shį́į́ nihe'anaa'í baa ni'deeltį́į nidi, doo bił ahidinits'a' da dóó doo bił ahidíníniIlnáa da. 'Áłahjį' daats'í nihá 'ata' hane' dooleeł? Náás silį́į'ii nilį́. Łą́ náához yee nilą́ąjį' naaghá. Nilą́ąjį' są́ yiih doogááł. Są́ yiih híyáago yéego bich'į' anáhóót'i' doo. 'Áajį' ahoolzhiizhgo, baa 'áháyą́ągi bił ahaa ch'í'ahidíígééł. Ákót'éego 'iináhígíí doo ná nisin da, she'awéé'. Naa hą́ąh nisingo biniinaa kót'éego nich'į' yáshti'." *Although you were given to our enemy in marriage, you do not speak the same language and you are not compatible with him. Will you always need an interpreter to communicate with one another? He is an older man. He is much older than you. He will enter old age before you do. When he enters old age, he will have a lot of hardship. When that time comes, you will be loaded down with caring for him. I don't want that kind of life for you, my baby. I do not want a hard life for you and that is why I am talking to you this way.*

Dédii felt tears form in her eyes. She turned away from her mother and felt the warm rays of the sun gently settle on her tears. For years, she had gently nourished the memory of the tall gray-haired one and her love for him. Her heart was breaking. "My family wants a rich life for me, one full of laughter, love, spirituality, contentment, faithfulness, peace, happiness, and safety. The tall gray-haired one cannot give me what my family wants for me," she thought. The tears she refused to cry for several years came to the surface and streamed down her face. Sobs shook her frail body. She had to admit her mother was right. Her mother always knew the way in which to lead her family. She never failed to make sense of confusion.

A few warriors left the camp when the sheep and the women and girls returned to their camping area. Before the young men left, they announced they were going to hunt for prairie dogs.

"T'áátá'í nootínígo dlǫ́ǫ́' bitsį' ła' dadoołghał. Dlǫ́ǫ́' bik'ah nihíla' bąąh nidaazlįįgo da'doołghał." *Each one of you will have prairie dog meat to eat. The fat from the prairie dog meat will be running down your hands as you eat the meat.* To their announcement, Nínáánîbaa' replied,

"Ádaa 'ádahołyą́ą́ dóó 'ałhaa 'ádahołyą́. Tsxį́įłgo nihaa níjíkah, sha'áłchíní." *Take care of yourselves. Take care of one another. Come back to us in a hurry, my children.* In answer, the young men swung their slingshots above their heads and walked quickly into the shallow hills, away from the Pecos River.

True to their word, the young men returned with a long string of prairie dogs. In preparation for the successful hunt, the young boys kept several fires going. After the skins of the prairie dogs were singed off, the boys used wide flat rocks to carefully remove the fires then used the same flat rocks to dig holes in the ground where the fires once burned. Being careful to maintain the heat, the boys carefully removed the hot sand. The prairie dogs had been cut open and their internal organs had already been removed. Using leaves the men gathered from the riverbank, they covered the prairie dogs and placed them in the ground and covered the rodents with hot earth. The fires were set back in place and the people sat in a circle telling stories. Their stories ranged from childhood experiences to stories of preparing and maintaining a dá'ák'eh *cornfield.* When the voices quieted, the men removed the fires and the hot earth covering the prairie dogs and gently lifted out the roasted prairie dogs. The men reverently announced,

"Dząądi da'ohsą́, . Dlǫ́ǫ́' bitsį' daołghał." *Eat over here. Eat prairie dog meat.*

The women were given a roasted prairie dog first. The children were asked to share their meal with their siblings. The men made sure everyone had a prairie dog before they took a roasted one. There was complete silence while the people ate. Only the sound of the smacking of lips was heard. The scent of roasted prairie dog meat hovered in the air above the people as they ate the delicacy that was obtained and prepared by the young men.

Nínááníbaa' broke the silence,

"Ahéhee', sha'áłchíní, nihada'sołtsood.
Dlǫ́ǫ́' bitsį' nínéiisisdlįh. Dlǫ́ǫ́' bitsį' nídasiidlįh. Ahéhee'gi 'ádanihoohłaa." *Thank you, my children, you have shared your meal with us. I have tasted prairie dog meat once again. We have tasted prairie dog meat once again. You have gratified us.*

The children held their collective breaths as they waited to hear their older brothers, fathers, grandfathers and uncles rub their fat-covered hands together, then rub their hands on their ankles and legs. The children heard an echo of the words among the men as they said,

"K'ad lá dinishjáád dooleeł." *Now I will run real fast.* Others rubbed the fat on their elbows and wrists and echoed the words,

"K'ad lá honishyóí dooleeł." *Now I will be helpful.* The boys repeated the actions of the men and repeated their words. The echo of the words continued as the light of the moon pulled the late-night constellations across the night sky. The people looked up and breathed a word of gratitude to the Creator. Nínááníbaa' and Dzáníbaa' and Dédii breathed,

"Ahéhee', shiTaa', nihik'i jiisínídli'. T'áadoo hasinígi da'iilghal." *Thank you, our Spiritual Father, you have blessed us. Unexpectedly, we ate meat once again.*

****

Hashké Yił Naabaah, his son, Kiizhóní and the warriors walked back into their camp at dusk of the next day. Without hesitation, Hashké Yił Naabaah walked to where his beautiful Nínááníbaa' was sitting. He sat down beside her and watched the last light of day disappear into the western horizon.

"Nídįh sélį́į́'," *I missed you,* he said quietly as he took her hand and pulled it close to his heart and held it there. Quietly, Nínááníbaa' responded,

"Shí dó' yéego níhásááh nít'ę́ę́' shaa néínídzá, nihaa nánohkai." *Me too, I really missed you and you came back to me, you all came back to us.*

"Nich'į' shíni' íí'áá nít'ę́ę́'. Ha'át'íi da shą' jiyą́ nisingo naa nitsídiiskos." *I was worried about you. I kept thinking about you and wondered what you were eating.*

"Ninaabaahii t'áá kǫ́ǫ́ hook'ee nííniligíí dlǫ́ǫ́' hádaashzhee'go t'áálá'í niitínígo nihik'eh dlǫ́ǫ́' nihá dayiishxį́į́ dóó nihá łeeh deist'é. 'Ayóó 'áhálniihgo, 'áda'azįįd bich'į' jidineezbin nahalingo, dlǫ́ǫ́' deiildéél." *The warriors you left here to watch over us hunted and killed one prairie dog for each one of us and roasted it in the hot ground. It was delicious and we ate the prairie dogs as if we had sat down to a feast.* Nínááníbaa' giggled when she said,

"Danihibid dah daasts'id." *Our stomachs stuck out.* She continued, saying, "Ts'ídá doo 'a'jółtsódígi 'áhálniihgo da'iilghal dóó nídadeegalígi 'áhoodzaa. 'Áłchíní doo daachagóó t'óó nihił hodéezyéelgo da'iilghaazh dóó danihiiską́. Doo 'íits'a'ígóó 'awéé' danilínígíí da'iiłhaazh." *It was so good, we could not even think of sharing it with someone as we ate it. It was as if we got our eyesight back. The children did not cry, it was peaceful when we went to sleep and we slept through the night. The babies went to sleep without making a sound.* Hashké Yił Naabaah licked his lips and swallowed the saliva that collected in his mouth from the description his wife gave of their feast from the night before.

"Nihíshą'? Niha da'iistsoodísh?" *What about you? Did they give you food?* she asked.

"Aoo', áko nidi 'atsį' dííldzid léi' nihitaadaas'nii'. Kóníłyázhí nidi doochohoo'íįgóó niłchon, áko nidi baa hóchį'go nihitaadaas'nii'. Níléí tó nílínígíí biih bee 'adzíiłne'. Háni'dii tó yii' naaldeehii yee hwiih daaleeh nisingo t'óó 'áajigo bee 'adzíiłne'. Chxosh yiists'ą́ą'ii' taah yilts'id." *Yes, but they only gave us rotten meat. As small as it was it smelled bad. They were stingy with what they distributed to us. I just threw it into the running water. When I threw it into the water, I thought, let the creatures that live in the water eat it and get full on it. When it fell into the water, it made the splashing sound of a solid object hitting the water.* Hashké Yił Naabaah went on to explain that his warriors gave the meat they were given to hungry women and children who did not have a man to obtain rations for them.

"Bił ayóó 'ádahoodzaa nahalingo 'ak'áán dóó gohwééh yił dah diijéé'." *They ran away with the flour and coffee as if something wonderful happened to them.* After there was a lull in their conversation, Nínáánibaa' told her husband their son had some important information to share with him.

****

Hashké Yił Naabaah assumed his son wanted to speak with him regarding the young girl who kept watch over him when he was extremely ill. He reluctantly called for his son.

"She'awéé yázhí, hágo," *My little baby, come here,* he called. Tł'ée'go Naabaah knew his father was calling for him. It was the way his father addressed him as his father's youngest child. Tł'ée'go Naabaah looked at his mother, smiled a weak smile, got up from his rug blanket, and sat down next to his mother who was sitting by his father.

"Ha'át'íí lá, shizhé'é?" *What is it, my father?*

"Níla'ísh yá'át'ééh náádleeł? Náádzíí'ísh?" *Is your hand getting better? Has it healed?*

"Aoo', shíla' yá'át'ééh náádleeł." *Yes, my hand is getting better.*

"Nimá yee' ha'át'íishįį bee shich'į' hanidziih ní. Ha'át'íí lá, she'awéé'?" *Your mother told me you wanted to speak to me about something. What is it, my baby?* Before he could lose his courage, Tł'éego Naabaah told his father,

"Éí yee' naat'áanii 'ídlįįgi bínashinínítą́'ígíí shił nilįį dóó 'ayóó'át'éego nich'į' baa 'ahééh nisin. Áko nidi naat'áanii na'abaahjí dahóo'áłígíí baa 'íhoosh'aah dooleełígíí doo bídínéeshnáa da dóó doo bíneeshdlįį da sélįį'. Shínaaí 'éí 'ááji naat'áanii nilįį dooleeł yiniiyé nits'ą́ą́dóó 'íhooł'aah. Shí 'éí dąągo dóó shįįgo naat'áanii danilínígíí binahat'a' ayóo bíneeshdlį. 'Éí lá hait'éego baa nitsíníkees, shizhé'é?" *I appreciate and value your teaching regarding becoming a War Leader. My older brother is already training to become such a leader. He is training and learning from you. It is my desire to become a leader in times of peace. My thoughts are not compatible to the thoughts of war and I do not enjoy it. I want to become one who leads in the spring and summer seasons. I enjoy learning about becoming a Peace Leader. What do you think of it, my father?*

"Dá'ák'eh baa 'áháyą́ągi dóó bína'niltin t'éí shinaanish ádeeshłííł dóó 'ááji t'éiyá shinaanish naat'i' dooleeł nisin. Áko nidi, nihe'anaa'í nihik'ijį' nídadibahgo 'éí ni dóó shínaaí t'áá nihíighah naashbaah dooleeł. Haaléit'éego lá bee nił hodeeshnih nisingo yee' ch'ééh baa nitséskees nít'ę́ę́'. Naa sistxi'go biniinaa t'ahdoo nił hashne' da. Ei shį́į́ naah hodinóokał nisingo biniinaa t'ahdoo bee nił hashne' da nít'ę́ę́'. Shimá 'éí bee bił hweeshne'. Díí yee' yéego baa nitsísékézígí 'át'é. T'áá hazhó'ó t'áá ni dóó shimá t'éí wohniih, shizhé'é. Shínaaí t'ahdoo bił hashne' da. Nił lá hait'é, shizhé'é? Haa lá yit'éego baa nitsíníkees?" *I want to make the care of the cornfield my main area of work. When our enemies make war against us, I will fight right alongside you and my older brother but I will not make that my life's work. I didn't know how to tell you because I wanted to spare your feelings. I kept thinking about the best way to tell you. I thought that if I told you about my desire, you might be real disappointed. I told my mother about it. I have put much thought into my decision. You and my mother are the only ones who know. I have not told my brother about it. How do you feel about it, my father? What do you think about it?*

"Hádą́ą́' shą' akót'éego níni' silį́į́', shiye'?" *When did you make up your mind, my son?*

"T'ah t'áá hooghandi danihighan yę́ędą́ą́'. Nóoda'í ła' shimá dah deidiilóosgo ch'ééh ádáát'įįd, áko yik'ee bádahazhchįįdgo shimá deidiyoołhééł yiniiyé k'asídą́ą́' shimá béésh yaa 'adeiz'ą́. Nóoda'í béésh yoo'áłę́ę sélkahgo 'índa nihik'ideeskai. Éí 'áádóó doo niizį́į' da.

Doo 'éí na'abaah bik'ee niseeshdáa da dóó doo binásdzid da nidi t'óó doo niizį́į' da. Shimá k'asídą́ą́' sélkahígíí biniinaa na'abaah doo niizį́į' da." *At the time when we were still living at home, some Utes tried to take my mother captive but failed. After that, they got mad and tried to kill her with a knife but in shooting the Ute warrior, I nearly shot my mother with an arrow, but I was able to shoot the enemy with one arrow. After that, they left us alone. Following that incident I did not want the life of a War Leader. I am not afraid of warfare, I just don't want it.*

"Aadę́ę́' nihidi'noolkał yę́ędą́ą́' shidine'é t'óó'ahayóí bąąh ádahasdįįd. Nihe'anaa'í 'éí doo bida'diił'áágóó t'óó náás danihinoołkałgo kojį' adanihineeskaad. Háida 'ádin yileehgo bik'ee haashį́į nisht'éego díkwíįjį shį́į ná'ádleeh ne'. Kwe'é nidi txi'hoo'níįh t'éí bii' ałk'ineiikai." *When we were forced to walk here, many of our people lost their loved ones. Our enemies did not care, they just forced our people forward and on to this place. When someone dies, I am affected by their loss for a few days. Here, we are walking in so much suffering and torture.*

"Shimá doo nízaadgóó bits'á shíni' da. Yéego txi'hooznii'ígíí biniinaa. Ni dóó shínaaí naat'áanii bił ahínínáohkahgo, shimá t'áá sáhí hooghandi sidáa łeh ne'. Éí dó' biniinaa t'áá hooghangi shinaanish naat'i' doo niizį́į'. Díí t'áá'át'é shá baa 'ákonínízin dooleeł, shizhé'é." *Another reason is that I do not want to be far from my mother. She suffered greatly. When you and my older brother attend War Leadership meetings, my mother used to stay home alone, that is the reason I want to stay around our home and work there. Consider all these reasons I gave you, my father.*

"Shiye', bee shił hwíínílne'ígíí shįį́ bits'ą́ądóó t'áá yéego níni' bii' hasdił. Díí yee' doo ts'íí'át'éégóó txi'dahwii'nííh. Hastóí daniidlínígíí nihe'iina' bídaneeldin yę́ę nihąąh yist'įįd. Bee 'iiná 'ádeiil'ínée 'ałtsoh nihighadaasya'. Nihe'anaa'í nihik'ijį' nídadiibaa'go, shidine'é bee bich'ą́ąh nideeshbah yę́ęni' t'áadoo bił hadóshchídí da, ádin. T'áá hazhó'ó shizaad t'éiyá shidine'é bee bich'ą́ąh nideeshbahgo shił hoo'a'. K'ad éí ch'éná, dichin, doo 'awosh, éhályáhígíí, díí t'áá'át'é nihik'ijį' nidaabaah dóó bik'ijį' nideiibaah. Díí t'áá'át'é nihe'anaa'í daazlį́į', áko nidi, doo daat'įį da. Doo daat'įį daaígíí biniinaa báádahadzid, bá'át'e' dahólǫ. Ił hodéezyéélji naat'áanii nishłį́į dooleeł dinínígíí, díí nihe'anaa'í doo daat'ínígíí bik'ijį' nanibaah doo. 'Ayóo nił aahojooba', she'awéé', éí beego naat'áanii yá'át'éehii nílį́į doo." *My son, what you have told me has affected your mind in a grave way. We are facing extreme suffering. Those of us who are men, our livelihood has been stripped of us. All the tools with which we made a living have been taken from us. If our enemy came against us in warfare, I have no weapons with which to protect my people. I have nothing to place in my hand. All I have is my words with which to protect my people. Loneliness, hunger, insomnia, homesickness, missing those you love are our enemies. They make war against us and we make war against them. These have become our new enemy but we can't see them. They are dangerous and deadly because we can't see them. You want to become a Peace Leader, even as a Peace Leader, you still have to fight against the enemies that can't be seen. You are kind, my baby, because of that, you will make a very good Peace Leader.* Hashké Yił Naabaah looked at his hands. Absent from his hands were his tools as a warrior, his bow and arrows, his lance, his spear, his shield and other items of warfare. He already knew from the time his son was still a toddler, his youngest son would not become a War Leader, but instead, a Peace Leader.

"Ha'át'íísh dó' náádideesh'niił? T'áá bahat'aadí yéego baa nitsísíníkééz. T'áadoo baa níni'í, she'awéé', shiye', shiyázhí. 'Akót'éego 'ádá hodíní'ánígíí baa shił hózhǫ́. Shiyázhí, hooghandi nániikaigo 'índa yá'át'ééh nídíídleeł. T'áá'ániit'é yá'át'ééh nídadiidleeł. Áájí 'iinánígíí béédahoniilzin dóó bídaneeldin." *What else can I say? It is obvious you have thought this through. Don't worry about your decision, my baby, my son, my little one. I am happy you have set plans for becoming a Peace Leader. When you go back home, you will regain your health. We will all become well again. We know that kind of life and are used to it,* his father said softly.

"Hágo, shiyázhí." *Come here, my little one.* Father and son fell into each other's arms and held each other. Hashké Yił Naabaah was so very proud of his youngest son.

"Shizhé'é, 'azhą́ shį́į́ naabaahii binaat'áanii nílį́į nidi, dá'ák'ehgi na'anish bínashiníníłtą́ą́'. Naadą́ą́' dóó naayízí dóó nímasii dóó tł'ohchin dóó naa'ólí k'idadilyéegi yiishchį́į́h dóó shá nidanise'. Kojí nihine'jí dá'ák'eh bá hosé!bį' dóó bii' k'í'di'deeshłééł. Bínashininíłtą'ę́ę shidine'é bee bínanishtin doo. 'Ahéhee', shizhé'é, 'ayóó'ánííníish'ní." *Even though you are a War Leader, you taught me how to maintain a cornfield. I know how to grow corn, squash, potatoes, onions, and beans. I have started to prepare my own cornfield behind our camp so that I may maintain the teachings of my people. Thank you, my father, I love you.*

"Shí dó', ayóó'ánííníish'ní, shiye, she'awéé'." *I love you too, my son, my baby.*

Nínáánibaa' listened to her beautiful son telling his older brother he wanted to become a leader who teaches the Naabeehó people about maintaining the health of the dá'ák'eh. "Our father taught us that the dá'ák'eh is our elder. There has to be someone in our family who does not neglect the teachings of the dá'ák'eh, our elder. My son, the Peace Leader," she thought as a smile brightened her face.

Chapter Six
The Dirty Runaway Soldier

Hashké Yił Naabaah's people had become more vulnerable as they explored areas further east from their camping area to look for pasture land to which they could herd the sheep. They found wolves had become a menace to the Naabeehó people who lived south of their camp. They heard stories about how the wolves tear a person apart limb by limb, then finally eat the heart last. The elder Peace Leader told his people that as long as they explored the area in a large group, the wolves would be less of a danger.

A small group of young women and girls did not need any convincing. They gladly complied, enjoying every opportunity to take the sheep out to graze on nearby pastures. A larger group of young women and girls became afraid and were reluctant to take the sheep out to pasture but forced themselves to do so. They did not want to be deprived of being near the flock of sheep that was bringing healing to their devastated bodies. The young women and girls gathered in a huddle to shield one another. Not only were there soldiers nearby in their picket forts, there was the lone soldier who was assigned to watch over the Naabeehó women. The young women and girls remembered the words of their leaders who warned them to be careful of the evil men who all dressed alike and who carried long guns. Stories had been told many times in different parts of the Fort Sumner Indian Reservation of evil men who could not satisfy their hunger for inflicting torture on the female Naabeehó prisoners of war.

When Hashké Yił Naabaah and the elder Peace Leader returned to their camp from their meeting with the tall gray-haired one, the young angry women gathered around their leaders and told them of a bold, repulsive skinny soldier and his bold revolting activities. The leaders listened intently to the women. They knew the old soldier was a danger to the women and girls and also to the young men who accompanied the women. The new concern was the avoidance of bloodshed and death of Naabeehó people due to the old soldier's careless actions.

The elder Peace Leader hastily sent a message to the tall gray-haired one, requesting a meeting with him. Days later, soldiers came to their camp requesting a meeting with the tall Navajo leader. The elder Peace Leader and Hashké Yił Naabaah were disappointed when the tall gray-haired one did not arrive with his soldiers. The elder Peace Leader bravely told the interpreters,

"Ei naabaahii binaat'áanii shą' háájí? 'Éí nihaa doogáałii' bich'į' nihíni' íí'áhígíí bee bił dahodiilnih nisingo biniinaa 'éí há'íił'a' nít'ę́ę́'." *Where is those warriors' (soldiers') leader? We wanted him to come so we could tell him of what we are worried about and that is why I sent for him.*

"Shinaanish hólǫ́ ní, jiní," *He said, he has work to do,* one interpreter answered without telling the soldiers what the leader asked.

"Yáadilá 'óolyéé dó', ha'ahoosdlí'ę́ę," *What a thing to say, we needlessly placed our faith in him,* Hashké Yił Naabaah said with disappointment and resentment in his voice.

"Éí binaabaahii ła' t'áadoo 'ákǫ́ǫ t'éí 'áát'įįł. T'óó nichǫ́'ígi 'áát'įįł. Ts'ídá doo hóyą́ą da. Diigisii daats'í nılı̨́. Sáanii yaatįįh nádááh. T'óó baa'iihígi 'áát'įįłgo biniinaa sáanii béédaasdzííd. Hanaabaahii doo 'áhályą́ą daígíí biniinaa haada hoodzaago, jó shidine'é da bik'íhodoot'ah. Éí shá bee bił hólne'." *One of their soldiers is doing things that are not acceptable. What he is doing is awful. He is not sensible. He may be someone who is stupid. He bothers the women. Because of his behavior that is unacceptable, the women are afraid of him. If something adverse happens because of the actions of their soldier, my people will be blamed, instead of him. Tell them that for me.* After waiting for the first interpreter, the second interpreter turned to a soldier and said,

"One soldier bother the ladies and girls. He not nice to them. Leaders said girls and ladies be scared of crazy soldier. He not nice. Leader said girls and ladies scared." The soldiers took note, turned and left, leaving their interpreters to talk with the elder Peace Leader and Hashké Yił Naabaah. The young soldiers did not acknowledge their understanding of the gravity of the situation facing the Naabeehó women and the people.

Every day the elder Peace Leader and Hashké Yił Naabaah waited for the tall gray-haired one to arrive at their camp, but each day ended without his arrival. The brave women and girls could not be discouraged from taking the sheep out to graze for the next few days, so the elder Peace Leader and Hashké Yił Naabaah were coerced into allowing the young women and girls to continue to herd the sheep. The older women were worried about the large number of young warriors who were assigned to accompany the young women and girls to protect them and to discourage the old skinny, crazy soldier from harming the vulnerable women. The women were also worried because they knew the blood-thirsty soldiers were known to shoot to kill before they became fully aware of a situation. They knew their sons, brothers, and nephews were vulnerable in their role as protectors, all because of the antics of the old pesky soldier.

Every day, the old pesky soldier appeared in the open areas near the place where the women and girls took the sheep. His body odor announced his presence long before the old soldier was seen by the women. The old pesky soldier was skinny, dirty, had dirty stringy hair that resembled straw, and had a big booming voice which he used to intimidate Naabeehó prisoners.

A message was sent back to Hashké Yił Naabaah and the Peace Leader by the young soldiers in which the tall gray-haired one explained that the old skinny soldier had volunteered to become a soldier and later had been assigned to protect the women when they took the sheep out to graze upon the sun-dried and wind-dried hills, hills that were dotted with precious few weeds. The old soldier is harmless, they were told. Hashké Yił Naabaah was disappointed by the flippant answer sent by the tall gray-haired one. It was evident to Hashké Yił Naabaah that the tall gray-haired one was not aware of what his old skinny soldier was capable of.

Nínáánibaa' consulted with her husband to tell him to support her in not allowing their daughters and daughter-in-law to join the young women and girls who were taking out the sheep.

"Hojoobá'ígo yee' shich'é'éké shaa nídashoo'eezh. Akéé' dookahígíí doo bá nisin da. 'Éí bee bił hodíílnih. Hastiin, k'adni' nihaadaaní (the tall gray-haired one) yileehígíí, binaabaahii t'óó baa'iihígi 'áát'įįłígíí doo bi'diił'áa da." *Our daughters were finally brought back to us. I do not want for them to follow. The man, who wants to be our son-in-law (the tall gray-haired one) so badly, is not concerned about his warrior who does shameful acts.*

The Naabeehó women and girls hated the presence of the pesky old soldier. They hated the stench that followed his skinny form, his dirty straw-like hair that hung in clumps down the sides of his head, and his booming voice that did not match his skinny body. Every day, the skinny old soldier came to watch the women and girls who were out with the sheep. With an evil smile, while holding his rifle, his actions became increasingly bold where he usually set his eyes on a young woman and stood nearby rubbing his chest through his thick shirt.

As time wore on, it never failed, the old skinny soldier would slowly unbutton his dirty shirt and as each button was popped out of its buttonhole, the old skinny soldier placed his dirty hand inside his shirt and rubbed his dirty chest rather vigorously. As he rubbed his chest, a crooked smile would appear on his face and show his yellow, jagged, crooked teeth.

Every day, the women and girls cautiously watched the crazy soldier step closer and closer to where they sat on the ground, watching the sheep. At different times, the skinny old soldier would take out his watch which was attached to a chain, stretch, yawn, belch loudly, then get up off of the rock he sat upon and walk slowly to where the young women and girls sat on the ground. Before he would reach their resting spot, the young women and girls would jump up and run toward the flock of sheep and herd them back to their camp, but the dirty, skinny soldier would usually run and place his skinny, smelly body between the women and their camp.

One day, the skinny soldier became even more bold after his usual antics and grabbed a young woman who was running toward the camp and started to drag her away from the others. The young woman screamed, kicked, bit, and tugged at the skinny soldier while the women hit him with rocks that were hot from sitting in the hot sun. As soon as he released the young woman, the women stopped throwing rocks at him because they were afraid of the dangerous gun he carried. The young women instantly remembered when they were still living on their land between their four sacred mountains, they had seen their men get shot and killed after the soldiers pointed their gun at the men and shot them. The women admitted they were afraid of retaliation in the case that the old skinny soldier told his superiors of how mean and unruly the women had become in their attempt to free one of their own. The young women regretted forgetting to gather pebbles beforehand to place in their slingshots to scare off the old skinny soldier. When they returned to their camps, their husbands, fathers, sons, and brothers chided them for not gathering pebbles with which to pelt the old skinny soldier with their slingshots.

The young woman who was nearly dragged off by the skinny soldier reported she noticed the old skinny soldier's neck was very wrinkled and his skin looked like the skin of a horned toad. The women laughed every time the young woman described her assailant's neck. The cries of the women yelling,

"We'! We'! We'! Wéée'!" *Yuck! Yuck! Yuck! Yuuuuck!* could be heard drifting on the wind at Hashké Yił Naabaah's people's camp. More screams of disgust were heard when the young woman told the others of the foul smell of the skinny soldier.

"Tł'ízí chǫǫh sání halchinígi 'áhálchin!" *He smells like an old billy goat!* and another round of,

"We'! We'! We'! Wéée'!" *Yuck! Yuck! Yuck! Yuuuuck!* could be heard.

As the days wore on, the women noticed the old soldier was placing himself nearer to their resting spot on the ground. He smiled wickedly every time his buttons were popped out of their buttonhole. He would settle into his routine of settling down on the ground or on a rock and stroking his chest. The girls and women did not dare to take their watchful eye off of the old wrinkly rascal.

Becoming bolder in his actions, the old skinny soldier was not only witnessed opening his shirt to expose his dirty hairy chest but he did not stop there like he did on earlier days. Instead, he reached his bony, chapped hand into his loosened pants. The women were afraid of what he would expose in his new daring antics. Already repulsed by his actions and the appearance of his skinny, wrinkly, dirty hairy chest, the women did not have to look up to see where the skinny soldier had stationed himself. A breeze carried his foul smell, alerting them of his close proximity.

Every day, fear rose within the women. They wondered if he was one of the soldiers the Naabeehó people talked about who had raped a Naabeehó woman in front of her children; he may have killed the fathers for protecting their families from the soldiers. Their horrified thoughts brought back the terrible memory of the soldiers who cut off the breasts of young girls and played a game where they batted the breast from one soldier's stick to another. They further heard the many horror stories that were told about a certain man the Naabeehó called, the One with a Red Shirt (Kit Carson) who along with his troops burned hogans with the Naabeehó family trapped inside when the fire was set to the entrance of the hogan made of cedar logs. They were told that only screams could be heard, which after an agonizing time would be silenced as the black smoke curled upward, making sad shapes in the sky.

Anxiety filled the women's minds when they were reminded of a time when the soldiers of the man named Red Shirt herded over a hundred goats and sheep into an enclosed area and set the herd on fire. Since that time, Naabeehó women retold stories of having been forced to watch in horror when the soldiers, who held them back to keep them from rescuing their livestock, reduced them to helplessness.

The older women reminded the young women and girls of the contribution the sheep and goats make to their well-being. The young girls knew the words by heart but they listened patiently as they were told again and again.

"Dibé dóó tł'ízí 'ayóó nihaa dajooba'go 'át'é. Deesk'aazgo nidaniichéhę́ędą́ą́' dibé dóó tł'ízí 'ayóó 'át'éego bits'áníłdoi łeh ne'. Tł'ée'go 'ayóó'íídéesk'aazgo, dibé naazhjéé'góó bita' nídanihiilkáah ne'. Ach'ą́h danihi'niighą́ągo t'óó ła' nínádeiil'ah łeh ne' dóó bitsį'ígíí deiilt'isii' nída'iilghał łeh. Áádóó danihi'éé' dibé bighaa' bits'ą́ądóó nishóhwiit'eehgo bii' nishiijée' łeh. Hastiin diigisii nilínígíí daats'í 'atah nihidine'é 'atxíyiilaa? Hatxíhíláanee'ę́ę́'!" *Sheep and goats are very kind to us. When we were running from the enemy (soldiers), the sheep and goats provided us with warmth, especially on the nights when it was extremely cold. We slept amongst the sheep and goats. And when we were very hungry for mutton, all we had to do was butcher a sheep or a goat and cook it, then eat the meat. And our clothing we wear is obtained from the wool of the sheep. It could be that the crazy man was among the ones who severely traumatized our people. What a scary thought!*

During the time when the old crazy, dirty soldier was terrorizing the young women and girls, Dédii and Dzáníbaa' frequently asked their father when the tall gray-haired one was going to remove the old soldier from his assignment of watching over the women. He usually responded saying,

"Díkwíidi shįį́ hastóí nihá 'ata' dahalne'ígíí bee bił nídahweeshne'. T'áá nihí baa tįįh yiikaigo shįį́ yá'át'ééh." *Several times I have told the men who interpret for us. It is probably better that we deal with it on our own.*

Not long after the incident where the old crazy soldier tried to drag the young woman away, the young women and girls noticed the crazy old soldier ventured even nearer to where they sat and looked from one face to another as he stroked various parts of his body. The old soldier increased his bold antics where he was seen removing his clothes in attempts to expose himself to the young women and girls.

Dédii and Dzáníbaa' reported the incidents to their mother, who informed other older women about the impending danger. After a long discussion, it was decided that several older women would go out and herd sheep with the young women and girls.

The women and girls cut off more pieces of the calico fabric for the older women to cover their heads to go out with the sheep. Once out, they all covered their heads with the fabric and sat in a huddle as if nothing changed.

Over the next few days the older women tried their best to ignore the old soldier. With every passing day, he became more reckless in his sordid acts. One day it was decided by the elder Peace Leader and Hashké Yił Naabaah the older women would be the only ones to herd the sheep. The older women hoped the old skinny soldier would not get close enough to them to realize older women had replaced the younger women when they took the sheep out. With every passing day, the old soldier kept up his despicable behavior.

One day after the old skinny soldier entertained himself by exposing himself while sitting on a nearby rock, the older women were relieved when they saw him disappearing over a small hill. Not long after, the women saw an unrecognizable figure running toward them. They feared it may be one of their enemies who was wearing buckskin clothing. Cautiously, the older women pulled their scarves up to hide their faces and sat still to watch the figure come closer. The women grabbed their sticks and slingshots while they tightly held several small pebbles in their hands. "All we need to do is aim right," Nínáánníbaa' thought.

The person running toward them was wheezing loudly. When the person came closer, the women realized it was the old skinny soldier. He had taken all of his clothes off! The women sat still and quietly observed his skinny naked body running toward them. Their hearts were pounding in their chests out of anger, but the women could not help but laugh as the pesky soldier's skinny body wobbled back and forth as he ran. The women lowered their heads so the skinny soldier would think the young women and girls were huddled together. Nínáánííbaa' was laughing so hard she could hardly talk to say,

" 'K'ad,' nihidííniidgo, danihich'ah nahgóó kódadohłíiłii' 'ayóó'íits'a'go hadadidołwosh." *When I say 'now', remove your scarves and yell really loud.* When they could hear the old skinny soldier's footsteps nearly upon them and when they could hear his raspy heavy breathing, the women pushed back their calico scarves. They waved their sticks in the air and yelled and screamed in unison,

"Shéebee!" *Go away!*

"Haash nit'į́, diigisii!" *What are you doing, stupid!*

Nílááh háadi da ni'éé' t'áágééd naanínáánáalwoł! Kodi 'éí dooda!" *Go somewhere else and run around without your clothes! Not here!* An older woman yelled,

"Nídinilgą́ązhgo hanii 'áníťį!" *You must be running because of a nightmare!*

"Nílááh nidine'é bich'į' nídílyeedgo 'áadi níłchxongo sínítłéé'!" *Go on, go back to your people and plop yourself down over there with your bad odor!*

"Kojį'!" *Go away!*

"Éé' ádaadindę́ę́' hanii yílwoł! *You must be running from a place where there are no articles of clothing available!*

"T'óó yee' naa'ih! We'!" *You are ugly looking! Yuck!*

"Níłchxon, níłchxonéíí! We'!" *Your smell, you really smell! Yuck!*

"Nílááh nánííchʼį́įdii! Tʼáadoo ʼaadę́ę́ʼ náádiilwoʼí!" *Go somewhere else. Don't come around here!*

"Tsíkʼeh hanii ʼánítʼé! Tʼóó yeeʼ niniłtsǫǫz!" *You aren't any good. You are all wrinkled!*

"Yáadishąʼ eidí! Tʼóó naaʼiih!" *What an awful thing! You are ugly!*

"Tłʼízí chǫǫh biláahdi níłchxon! Tłʼízí chǫǫh nidi doo nigi ʼátʼéego niłchxon da! Weʼ, nikéyahgóó naníchʼį́įdii!" *You smell worse than a billy goat! A billy goat doesn't even smell as bad as you! Yuck! Take your evil back to your own land!*

The women watched in surprise and amusement when the old skinny soldier's facial expression turned from a wicked smile to a look of sheer terror. When the women screamed at him, they pulled out the sticks they brought with them as additional weapons and swung the sticks at him as if they were going to hit the skinny soldier's body part that he loved to expose. The dirty soldier shrieked loudly as he clumsily ran in a zigzag pattern to avoid being hit or tripped by the extended legs of the women. His body was red from fright as he nearly tripped over the women's legs that were extended in front of him. Screams and yells began again with an older woman screaming,

"Tsʼídá yéego bitłʼaaʼ yiishtxąsh, yaʼ?" *I'm going to shoot a pebble at his buttocks, okay?* Another woman yelled,

"Aooʼ, tsʼídá yéego bitłʼaaʼ yiiłtxąsh. Bee ʼadiltxąshí yéego díłtsʼǫǫd!" *Yes, hit his buttocks really hard with the pebble. Put more strength into extending the slingshot!* Nínáánîbaaʼ yelled,

"T'ahdoo nízaad niilyeedí, bee 'adiltxąshí tsé yázhí biih dahohníiłgo bee nídanołtxąsh! Tsxį́įłgo! Náániá! Náániá!" *Before he runs too far, hit him with a pebble using the slingshot! Hurry! Again! Again!* The old skinny soldier tumbled forward when he was pelted with pebbles that stung his skin. The women quickly put another pebble in their slingshots and aimed again, hitting the skinny soldier in various spots on his body, sending him running even faster over the open hilly plain. Nínááníbaa' noticed that even the sheep were watching the old skinny soldier run away. She could not talk, she could only point to the sheep. The women rolled over laughing so hard they were wheezing.

When they sat up, the women laughed at his bowed hairy red legs clumsily carrying him over the next shallow hill. The pesky soldier disappeared and was seen again running over the next low hill. They could hear him still gasping for air as he wildly ran with his arms flapping in the air. Even out of sight, the women could still hear him gasping for air. The women put their hands over their mouths and sat laughing uncontrollably. Every time another round of laughter sounded, the women held their stomachs.

Behind them, the women heard peals of laughter. A few Naabeehó men had been hiding in a shallow ditch.

"Doo lá dó' sáanii da'diłtxąsh da! Hastiin sání yę́ę shį́į bijéí niiltłahgo t'áá 'áhoodzaagi naa'íígo'go t'óó baa 'anídaohdloh!" *Wow, the ladies can sure shoot with their slingshots! The old man's heart probably stopped and he fell in an uncertain area, and here you are laughing about him!* one man said in between peals of laughter.

"Hxííhxí ya'!" *Woohoo!*

"Nihéédasiildzííd yee'!" *We are afraid of you now!*

"Doo lá dó' dahonohyói da!" *You are all very capable!*

For the next few days the people who lived at Hashké Yił Naabaah's camp laughed so hard their tears were running down the sides of their cheeks. For safety, the older women continued to take the sheep out for several days. The old filthy soldier never appeared again. The women figured he was still running in different directions, days after the incident.

The old skinny soldier never appeared again so the people felt it was safe for the young women and girls to herd the sheep again. Their laughter continued for days. The incident filtered its way through the Naabeehó camps to unify whole groups of Naabeehó people in laughter. With each retelling of the incident, new information was added as a new round of laughter sounded again. Many times a day, the older women were heard to say,

"K'asídą́ą́' la' adasiidlo'! *We almost died laughing!* The laughter would start all over again, particularly when the young men added their observations of what they witnessed.

Every time Hashké Yił Naabaah and his warriors saw an old soldier at the parade grounds, they snickered and wondered if he was the one their women scared half to death. In their minds, they could still see him running toward the east, never stopping, possibly still running through Anaa' Łání bikéyah *Many Enemies' territory (Oklahoma).*

****

At the parade grounds the tall gray-haired one kept a watchful eye, looking for the maroon leadership stick that would signify Hashké Yił Naabaah's presence. Many men walked past tall gray-haired one when they walked to where the line for counting and rations was forming. Peering out of his one eye, the tall gray-haired one squinted as many young, middle-aged, older, and old men walked past. A young soldier approached him and hissed,

"I think more Navajo men have run away, sir. There are fewer and fewer being counted. Do you want us to go after them, sir?"

"Well, I don't think that is the reason there are fewer men. Most of them are very sick. Think about it, soldier, if you had to live under these conditions, how long would you last? The Army makes sure you get three full meals a day, not always filling, but you get regular meals. These men have in their hands all they and their families are going to eat for the next three days and that is not much. Have you tasted the bacon lately? The beef we promised them were in the form of skinny, falling down cows that were driven over hundreds of miles of prairie land. And yet, the Navajo men come to be counted and when they pick up their meager rations, they gratefully accept what we give them. I fought in the Civil War. We were starving, but not like this. No, they have not escaped the reservation. They are dying. Every day, they are dying. When a male captive dies, he leaves a woman and children with no one to obtain rations for them. I did not give my life to the Army so I could stand by and watch people starve to death, but my hands are tied. I have my orders and so do you." Slowly and shamefully, the tall gray-haired one looked among the crowd of men, looking for Hashké Yił Naabaah.

Catching sight of the maroon fabric that was attached to the leadership stick, the tall gray-haired one felt a sense of calm come over him. He was a little closer to his Sunflower.

"My beautiful Sunflower," he whispered. He asked for the interpreters to be brought to him, then watched the peaceful line of men waiting for their rations. He was ashamed of the food for which the men stood patiently in line. Shiny tokens could be seen in their thin protective hands.

The tall gray-haired one asked the interpreters to bring Hashké Yił Naabaah to him. Hashké Yił Naabaah and his sons, the elder Peace Leader, Kiizhóní and the young Naabeehó 'Ashkii approached the tall gray-haired one. Hashké Yił Naabaah noticed his grandson, Dédii's oldest adopted son, did not greet the old soldier like he used to. Instead the young boy stood behind him as if he was afraid. Hashké Yił Naabaah stepped aside to encourage the tall gray-haired one to converse with the elder Peace Leader. Ignoring the elder Peace Leader, the tall gray-haired one stepped back to face

Hashké Yił Naabaah. Out from the crowd of soldiers stepped the interpreters.

Without addressing the dangerous actions of the old skinny soldier as Hashké Yił Naabaah expected, the tall gray-haired one told his interpreters to interpret a message between himself and Hashké Yił Naabaah,

"Ask him how his daughter is doing. I want specifics, gentlemen." The tall gray-haired officer waited patiently as messages were spoken between the interpreters and the leader.

"She be good." The tall gray-haired one was not satisfied with their responses. He turned to the young Naabeehó 'Ashkii to "send messages between your grandfather and me..." Looking into the young boy's eyes, the tall gray-haired one said,

"Ask him if his daughter is enjoying the sheep I placed in their care. Tell him if I had my way, I would have given the sheep to his daughter but the sheep are the property of the U.S. Army." The tall gray-haired one turned back to the interpreters and asked to have his message given to the leader. He stared at the mouths of the interpreters as the messages went from one interpreter to the other and finally to Hashké Yił Naabaah. The tall gray-haired one intently watched the face of the tall leader, hoping to obtain a clue of his response to his question. He saw a frown bring out the creases in the forehead of the tall leader. Agitated, Hashké Yił Naabaah responded, saying,

"Shitsi' bína'ízhdídóołkił biniiyé 'éí doo díkwíidishįį́ hágo hodíiniid da. Níláahdi yee' hanaabaahii sáanii dóó 'at'ééké dibé nideinihkaad yę́ę yaatįįh nádáahgo nahashzhiizh. Éí daats'í hó bich'į' jíít'aad? Danihizáanii yee' hanaabaahii yik'ee niseekai. Hanaabaaii sáanii dóó 'at'ééké yich'į' t'óó nichǫ́'ígi 'áát'įįłgo biniinaa ch'ééh hágo hodíiniid." *I did not want to speak with him just so he could ask about my daughter. Back over there (where his people live), his warrior kept bothering the young women and girls who were herding the sheep. Maybe he is the one who told him (the old skinny soldier) to do that. Our women were afraid and got tired of him bothering them. His warrior acted terribly toward our women and girls and that is why I asked him to come to our camp to talk with us.* Hashké Yił Naabaah placed his hands on his grandson's shoulders and watched as his grandson conveyed his message to the tall gray-haired one.

The tall gray-haired one lifted his head, pointed to the tall leader and said,

"Tell him I did not think it was important for me to go to him to discuss with him the actions of my soldier who would soon be leaving the Fort Sumner Indian Reservation. I had to obtain permission from my superiors to release Mr. Calvette from his duties as a soldier in the U.S. Army. I don't like what Mr. Calvette has done. He will be escorted from the fort and the Indian Reservation. The interpreters did not inform me that it was this leader who requested my presence at their meeting. In addition, their description did not match that of this leader."

"He was not the man holding the stick for leader. Old short man hold stick," one interpreter interrupted.

"You knew! You were there when we first spoke to him!" accused the tall gray-haired one while staring at the interpreters. Still looking at them, he said,

"Tell him the unruly soldier is serving his last few days at Fort Sumner. He will be sent back to the states, back to where he lives. It is far away from here.
New soldiers will be sent to watch over his people so they can herd their sheep in peace." Hashké Yił Naabaah, turned away from the old soldier and walked away.
His sons, Kiizhóní, the elder Peace Leader and the young Naabeehó 'Ashkii followed their kind leader.

Chapter Seven
Arrival of the Tall Gray-Haired Soldier

At the time when Dédii reunited with her mother, her father, her adopted children, and her brothers she informed her mother about the father of her little one, but she did not elaborate on him much. Since her mother made comments about the tall gray-haired one, Dédii decided to tell her mother about the father of her child. Still hesitant to talk about him she began with the story of her and her younger sister's kidnapping, saying,

"Shí dóó Dzáníbaa' t'óó nihi'disnáhę́ędą́ą́', nihe'anaa'í danihisnáhígíí shił dah diikaaí, níléí ha'a'aahjigo shił adaaskai. Łį́į́' t'ááłáhígi 'át'éego nihił deiyíjeehgo dį́į́' éí doodai' ashdla' daats'í yiską́." *When Dzáníbaa' and I were first kidnapped, the enemy who kidnapped us took me toward the eastern direction. We rode the horses really fast for four or five days.*

"Nihe'anaa'í bitsį' daalgaaígíí níléí kéédahwiit'ínéedóó ha'a'aahjigo binaabaahii danilínígíí kin tsin bee 'ádaalyaago díkwííshį́į́ nideiznil. Éí kinígíí ła' yii' dabighan lá.

Kin nááná ła' éí yii'dóó nihik'ijį' nidadoobah yiniiyé nihinidaha'áá lágo baa 'ákoniizį́į'. Éí 'áajį' nihe'anaa'í dashisnáhígíí shił adaaskai dóó 'ei hastiin na'niłhodígíí yich'į' nidashiisnii'. Shą́ą' shizhé'é yáál dadisǫsígíí neijaah yęę, 'éí yáál nahalinígíí t'áała'ígo nihe'anaa'í dashisnááh yęę ła' yeiní'ą. Éí yáálígíí shį́į shidéená dooleełígíí 'át'éé lá." *To the east from where we lived at Black Mesa, our enemies built several square buildings that were made with logs. They lived in some of the houses. I realized they met in a separate building to plan ways they could wage war against us. My kidnappers took me there and sold me to the man who limps (the tall gray-haired one). Do you remember the shiny coins my father had? It was a coin like those the man who limped gave my kidnappers. The coin was given in exchange for me.*

"Nihe'anaa'í bitsį' daalgaaígíí bił haz'ánígi hastóí ts'ídá doodahígi 'ádashiilaa. Bits'ą́ądóó ła' bá 'a'niistsąąd, áko nidi t'áá 'ákódashiił'įįgo bits'ą́ądóó shitsą ha'íí'éél lá. 'Ákónáádashidléehgo 'ei hastiin na'niłhodígíí shaa 'ákoniizį́į' lá, áádóó hastiin yee 'a'ásizínée yik'iilwod dóó yiyaadóó hashíídzį́įz." *At the place where our enemy with white skin lived, the men did horrible things to me. Because of their actions, I became pregnant but when they kept up with their actions it caused me to have a miscarriage. They were going to do the same thing to me again when the man who limps noticed what they were doing to me. He got in a fight with the man who was the main one who assaulted me, then he dragged me out from under the man who was assaulting me.*

'Éí bijį́įdóó hastiin na'niłhodígíí shaa 'áhályą́ągo hahoolzhiizh. Bá'át'e' ádííníyee' dóó 'ayóo 'aajooba' lágo baa 'ákoniizį́į'. Shiyáázh bizhé'é t'áadoo shich'ą́ąh naazbaa'góogo 'éí nihe'anaa'í dashiishxį́į doo nít'éé'. Doo kǫ́ǫ naasháa da doo ni', áádóó nitsóí t'áadoo hazlį́į' da doo ni'. Biniiłt'aa shikáa'jį' hazlį́į'." *From that day on, the man who limped took care of me. I came to find that he is mild mannered and is very kind. If my son's father had not intervened on my behalf, my enemies would have killed me and you would not have a grandson. My life was spared because of him.*

Dibé yázhí ła' sheiníłtį. Dibé yázhí baa 'áháshyą́ągo bee shíni' hast'edíít'e'. She'awéé' bizhé'é díkwíí shį́į nídeezidjį' shaa 'áhályą́ągo nahashzhiizh." *He gave me a lamb. In caring for the lamb, my mind settled down. The father of my baby took care of me for several months.*

Łah hastiin sání léi' yidááhdóó nishinílóóz. Ha'át'íishį́į bínashídéékid, áko nidi doo 'ak'i'diishtįįhgóó biniinaa t'óó, 'Aoo',' diní shi'doo'niidgo, t'óó lą́ 'asélį́į'. K'adshą' iigeh nihá yii'a' léi' doo nidi shił bééhózin da. Éí bikéédóó kin áłts'íísí léi' bii' kééhasht'ínéegóó nináshiit'áázh, áádóó 'éí hastiin shikéé' yah ííyáá dóó shił biiską. Díkwíidishį́į sha'ałk'ee biiską. T'áadoo kót'é ha'níní t'ah nít'ę́ę' doo bééhoozin da. T'áadoo shaa nádzáa da." *One day he led me to stand before an old man. When I was asked a question, I did not understand the question and so I was told to say, 'Yes,' and so I said, 'Yes". What happened was that a wedding was held for us. After that, we went back to the little house that I lived in and the man came in and he spent the night with me. He spent several nights with me, then all of a sudden, he disappeared without a word. He never came back to me.*

Lifting her hand to point out the young Naabeehó 'Ashkii *Navajo Boy,* Dédii continued telling her mother about the tall gray-haired one.

"Ei 'ashkii t'ah ashkii yázhí nilį́įgo nihá 'ata' halne'go binahjį' ahaanihi'dee'nilígíí shił bééhoozin. Hastiin bidine'é 'iigeh nídayiił'aahígi 'át'éego 'ahaanihi'dee'nil lá. Hastiin háájíshį́į 'ííyá, hóla. Biba' siikéego łą́ yiską́. T'áadoo nihaa nádzáa da. T'óó yóó 'ashi'doot'ą́ niizį́į'. Yóó 'ashi'doot'ánígíí biniinaa shíni' yisdiłígi 'ádzaa. Biba' ánísht'éego dóó bíhásáahgo łą́ nídeezid. Hojoobáá'ígo 'índa bik'idéyá. *When that boy (the young Navajo Boy) was still a little boy, he interpreted for us and it was through him that I learned we were put together in marriage. The wedding was in the way of the man's people. I did not know where he went. We waited for him for many days. He never came back. I just thought he abandoned me. My mind was injured because of him leaving me. I waited for him and missed him for many months. It took me a long time to get over him.*

"Naaki daats'í nááhai yę́ędą́ą́' índa t'áadoo hasinígi bił ná'ahiistsą́, 'áko nidi t'áadoo bich'į' haasdzíí' da, 'áádóó bí dó' t'áadoo shił nahasne' da. Be'awéé' yiyiiłtsą́ą nidi t'áadoo be'awéé' k'é yidííniid da." *I had not seen him again until all of a sudden, I saw him two years ago but I did not speak to him and he also did not talk to me. He saw his baby but he did not greet his baby.*

Nínááníbaa' felt conflicted but she knew her daughter was also left with conflicting feelings, which would most likely include feelings of loyalty to her people and their imprisonment as well as feelings of gratitude to the man with white skin who was the father of her child and on the other hand, an enemy of her Naabeehó people. She noticed that ever since her daughter caught a glimpse of the tall gray-haired one at the parade grounds, her daughter was quiet and more protective of her little one.

****

The tall gray-haired one smiled at himself in the round framed mirror that hung on the wall near his bureau. He told himself he was just as cunning as a fox.

"The plans of moving the Navajo people to reserved lands in Oklahoma came at an opportune time. I have been looking for my beautiful Sunflower for nearly two years now. Fortunately, I didn't need to search all day for her, the young Navajo boy who served me at Fort Canby led me straight to her Navajo leader." He smiled at himself in the mirror and continued,

"You even had soldiers accompany Sunflower and her group to their camp. It will only be a matter of hours before I get to see my beautiful Sunflower again." After he combed his hair, he winked his "good eye" before he placed his patch over his damaged eye, then said,

"Sunflower darling, I can't wait to look into those beautiful eyes of yours. The memory of our last few days and nights together kept me alive the past few years.

You don't realize that your memory made me brave so I could come back to you. Your memory also made me fight for my life at a time when my men were outnumbered. Although I lost many brave soldiers, a good number of us still made it out alive. It was a struggle getting back out west but once I saw your eyes two years ago, all memories were wiped from my mind. We will create new beautiful memories, my darling."

The tall gray-haired one could not wait for his interpreters to arrive so the soldiers could lead them to the leader who carried the leadership stick with a maroon strip of fabric attached to it. With lightness in his step, the tall gray-haired one stepped out onto the porch and down the steps to be helped onto his horse. With little conversation, the three men rode on their horses to follow a few soldiers who were assigned to the picket forts near the eastern edge of the Indian Reservation.

The tall gray-haired one remained mindful of their surroundings and the path that led to the camp of the leader with the maroon strip of fabric attached to his leadership stick. He wanted to whistle a familiar happy tune but the men surrounding him kept him quiet and kept his level of happiness in check. Seeing the sun had slipped up from the eastern horizon to rest overhead he wondered how long it took his beautiful Sunflower to walk to the parade grounds. When the sun began its downward glide toward the western horizon, the tall gray-haired one asked if they were close to their destination. The soldiers pointed out a bend in the river and identified it as near the camp of the leader their superior officer had selected to inspect.

The tall gray-haired one drew in his breath when he realized he had not ordered the cooks to prepare a lunch for him and his group. He was even more taken aback by the fact that they had traveled a good portion of the day and were just now reaching their destination. He admitted he had no idea the leader with the maroon leadership stick lived so far from the parade grounds. Becoming pensive, he wondered how his beautiful Sunflower could have walked so far. He further wondered how long it took for her to walk so far. He felt guilty for not having the foresight to have fed Sunflower and her people. His thoughts were interrupted when the soldiers announced they had arrived at their destination.

****

The sound of horses' hooves pounding on the soft, moist earth, sent the Naabeehó women, young and old alike, scattering frantically searching for a place to hide. The tall gray-haired one arrived at Hashké Yił Naabaah's camp without warning. Before the horses rounded the corner, all the women and the young women and the girls had hidden beneath their thick rug blankets that were still damp from the recent rains. It had been many days after the meeting at the parade grounds. The people were anxious at the arrival of the soldiers.

The tall gray-haired one brought two interpreters, one, a young Mexican man who spoke Spanish and Navajo and Apache and the other spoke English and Spanish. The tall gray-haired one's eye darted from one area of the camp to another as he quickly took in the scene before him. He looked from one group of Navajos to another, searching the faces of the people. He did not see any young women in the vicinity. After listening to the first interpreter voice the request of the officer, the Apache interpreter asked,

"Nihinaat'áanii shą'?" *Where is your leader?*
He struggled with the Navajo words. Hashké Hił Naabaah asked the interpreter,

"Ha'át'íí lá biniiyé nihinaat'áanii yína'ídíłkid?" *Why is he asking about our leader?*

"Naat'áanii ní. Hóla," *He said the leader. I don't know,* answered the interpreter. Hashké Hił Naabaah pointed to their elder Peace Leader and said,

"Ei nihahastóí nihinaat'áanii nilį́." *That elderly man is our leader.* The interpreter looked at the tall gray-haired one and nodded in the direction of the Peace Leader. The tall gray-haired one looked confused. Pointing to Hashké Yił Naabaah he demanded,

"No, tell him I want to see him. He was the one holding the leadership stick the other day."

"Dooda, ni dooleeł ní." *No, he said you.* The tall gray-haired one shook his head as his level of confidence began to fade. He felt at such a disadvantage because he could not speak directly to the leader he met a few days ago at the parade grounds. He studied the elder man who was pointed out as a leader. "Was the Navajo leader who held the leadership stick lying to him, an officer of the United States Military?" he thought.

The young Naabeehó 'Ashkii *Navajo Boy* returned from the river with the young men. Without hesitation, he walked up to the tall gray-haired one who was still on his horse and called out,

"Folton." The tall gray-haired one felt his confidence returning, knowing he was at the correct camp. He turned to the young boy and asked,

"Where is the leader I spoke to when you were at the parade grounds?" The young boy pointed to his grandfather, Hashké Yił Naabaah, then turned toward the elder Peace Leader and said,

"Our leader." The tall gray-haired one was so confused. The young boy had not witnessed the earlier conversation so he would not know that Hashké Yił Naabaah had also pointed out the elder man as the leader. The tall gray-haired one asked the soldiers to place the stool near his horse. Two soldiers brought a stool with steps near their officer's horse. With difficulty, the tall gray-haired one got off of his horse and stepped onto the ground to stand near Hashké Yił Naabaah and the young Naabeehó 'Ashkii. He placed his hand gently on the shoulder of the young boy and told the young boy,

"I came here riding on a horse because I want to visit your leader. I want to see him, not someone else. He was the one holding the leadership stick at the fort." The young boy turned to his grandfather and said,

"Naat'áanii bił nahozhdoolnih biniiyé kodi łį́į́' hoł yíldloozh lá. Ni naa níyá niłní, nááná ła' éí dooda. Ni níléidi tsin dah yítį́į́ł nít'ę́ę́', ní," *He rode his horse to come here to visit with you. He told you he came here to see you, not another person. You were the one holding up the leadership stick over there,* the young Naabeehó 'Ashkii *Navajo Boy* reported.

"Shí yee' naat'áanii 'ídlį́įgi nahgóó nidiní'ą́." *I placed being a leader to the side.* The young boy told the tall gray-haired one what his grandfather said and watched the old soldier shake his head. The tall gray-haired one thought for a bit then told the interpreters to return to their horses and ordered the soldiers to lead the interpreters out of earshot of the conversation he was having with the leader. Thinking about his Sunflower and knowing her young son would lead her to him, he nervously asked,

"Where is the little boy who was born for a soldier?" The young boy relayed the message at which Hashké Yił Naabaah boldly responded,

"Ha'át'íísh biniiyé shicheii yázhí bína'ízhdíłkid?" *Why is he asking about my little grandson?* The young boy turned to his grandfather, cleared his throat, shifted his position, and nervously said,

"Hóla." *I don't know.* Turning to the young Naabeehó 'Ashkii *Navajo Boy,* Hashké Yił Naabaah quietly asked,

"Shicheii yázhí daats'í díí hastiin yáshchíín." *Maybe my little grandson is born for this man.* The young boy put his head down and muttered,

"Aoo', shitsilí 'ei hastiin yáshchíín." *Yes, my younger brother is born for that man.* Turning back to the tall gray-haired one, the young Naabeehó 'Ashkii asked,

"Why you ask?" The tall gray-haired one was not prepared for the question. He stuttered for a minute then said,

"Sunflower and I were married at Fort Canby. You were there. For several years I trained young soldiers to fight in the Indian wars. After we were married, I was sent to the east to train soldiers for the big war. I was there for several years. Two groups of white soldiers were fighting and that was where I was sent. It has been nearly two years that I have been sent back to the west. I was glad because I have been looking for Sunflower."

"Díí hastiin dóó shimá 'ahaabi'dee'nil. 'Áadi nihe'anaa'í ła' na'abaah hats'ą́ądóó yídahoołaahgo 'ákwe'é hanaanish ájiilaago díkwíishįį́ nááhai. 'Áádóó níléí ha'a'aah biyaadi naabaahii bitsį' daalgaiígíí 'ałk'iijée'go 'ákǫ́ǫ aho'dool'a' lá. K'ad naaki nááhai yę́ędą́ą' kojį' anídahas'a' lá. Doo nihe'anaa'í hashkéhígíí nilįį da. Naabeehó dine'é bił nilį. Kodi níjídzáhígíí baa hoł hózhǫ. Shimá bich'į' hazhdoodzih biniiyé 'áádę́ę' łįį' hoł yíldloozh lá." *This man was married to my mother. He was there for several years making the training of soldiers his work. He left from there because he was sent to fight in the war between two groups of white soldiers in the east. Now it has been about two years since he has been sent back here. He is not a mad soldier. He respects the Navajo people.* The tall gray-haired one waited patiently as the young boy conveyed his message to the tall leader.

"Tell him I came here to speak to Sunflower. I know she is here because she was with you at the parade grounds." Nervous of his grandfather's response the young boy bravely said,

"Shimá bich'į' hazhdoodzih biniiyé kwe'é nihaazhníyáá lá." *He came here to speak to my mother.*

There was a long silence. Hashké Hił Naabaah thought of his beautiful Nínááníbaa'. She had recently reunited with her daughters and now a member of the enemy with white skin wanted to see their daughter. He had seen how the enemy with white skin treated the young women and fear gripped his heart, but at the same time, he did not want to place his family in jeopardy by fully denying the soldier of his request. The tall gray-haired one called for his interpreters, hoping he could obtain more information.

Nínááníbaa' and her sons and Kiizhóní all held their breath as they listened to Hashké Yił Naabaah say,

"Nihe'anaa'í bitsį' daalgaiígíí yee' shitsi' yisnááh ádayiilaa. Shitsi' yee' nihe'anaa'í bił haz'ánígi 'atah ąąhéeshjéé' nilį́įgo doochohoo'į́įgóó txi'hooznii'. Shitsi' txi'hooníihgo t'óó bits'ą́ą' ajoolwod. T'óó bik'izhnííchą́ą'. Yówéé 'ázhdooníít. Naabaahii diné bił nilį́įgogo 'éí doo 'ákódooníił da. Doo ba'áłchíní yik'i dínóochéeł da! Ts'ídá dooda lą́ą! Naabaahii nidanétą́'ígíí ts'ídá doo 'ákó dadooníił da, háálá bił aadahojooba'. Hó shį́į 'éí doo yá'át'ééhgóó nahodi'neeztą́ą' da. T'óó daats'í nihe'awéé' yisnááh ánáázhdoodlííł biniiyé nihaazhníyá." *Our enemy with white skin are the ones who took my daughter captive. My daughter really suffered while she was held captive at the place where our enemy live. He ran off from my daughter when she was suffering. What a thing to do?*

He just abandoned her. If a warrior respects a person, he would not abandon his family! Absolutely not! The young men I trained in warfare would never do that because they have sympathy for others. He was probably not taught very well. Maybe he came here just so he could kidnap our baby again. The tall gray-haired one felt heat flow into his face after hearing of the accusations of the respected tall leader. The tall gray-haired one was not aware the tall leader was the father of Sunflower until the interpreters relayed the tall leader's words. He did admit that the tall leader had every right not to trust him.

The tall gray-haired one felt his power leave him. "She still has power over me, after all these years," he thought. To show his strength, he pointed at Hashké Yił Naabaah, looked at the Naabeehó 'Ashkii and demanded,

"Tell him I will come back and speak to his daughter. It will be a quiet meeting. Tell him," the tall gray-haired one demanded pointing to the young boy. After politely hearing the old soldier's message, Hashké Yił Naabaah looked at his adopted grandson and told the young boy that as a father and a leader he did not want a member of the enemy speaking to his daughter alone. Her protectors would be surrounding her. Looking in Nínáánîbaa''s direction, he said,

"Díí yee' Naabeehó binaat'áanii 'atah nishłį́. Doo 'éí shitsi' t'áá sáhí bił ałch'į' jizkéego bich'į' hazhdoodzih da. Shí dóó shitsi' bimá bił ahił nidahwiilne'go t'éiyá nihich'į' hazhdoodzih." *I am one of the leaders of my people.*

He cannot speak to my daughter alone. He can speak with me and my daughter's mother. Hashké Yił Naabaah was worried. While his grandson was conveying his message, he saw that the old soldier's eyes were darting back and forth looking into the faces of the Naabeehó women sitting nearby. He knew the old soldier was looking for his daughter Dédii. The old soldier impatiently listened to his grandson then slowly turned and limped toward his horse and with help, got on his horse.

Hashké Yił Naabaah remembered the words of Nínááníbaa' when she told him their daughter Dédii was still in love with the man who spared her life and whom she claimed was the father of her child. Hashké Yił Naabaah's voice took on an authoritative tone when he said,

"Nihinááł shitsi' bił ahił nahozhdoolnih. T'áá'aaníí hoł da'niidlį́įgogo 'éí t'áá kwe'é nihinááł shitsi' bił ahił nahozhdoolnih." *He will speak to my daughter in our presence. If we really are respected by him, he will speak to my daughter in our presence.* The tall gray-haired one was confused.

"Did you tell him what I asked you to tell him? I don't want to speak to just any Navajo girl. I want to speak to Sunflower. You know who I am speaking of. She used to ride in front of you when we went up the hill to the beautiful pasture."

Before the tall gray-haired one turned his horse toward the path that led toward the parade grounds, he turned and said he agreed to speak with Dédii in the presence of her father and her mother.

****

Two days later without warning, the tall gray-haired one arrived with only one interpreter and several soldiers. The women scurried out of sight while Hashké Yił Naabaah and his sons and Kiizhóní settled in their meeting area. The interpreter was asked to stay with the soldiers as the tall gray-haired one moved forward to meet his Sunflower and her family. The tall gray-haired one caught his breath when he caught a glimpse of Dédii.

Dédii was brought out of hiding by her brothers and was brought to the cooking area accompanied by Kiizhóní. Her mother declined to be in attendance because the tall gray-haired one may possibly be her son-in-law and if indeed he was, she would be considered his "doo yoo'íinii" *the man a mother-in-law is not to be in the presence of.* Dédii sat between her father and her brothers. Kiizhóní sat directly behind her. She pulled the Naabeehó 'Ashkii near her for support. Sitting near her family and the young Naabeehó 'Ashkii gave her the strength to see the man she once loved and for whom she waited many years.

The tall gray-haired one tried getting her attention by speaking the name he called her.

"Sunflower," he said in a gentle voice but Dédii ignored him. Her father asked her,

"Díí hastiinísh bééhonísin, shiyázhí?" *Do you know this man, my little one?* Without looking up she answered,

"Hóla," *I don't know.* She thought of her little one who was sitting on her mother's lap and was hidden by her rug blanket. She heard her son whimpering. Her mother was speaking soothing words to calm her little one down.

The young Naabeehó 'Ashkii felt uncomfortable in being the one through which the tall gray-haired one communicated with his mother. He listened as the tall gray-haired one continued in a kind voice,

"Please tell her, I was sent to fight in a war in the south. I never wanted to leave her." Turning to Dédii, he said,

"I missed you terribly when I was away from you. I asked to be sent back to the west when the war was over. When the war was over I went to Fort Canby where there were just a few soldiers and when I did not find you there, I went to Fort Fauntleroy. I kept hoping and praying that you were not sent here to this horrible place." Blinking at the number of words he was expected to interpret, the young boy thoughtfully told his mother what he understood of the tall gray-haired one's message.

Looking directly into Dédii's face, the tall gray-haired one asked,

"Sunflower, I suspected you lived here because my soldiers followed the young boy who was my helper at Fort Canby. Do you like the sheep I had my soldiers bring over? I know you like sheep. Do you remember the lamb I gave you when I first got to know you at Fort Canby? I still remember the image of you walking among the sheep while you were talking to the sheep. That memory is the reason I had the sheep brought over to your camp so you and your family and your people could take care of the sheep. I hoped we sent them to the right place. I'm glad the sheep are here with you. I remember the little lamb that made you very happy and you opened up to me after you started taking care of the lamb. I wish I could give you the sheep but they belong to the federal government so they cannot be given to you. I just want you to be happy, my sweet Sunflower," the soldier said as his heart was breaking. He looked nervously at the young Naabeehó 'Ashkii *Navajo boy* and said in a low voice,

"Will you tell her what I said? Make sure she understands you." The young boy delivered the message to his mother but he was confused about the reason for the use of the word "sweet" in the tall gray-haired one's pleas. After the young boy relayed the message to his mother, he thought for a minute and finished by saying,

"Nidiyilii łikanígíí nílį́, niłní." *He said you are a sunflower that is sweet.* Hashké Yił Naabaah and his sons and Kiizhóní all snickered at the last message.

Dédii busied herself by brushing her rug dress with her hand and ignored the tall gray-haired one who was not used to being ignored. The tall gray-haired one looked helplessly at her father but Hashké Yił Naabaah kept an eye on his daughter who had been through so much uncertainty, pain, horror, and loss. Dédii did not show any emotion and did not speak. The tall gray-haired one, desperate to get a reaction from Dédii said with emotion,

"Sunflower, I love you." He waited for the young Naabeehó 'Ashkii to tell Dédii about his undying love for her.

"Nidiyilii shił ayóó 'át'é, ní," *I love sunflowers, he said,* the young boy said. Hashké Yił Naabaah sat quietly. He wondered why the tall gray-haired one became so filled with emotion when he declared he loved sunflowers. Looking past Dédii and scooting back a little on the wide stool, the tall gray-haired one looked from one face to another wondering why his Sunflower did not respond to his message of love. Nervously, he told his Sunflower,

"I don't mind that you had a baby for another soldier. I want to take care of you. You and I can make a home for ourselves. I can ask to be stationed at Fort Canby and you will come and live with me. Your son can say with your family. I came all the way back to New Mexico Territory to look for you. I will be good to you. Let me protect you. We can have children..." The young Naabeehó 'Ashkii, stared at the tall gray-haired one. Without relaying the message to his mother, the young boy said,

"My mother baby, your baby. My brother, your baby. Your baby! My mother hide your baby. She carried your baby here! My mother cried. Lots she cried for you!" the young Naabeehó 'Ashkii nearly shouted. The young boy was embarrassed and disappointed in the man he had looked up to. He left out most of the message in his interpretation of the tall gray-haired one's words so as not to offend his mother and his grandparents.

The tall gray-haired one was confused once again.

"Why is she your mother? You were an orphan. I took you in."

"She my mother now," the young Naabeehó 'Ashkii announced proudly. Hashké Yił Naabaah decided not to ask his daughter to answer the old man's pleas. To get the young Naabeehó 'Ashkii's attention, Hashké Yił Naabaah asked,

"Shicheii. Shicheii. Ha'át'íí lá bidíníniid?" *My grandson. My grandson. What did you say to him?* The young Naabeehó 'Ashkii was near tears. He was so disappointed in the man he called "Folton". He could not tell his mother about the tall gray-haired one's words, words that he felt were selfish. He regretted being placed in the position of interpreter. He was determined not to tell his mother about the selfishness of the tall gray-haired one. His adopted brothers were his mother's children too. "I am her son too!" he thought. His mind was racing. "What's going to happen to all of my little brothers? What's going to happen to my old shicheii, the man my mother rescued from the mean soldiers on the way to this place?" he thought in defiance.

When Dédii continued to ignore him, the tall gray-haired one wondered if the Navajo boy related his message as he spoke it.

"Did you tell Sunflower what I said?" he asked of the boy. The young boy looked from his mother to his grandfather, then turned to the tall gray-haired one and stated while pointing in Nínáánibaa"s direction,

"My mother, bichildren, *her children*. My brothers with your baby." With big tears in his eyes he turned to his mother, Dédii, and spoke in words that were deliberately spoken.

"Shimá, ni téiyá nił shighan dooleeł, ní. Nihighan hólǫ́ǫ dooleeł, ní. Shitsilí 'éí shicheii dóó shimá sání yił bighan doo, ní. Ni t'éiyá, ní. Shitsilí 'éí dooda, shí dó' dooda, shitsilíké dó' dooda. T'áá ni t'éiyá. Nízaadę́ę́' níkánootáałgo kodi níyá, ní." *My mother, only you I will live with, he said. He said, we will have a home. My younger brother will live with my maternal grandfather and my maternal grandmother. Only you, he said. Not my younger brother, me too no, my younger brothers too, no. Just only you. He came from a long way away looking for you, he said.* The young Naabeehó 'Ashkii's tears spilled out of his eyes and the young boy covered his eyes with the back of his hands and silently cried. Hashké Yił Naabaah broke the silence with a loud voice and announced,

"ShiDédii 'éí ba'áłchíní doo yits'ą́ą́' dah didoogááł da. Biyázhí há yizhchínígíí doo yits'ą́ąjį' dah didoogááł da. Ts'ídá dooda lą́ą. Hó shįį́ hodine'é 'ákódanooníił. Nihí 'éí niha'áłchíní t'áá nihídaastł'ǫ́ǫgo nideiikai. Ha'át'íísh ą' bíká nijibaah? Háíshą' bich'ą́ąh nijibaah? T'áá'íídą́ą́' yee' hwééhoozin. Shiyázhí dóó shicheii yázhí bik'izhníícháą́', dóó t'áá náábiláahdi bits'ą́ą́' dashdiiyáhę́ędą́ą́' yóó 'azhdíí'ą́. T'óó 'ákónáázhdoo'nííł t'éí biniiyé, wóshdę́ę́' jiní. Dooda lą́ą. Hait'éego shą' shiyázhí dóó shicheii yázhí bik'i nijildzil dooleeł? Yéego yee' hach'į' anáhóót'i'. Sáanii táá 'ákót'éego nitsídaakees. T'áá hó hadine'é bich'į' níjoodáłíjí t'éí há yá'át'ééh." *My Dédii will not walk away from her children. She will not leave her little one who was born for him. Absolutely not. It is possible that his people will do that. As for us, our children are tied to us as we walk around.*

What is he fighting for? Who is he defending? We have already found out what he is like. He walked away from my little one and my grandson, and besides that, when he left them behind, he abandoned them. He will do that again, that is why he is asking for her (Dédii) to go live with him. Absolutely not. How can he provide for my little one and my grandson? He needs a lot of help. It is better that he return to his own people.

When the young boy told the tall gray-haired one what his maternal grandfather said, the tall gray-haired one frowned deeply at the young boy's interpretation of the message. Hashké Yił Naabaah watched as the tall gray-haired one's lips began to tremble and tears ran down his face.

The tall gray-haired one attempted to get up from the little stool but was not able to. In a second attempt, he used his cane to push himself up and with great difficulty, amid grunts, he stood up and stood still for a minute before taking short steps toward his horse. Thinking about his actions, the tall gray-haired one returned to the meeting area and sat down.

With disgust, Hashké Yił Naabaah hissed,

"Doo nihaadaaní jílį́į da! Hajéí 'ádin! Doo 'áłchíní bich'ą́ą́h nizhdoobahígíí jílį́į da. Na'abaah doo bízhneel'ą́ą da. Hwe'anaa'í doo hwéédadooldzííł da." *He is not our son-in-law! He does not have a heart! He is not one to go to war on behalf of children. He is not strong enough to be a warrior. His enemies will not be afraid of him.*

Nínáánábaa' felt torn. She felt the weight of her husband. He was a respected War Leader among their Naabeehó people. He would lose the respect of his people if he accepted a member of their enemy into his home as a son-in-law, especially one who kept the Naabeehó people captive and starved and tortured them. Nínáánábaa' knew her husband was embarrassed by the tall gray-haired one's pleas to his daughter. A respected Naabeehó War Leader had to gather healthy men to go to war with him at a moment's notice. He needed a strong son-in-law, not a member of the enemy who was not well.

Nínáánábaa' also felt for her Dedii. Her daughter had waited for the tall gray-haired one for many years. Nínáánábaa' watched and listened closely from behind a rug blanket. Knowing her daughter had survived such adversity, she asked Hashké Yił Naabaah to send their daughter to rejoin her and Dzánábaa'. Nínáánábaa' knew her daughter's heart was breaking, but she was angered that the tall gray-haired one did not seem interested in his son, her grandson. She spoke up with emotion when she chided her husband and her sons, saying,

"Be'awéé' nidi t'áadoo yína'ídéé łkid da. 'Ádin, t'áadoo nidi biyázhí bá yizhchíinii k'é yidíiniid da. 'Éí shą' hait'éego baa nitsídaohkees?" *He did not even ask about his little one. He did not even greet his little one who was born for him. What do you all think about that?* Without waiting for an answer, she continued, "Naabeehó dine'é yee' nicheii yázhí dóó nihida' doochohoo'į́įgóó deijoołá. Shitsóí yázhí 'ei hastiin yáshchíín, éí biniinaa nihidine'é 'ayóo shitsóí deijoołá. 'Ei hastiin 'ąąhéeshjéé' ánihiilaaígíí biniinaa shitsóí yázhí deijoołá. 'Áko nidi, nihidine'é binaat'áanii nílínígíí biniinaa nicheii yázhí yaa 'a'ááh daniizį́į́'. Bináál nicheii yázhí k'é bidíníniid, azhą́ shį́į́ nihe'anaa'í yáshchíín nidi 'ayóó'ó'ó'ni' bee k'é bidíníniid." *Our people have such hatred for your grandson. That man made us prisoners of war and for that reason, our people hate my grandson. Our grandson is born for him (the enemy) and that is why our people hate our grandson. Our people, of whom you are the leader, have compassion for our grandson only because you greeted him out of love in their presence, although he was born for our enemy.*

Nínááníbaa' held her grandson tightly because she did not want the tall gray-haired one to take her grandson from them. She was also afraid the tall gray-haired one with a cane, a large eye patch, and many scars on his face would scare her grandson. She had sympathy for the tall gray-haired one but she could not let herself give her grandson over to him.

When the tall gray-haired one realized he would not be able to speak to his Sunflower alone, he put his head down. His face turned red and tears dropped from his eyes to the ground below. The tall gray-haired one turned his face away from the group before him.

In the suspended silence, Dédii heard his tears drop to the ground. She remembered he had the same expression the last night they spent together. He cried then too. "I think he cried because he loved me so much then," she thought, but she did not realize that he also cried because he would be leaving her to go fight in the war that raged in the east called the Civil War.

Just as she did on that night long ago, her heart wanted to take him into her arms and cradle his head against her breasts, but her eyes told her he was not the same man she fell in love with long ago. Her thoughts brought a tingling feeling to her breasts. She looked at his lips. They were full and pouty. "Those are the same lips that nibbled on my breasts and explored my body. Those lips awakened a deep wanting in the central part of my body. Those lips awakened a passion that rose within me that I wanted him so much to satisfy," she thought. She looked at his body. "It is not the same body with which he made gentle, yet selfish, love to me when he thrust his body into mine and made us move as if we were one body," she thought. Embarrassed by her thoughts, she looked around, looking first at her father, then her mother, then glanced at Kiizhóní. She was relieved to see they were focused on the tall gray-haired one.

Wanting to reclaim her memories, she closed her eyes and listened to his voice. It was void of its low sensuous sound that was soft and loving and inviting. She thought of the sound of his pleas for satisfaction as he held her body close to his and caused them to move as one. Her mind lingered on his sound of satisfaction that started from deep within him and rumbled out into the still, cold air of night. She tilted her head to listen closely to his voice. "His voice is harsh, demanding, and void of his kind personality that drew me close to him all those years ago," she thought.

She was conflicted. She raised her hand to her forehead and gently wiped her forehead to rid her mind of the thoughts of love with the man sitting before her.

"Háish áníťį?" *Who are you?* she quietly whispered. She looked at her son sitting on her mother's lap. "Shiyázhí bizhé'é nílį́." *You are my little one's father,* she breathed. As soon as she spoke the words, her love for him that she harbored within her heart and lovingly protected, spilled forth. Tears gathered in her eyes and spilled onto her face. She turned her head so no one could hear her whisper,

"Sáanłáawah..." *Sunflower...* "Yes, I can still love him. Our love will not be the same innocent love we once claimed, but my love for you will forever be rooted in the son you gave me," she thought as she looked upon the tall gray-haired one with kind, sympathetic eyes. Tears continued to make patterns on her face as they picked up particles of dust and carried them down her face to pool in her lap.

Although she had sympathy and felt kindness and love for him, he was the reason her people were suffering. The tall gray-haired one used his right arm to lift himself up from the stool, winced and had trouble getting up off of his stool. When the soldiers rushed forward and offered their hand, the tall gray-haired one refused their help. With great effort, he stood up, and using his cane he walked to his horse. The stool was placed beside his horse. With great difficulty and effort, tall gray-haired one got on his horse and barked orders to his men and was gone.

Nínáánîbaa' gasped when her husband said,

"K'adę́ę la' shaadaaní jileeh. Hait'éegoshą' shiyázhí bik'i nijildzil doo? Hó yee' honiinaa doo ts'íí'át'éégóó txi'dahwii'nííh. Dooda lą́ą." *He sure is in a hurry to become my son-in-law. How will he be able to care for my little one? It is because of him that we are severely suffering. Absolutely not!* Nínáánîbaa' sensed the heartbreak of her Dédii while her own heart was breaking for her daughter. She knew her daughter was strong enough to survive such adversity. To lighten her Dédii's load, Nínáánîbaa' quietly said,

"Dédii, hágo, shiyázhí." *Dédii, come here, my little one.* Dédii jumped up and quickly walked to her mother and collapsed in her mother's arms. Pulling her little one toward her, Dédii whimpered softly. Her thoughts were crashing into one another. She wanted to look into the face of the tall gray-haired one but the patch over his eye was so prominent she refused to look into the other eye. She remembered her first thoughts of his eyes so many years ago, she snickered at the thought. She remembered she thought his eyes resembled the eyes of the fat horned toads that were found near her home at the base of Dziłíjiin *Black Mesa.*

She wanted to touch his soft lips that were partially hidden by his thick mustache. She remembered the way his mustache burned her lips when he kissed her so passionately. She wondered how many women he had made love to after he abandoned her and her little one. She remembered the sound of the soft words he murmured into her ear when they made passionate love to one another. She wondered how many of the enemy he had killed. The scars that lay on his face were testimony of how hard he had to fight against the enemy. She wanted to look into his eyes and see the kindness she once saw that won her heart and made her trust him. She shook her head to rid her mind of her thoughts.

"Biyázhí nidi t'áadoo yína'ídéełkid da." *He didn't even ask about his little one.* Her heart was breaking once again.

Sensing her heartbreak, Kiizhóní ignored cultural protocol and entered the area that was set aside for the women and children, and sat down near Dédii. Not knowing what to say, he pulled out a slingshot he recently made and held it out to Dédii.

"Na', díí ná 'íishłaa. Bee 'adíłtxąsh doo biniiyé." *Here, I made this for you. You can shoot things with it.* Dédii could not keep her face turned away from the kind-hearted Kiizhóní. She turned her tear-stained face toward him and said,

"Biyázhí t'áadoo k'é yidíiniid da. T'áá shǫǫh, 'Shiye',' bizhdidooniił." *He did not greet his little one. At least, he could have claimed him and called him, 'My son.'* In a gentle voice, Kiizhóní stated,

"T'áadoo 'ákǫ́ǫ́ nitsíníkeesí. Niyáázh doo ts'íi'át'éégóó 'ayóó'ábi'dó'níigo 'át'é. Nimá 'ayóó'ábó'ní. Nizhé'é 'ayóó'ábó'ní. Bił hainíjéé' 'ayóó'ádabó'ní. Shí nidi niyázhí t'áá shí shiye', shá yizhchíinii nilį́ nahalingo baa nitséskees. K'adí, t'áadoo 'éí níni' si'ání. Shee ha'íínílní. Shinahjį' áníť'é." *Don't think like that. Your son is dearly loved. Your mother loves him. Your father loves him. Your siblings love him. I too, I think of him as my son, one who was born for me. Now stop, don't let those thoughts remain in your mind. Take comfort in my presence. Be strong in me.*

"Ákó ho'dó'ne' nisin łeh. Saad bee ha'ahónínígíí 'ayóo bídin nishłį́." *I have been wanting to hear that. I am desperate to hear words of comfort.* Shaking her new slingshot, Dédii continued, with sarcasm,

"Doo haniih díí shiyázhí bizhé'é bee yiiłtxąsh da!" *Why didn't you shoot my little one's father with this!* she said holding up the slingshot Kiizhóní gave her. Kiizhóní snickered and said,

"Éí hanii biniiyé ná 'íishłaa." *That's not the reason I made it for you.* With all the sympathy and kindness for the tall gray-haired one absent from her voice, Dédii said,

"Biyázhí t'óó yóó 'iidíí'ą́. Hayázhí hó honiinaa doochohoo'į́įgóó txi'hooníłh. Háshchínígíí biniinaa nihidine'é doo ts'íí'át'éégóó dabijoołá." *He just gave his little one away. It is because of him that my little one is suffering greatly. Our people resent my little one because he was born for him.*

Kiizhóní opened his heart and told Dédii,

"T'óó níni' bii'di bits'ánínááh. Doo 'éí t'áá sáhí na'ałchíní ch'ídíí'ish da. Ni dóó na'ałchíní nihaa 'áháshyą́ągo bínéshdin. Aadę́ę́' nihidi'noolkałgo, doo nidi 'atah ąąhéeshjéé' nishłį́ nisingóó 'akéé' níshtł'áh, háálá t'áá hazhó'ó nihíighah yisháłígíí t'éí bee ha'íínishníigo 'aadę́ę́' nihiyéél níłjid. Doo lá dó' shí da, nisingo nibeedí ná bił na'ashjoołgo dóó doo nidi shił nidaazgóó ná níłjid.

T'óó nihíiyáhę́ędą́ą' ílį́įgo sha'nídéél nisingo baa shił hóózhǫǫd." *Just get away from him in your mind. You will not walk alone with your children. I have become very much used to taking care of you and your children. When we were forced to walk here, I did not feel as if I was a prisoner along with the others as I walked, because I felt hope when I walked with you, carrying your belongings. 'How fortunate I am,' I thought as I carefully carried your things that were not at all heavy. When I first joined you, I felt I had been given a valuable gift and I was happy about it.* Dédii knew Kiizhóní was speaking from his heart. He had proven himself and had proven his loyalty to her, whereas, the tall gray-haired one had also proven himself by abandoning her and her little one.

She decided to speak with her adopted son as soon as she could to ask him about the true message the tall gray-haired one spoke. Had her son misunderstood the tall gray-haired one when he said the tall gray-haired one wanted only her and not her children? "I carried his little one over all those hills and down into the valleys, over the rocks and cacti of all shapes and sizes, and I did that because I loved my little one and I loved the one who gave me my child." Dédii could not believe a man could place words in the air just to be carried about by the wind, words that said, 'I want you but I don't want your children'. She shook her head and stomped her feet, doing her little dance that demonstrated how upset she was.

Long after the tall gray-haired one left, Dédii found her oldest son sitting with her brothers and Kiizhóní.

She and her son walked slowly back to their camp. While they walked, she asked the young boy what the tall gray-haired one actually said.

"Shí dóó shiyázhí bizhé'é nihá 'ata' hólne' yę́ędą́ą' ha'át'íí shį́į́ t'áadoo bee shił hwíínílne' da. Shí daats'í shaa sínítxi'go biniinaa t'áadoo t'áá'át'é bee shił ch'íhwííní'ąą da. She'awéé' bizhé'é lá ha'át'íí ní?" *When you were interpreting for us, there was something you did not want to tell me. Maybe you wanted to protect me and that is why you did not tell me. What did my baby's father say?* The young Naabeehó 'Ashkii lowered his head to hide his trembling lips. In between tears, the young boy told his mother what the tall gray-haired one said that caused him so much hurt that he could not repeat it in front of her family.

"Shitsilí yázhí nááná ła' hastiin bá shíníłchį, níiga'. Binaabaahii ła'," *He said you had my baby brother for someone else. One of his soldiers,* her young son answered with tears pouring down his face. He knew how much his mother loved and desperately missed the tall gray-haired one.

"Ha'át'íí ní diní?" *What did you say he said?* gasped Dédii. The young Naabeehó 'Ashkii repeated what the tall gray-haired one said. Dédii felt a deep hurt in her heart.

"T'óó la' shitah hwiisxíí'! Ts'ídá hanii doo 'ákóshidídooniił da nisin nít'ę́ę́'." *I feel numb! I never thought he would say that to me!* she blurted out. Dédii looked around her. She had to sit down on the ground. She did not expect the tall gray-haired one to deny he was the father of her son.

She thought of being forced to work when she was pregnant with her little one. She thought of nearly going into labor while she was busy washing the soldiers' dirty clothes, sheets, and blankets while her Naabeehó people slept under the stars with no blankets on cold, cold nights. She thought of the heavy baskets full of wet clothes, sheets, and blankets she had to carry from one place to another in completing her work at the laundry room. She thought of having to deliver her little one with no help from anyone else except her father and mother who were not really present at the birth of her little one. She thought of the many nights she waited for the tall gray-haired one. She thought of being held prisoner by the tall gray-haired one's soldiers at Fort Canby. "When he disappeared, I was abandoned. I had no one except this young Naabeehó 'Ashkii and my brother," she thought. She wondered if she and her little one and all of her adopted sons and the man she called her maternal grandfather would have survived the many days of walking if it had not been for her brother and Kiizhóní. She felt abandoned by the tall gray-haired one once again. Her heart was breaking. Her heart felt heavy, very heavy. She leaned to one side and supported herself with her arms so she would not topple over.

With his face contorted from crying, her son said,

"Shí dóó shitsilíké 'ałdó' doo nihidi'nidzin da.
Nihí nihicheii dóó nihimá sání bił danihighan doo shą́ą́' nihiłní. T'áá hazhó'ó ni t'éiyá shił nighan doo, níi ne'."
Me and my younger brothers are not wanted. Remember he told us we would have to live with our maternal

grandmother and maternal grandfather. He said you were the only one who would live with him. Dédii reached out to her son to reassure him with her words, saying,

"Shí doo bich'į' shíni' da." *I do not want to go to him.* Still stunned, she continued, "Doo bikéé' shíni' da. Nihí yee' shik'ídahołta'go bee shí dóó nitsilí yázhí nihikáa'jį' hazlį́į́'. K'adí, t'áadoo nichaaí. Shí nihimá nishłį́. Ts'ídá doo nihits'ą́ą́' dah dideesháał da. Ních'aad, shiyázhí. 'Azhą́ shį́į́ doo nihishéłchį́į da nidi, t'áá shí sha'áłchíní danohłį́į go nihaa nitséskees." *I don't want to follow him. It was you all who comforted me and because of that, your little brother and I survived. Stop, don't cry. I am your mother. I will never walk away from you all. Don't cry, my little one. Although I did not give birth to you, I think of you as my very own children.* With her soothing words comforting him the young Naabeehó 'Ashkii stopped crying and hugged her so tightly, murmuring,

"Shimá... Shimá..." *My mother... My mother...* He placed his head in her lap and rested beside her. Dédii decided then and there that she would never consider life with the tall gray-haired one ever again. She felt extremely hurt and sad, but she felt strong. The tall gray-haired one denied the love they had for one another when he denied her little one of a father's love.

****

Sitting alone with her husband that evening, Nínáánínbaa' scolded her husband.

"Azhą́ shį́į́ naadaaní doo baa dzíínílíí da nidi, 'ei hastiin nihiyázhí Dédii yisdáyíílóóz. Éísh doo naabaahii 'ílíinii wolyée da. T'áadoo nitsi' binááł nihaadaaní bá nahółt'i'í. Nihiyázhí bíni' yiniłʼa'. Nihitsóí 'ei hastiin yáshchíín." *Even though you don't think much of your son-in-law, he rescued our little one, Dédii. Because of what he did, isn't he what you would call a warrior? Don't say demeaning things about him in the presence of your daughter. You hurt our little one's feelings. Our grandson is born for that man.* Hashké Yił Naabaah was squatting on the ground as he listened to Nínáánibaa'. Feeling bad about his words and his actions, he wanted to lighten the moment. He got up and knelt down on the ground and put his face down toward the ground with his buttocks in the air, acting as if he was pouting.

"Da' t'áadoo 'íits'a'í kojí hatł'a'iish'á?" *Shall I be quiet and remain in this position, on my hands and knees with my buttocks in the air?* Without waiting for an answer, he said, "Hágoshį́į́, t'áadoo 'íits'a'í kojí hatł'a'iish'áa dooleeł." *Okay, I will be quiet and remain in this position?* When Nínáánibaa' heard her husband's words and saw the position he was in, she started laughing. Her husband was in a funny position. She thought of stinkbugs that raise their hind end up in the air when they feel threatened.

Without warning, Hashké Yił Naabaah jumped up from his awkward position and in one long step he effortlessly lifted Nínáánibaa' to her feet. In the swiftness of his action, Nínáánibaa' found her husband standing directly behind her. He hugged her so close that she could feel his breath on her hair.

"T'óó la' nízhóníyee'," *How beautiful you are,* she thought as she leaned her head on his strong thin shoulder. He hugged her tightly again and sensuously whispered in her ear,

"Ch'ídíiníldlo'go 'ayóó 'ánoolningo ne'iinéé' diséts'ą́ą́'. Háshinee', shiyázhí," *I heard a beautiful sound when I heard your laughter. Dear one, my little one,* her husband said in her ear in a hoarse whisper. "Hádą́ą́' shį́į́ t'éí 'anánídlohgo sidéts'ą́ą́'. Ne'iinéé' diséts'ąą'go bee ha'iisisniid. Ahéhee', shiyázhí. 'Ayóó'ániíínísh'ní." *It has been a long time since I heard you laughing. When I heard the sound of your laughter, I was given hope. Thank you, my little one. I love you.*

Nínááníbaa' felt her tears rise to the surface and spill over onto her face. She leaned against her husband and allowed her body to feel his closeness. Nínááníbaa' fought her emotions. She wanted so much to hold her husband. He needed hope, love, encouragement, strength, and he needed her.

****

Many times, since they became prisoners of war at Fort Sumner, Nínááníbaa' remembered hearing Hashké Yił Naabaah telling his warriors not to sleep with their women because they would not want any of their children to be born in a repulsive enemy's land. Neither would the warriors want their women to suffer because of a pregnancy. It seemed as if it was yesterday that she heard her husband tell his warriors,

"Doo ts'íí'át'éégóó txi'dahwii'níih kodi. T'áadoo danihizáanii bit'áahjį' anídaniichéhí doo. Danihizáanii yéego txi'dahooníih. Nihá da'niltsąądgo 'éí t'ah nááyówehgo da txi'dahooníih doo. Ha'át'íísh deiyą́ą doo? Hait'éego shą' hak'az yídaníłdzil dooleeł? Hait'éego shą' hadoh yídaníłdzil dooleeł? Danihizáanii baa hą́ąh danohsin, t'ááshǫǫdí. Éí baa nídanihooshkąąh. Díí yee' nihe'anaa'í bikéyah bii' ąąhéeshjéé' daniidlį́. Nihe'anaa'í ts'ídá bíighahí bik'ee txi'dahwii'níihgo 'ánihiilaa. Nihí bídaniildzil. Naabaahii bitsxe'ígíí dadiidleeł biniiyé, ts'ídá t'áá 'óolyéego na'íhonitaah bii' tádiikai, 'áko nidi, danihizáanii dóó nihada'áłchíní danilínígíí 'éí doo 'ákót'éego nidabidi'neeztą́ą' da. Baa dahojoobá'íyee'. T'áá nihí nihikéyah biih ninádaheekaigo 'índa nihá nida'iichíihgo yá'át'ééh dooleeł. K'ad éí dooda." *Although we are suffering greatly here, let's not run behind our spouses for protection. Our spouses are really suffering. If they become pregnant with your child, they will be suffering even more. What will they eat? How will they withstand the cold? How will they withstand the heat? I plead with you, please be considerate of and be kind to your spouses. We are living in enemy territory. Our enemy has made us suffer from many bad things. We who are warriors are strong enough to withstand the suffering. In becoming warriors that have strength, we have put our bodies through many tests, but our spouses and our children did not train themselves in that way. We have to have compassion for them. Only until we return to our own land will it be suitable to have babies born for us. Not now.*

Nínáánībaa' could hear her husband's words in her ear as she felt his words surround her and bind her to her husband. She knew her husband was thinking of her and his daughters when he spoke to his warriors. Many times Nínáánībaa' yearned for the feel of her husband's breath on her hair. Here he was, standing behind her, holding her close, and breathing soft breaths in her hair! Hashké Yił Naabaah whispered into her ear the beautiful words she loved to hear,

"Ayóó'ánííníshní, shiyázhí. Háshinee' dó' ánít'į. T'áá łáhígi 'át'éego shíighah ahidííníz į́. *I love you, my little one. You stand by me without faltering.* Nínáánībaa' felt weak. She wanted to hear more of his low sensuous voice and his soothing words of strength. She wanted to turn to face him to look deep into his strong eyes so their souls could meet and touch. She was becoming weak fighting the urge to turn toward her husband to kiss him as if they were alone. She could feel his mound of passion pressing on her.

Nínáánībaa' looked up and noticed their children were surrounding them. They were not alone! Her children had worried looks in their faces. Nínáánībaa' was horrified. To hide her wanting of her husband, she pretended she nearly fainted. What she really wanted and needed was to be alone with her husband so they could laugh and giggle and be happy.

Hashké Yił Naabaah gently lowered Nínáánībaa' down onto her tattered rug blanket. Naabeehó women came to ask if she was feeling strong. She looked at her husband and their eyes met. Hashké Yił Naabaah smiled back with a faint guilt-filled smile. Nínáánibaa' felt a sense of satisfaction that had to serve as the closest emotion to making love to her husband. "This is going to be one of my favorite memories," she told herself. On many days and many times following, Nínáánibaa' found this memory would sustain her through difficult times.

Many times that evening, Nínáánibaa' thought of the tall gray-haired one who bravely came to see her daughter to declare his love for her. She scolded herself for never asking her Dédii how she felt about the soldier coming to see her. The sight of his failure to prove he was as strong and as well-trained as one of Hashké Yił Naabaah's warriors was pitiful.

She regretted scolding her husband earlier in the day. She admitted she nearly allowed a snicker to escape her lips. She knew others were talking about and laughing at the tall gray-haired one in the presence of her daughter. She was ashamed of herself. She had not defended the father of her precious grandchild. She felt her husband had a reason to criticize the tall gray-haired one because her husband was a War Leader and a respected warrior but she did not have a reason to laugh. She made a vow to be respectful toward the man her daughter claimed spared her life and gave her a little one. "There is a reason my daughter has loved him for so many years," she thought. Nínáánibaa' declared to herself that she would thank the tall gray-haired one for sparing her daughter's life. "In an indirect way, the tall gray-haired one gave my husband and I a tender moment that would be one of my favorite memories," she thought.

That night when Nínáánbaa' and Hashké Yił Naabaah were alone, she gently told him he needed to apologize to his daughter Dédii.

"Díkwíí shįį́ náhááh k'ad, nihiyázhí nihaadaaní 'ayóó'áyó'níigo. NihiDédii t'óó shił baa hojoobá'íyee'. Ch'ééh ha'oolniih. Nihiyázhí bich'į' hadiidzih. Níni' yiil'a'ígíí baa nihíni' bididii'niił. Íishjąą́shįį́ ha'át'íí níi doo." *It has been several years that our Dédii has loved our son-in-law. I feel so much sympathy for her. She is trying so hard to have hope. Let us speak to her. We will tell her we are sorry for hurting her feelings. Let's see what she has to say.*

Tears fell from Hashké Yił Naabaah and Nínáánbaa''s eyes as they thought of what their Dédii had been through. They held one another and cried for their daughter. Their tears mingled on the tattered rug blanket beneath them. Hashké Yił Naabaah made a promise to himself that he would never again make fun of his son-in-law, who was their enemy. "He deserves my sympathy and respect," he thought. He kissed his Nínáánbaa''s forehead and thanked her for reminding him of his responsibility of being a leader who was kind. "Even a War Leader has to be kind," he thought.

He watched the constellations march across the sky as he thought about the activities that transpired through the day. With the white light of dawn pressing up on the black sky on the eastern horizon, he sighed a heavy sigh. He noticed thin strands of his Nínáánbaa''s hair were disturbed by his breath from his deep sigh. The loose strands of her hair moved and tickled his nose. He sighed again deeply into his beautiful Nínáánbaa''s hair and fell into a deep sleep.

Chapter Eight
A Happy Sad Meeting

The cry of a woman crashed through the air near the large parade grounds,

"Shooh, háíshą' bibiil éé' bii' sínítį́?" *Whose rug dress are you wearing?* The accusatory question was followed by a loud, long drawn out sob that came from the depths of the woman's chest. The woman screamed again as she ran toward a small crowd of people who surrounded a young girl who had fallen into a crumpled heap on the ground. An older tall Naabeehó man tried in vain to hold back the screaming woman, but the woman broke loose, rushed through the crowd and pushed forward. Soon, a throng of people moved as one as they followed the woman who was running toward the young girl. Everyone held their breath.

Puddles of dirty brown water pooled on the ground from the rainfall the night before. Oblivious to the deep puddles, the woman did not bother to side-step or hop over the puddles, she just raced through the puddles, splashing dirty water on the Naabeehó people who stood nearby and watched the meeting unfold before them. The woman pushed the crowd aside and planted herself in front of the young girl who stared back at the crowd in confusion. Tears flowed down the woman's face as she reached out with wrinkled thin hands toward the young girl.

The woman stared into the face of the young girl with great apprehension. The woman was shaking. Leaves that were once stuck to her rug dress fell off one by one. The woman bent over and looked into the face of the young girl and asked,

"Shooh, díí biil éé' bii' sínítínígíí shą' háádę́ę́' shóisíníłt'e'?" *Look, where did you obtain this rug dress that you are wearing?* Without waiting for an answer, the woman continued,

"Shich'é'é hanii 'áníť'į́ nisin nít'ę́ę́'. Shiché'é shą', yį́į́'į́?" *I thought you were my daughter. Where is my daughter, huh?* The young girl's body shook as she stared back at the woman with empty eyes. The young girl's tangled hair was stiff with dried blood, dirt, twigs and leaves. What was once a tsiiyéél *hair knot* hung disheveled on one shoulder. The sheen was absent from her hair. Blood trickled down the left side of her face, staining the left shoulder of her rug dress. Her face was badly swollen. Whatever had badly scratched her face, barely missed her left eye, leaving the white of her eye a deep red color. The outline of her lips was distorted by a large bruise which made it difficult for the young girl to speak.

Reaching out for the young girl's hand, the woman softly said,

"Nídii'nééh. Yiizį́įhgoósh bíninil'ą́? Nibiil éé' hazhó'ó nésh'į́." *Get up. Can you stand up? Let me look closely at your rug dress.* The young girl unfolded her arms for balance as she lifted her torso. Slowly, she unfolded her legs, one after the other, and slowly stood up on her wobbly legs. She looked down and smoothed her rug dress that was stained with mud and blood. Looking down at her feet, she stomped her feet to dislodge red ants that had made a path along the soles of her moccasins which had large holes worn into them.

A distinct design was woven into the young girl's tattered rug dress that identified her with the weaver's family. The design was interrupted by holes in her dress but warp yarns still carried the dye color of the weft yarns that had been woven into the dress.

The woman studied the design she knew she wove into the dress as she walked around the young girl. Looking deep into the young girl's face, she slowly whispered,

"Shiyázhí shą'? Háíshą' bibiil éé' bii' sínítį?" *Where is my little one? Who's rug dress are you wearing?* she asked, looking at the young girl's dress. All recognition slowly left the woman's face as her body became limp and slowly slumped towards the ground. The tall man who followed his wife bolted forward and lifted his wife's thin body just before she fell to the ground near a puddle of water. Quietly, the woman whispered,

"K'asídą́ą́' la' shich'é'é bił ná'ahiistsą́. 'Ei biil éé' at'ééd yii' sitínígíí shiché'é bá sétł'ǫ́. Shí 'akót'éego naashch'ąą'go shiché'é bibiil 'éé' bá náshtł'óóh nít'ę́ę́'. Ei 'at'ééd shą' háí 'át'į́? Biniiji' háíshį́į́ 'íiyisígi 'áhoot'é. Shich'é'é bibiil éé' yii' sitį́. Nihiyázhí da shą' háadi t'áá sáhí txi'hoonííh? Doo lá dó' dooda da!" *I almost saw my daughter again. I wove that rug dress for my daughter. I used to weave that design into my daughter's rug dresses. Who is that girl? Her face looks extremely bad. She is wearing my daughter's rug dress. Where is our daughter? She is suffering all alone. What a terrible thing!*

Not having heard the woman's words, the young girl stared at the woman's thin, limp body. Slowly, the young girl looked into the face of the tall man holding the woman in his arms. She shut her injured eye in hopes of focusing upon the tall man who held the woman in his arms.
The young girl's head shook from side to side as she stared at him. A tear formed in her open eye before the young girl whispered words no one heard. The tall man turned to carry his wife's crumpled body back to the place where their leader and his people camped, but before he fully turned around to leave, the young girl lifted a weak hand to stop the man from leaving. In barely audible words, she asked,

"Da' niísh Łį́į́łgai Bito'dóó naniná?" *Are you from White Horse Lake?* The man, more concerned for his wife, turned and took a step away from the young girl. Out of desperation, the young girl called out in a hoarse voice,

"Da' niísh Łį́įłgai Bito'dóó naniná?" *Are you from White Horse Lake?* The man turned toward the question. He did not know how to answer. The woman in his arms weakly stirred, whispering,

"Aoo'," *Yes.* Tears formed in the young girl's open eye.

"Shí dó' áádę́ę́' naashá," *I am also from there,* the young girl replied with great difficulty. The man squinted his eyes and stared at the young girl and asked,

"Háísh ánít'į́?" *Who are you?*

Shaking as if she was cold, the young girl answered,

"Shimá 'Asdzą́ą́ Télii Neiniłkaadí deiłní." Shimá t'élii t'éí bilį́į́', éí biniinaa 'ákót'éego diné dabíízhi'." *They call my mother the Woman Who Herds Donkeys. She only has donkeys, that is why the people gave her that name.* The tall man nearly dropped his wife when he heard the young girl's answer. The woman in his arms twisted her body to look at the girl. The young girl's body shook, waiting to see if the couple recognized the name of her mother. She stood motionless, her head slightly shaking from side to side. The tall man tried to hold back his weak wife, but she poked his thin rib cage as hard as she could with her bony elbow and demanded that her husband put her down. Nearly dropping her, the tall man lowered his wife's feet to the ground and placed an arm around her waist to support her.

The air was held in suspense as the three people stood motionless, staring at one another. The people around them did not breathe. Reaching out with a painfully thin hand, the young girl said,

"Shimá 'éí 'Asdzą́ą́ Télii Neiniłkaadí wolyé." *My mother is called the Woman Who Herds Donkeys.* The tears the three people had held back for many years found their way first to their hearts, their throats, their eyes, and then exited through their mouths in high mournful loud cries. People who stood near them reached out to grab hold of the three people but could not hold them up as mother, father, and daughter slid down as one to the ground and into a dirty cold puddle of water.

The tall man cried,

"She'awéééééééééé'," *My baby,* while the woman cried,

"Shi-, shi-, shiyá-, shiyázh-, yázhí!" and when the young girl found her voice, she cried,

"Shimá! Shizhé'é! Ch'ééh hánihidésh'į́į́' nít'ę́ę́'!"
My mother! My father! I tried several times to look for you! Loud sorrowful cries were lifted by the wind and carried across the valley floor of Fort Sumner. To protect the newly reunited family from the evil eye of the soldiers, the Naabeehó people surrounded the three family members who found one another after three long years of separation. Tears flowed down the faces of the people who were witnessing the happy reunion. The people tried to coax the three huddled bodies out of the cold dirty puddle of water but the three people held tightly on to one another and wailed loudly in waves.

After what seemed like a long time of wailing, the young girl lifted her head and said between sobs,

"Háshinee', shimá! Háshinee', shizhé'é! Háshinee' shimá! Háshinee' shizhé'é!" *Dear one, my mother!*

Dear one, my father! Dear one, my mother! Dear one, my father! At the sound of the young girl's words, her mother's cries loudly burst forth into the air again. As if her breath refused to come to the surface, the young girl hoarsely whispered,

"Doo ts'íí'át'éégóó nihídin sélį́į' nít'ę́ę' dóó yéego bik'ee kadéyá..." *I was desperately lonely for you, and because of it, I became really sick...* She choked on her tears, coughed and wailed,

"Shizhé'é! Shimá! Shizhé'é! Shimá!" *My father! My mother! My father! My mother!* in a high-pitched voice. Her father grasped his chest and grimaced. The sound of his daughter's voice and greeting left him breathless. Finally finding his voice, the tall man said in between sobs,

"Haa'ígi doo niniit'áazh da, shiyázhí, níkaniitáago. Yisnááh áni'diilyaa ha'níigo, yéego bik'ee txi'hwiisii'nii'. Nénáhoosdzinígíí doo ts'íí'át'éégóó baa 'ahééh nisin. Nimá yéego txi'hooznii', ni'disnááh yę́ędą́ą' dóó wóshdę́ę́'." *We went far and near, my little one, we were looking for you. It was said that you were kidnapped, we suffered greatly because of that. I am extremely thankful that you have been found. Your mother suffered greatly from the time you were kidnapped until now.*

"Háadishą' nanináá nít'ę́ę', she'awéé'?" *Where were you, my baby?* the tall man and woman screamed in unison at the top of their lungs as they held and questioned their long-lost daughter, their only daughter.

The tall man was running out of breath when he gasped,

"Ayóó'ánííníshní, she'awéé'. Doo nééhoozingóó biniinaa shijéí doochohoo'į́įgóó bich'į' nahwii'ná. K'ad nída'ahiiltsánígií beego nihikáa'jį' hazlį́į́'. K'ad ahaa 'ádahwiilyą́ą doo. Doo ts'íí'át'éégóó nihich'į' nahwii'náa nidi, k'ad dóó kodóó nihił dahózhǫ́ǫ dooleeł. Doo lá dó' ahéhee'gi 'áhoodzaa da hééííííííííí!" *I love you, my baby, my heart has faced hardship because we did not know what happened to you. Now that we have seen one another again, we will survive. Even though we are facing extreme hardship, we will be happy. What a wonderful happening for which we can be thankful!* With those words, the tall man gripped his thin chest again and fell forward, hitting his head on a rock that jutted out of the dirty puddle.

The people moved forward in unison and tried in vain to talk to the tall man but his labored breaths came to an end. Two soldiers rushed in to see what the commotion was about but turned away when they saw three pitifully thin people hugging one another as the woman cried.

The woman leaned heavily on her husband and shouted,

"Haash yinidzaa? Haash yinidzaa? Deh kónínééh! Deh kónínééh!" *What happened to you? What happened to you? Lift up your head! Lift up your head!* She looked at the people surrounding them and in a loud scream she wailed,

"Doo lá dó' doodahígi 'áhoodzaa!" *A horrible thing has happened!* The people reached down and pulled the woman and the young girl to their feet and held on to them to support their weak bodies. The wound above the young girl's eye opened as fresh blood trickled down her face and mingled with her hair, sending the blood flowing even faster down her face. All she could do was scream a high-pitched scream that alerted the soldiers and brought them running with their rifles.

When the soldiers saw the deceased man lying in the puddle of dirty water, they poked several Naabeehó men with the end of their rifles and ordered,

"Pick up the body, take it to the river and throw him in the river!" No one moved. Looking over their shoulders, they yelled for the interpreter.

"The current will carry him out of here in no time," one soldier announced nonchalantly.

"I'm glad that the river water is running at its crest from all the rain. Come on! Giddy up! Get this body out of here!" An interpreter appeared. He was out of breath. The message was repeated to the interpreter. He winced as he reluctantly relayed the message to the Naabeehó men. The Naabeehó men who witnessed the dramatic reunion were appalled at the soldiers' demand.

The interpreter explained the unwillingness of the Naabeehó men to pick up the body of the tall man. The soldiers were unconcerned of the taboo the Navajo people observed regarding dead bodies.

"Better that they do it than us. If they throw him in the water, we don't have to report his death. We don't have time to report the death of another savage. To me, it's just one less mouth to feed. Don't let the word get back to Folton, the savage lover! He will make us dig a grave and properly bury this vermin-infected savage."

With guns pointed at their heads, four Naabeehó men were forced to carry the tall man's body behind the parade grounds and toward the fast running water of the Pecos River. Out of the corner of his eye, Lt. Col. Folton saw Navajo men carrying a body past his office window. His office was housed in a large building with several large windows in each wall. His desk sat in front of one of the windows so he and other officers could keep an eye on the activities of their soldiers and Navajo captives. The officer hopped up as quickly as he could, grabbed his cane, and stumbled out after the soldiers following the four Navajo men. At his orders, the two soldiers lowered their rifles, turned, and stood at attention after they saluted their superior officer.

"What is the purpose of this? Why are you walking away from the designated burial ground?" he demanded.

"We are escorting these sav-, men to the burial grounds to bury their deceased, Sir." Using his cane to point toward the burial grounds, the officer yelled,

"The burial grounds are in the opposite direction from where you are headed! Why are you directing them in this direction? Answer me! You know we have been told the Navajo captives have been throwing their dead into the river because they are afraid of the dead! It is one of the reasons the Mescalero Apache Indians stole away from here! Their waters were being contaminated by dead bodies. It was not the Navajos, it is my own soldiers who contaminated the waters and drove off the Mescalero Apaches! Now tell me why you are throwing the dead bodies into the Pecos River?" the officer demanded. The two soldiers stood with their heads down and did not answer. Shivers ran up and down Lt. Col. Folton's spine. His beautiful Sunflower and her family, along with the people of whom her father was the leader, had been settled down the river. "They have been exposed to the contaminated waters," he thought as he shivered. He thought of the little toddler who was supposedly his son. He thought of the cleanliness of his beautiful Sunflower's people. He was so ashamed of his soldiers.

"Stay here!" he demanded and walked back into his office building. Calling the officers together, he informed them of the situation. The officers discussed the incident and what was to become of the soldiers who committed the infraction. The officer told his soldiers they had to bury the body in the graveyard that was "created and set aside for this very purpose!" he yelled. The two soldiers were assigned to work in the graveyard until summer.

"That means digging graves, protecting the graveyard, documenting the ones who pass, and so on and so on..." the officer yelled. The two soldiers looked at the Navajo men with hatred in their eyes. What they were trying to avoid, they were required to complete. The first grave they had to dig was the one for the tall Navajo man after they completed a full report of his death. The grave they dug was measured to ensure they followed guidelines, at which the two soldiers complained to no end.

****

The young girl and her mother sadly returned to their leader's camp. Their people consoled them after they learned of their plight. Mother and daughter shared their stories to enlighten the others of their experiences of how they became separated from one another when Kit Carson's soldiers stole all the donkeys from the mother, who owned a herd of donkeys. As an afterthought, the soldiers grabbed the young girl and took her from her home.

The young girl reported to her mother that she was very hungry so she followed an old soldier who promised to give her food to eat and more for her family. Instead, the old soldier gave the young girl to the soldiers who chased her from one end of the valley to the other, laughing and taunting one another about who would ride the young girl first.

What the soldiers were not prepared for was the loyalty of the donkeys to the young girl's mother. When they attempted to ride the donkeys to rest their horses, the donkeys heard the young girl's high whistle and started bucking the heavy soldiers off of their backs. The soldiers jumped up with dirt pouring off of their clothes and their hats. Although she was running for her life, the young girl had to stifle her laughter. Her laughter was stifled and replaced by a scream when shots rang out across the valley. One of the soldiers was badly hurt when he was bucked off of a donkey. In retaliation, the soldier lifted his rifle and shot the animal several times making sure the donkey was dead.

A man the Naabeehó people called Adilohí *Roper* (Kit Carson) shouted out an order. The man was short, stocky and was mad at the environment. He did not look strong, but he was impulsive, shooting at whatever scared him. He never tried riding one of her mother's donkeys but he did not want his soldiers to kill any more donkeys.

"We need them for packing the meat," he growled. He also told the soldiers the donkeys are more agile than their horses and are valuable to the assignment of rounding up the Navajos. The donkeys were unruly and seemed wild but the soldiers noticed the donkeys moved toward the young Navajo girl and were relieved that she knew how to control them. The leader of the soldiers acknowledged the young girl was essential to the usefulness of the donkeys.

"Shimá, nitélii biniit'aa 'aníícháą'go bee yisdzíí'. Nihe'anaa'í bitsį' daalgaiígíí t'áadoo yéego 'atxídashiléhí kojį' adanihineeskaad. Áko nidi, shimá, nitélii nihe'anaa'í bitsį' daalgaiígíí ayóo deijooła. Ts'ídá doo 'ádabi'di'níi dago biniinaa jó shí da nilį́į' nihe'anaa'í bá baa 'áháshyą́ągo 'ádashiilaa. 'Éí bee shikáa'jį' hazlį́į'. Háájí shį́į 'adeineeskaad, sha'shin, hóla. 'Ayóo bídahasááh. Télii ayóo nídahasáahgo biniinaa ts'ídá doo 'ádabi'di'nínígi 'ádaat'ée da daazlį́į'. T'óó baa yíníh hasingo baa 'ákoniizį́į'." *My mother, it was because I sought solace behind your donkeys that I was spared. I wasn't tortured much by our enemies with white skin during the time they forced us to walk here. But our donkeys really hated our enemies with white skin. They just would not listen and that is why I was told to take care of your donkeys and that was the reason I was able to survive. I don't know where they herded them. I don't know. I really miss them. The donkeys really missed you and that was the reason they would not behave. I felt so sorry for them.*

"Ch'ééh hánihidésh'íį' łeh nít'ę́ę́'. Kojį' anihidi'noolkaad yę́ędą́ą́' t'áá sáhí nikidiitłizh. Ch'énáh dóó dichin bik'ee txi'hooshníihgo hahoolzhiizh. Hastóí t'éiyá ch'iiyáán bich'į' ch'éédadit'áahgo biniinaa dichin bik'ee txi'hooshníih nít'ę́ę́'. Áko nidi sáanii dóó 'áłchíní t'óó'ahayóí ch'iiyáán doo bich'į' ch'éédadit'áah da lágo baa 'ákoniizį́į́'. Hastóí t'óó hak'i nidanilne'go biniinaa shí sáanii dóó 'áłchíní 'ada'diyoołnah biniiyé bá hásht'į́įgo nahashzhiizh. Sáanii dóó 'áłchíní bąąh ádahasdįįdígíí bá hásht'į́įgo, łą́ądi nihe'anaa'í shich'į' bináák'is ánídayiil'įįhígíí bit'éíyáago 'át'é, shimá." *I also have been looking for you too. Ever since we were forced to walk to this place, I have been alone. I suffered from homesickness and extreme hunger. The men are the only ones who are given food and that is the reason I really suffered from extreme hunger. But I saw many women and children who did not receive any food. The men ignored them and that is the reason I began to obtain food for them to eat. Many times, I met our enemy who winked at me and got under his clothes in order to obtain food for the women and children who lost their male relatives, my mother.*

Tears filled the young girl's eyes as the memory took her down a painful remembrance, but her mother, noticing her pain, interrupted her and asked,

"Hait'éego shą' bá háníťįį́ níťę́ę́, shiyázhí?" *How were you able to obtain supplies for them, my little one?* The young girl's eyes clouded just before she began to tell her mother how brave she tried to be for all the women and children who depended on her. She told of an old skinny soldier with wiry yellow hair who used to smile and wink at her. She told of how she understood the smile but she did not understand why the old soldier winked at her so much. The young girl's mother frowned when she heard her daughter talk about the soldier who winked.

"Shich'į' bináák'is ánáyiil'įįh díníniid, éísh ha'át'íí 'óolyé? Bináá' lá haa náyiil'įįhgo?" *You said he winks his eye, what does that mean? What did he do with his eye?* the mother asked. The young girl tried to wink but instead her face became contorted and her mother started laughing at her and pretty soon, they were both laughing, after her mother said,

"Haash nit'į́? Ninii' tóó dah yishch'il. T'óó la' nichǫ́'í. Hoł hodiniih nahalingo la' ninii' dah yishch'il." *What are you doing? Your face is all contorted. Your face is wrinkled like someone who is in a lot of pain.* Following her mother's comment, the young girl placed two fingers over her eye and quickly pushed her eye closed while keeping the other eye open and smiling. When she lifted her fingers off of her eye, her mother started laughing again because her upper eyelid remained stuck to her lower eyelid. After some stretching of her face, her eyelid popped up and both mother and daughter laughed, hugged and cried knowing that laughter was so rare as prisoners of war.

The young girl returned to her story about the old skinny soldier who lured her toward the large building where food supplies were stored. Once they entered the massive building without being noticed, the old skinny soldier knocked the young girl off of her feet by overpowering her. The young girl underestimated the power of the old soldier and soon succumbed to his evil wishes, hoping he would keep his word regarding the offer of food for her and her family. Gone were his crooked smile and his winking eye. Raw desire took their place as he grunted and moaned with wild satisfaction as he crushed the young girl's body onto the dirt floor with his need for sordid satisfaction.

Crying, the young girl accepted his stingy offer of flour, coffee grounds, and meat that was covered with slime and smelled awful. She retold of how the old soldier would straighten her rug dress and pat the dirt off of her dress then look out between the thick lumber boards that made the door, then shove her out the door to quickly shut the door behind her.

The young girl looked away from her mother and resentfully thought, "I did not have a man to accept food for me but the old soldier became the man who gave me food although it was rotten, which I shared with the women and children who also had no man to represent them." Tears formed in the young girl's eyes as she continued to tell her mother of her desperate fight for her life and for that of the others who depended upon her. Her mother, wanting to comfort her, said,

"Jó níni' ayóo bidziil lá, shiyázhí. Sáanii dóó 'áłchíní bich'ą́ąh nisíníbaa'go 'át'é. Ła' shį́į́ nik'éí danilį́įgo biza'íłtso'go bee bich'ą́ąh nisíníbaa'. Nihe'anaa'í bit'éíníyáhígíí t'áadoo biniinaa yaa nanít'áhí dóó t'áadoo baa níni'í. 'Áko nidi kodóó náasjį' éí doo 'ákót'éego ch'iiyáán hánít'į́į da dooleeł. Hastóí ch'iiyáán bich'į' ch'éédadit'ááhgóó 'ałnánéiit'ash doo. 'Ei shį́į́ t'áá shǫǫ ła' nihik'i jiidoobaałgo da 'át'é. Nihí nihinaat'áanii nilínígíí bąąh áhásdį́įdgo yits'ą́ądóó bíni' bąąh dahoo'a'go yik'ee t'áá yéego kadeeyá. 'Éí 'éí doo ba'jóolíí' át'ée da. 'Nihikéyahgóó náshí'ni',' níigo yaa nisé'áłdił. T'óó baa hojoobá'ígo bił hoo'a'. T'áá nihí 'ák'inidiidáago t'éí nihikáa'jį' hodooleeł. Ayóó 'át'éego naa'a'ááh nisin, shiyázhí. T'áá 'ákónéehee 'íinidzaa lá." *Your mind is very strong, my little one, you have gone to battle against hunger on behalf of the women and children. Some of the ones you went into battle on behalf of were probably your relatives. It is a good thing you did that. Don't be ashamed that you went underneath one of our enemy's clothing and don't be sorry about it. But from now on, you will not need to obtain food like that again. We will go where the men are given food. We hope one of them will show kindness to us and give us some food to eat. Our leader lost his loved ones and because of that, his mind was affected and he became very sick from it. We cannot expect him to help us. He keeps saying he wants to go back to our own land. His situation has become so pitiful. In order to survive, we will have to depend on ourselves. I am in awe of you, my little one. You survived because of your actions.*

"Háshinee'gi 'áshidíníniid, shimá. Jó k'ad éiyá 'ałk'íhwiilta'go binahjį' doo díníi'néeł da." *What a wonderful thing to say to me, my mother. Well, now we will help one another and we will not die.*

"Nihe'anaa'í baa hólne'ígíí shą' haa nóolnin? Yiiłtsą́ągo ts'ídá yéego bibid nídideests'į́į́ł," *What does the enemy that you were talking about look like? When I see him I will hit him real hard in the stomach with my fist,* the mother said in an attempt to erase some of her daughter's painful memories of survival.

"Éí hastiin nihe'anaa'í nilínígíí bitsii' łitsoh dóó tł'oh nahalingo t'óó bik'idéjool. Binii' yéego yishch'il dóó bináá' éí yá nahalingo dootł'izh áádóó t'óó yéego bííts'iiní. Łah t'áá łichíi'go shidááhdóó yiizį' nít'ę́ę́' biyid t'óó biih yíts'ǫ́ǫ́d nahalin. Áko t'óó'ayóo bich'íí' dootł'izhí t'áá 'ííshjání bitsą́ shijoolgo shidááhdóó nijíídongo hak'íníghal. T'óó ga' béésísdzíidgo t'óó niishch'iil." *That man who is our enemy has yellow hair that looks like hay as it is plopped on his head. His face is really wrinkled and his eyes are of the color of the blue sky and he is really skinny. Once, he stood in front of me with no clothes on and his chest looked as if it caved in and I could easily see what looked like his blue intestines in his stomach as he planted himself in front of me. I just closed my eyes because he looked scary.* The young girl's mother shivered and reached out to her daughter and held her to comfort her and to erase a few of the horrendous memories she carried.

All of a sudden, the young girl felt her mother's body shaking. Out of fear, she loosened her grip on her mother and took a step back. Relieved, she realized her mother was trying so hard to stifle her laughter. In a hoarse voice the mother said,

"We', yish'į́į la'. T'óó la' bááhádzidígi 'át'éego bits'íís baa ch'íhwííní'ą́!" *Yuck, I can see him. Your description of him is fearful!* Another round of laughter shook the mother's body. In her mind, the young girl could still see the old soldier's naked body, as she too joined her mother in another round of laughter.

"Anáshdlohgo la' shii' hááhwiisdoh, shiyázhí. Yáadilá t'óó bááhádzidgo baa hwííníłne'." *Laughing has been a relief for me, my little one. You told about an awful thing!*

Out of their desperation to survive, the mother asked her daughter to join her to walk to the horse corrals. There, under the cover of dusk, they collected horse manure and took the manure back to the outskirts of their camp and sifted through the horse manure, hoping to find corn kernels the horses had not digested. They noticed other Naabeehó women were there for the same purpose. After the mother and daughter were able to obtain several handfuls of kernels, they returned to their camp and boiled the kernels then ate the kernels. They found the corn kernels tasted similar to the short variety of sagebrush. Their meal was comforting to them. They came to rely on the tainted corn kernels as they shared their meager meals with several other women and children.

****

Leading his warriors, Hashké Yił Naabaah turned to walk along the path they follow going back to their camp.

He saw a very thin woman sitting with a thin young woman who looked weak and undernourished, just like the woman she sat near. He remembered he had seen the two women sitting in the same spot before. He had not taken their presence into consideration but seeing them again, Hashké Yił Naabaah felt sorry for them. He approached the two women and greeted them and asked them what area of Diné bikéyah *Navajo land* they were from. He then asked,

"Háí lá biba' sooké? T'óó kǫ́ǫ́ sookéego nánihiistséé h." *Who are you waiting for? Several times I have seen you two sitting here.* The older woman responded, saying,

"Díí yee' nihąąh áhásdįįd. Díí hazhé'é be'iina' bits'ą́ą' náádiilyáago biniinaa ch'iiyáán bich'į' ch'éédít'ááh yę́ę nihits'ą́ą' ásdįįd. T'áá shǫǫ da t'áá háida nihaa jiidoobaał niidzingo biniinaa kǫ́ǫ́ sikée łeh." *We have lost a family member. Her father's life was taken from him and the ration that used to be given to him stopped. We sit near the place where they distribute rations, hoping someone would be kind to us.* All Hashké Yił Naabaah could say was,

"Yáadilá 'óolyéé dó'. Sáanii dóó 'áłchíní t'óó'ahayóí bich'į' ákódahoodzaa. T'óó shił baa dahojoobá'ígo biniinaa kéédahwiit'ínídi ninádahiit'éésh. Nihikéé' nánihí'ni'gogo 'éí tsołtxį', nihikéé' woh'ash." *What a thing to say. That has happened to a lot of women and children. We have had sympathy for them and for that reason, we have led them back to where we are camped. If you are willing to follow us, let's go.* The mother and her daughter did not have to be coaxed into joining Hashké Yił Naabaah and his group.

They followed their new leader down the path that led toward their camp.

Hashké Yił Naabaah and his warriors walked slower because of the two women. They worried about the strength of the older woman but the woman and her daughter insisted on keeping up with the men. On their way, Nahat'á Yinaabaah and Tł'ée'go Naabaah as well as Kiizhóní gave up the pieces of jerky that was packed for them before they left for the parade grounds.

While snacking on the jerky, the two women told the men their story starting from the time when the soldiers kidnapped the daughter and forced the mother and her husband to walk to Fort Fauntleroy, and a few days later, forced them to walk to Fort Sumner. When the sun shed its dim, predawn light to illuminate the landscape around them, Hashké Yił Naabaah and his group arrived at their camp. He announced,

"Ła' hoł nániikai. T'óó haa hojoobá'ígo ch'iiyáán ch'éédít'áhígi jizkéego haa 'ákodaniidzį́į́'. K'é dabididoohniił dóó baa dajiinohba' doo, t'ááshǫǫdí, shidine'é danohłínígíí." *We came home with someone. I had sympathy for them as they sat near the area where the rations are given out. Greet them and be kind to them, please, those of you who are my people.* Hashké Yił Naabaah was proud of his people when he saw them obeying his request.

Hashké Yił Naabaah sought out Nínáánníbaa', and when he saw her sitting on the ground, brushing her hair, he hurried to her and plopped himself down on the ground next to her. He told her about the mother and daughter he invited to come and live at their camp. In her soft soothing voice Nínáánîbaa' said,

"Ayóo 'aajiiníba'. Azhą́ shį́į́ sáanii dóó 'áłchíní dichin yik'ee txi'dahooníhígíí nináhí'éesh nidi, nihich'iiyą' t'ahdoo 'ádįįh da. Ne'ajooba' binahjį' nihik'ihojidlí. 'Ahéhee', shinaat'áanii, nizhónígo nihidine'é bá nahó'áago binahjį' bikáa'jį dahazlį́į́'." *You are very kind. Even though you bring back women and children who are suffering from lack of food, our food supply has not vanished. Thank you, my leader, because you are a good leader our people will survive.* Nínáánîbaa''s words encouraged Hashké Yił Naabaah's heavy heart. He turned to her, picked up her hair that drifted down into a soft mound on her rug blanket and lifted it to his nostrils and took in the sweet scent of his Nínáánîbaa''s hair then said, while still smelling her hair,

"Jó 'ił ahojooba' nits'ą́ądóó nídiiláhígíí 'át'é. T'áá'ákwíí jį́ shaa jiiníba' łeh. Áłchíní bee shaa jiisíníba', ninahjį' shicheii yázhí naakigo hazlį́į́'. T'áá nihí nihikéyah biih néiikaigo hooghan nímazí bii' sínídáa dooleełígíí ła' ná nideesh'ááł dóó dibé ła' ná shóideesht'eeł. Éí bee náádidíídááł. Shí 'éí ninahjį' shitah yá'ánááhoot'éeh doo, shiyázhí. T'áá 'ákónéehee shaa ni'deeltį́į́ lá nisin łeh. Ayóo naa 'ahééh nisin. Háshinee', shiyázhí. *I picked up kindness from you. You are kind to me everyday. You have blessed me with children. It is through you that I have two grandsons. When we enter our own land, I will make a hogan for you to live in and I will obtain some sheep for you. Those will make you well again. I will get better because of you, my little one. I always think it was good that you were given to me in marriage. I am very thankful for you. My dear little one.* Nínáánîbaa' smiled and nuzzled against her husband's strong tired shoulders. She thanked the Creator for bringing her husband back safely.

Nínáánîbaa' listened to the soft sounds of the early dawn that drifted throughout their camp as she held her exhausted husband in her arms. She could feel his breaths softly settling on her neck. She wanted him to hold her, but he needed his rest.

When the sun's bright rays of dawn announced the beginning of a new day, Nínáánîbaa' moved and slowly moved her arm out from under him. In soft whispers, he said,

"Hágo, shiyázhí. 'Ádíniistsóód." *Come here, my little one. Let me hold you close to me.* Slowly she lifted her torso and slid right into his arms. Her husband let her sleep while he listened to his people quietly talking to one another.

Chapter Nine
Preparations for Negotiating the Naaltsoos Sání *Old Paper*

Interpreters arrived with a hasty message informing the Naabeehó people of a meeting that would be held with leaders with white skin. The Naabeehó people learned a group of people would arrive from the east to tell them about land that was set aside for them to claim as their own.

The elder Peace Leader planned their walk to the parade grounds near the fort. Nínáánibaa' looked upon Hashké Yił Naabaah with pride. He observed cultural protocol that dictated he lay aside his leadership to allow the elderly Peace Leader to lead their people while remaining a constant source of strength, support, and wisdom for the new leader. Her husband had complied with the protocol since he had become a War Leader. She admired her husband for not ignoring cultural protocol and his lifestyle as a War Leader.

Her thoughts were drawn back to the discussion when she heard murmurs among the women who refused to accept the orders of the soldiers who wanted to resettle the Naabeehó people on lands in the eastern direction. An elderly woman who spoke loudly and clearly said,

"Nihinaat'áanii níłíinii, bee síníłtxee' dooleeł, t'áá hazhó'ó t'áá nihí nihikéyahgóó t'éí nídanihí'ni', náána łahgóó 'éí ts'ídá dooda. Ts'ídá doodaí bee doodaí bee dooda! Áadi shįį́ t'áá kónááhoot'ée dooleeł." *Our leader, be adamant about it, we only want to go back to our own land, not to another place. Absolutely not, no, no! It will probably be just like it is here."* Nínáánibaa' heard the women echoing the words of the elderly woman. In agreeing with the elderly woman's words, many women spoke up saying,

"Aoo', aoo', aoo'." *Yes, yes, yes.*

Hearing the objections of the women, the elder Peace leader looked at Hashké Yił Naabaah, and said

"Jó 'ákót'éé lá. Bee sistxee' dooleeł." *Well, that is the way it is going to be. I will be unwavering about it.* The women turned toward Nínáánibaa' to read the reaction on her face but she wanted to speak with her husband before she gave any clue regarding her thoughts on the new peril her people were facing. The Naabeehó people did not realize the federal government had already decided to remove all the Navajo people to the lands in the eastern direction they called Indian Territory (Oklahoma).

Hashké Yił Naabaah asked his daughter Dzáníbaa' to relay the interpreter's message to his Mescalero Apache son-in-law. The young Mescalero Apache man immediately asked Dzáníbaa' to translate his message to her father. The young man warned the elder Peace Leader against moving the Naabeehó people to the land in the eastern direction.

"Shidine'é bikéyah kodóó shádi'áahjigo bił haz'ą́. Dziłtahdi kéédahat'į́į́ dóó 'ayóó 'áhonoolnin léi'gi bikéyah bił haz'ą́. Ei kéyah nihidiné'é bá náhodiit'ánígíí 'éí Naashgálí dine'é bikéyahdóó ha'a'aahjigo bił haz'ą́, ní." *My people's land is located south of here. Our land is in the mountains and is located in a beautiful area. The land they say has been set aside for your people is located east of the Mescalero Apache lands, he said.*

Bitsį' Yishtłizhii danilínígíí, t'óó'ahayóí 'áajigo kéédahat'į́į́ lá, ní. Naashgálí dine'é beda'anaa'í Bitsį' Daashtłizhii danilį́įgo t'óó'ahayóí 'áajį' ch'ídabidi'neeskaadgo 'áadi kéédahat'į́, ní. 'Áko t'áá 'ahą́ą́h 'áádę́ę́'go, ha'a'aahdę́ę́'go, hadine'é yik'ijį' nídadibah nít'ęę́'. Sáanii dóó 'áłchíní yisnááh ádcidoolíłígíí shį́į́ biniiyé. Ts'ídá doo daats'íid da dóó doo 'aadaastxi' da, jiníigo baa hojilne'." *Over there, there are many different people with brown skin (Indians) who live there, he said. Many enemies of the Mescalero Apache people who have brown skin have been chased to that area and now live there, he said. And so from there, they make it a regular practice to wage war against the Mescalero Apache people. They were searching for women and children to kidnap. They are not friendly and are not kind, he said.* Dzáníbaa' listened to her husband offer more information before she relayed the message.

"Aadę́ę́' nihich'į' yinééł ha'nínígíí 'éí bizaad k'ehgo 'e'e'aahjigo kéyah ła' náάhódlǫǫdi nihá nídahodii'ą́ą, nidi 'éí kéyah bikáá'góó t'óó halgai dóó hodilkǫǫh, ní. Hodilkǫǫhígíí biniinaa nízaadgóó hoot'į. T'áá kwe'é 'áhoot'éhígi 'áhoot'é' áadi. Hwe'anaa'í hak'ijį' nídadibahgo t'áá bahat'aadí hach'į' yinéeł łeh, jiní. Díí kéyah bikáa'jį' anihi'di'noolkaadígíí t'áá bihoołt'é 'áadi." *The people who are coming (Washington delegation) have selected land that is available in the east, but that land is land that is barren and flat, he said. One can see far because the land is flat. It resembles this land. Whenever an enemy is approaching for warfare they can be easily seen, he said. This land we have been chased onto is much like that land.* Dzáníbaa' could hear the people murmuring, voicing their dislike for the information she relayed to the elder Peace Leader.

"Kéyah ha'a'aahjigo nihá náhodiit'ánígíí doo nihá yá'át'éeh da, ní. 'Áadi hoołtsą́ą́ lá. Bí díkwíidi shįį ákǫ́ǫ́ 'akéé' naazbaa'. Haté'áziní ła' hats'ą́ą́' yisnááh ádabi'diilyaago biniinaa 'ákóó bikéé' nidajizbaa'. Tó 'ayóo bídin hóyéé', jiní, áadi. T'óó tsédaatah dóó łeezh bee halgai dóó ch'il deeníní t'éí bił nidaayol, níigo yaa halne'." *The land in the east that has been selected is not good for us, he said. He has seen the place. He went there several times when he went along for the purpose of warfare because some of his relatives were kidnapped. There is a shortage of water there. There are many rocks and the sand is white and tumble weeds are blown all around, he said.* Dzáníbaa' could sense the burden of leadership the elder Peace Leader took on when they heard the first thunder. She trusted her husband. He would not lie about the land her people may be forced to settle upon. She too, wanted to return to her home at the base of Dziłíjiin *Black Mesa.*

Hashké Yił Naabaah felt a deep sense of sadness. He looked into the distance and felt an unbearable sense of sadness. When consulted by his elder Peace Leader, he encouraged his leader not to agree to resettle his people on land that was similar to where they were held prisoner, land that was unproductive, unwelcoming, deserted and plain. It was land that was not between their sacred mountains. It was land that was selected for his people by their enemies. He knew in his heart their enemy would select land that would be the death of all his people. "Why should our enemy select land that is beautiful, productive, welcoming, and abounding in life?" he questioned.

He looked up into his young Dzáníbaa''s face and saw features that resembled his beautiful Nínááníbaa'. He also looked into the face of his little grandson who sat on her lap. He was grateful to the young Mescalero Apache man for giving him and their elder Peace Leader insight to the land to which their enemy had decided to send them. In a soft voice, he said,

"Ahéhee', shiyázhí, yéego nihíká 'íínílwod. Nihá 'ata' hwíínílne'. *Thank you, my little one, you have greatly helped us. You interpreted messages for us.* He approached his Mescalero Apache son-in-law with an outstretched open hand and clasped the young man's hand and held it tight, saying,

"Ahéhee', shaadaaní. Nizaad bee nihidine'é bich'ą́ąh nisíníbaa'. NihiDzáníbaa' dóó niyázhí bich'ą́ąh nisíníbaa'. 'Nihe'anaa'í kéyah doo nihá yá'át'ééhígíí nihá nídahodii'ą́ą lá,' diníigo bee nihił ch'íhwíiní'ą. T'áá'íídą́ą' éí kéyahígíí bii' hwiiniłtsą. T'áá kónááhoot'é diníigo baa ch'íhwíiní'ą. Naat'áanii t'áá'át'é bee bił dahodoonih. Ałtso nanihi'di'dooltsxił t'éí biniiyé 'áajį'go nihá nídahodii'ą. Éí dó' deiniih dooleeł." *Thank you, my son-in-law. You served as a warrior by means of your words to protect our people. You protected our Dzáníbaa' and your little one in serving as a warrior. You told us our enemy has selected land that is not good for us. You have already seen the land. You reported the land is the same as this land here. All the Naabeehó leaders will be told. They also need to know.* Hashké Yił Naabaah knew his Mescalero Apache son-in-law was very concerned for his wife's people.

Hashké Yił Naabaah discussed his son-in-law's warnings with the elder Peace leader. Following his meeting with Hashké Yił Naabaah, the elder Peace Leader listened intently to the words of his people in preparation for the meeting Naabeehó leaders would have with the people who are coming from the eastern direction (Washington, D.C.)

Hashké Yił Naabaah and the elder Peace Leader always made it a practice to include the young warriors in all their plans and listened to their budding wisdom regarding leadership. Hashké Yił Naabaah had an additional concern. He noticed his youngest son sat near the elder Peace Leader. He thought back to the last few meetings. He felt a sadness in seeing his youngest son sitting with the young men who had been selected to be trained as a Peace Leader. Hashké Yił Naabaah knew his son, as a Peace Leader, would protect his people by his words instead of by warfare. Hashké Yił Naabaah decided to wait and observe his son. He trusted the years he spent training his sons to become effective War Leaders. He mentioned his worry to Nínááníbaa'. She advised him to observe his son before he made a hasty judgment.

Hashké Yił Naabaah convinced his young Mescalero son-in-law to accompany them to the parade grounds. He pointed to his ears and said,

"Adiits'a'í nihá nílį́į doo 'áadi. Nihidine'é bá 'adinits'a'go bich'ą́ą́h nidííbah. Shicheii yázhí, ne'awéé', dóó nihiyázhí Dzáníbaa' bich'ą́ą́h nidííbah. Saad bee na'abaahgo 'át'é. Yéego shidine'é bíká 'ííníilwod dooleeł. Shidine'é t'óó shił baa dahojoobá'íyee'. Nínááníbaa' doo ts'íí'át'éégóó txi'hooznii'. Naakidi nihiDzáníbaa' bich'ą́ą́h nisíníbaa'. Nit'áahjį' aníícháą́' áádóó bí dóó nihicheii yázhí nihá baa 'áhólyą́ągo binahjį' nihiyázhí bikáa'jį' hazlį́į'." *You will be an interpreter for us. As you listen on behalf of our people, you will become a warrior for our people. You will fight on behalf of your baby and our little one Dzáníbaa'. A person can enter into battle with words as their weapon. You will have helped us in a great way. I have such sympathy for my people. Nínááníbaa' really suffered. Twice, you went into warfare on behalf of our Dzáníbaa'. She found safety in your care and when you cared for her and our little grandson, you saved their lives.* Dzáníbaa' smiled as she spoke in the Mescalero Apache language and conveyed her father's message although she knew her husband understood many words her father spoke with such passion.

With them were Hashké Yił Naabaah and his family and the warriors, as well as many of their people from other camps, and additional War Leaders and Peace Leaders. With the leaders, were their families and people under their leadership. All arrived at the parade grounds in a large group, one day before the pretreaty talks would be held. The Naabeehó people were nervous and not comfortable with their surroundings. Many troops had their guns drawn and had them pointed at the Naabeehó men. Others were on horseback with their guns drawn while additional troops holding rifles stood on the roofs of the buildings that surrounded the large parade grounds.

Nínáánímbaa' and her daughters followed Hashké Yił Naabaah and their elder Peace Leader to the parade grounds. They were shocked to see so many Naabeehó people, more than they could count, sitting on the ground, waiting patiently. Hashké Yił Naabaah told them many more Naabeehó people were still at their camps who could not attend the meeting because they had loved ones to care for or they wanted to protect their camps from intruders and many had small babies and children to care for.

Tears danced in the eyes of Hashké Yił Naabaah as he looked over the large population of Naabeehó people. Many Naabeehó were wrapped only in thin pieces of cloth, others had no shoes, still others had nothing covering their bodies except for a string that held small pieces of cloth in place to cover their crotch and their backside. Many men wore gray blankets around their shoulders. A few of the women wore rug dresses while others had wrapped calico fabric around their bodies and shared their gray blankets with others. Hashké Yił Naabaah looked back at his own group of people, they were clothed in tattered and worn out rug dresses and a few covered themselves with their tattered rug blankets. No one wore the gray blanket the tall gray-haired one gave them. Looking back at the multitude of Naabeehó people before him, he whispered,

"Tóó la' bik'ee jóchaaígi 'ádajít'é. Hojooba' ádeizhnízingo kodi nijiiskai. T'óó la' haa dahojoobá'íyee'. T'áá'ájít'é yéego dahwííts'iiní. Daházhi'ęę doo k'ídaazdon da, t'óó yéego dahwíishghánée nídaazhah. Ha'át'íishįį́ hadazhnitá nahalingo ni'jį' yaa 'adazhnool'ą́. Yáadishįį́ kódanihííł'įįd! Doo bíla' ashdla'ii danilįį da. Dooda lą́ą!" *One could shed tears over this. The people gathered here because they want to hear good news. I feel so sorry for them. They are all so very thin. The form of their bodies are not straight anymore, instead their backs are rounded. Their faces are close to the ground as if they are looking for something that is on the ground. What awful things did this to us! They are not five-fingered ones. Absolutely not!*

Noticing the soldiers placing a table in the area before the parade grounds in preparation for the treaty negotiation between the representatives of the United States government, the soldiers, and the leaders of the

Naabeehó people, Hashké Yił Naabaah took a few steps back to return to his people, then sat down on the ground in front of his Nínááníbaa'.

Dédii and Dzáníbaa' watched their mother brush their father's long hair with a bé'ázhóó' *a hair brush* made of long stems of grass that are tied tightly together. Skillfully, Nínááníbaa' placed the end of the bé'ázhóó' against her husband's head and brought the bé'ázhóó' down to smooth the loose strands of hair. Each time she placed the end of the brush against his scalp, she gave him a little bit of advice. Dédii and Dzáníbaa' heard their mother quietly, but firmly, give their father advice, telling him to remain firm on their need to return to their own land between their sacred mountains.

"T'áá nihí nihikéyah t'éí bich'į' nídanihí'ni'. Éí bee sínííltxee' doo. Niha'áłchíní dabits'éé' nihighandi, dibé bighan bitsįįgi dóó táchééh bitsįįgi łeeh naaztą́. Nihikéyah doo yits'ą́ąjį' dah didookahígíí biniiyé niha'áłchíní dabits'éé' áadi łeeh niniilyá. Nihi'í'óol'įįł dóó 'iiná bee 'ádeiil'íinígíí dóó bik'ehgo dahinii'nánígíí doo yits'ą́ąjį' dah didookah daígíí biniinaa niha'áłchíní bínaniiltingo daneeyą́. Nihahastóí, k'ad nihinaat'áanii nilínígíí, nihá bee bił hodíilnih, azhą́ shįį́ nihíni' danilínígíí bił bééhózin nidi, naat'áanii yił ahínéikahígíí yił saad t'áála'ígíí yee hadadoodzih dóó yee daastxee' doo. T'áá nihí nihikéyah bich'į' dah nídidiikah bididíiniił." *We want only to return to our own land. Be adamant about that. Our children's umbilical cords are buried at our home, specifically at the base of the sheep corral and at the base of the sweat hogan. We buried their umbilical cords there so they would not walk away from where they were raised. When we raised our children, we taught them about our culture, our traditions, and our lifestyle so they would not walk away from them. Tell the elderly man who is our current leader to tell the other leaders he meets with so they can speak with one voice and be adamant about our wishes to return to our own land. Tell him to lead us back to our own land.*

Nínáánîbaa' watched little gusts of wind pick up the loose strands of Hashké Yił Naabaah's white and gray hair. She whispered,

"Hódzą'." *Wisdom.* Still watching the strands drift up in the air and play with the brisk breeze, she stated,

"Nitsii' daalgaiígíí ch'ééh shizhéé' bee nínáshtłoh dóó yaa kónídeiish'įįh nidi t'óó dah ninááda at'a'." *I keep trying to moisten your white hairs with my saliva and push them down but they just keep flying up.*

"Jó ne'ahódzą' bee hadínísht'ée dooleełígíí shįį biniiyé t'óó dah nidaasaał. Asdzání bizhéé' bee hojíyą́ą doo shįį dashó'ní," *They probably keep popping out and fly up in the air so I could put on your wisdom. They probably want me to be wise by means of my young woman's saliva,* Hashké Yił Naabaah said smiling at the thought of wearing his wife's saliva as a covering to bring wisdom. Nínáánîbaa' chided her husband saying,

"T'áá 'íídą́ą́' yee' honíyą́. Hastiin náás silį́'ígíí nílį́. Nitsii' yiigááh. Nihinaat'áanii nílį́." *You are already wise. You are a man who is older. Your hair is turning white. You are our leader.* At her words of confidence in his leadership skills,

Hashké Yił Naabaah reached up and caught Nínááníbaa"s hands, pulled them toward him, kissed them gently, and said,

"Háláane'ęę', shiyázhí. 'Ayóo dó' shaa dzííníłí. 'Atah shidine'é bá nahash'áago, t'áá shíighah áníť'ée łeh." *Dear one, my little one. You have so much confidence in me. When I join in the planning for my people, you support me.* When Nínááníbaa' had settled all the loose strands of hair, she took his long hair that draped down and lifted his hair from the bottom and gently folded it up, then folded it again and again until she had a large four-inch sized rectangle. She took his tsiitł'óół *hair tie* she made many years ago from freshly spun wool, and quickly wound it around the middle of the folded rectangle. With Hashké Yił Naabaah's hair securely bound in a knot at the back of his head, Nínááníbaa' loosened her hair, pulled it to one side of her head then took her bé'ázhóó' and brushed her hair. Her hair draped down one side of her chest, covered her abdomen and lay in a soft heap on her lap. Sighing softly, she picked up her brush and brushed her hair a few more times then lifted a long faded thin white tsiitł'óół *hair tie* and tied her hair at the back of her head then asked Dzáníbaa' to fold her hair into a tsiiyéél *knot.* Dzáníbaa' took her time placing her mother's hair into a tsiiyééł. She remembered how black and thick her mother's hair was when they still lived at their home on Dziłíjiin *Black Mesa.* Just before she placed her mother's hair in the tied knot, she held her mother's hair in her open hand and was amazed at how heavy her mother's long hair was.

"Nitsii' ayóo nidaaz, shimá." *Your hair is real heavy, my mother.*

Hashké Yił Naabaah responded to her comment,

"Nimá bitsii' hódzą' bee hadít'é. 'Éí biniinaa hatsii' doo dajiigéesh da daaníigo nihahastóí dóó danihizáanii nida'neeztą́ą́'. Hatsii' k'íjígishgo 'éí, 'Hódzą' doo nisin da,' jiníigo t'éí 'ákózhdooníił. Nimá t'ah ánii naagháhę́ędą́ą́' nidi 'ayóo hóyą́ą́ nít'ę́ę́'. Éí shį́į́ biniinaa bitsii' nineez dóó 'ayóo nidaaz dóó yiigááh." *Your mother's wisdom is a part of her hair. That is why our older men and women taught us not to cut our hair. When a person cuts their hair, they are saying, 'I don't want wisdom'. When your mother was young, she was very wise, that is why her hair is very long and heavy and turning white.* Dédii looked at her sister's hair. Her sister's tsiiyéél *hair bun/knot* was thick and bursting out of its tsiitł'óół *hair tie.* Her sister-in-law's hair looked very full and heavy as well. Knowing all the women in her family had thick long hair, Dedii knew their many experiences had given them wisdom. She looked at the men in her family and they all had a very thick tsiiyéél snugly tied to the back of their heads as well. She loosened her tsiitł'óół to see if her hair was also heavy, which she proved to be so by the weight of her hair. Satisfied, Dédii watched her sister lean against her husband and softly touch his hair. His hair was very thick and coarse and long. Dédii knew her father, her brothers and their elder Peace Leader had earned a place at the negotiating table when the leaders would come together the next day. Her mind drifted to the tall gray-haired one.

His hair was short and very thin and was always tucked under his hat.

"Doodaiínee'. Hódzą' bee 'ádin," *Not so. He does not have wisdom,* she whispered, then turned her eyes to the clouds that drifted overhead. Looking to see if anyone was watching her, and once she noticed everyone was busy, she glanced at Kiizhóní. His hair was not bound by his tsiitł'óół, but was loose, thick, and very black with a slight curl as it cascaded down his back. Dédii whispered,

"Mmmmm, hódzą' yee hadít'é." *Mmmmm, he is made up of wisdom."*

The two sisters watched their sister-in-law, Tsék'iz Naazbaa', place Nahat'á Yinaabaah's, their brother's, thick long hair in a tsiiyééł. They noticed his tsiitł'óół *hair tie* was white but thin. The rectangular shape of his neatly folded hair was much longer. Compared to their father's tsiiyééł, it was a lot longer. Almost simultaneously, the two sisters teased their brother, calling him,

"Tsiiyééł Nézii," *One with a long hair bun,* and smiled timidly when their sister-in-law giggled at the name they gave their brother. The two sisters had missed over four years of their brother's teenage years and realized they had reverted back to the time before they were kidnapped. They chided one another and reminded each other that their brother was training to become a respected War Leader like their father. Dédii and Dzáníbaa' remembered the words of their father who scolded their brothers whenever they teased them. Their father had said many times,

"T'áadoo nihilahkéí bí'óhts'ihí. Náásgóó, nihíídéeskąąągóó nihilahkéí bí'óhts'ihgo doo nihaa jooba' da doo. Háadi da léi' dichin biih noodee'go 'áádóó jooba' nohsingo bighandi nooyáago, 'ánihididooniił, 'Shąą' ałchíní daniidlínéedąą' ałahíįį' nihí'óhts'ih łeh ne',' áko tó t'éí nihiyaa niidookáałii' bikiin iidoołhosh. Bí 'éí 'áda'azįįd yich'į' sikéego yee nidínóochał, nihí 'éí t'óó nihinááłgo. Baa jiinohba'. Háadi da léi' yisdánihidoo'ish. T'áadoo nihilahkéí bí'óhts'ihí. K'adí." *Don't tease your sisters. If you tease your sisters, they will not be kind to you later in life. If you fall into hunger sometime in the future, and you go to their home and want kindness, they may say to you, 'Remember when we were children you used to tease us all the time?' All they will give you is water while they sit at a feast and get full while you watch. Be kind to them. They may help you survive in the future. Don't tease your sisters. That's enough.* Remembering their father's words, the two sisters felt safe in teasing their brothers.

****

Dédii and Dzáníbaa' watched their father dust off his worn deerskin leggings. His leggings that once fit him well were loose but made tight at the waist and held up by a rope made of freshly cut and braided yucca leaves. His shoulders which were once strong, straight and squared, were now slightly hunched forward and thin. His tattered loose deerskin shirt did not hide his collarbones that protruded against his fair, browned skin. The two sisters nudged one another and giggled when their mother reached up and pinched off little particles of dust that stuck to their father's eyelashes, which made his black eyelashes appear to be of a light brown color.

"Ninádiz daalgááhíyee'." *Your eyelashes are of a light color,* she said softly. Hashké Yił Naabaah stood still and stared into his Nínááníbaa''s face and whispered,

"Shaa 'áhólyánígíí 'ayóo baa 'ahééh nisin, shiyázhí." *I am thankful that you take care of me, my little one.*

"Jó shinaat'áanii nílį," *Well, you are my leader,* she said, moistening her fingers with her tongue then catching loose short strands of white hair and pulling them behind his ears. Once again, she moistened her fingers and pressed the loose strands down.

Dédii and Dzáníbaa' felt chills run up and down their spines as their father squared his shoulders and looked at Nínááníbaa' and his children, allowing his eyes to rest on each face. He then raised his gaze to look out over his people. Memories from childhood were stirred as Dédii and Dzáníbaa' watched their father prepare for the meeting that was to determine the future of their Naabeehó people.

Taking his walking stick in his hand, their father invited his oldest son and his warriors to walk with him. He nodded to his youngest son then nodded to their elder Peace Leader. He gestured to his son that he was free to join their elder Peace Leader. The Peace Leaders would lead them throughout the spring and summer seasons. Tł'ée'go Naabaah smiled at his father and his brother and bravely walked to join the elder Peace Leader and his men.

Hashké Yił Naabaah and the elder Peace Leader had met many times with all the men under their leadership, after which they met with additional Peace Leaders to ensure they would speak with one voice the desires of their people. They met with and consulted additional Naabeehó leaders from across the Fort Sumner Indian Reservation.

Hashké Yił Naabaah quietly told his children and his people to respect the upcoming meeting with the enemy. He also encouraged his War Leaders to support and encourage their Peace Leaders during their time of leadership. Hashké Yił Naabaah and the leaders disappeared into the midst of the large gathering of Naabeehó binaat'áanii *Navajo leaders.*

****

Hashké Yił Naabaah stood in the parade grounds amidst many naat'áanii and Naabeehó people who followed their leaders to witness the treaty negotiations. He was reminded of the time when he and his people were first forced to enter the Fort Sumner Indian Reservation. He remembered how disheartened he felt and how ashamed he felt for leading his people to a place where their hateful enemy, Kit Carson, was the Indian Agent. At the time, Hashké Yił Naabaah realized they had been forced to walk to a place of hatred and anger and destruction and complete annihilation of his people because that was what their hateful enemy stood for. Even after his people became prisoners of war, their evil, foul, dishonest, indecent, and destructive enemy Kit Carson never lost his anger and hate even after killing so many Naabeehó women and children and men.

The Naabeehó people agreed that their hated enemy came out of his mother's womb with such anger and hatred that evil followed him. Many times the Naabeehó women were heard to say,

"Bimá bik'i nídínóodaał nít'ę́ę́'!" *His mother should have sat on him when he was born!* The Naabeehó called him "Doo Yildiní" *the Angry One* or Bi'éé' Łichíí'ii" *Red Shirt* or "Adilohí" *the One Who Ropes* and others called him "Tł'ohchin" *Onions* because he smelled like rotten onions and still others called him "Díítdzidii" *Rotten One* because of the stench that preceded his appearance. When Doo Yildiní came near a Naabeehó camp, the women ran, holding their noses and spitting. Once they found a safe spot nearby, the people spit and blew their noses so as to rid their bodies of the evil Díítdzidii. Mothers forced their children to do the same. Hashké Yił Naabaah shook his head in sadness. His memories had become his enemy.

It was Doo Yildiní *the Angry One* who insisted the Naabeehó people have one leader to meet with the military officers and speak for all the Naabeehó. However, the people were set in their ways with twelve Peace Leaders who led in the spring and summer seasons and twelve War Leaders who led in the fall and winter seasons. For a time, the people remained true to their ways and ignored the orders of Doo Yildiní and the officers, but as time wore on, many groups of Naabeehó people gave in to the wishes of Doo Yildiní and began to accept the leadership and voice of the leaders chosen by their enemies.

Hashké Yił Naabaah could hardly blame the Naabeehó leaders or their people. He was fully aware that it was the incredible hardship of being prisoners of war that made many Naabeehó leaders cave in to the demands of their enemy. The enemy knew when the people had reached their desperation point during times of destitution due to the shortage of food (even if the food was in the worst condition and the meat was rotting), extreme cold, extreme heat, and when dire loneliness set in because so many people died from various diseases, dysentery being the leading illness.

He knew War and Peace Leaders had to live and model their culture. Hashké Yił Naabaah could name the many cultural observances that were dying right alongside the elders who once held their culture so dear to their hearts. "There was the Kinaaldá *Puberty Ceremony* for the ch'ikéí *teenage girls* and a ceremony for the tsíłkéí *teenage boys* when their voices changed; there was the hooghan álnéehgi *building of a hogan*; there was the Alį́į́' neelkaad *Wedding*; there was the Awéétsʼáál álnééh *the making of a cradle board for the newborn infant*; there was the Awéé' ch'ídeeldlo' *Baby's First Laugh*, a celebration of life and laughter, and now there is so little to laugh about," he thought as his shoulders became hunched once again. There was the frenzy of "dibé tádadigéésh" *shearing of the sheep*, a deep sigh left Hashké Yił Naabaah's body when he thought, "there's the dá'ák'eh bina'anish" *work on the cornfield*, and "hasht'eelnéehgi" *preparing it* and "bii' k'i'dilyéegi" *planting in it* and "k'idadeesya'ígíí hadaneesą́ągo baa 'ádahayą́ągi" *caring for the new crop* and "da'nit'ą́ągi" *harvesting* and "agizhgi" *gathering of the husks* and "dá'ák'ehdi bee na'anishí 'ádaalne'gi" *making of planting tools* and "hasht'éédalne'gi" *repair of the planting tools.* Hashké Yił Naabaah felt an even more heavy burden fall on his shoulders. All these activities have been left behind. "Nihi'í'óol'įįł bii' haikááh. Hatxíhíláane'ęę'!" *We are walking out of our culture. What a dreadful thing to happen!* he said.

"Hait'éego shą' Naabeehó daniidlínígíí bee nihééhо'dílzin dooleeł?" *How will it be known that we are Navajo?* he whispered. "Nihi'í'óol'įįł dóó bik'ehgo dahinii'nánígíí dóó bee dahinii'nánígíí t'áadoo bee nida'neetą́'í k'adę́ę dį́į' nááhááh. Ła' shį́į t'áá nihitséedi kojį' adabidi'neeskaad. Ts'ídá la' t'áá'ałtsoní nihééldizgo dineebin. Hatxíhíláane'ęę'. T'áá hazhó'í nihikéyah biih néiikaijí t'éí sih hasin. T'áá shǫǫh nihi'í'óol'įįł náábidiyoolnaał ákogo 'índa Naabeehó daniidlínígíí bee nihéénááho'dílzin dooleeł." *For nearly four years, we have not taught our culture and our traditions and our lifestyle. Some were most likely forced to walk here before we were forced to walk here. We have been deprived of everything. What a scary thing to happen. The only consolation for us is to walk back into our own land. We can revive our culture and in doing so, we will be known as Navajos once again.*

His tears had dried, which made marks on his smooth thin face. To console himself, Hashké Yił Naabaah looked down at his hands and said,

"Nídahidizíid nídeiiyíníijiihgo, nihi'í'óol'įįł yéénihiyiiłníihgo 'át'é. Nihi'í'óol'įįł ayóo nihaa jooba'go 'át'é." *When we name the months, they remind us of our culture. Our culture is very kind to us.* He recited the names of the months, beginning with October,

"Ghąąjį' *(October) Parting of the Seasons,*
Níłch'ih Ts'ósí *(November) Slender Winds,*
Níłch'ih Tsoh *(December) Big Winds,*
Yas Niłt'ees *(January) Crusting of the Snow,*
Atsá Biyáázh *(February) Eaglets Hatching,*
Wóózhch'į́įd *(March) Cry of the Eaglets,*
T'ą́ąchil *(April) Miniature Leaves,*
T'ą́ątsoh *(May) Large Leaves,*
Ya'iishjááshchilí *(June) Miniature Corn Tassels,*
Ya'iishjááshtsoh *(July) Large Corn Tassels,*
Bini' Anit'ą́ą Ts'ósí *(August) Within It There Is A Slender Harvest,*
Bini' Anit'ą́ą Tsoh" *(September) Within It There Is a Big Harvest.*

Hashké Yił Naabaah hugged his grandsons tightly when he heard them recite the names of the months with him. Looking at them, he stated,

"T'áá nihí nihikéyah biih néiikaigo díí náhidizíid yíízhi'ígíí bee nihi'í'óol'įįł náábidiyoolnaał. T'áá 'ákónéehee danihizází yéę náhidizídígíí 'ákót'éego dayíízhi'. Háadida léi' nihich'į' kóhodooníłígíí shį́į biniinaa. Háláanee'ęę'go nihá 'ádajíít'įįd." *When we reenter our own lands, we will revive our culture by means of the naming of our months. It is a good thing our ancestors named the months accordingly. It was most likely they named the months because of the hardship we would be facing. Dear ones that they did that.*

Tears rolled down Hashké Yił Naabaah's slender cheeks. Not wanting his tears to fall on the area where his enemies walked, he lifted his hands and with the palms of his hands up, he watched the tears fall into his hands. His tears made tiny reflections of the blue sky before they burst and disappeared into the many creases of the palms of his hands.

He looked up and noticed his people were watching their leaders. He saw hope in the people's eyes.
The leaders were discussing their plight and their desperate desire to return to their own lands between the four sacred mountains when Hashké Yił Naabaah was called forward and was given an opportunity to speak to the Naabeehó leaders. Remembering his earlier thoughts and words, he began his speech with the words,

"Éhályáhígíí doo sohodoobéézhgóó txi'nihiyoołníih.
Nihité'ázíní be'iina' baa náádadiilyáhígíí bídahwiilzááh.
Danihilįį' bídahwiilzááh.
Danihikéyah yęę bídahwiilzááh.
Danihighan bii' kéédahwiit'ínée bídahwiilzááh.
Danihich'iiyą' bídaneeldinée bídahwiilzááh.
Nihi'í'óol'įįł ayóo nihaajooba' yęęni' nihąąh yist'įįd,
éí bídahwiilzááh.
T'áá nihí nihikéyah bikáa'gi bik'ehgo dahinii'nánée
bídahwiilzááh.
Éí lá baa yáshti' ni. 'Éhályáhígíí doo ts'íí'át'éégóó bik'ee
txi'dahwii'níih. T'áá nihí nihikéyah bich'į' nihéé'ílnii'go

t'éiyá t'áá'aaníí nihikáa'jį' dahodooleeł. Nihikéyah bits'ą́ąjį'go nihida'jisnii'gogo 'éí 'ałtso 'ánihi'di'dooldįįł."
We are desperately suffering because of loneliness.
We are lonely for our relatives whose lives have been taken from them.
We are lonely for our livestock.
We are lonely for what was once our land.
We are lonely for the home we used to live in.
We are lonely for the food that we were used to eating.
We are lonely for our culture that was kind and that was taken from us.
We are lonely for our lifestyle that we practiced on our own land.
That is what I am speaking of, we are desperately suffering because of loneliness.
We will survive only if we are released to our own land. We will all die if we are released to lands that are not our own.

His elder Peace Leader stood up and added his thoughts, saying,

"Nihe'anaa'í k'asídą́ą' ádanihisdįįd. Nidi, t'ah nidii t'áá kǫ́ǫ dahoniidlǫ. Háshinee, shidine'é, danihitsxe'go bee nihikáa'jį' hodooleeł. Nihiyiin bee nida'dii'a'go bee nihikáa'jį' hodooleeł. Danihisodizin bee 'ánídadii'nihgo bee nihikáa'jį' hodooleeł. Háláanee'ęę' dó' ádaoht'įį dooleeł. T'óó nihaa dahojoobá'í yee'. *Our enemies nearly killed all of us. But we are still here. My dear people, we will survive because we are strong. We will survive because of our songs that we sing. We will survive because of our prayers that we speak. Dear ones, you will do that to survive. I have such sympathy for you.*

****

The Peace Commissioners told the Naabeehó people that peace would be captured on paper and called a Peace Treaty. The Naabeehó leaders declared it was a mistake for the tall gray-haired one's warriors to kill, torture, and rape many of the Naabeehó women and children and then attempt to discuss peace. The Naabeehó leaders did not trust the words of promise these strange soldiers spoke when they discussed the meaning of peace. "If they killed so quickly, they would lie even faster on paper," Kiizhóní thought and then he said,

"Ei naaltsoos bee 'ałgha'diit'aah di'į́díyee' dóó 'ayóo łikon, áko nidi saad bee hadahiidziihígíí 'éí nihinaagóó dahólónígíí deidiits'a'. Nihizaad bee ałhada'di'diit'áłígíí 'éí níyol yidiits'a'. Níyolígíí 'éí 'oo'íinii nihá nilį́. *A piece of paper they call a treaty is brittle and can easily be burned, but the words that we speak are heard by the elements that surround us. Our words of promise are heard by the wind. The wind is our witness."*

The great Peace Leader, Ganado Mucho who was a veteran at treaty negotiations, still voiced concerns regarding these negotiations. The young men who were training as Peace Leaders sat in awe of him as he announced, after taking a moment to look around at the Naabeehó people who were so miserable,

"Saad bee hadahiidziihígíí dóó saad bee 'aha'diit'aah bee hadahiidziihígíí níyol yił nídiilwo' dóó saadígíí níléí dziłtahgóó dóó tsin adaaz'áhígóó dóó ni'góó dóó yá bii'góó dóó táyi' góne' da yił naanáalwołgo bitaa' íízhi'ígíí deidiits'ą́ą́h dóó saadígíí nihá dayótą'go nihá yił nida'ałjooł łeh. *The wind carries the words and promises that we speak into the mountains and to where the trees grow and carries them along the ground and into the sky and into the water, and when these elements hear our words they hold and gently protect our words.*

Shinaat'áanii danohłínígíí, na'ídíshkid. Dził bii' dahólónígíí dóó dził binaagóó dahólónígíí saad bee 'aha'diit'aah bee hadahiidziihígíí bídaheestł'ǫ́ǫgogo shą' hait'éego saad bee hadasiidzí'ígíí k'ídoo'nish? Nihinaagóó dahólónígíí nihizaad nihá yaa 'ádahalyą́ą łeh. Áko nidi díí kéyah bikáa'gi doo bąąh hólóní da, ádin. T'áadoo le'é yá'át'ééh nilį́į dooleełígíí bąąh ádin. Ádin! Áko shą' hait'éego nihe'anaa'í 'ąąhéeshjéé' ádanihiilaaígíí bił ahada'di'diit'ááł, nihita'gi k'é náhodoodleeł biniiyé? Ha'át'íishą' nihá da'oo'į́į doogo? Nihe'anaa'í danihijoołá, t'áá'óolyéego danihijoołá. 'Awéé' dóó 'áłchíní dóó ch'ikéí dóó sáanii dóó náás daazlį́į́'ii deijoołá. Nihe'anaa'í 'ąąhéeshjéé' ádanihiilaaígíí bá'át'e' dahólǫ́. Dił yíká dadichin, ákónáádaadzaago bizaad yee 'ahada'deest'ánée yaa deidiyoonahii' nihik'ijį' nídadidoobah. Hatxíhíláane'ęę' nááhwiinidzin doo. Nihe'anaa'í danihijoołáhígi 'át'éego díí kéyah nihijoołá. T'áá nihí nihikéyah t'éí bich'į' nídanihí'ni'. Náána łahgóó 'éí dooda! Dooda lą́ą! *I ask you, those of you who are my leaders, how can a person's word of promise be cut when they are bound to the mountain and its contents and all that is around it? All the elements around us take care of our words for us. But this land has nothing on it, nothing. There is nothing on this land that can be called good. Nothing! How can we discuss peace with our enemies who have made us prisoners of war? What elements will be our witnesses? They hate us, they truly hate us. They hate babies, children, teenage girls, women and old people! Our enemies who made us prisoners of war are dangerous. When their thirst for blood reappears, they will forget their words of promise. It will be a dreadful time again. This land hates us just like our enemies hate us.* Hashké Yił Naabaah was surprised at the words the great Peace Leader Ganado Mucho spoke. "He sounds more like a War Leader than a Peace Leader," he thought. From the surprised looks on his young warriors' faces, he knew they were thinking the same thought.

Worried about the promises being placed on paper, Nahat'á Yinaabaah said after he addressed the leaders,

"Shimá 'ání, 'ei yee 'ałhada'deest'ánée dabízhi' naaltsoos bikáá' ádaalne' lá ne'. Hait'éego da naaltsoosígíí 'eedǫ́ǫzgogo daats'í bikáá' yisdzohígíí doo 'íłį́į da dooleeł, háálá saad bikáá' nídahéesdzoh yę́ę 'ałts'ádaheesdǫ́ǫz doo. Níyol naaltsoos nidaheesdǫ́zę́ę yił nídidoolwołii' nááná łahdi, t'áá 'áhoodzaagi nikíidoonił. Ákóhoodzaago shį́į dahazaad dóó daházhi' naaltsoos há bikáá' bik'eda'ashchínée dóó bidazhdeeshchid yę́ę doo 'íłį́į da dooleeł. Éí nihá bééhániih doo. Baa nánihooshkąąh, shinaat'áanii danohłínígíí." *My mother said she remembers the promises agreed upon and the names of those agreeing to the promises are written down on paper. If somehow, the paper is torn, it is possible that what was written on the paper is no longer observed because the words would have been torn apart. The wind will take the pieces of paper and drop them in uncertain places. If that happens, the words and the names and your thumbprints no longer have value. I plead with you, those of you who are my leaders, remember that for us.* Dédii heard Kiizhóní clear his throat before he spoke, saying,

"Nihe'anaa'í t'ahdoo bił ahíikááhdą́ą́' nihinaat'áanii biye' yee hahaasdzí'ígíí baa nitsídaohkees doo, baa nánihooshkąąh, shinaat'áanii danohłínígíí. Nihinaat'áanii dabizaad dóó dabízhi' dóó naaltsoos yidadeeshchidígíí 'ílį́įgo baa nitsídeiikeesgogo 'éí naaltsoos di'į́díígíí doo bikáá' daasdzoh da dooleeł." *I plead with those of you who are my leaders, my kind leader's son speaks words that we need to think about before we go to meet with our enemy. The words and names and thumbprints of the Naabeehó leaders cannot be bound to a piece of paper that is easily destroyed!*

Many more young leaders spoke their concerns, many of whom had not witnessed a treaty signing during previous treaty negotiations. Hashké Yił Naabaah had witnessed two earlier treaty negotiations, the first being when the treaty was negotiated and signed at Tséyi' *Canyon de Chelly* and another near Tó Niłts'ílí *Crystal.* Both times he appeared as a War Leader in training and did not take part in the negotiation or the signing of the treaty.

The great orator, Barboncito listened to the Naabeehó leaders and warriors speak about the treaty negotiations which would be held the next day. He rubbed his face with his hands and told the young leaders and warriors about the process that had been followed in earlier treaty negotiations.

"Danihiiłkáahdi ninâhisohkaigo, haashílá t'óó da'jiiłhosh. Nihe'anaa'í bił ahíikáhígíí 'áłtsé sáanii bee bił dahodoołnih. Bí dó' bił nidahoh'á. T'áadoo nihí nihizaad t'éí dadiits'a'í. Danihizáanii t'áá nihíighah txi'dahooníihgo nahashzhiizh. Íishjááshį́į́ ha'át'íí daaníi dooleeł. Bada'áłchíní yá yádaałti'. Dabizaad nihił danilį́įgo 'áda'díínółzin, íishjááh." *When you warriors return to your camps, don't just go to sleep. Instead, discuss the information with the women in your camps so that you are representing the women and that your words are not yours alone. The women have suffered right alongside you. See what they have to say. They are speaking on behalf of their children. Make sure you respect their words.*

The leaders knew they still had so much to think about and much to discuss with their families and their people. They thanked each other for their important insight and input and vowed to consider what the young warriors spoke.

Chapter Ten

The Women Raise Their Voices, the Old Paper Concurs

At a nearby table sat a scribe, the one who was prepared to write the items of discussion regarding the treaty negotiations that focused upon the thirteen Articles of the new Navajo-U.S. Treaty. The Peace Commissioners and military officers also sat at the table. Facing the Commissioners was Barboncito, who was chosen by the Naabeehó Peace and War Leaders to be the spokesman for their Naabeehó people. He stood in front of the table facing the Peace Commissioners and the Washington delegation. He seemed calm, his back was straight, and his demeanor unaffected by the formal activities surrounding the negotiations of the newly titled, Navajo-U.S. Treaty of 1868. He was just as distinguished as the Peace Commissioners General William T. Sherman and Colonel Samuel Tappan, who was also a Senator. The Commissioners, military leaders, and Navajo leaders discussed their negotiations through the voice of three interpreters who were present to relay information.

A practice session was held to ensure important information was conveyed accurately from one entity to another.

Barboncito and the Naabeehó leaders and the people watched as the first interpreter who spoke English and Spanish stood nodding his head as he listened to the bossy soldier with a gruff voice, greasy hair, and thin build. With eyes that seemed ready to pop out of their sockets, the first interpreter turned to the second interpreter and spoke in a slow version of Spanish and relayed the message from English to Spanish. The first interpreter closely watched the second interpreter's mouth and moved his lips as the second interpreter relayed the message to the third interpreter who was another Apache scout who spoke a dialect of the language of the Western Apache as well as a crude form of the Navajo language. Often repeating Navajo words, the third interpreter shifted his weight from one foot to the other as he nervously spoke. The first interpreter shoved the second interpreter urging him to listen to the message, which would be helpful in that the second interpreter recognized many Navajo words which were very similar to his language.

The Peace Commissioners acknowledged the presence of the Washington delegation, the military presence, and the presence of the Navajo leaders standing before the Peace Commissioners. They admitted to Barboncito their shock at the horrible conditions in which they found the Navajo people at the Bosque Redondo Indian Reservation. The Peace Commissioners announced they had come with the plan to move the Naabeehó people to Indian Territory (on and near what would become the state of Oklahoma), which had been set aside for Indian nations who would be placed on Reservations. They reported that the Indians who had been relocated to Indian Territory were contented and happy. The Commissioners asked the Navajo leaders to select several leaders who could travel eastward to Indian Territory to see for themselves the land that had been set aside for them.

"Forty-Two Indian tribes have been relocated to lands within Indian Territory and they are happy and contented there. You will be content and happy there too. You can raise your families there. You can build your own homes to live in. Each of you will receive forty or eighty or one hundred sixty acres of land that you can call your own. It is the best solution for all of us. You will see. Choose the leaders you want to go there so they can see for themselves," one man excitedly stated who was possibly Senator Tappan or General Sherman.

The Navajo leaders and their people patiently waited while the words were formed in three different languages on the interpreters' lips. When the Naabeehó people heard the plan was not for their people to return to their own land between their four sacred mountains, the Naabeehó women raised their voices in defiance. The message was repeated countless times as women raised their voices throughout the crowded parade grounds. Dédii and Dzáníbaa' looked from one defiant face to the other as they listened to the angry women yelling,

"T'áhálǫh! T'áhálǫh!" *Wait! Wait!*

"T'áá nihí nihikéyahjį' t'éí nídanihíni', dooda!" *We only want to go back to our own land, no!*

"Ge' shooh!" *Watch out!*

"Áłtsé, shą́ą́' dooda danihidii'ní!" *Wait, remember we told you 'no'?*

"T'áadoo deiyísínółts'ą́'í, nichxǫ'!" *Don't listen to them, don't bother!*

"Yáadilá! Shą́ą́' dooda góne' bee nidasołtxee' danihidii'niid." *What a thing! Remember we told you to be adamant about saying 'no'?*

"Dóódahéii, dooda!" *No, no!*

"Áłtsé danihidii'ní. T'áadoo t'óó nihik'i nidanołne'é, 'Háhyǫǫhį́į́,' dadohníigo." *We are telling you to wait! Don't ignore us and say, 'okay.'*

"T'áá 'ádzaaí góne' nihá nidaha'á. Bikéé' dah doohjeeh lágo!" *They are not wise about their plans for us. Don't follow them!*

"Dooda, dooda, doodaí bee dooda!" *No, no, absolutely not!*

"K'adí, t'ą́ą́' dahidohkááh!" *That's enough, step back!*

"Ge' shooh! Akéé' ninohkááh lágo!" *Watch out! Don't go along with them!*

When the voices died down, Nínááníbaa', who was usually quiet cried out,

"Dooda! Doo 'ákót'ée da! T'áá nihí nihikéyah bikáa'gi t'áá'íídą́ą́' táa'di kéyah nihá hadahaasdzoh. Ei naaltsoos bee 'ałgha'diit'aah táa'go 'akót'éego hadadilyaa. 'Éí bii' dadóh'į́į́' dabidohní. T'áá nihí nihikéyah bikáa'gi kéyah nihá hadahaasdzoh, dabidohní!" *No! That is not right! Three times land has been set aside for us on our own lands. It is written in three treaties. Tell them to look in them (treaties). Tell them, land has already been set aside on our own lands.* Feeling she was being ignored, Nínáánībaa' raised her voice again and repeated,

"Naaltsoos bee 'ałgha'diit'aah táa'di bee bił ałghada'sidoot'ánée bii' daasdzoh! Haashílá baa hoyoo'nééh lágo! Táa'di naaltsoos bee 'ałgha'diit'aah bii' nihí Naabeehó dine'é daniidlínígíí kéyah nihá hadahaasdzoh. Éísh éí doo béédaołniih da, nihinaat'áanii danohłínígíí? Ge', áłtsé bínida'ídółkid." *Three times it has been written down in treaties that you negotiated with them. Don't let that be forgotten! Land has been set aside for us who are Navajos in three different treaties. Don't you remember that, those of you who are our leaders? Stop! First ask about it.*

Disappointed, Nínáánībaa' would not be silenced. The weight of her grandsons who were sitting on her lap made her more defiant in demanding that the earlier treaties be consulted first before asking Naabeehó leaders to travel to lands toward the east called Indian Territory. She also remembered the words of the young Mescalero Apache man who was her son-in-law, who warned them of the poor condition of the lands that were being offered to her Naabeehó people. Not willing to be silenced, she cried,

"Ei Bíís Kamisii (Peace Commission) dabidohnínígíí bínida'ídółkid dabidohní. T'áadoo t'óó nihá nidaha'áhí." *Tell those whom you call the Peace Commission to ask about it. Don't just allow them to make plans for us.* Additional women echoed the cry of Nínáánibaa'. Before the treaty negotiations could begin, they were stopped by the cries of the women.

Peace Leaders Barboncito, Armijo, and Ganado Mucho as well as War Leaders Manuelito, Hashké Yił Naabaah, and Manuelito's brother discussed the demands of the women. They knew that in Naabeehó society, women are revered so to ignore their words would be a grave infraction.

Barboncito asked the interpreters to let the Bíís Kamisii know that it was their request that the pre-treaty talks be stopped for two reasons. The first was because their women had brought up the subject of their land in the west which was situated between their four sacred mountains. The land had been promised to the Naabeehó people in earlier treaties. The Naabeehó leaders encouraged Barboncito to tell the interpreters to ask the Bíís Kamísii (Peace Commissioners) to consult three earlier treaties in which land boundaries had been established for the Naabeehó people. The Peace Commissioners became flustered when they heard the Navajo leaders were discussing land boundaries that had been drawn in earlier treaties.

The second reason for halting the pre-treaty talks was because the process of interpretation was consuming so much time. The Naabeehó leaders requested that the young Mexican the soldiers knew as Jesus Arviso, a young man who grew up with the Naabeehó people after he was kidnapped and sold to the Naabeehó people, be allowed to serve as an interpreter.

"Bił da'ahidiits'a'," *We understand him,* the leaders explained. It would also eliminate the need for a third interpreter, the Peace Commissioners agreed. The first interpreter remained while the two Apache scouts were eliminated as interpreters. In their place, Jesus Arviso spoke Naabeehó words that flowed off of his tongue, bringing the pre-treaty talks alive.

With confidence that his message would be understood by the Bíís Kamisii, the great War Leader, Manuelito stood up and said in a big booming voice,

"Sáanii yaa hadahodííłdládígíí t'áá'aaniigóó 'áhá'ní. Shí díkwíídi shį́į́ naaltsoos bikáa'gi shízhi' bíighah ałná 'asézoh. Kéyah baa saad hoséłį́į'go biniinaa naaltsoos bee 'ałgha'diit'aah hadilyaa. T'áá'aaníí 'éí naaltsoos bii' kéyah nihá haadzoh, bii' kéédahwiit'į́į́ dóó bii' nida'niilkaad dooleełígíí. 'Éí shį́įgo bii' nahalzhiishgo, Tséhootsohdóó náhookǫsjigo nihe'anaa'í bitsį' daalgaiígíí bił ahíikaigo naaltsoos bee 'ałgha'diit'aah hadilyaa. Kéyah nihá haadzoh. Díí nihí nihikéyah doo dajiníigo t'áá nihí nihikéyah nihich'į' kódajiilaa. Yáadishį́į́ t'éí 'ákódaat'į. T'áá 'ákónéehee 'ákódajiidzaa." *What the women raised their voices for is true. I was there. I placed my X mark near my name. A treaty was negotiated because I raised a dispute over land. In that treaty, land was set aside for us to live upon and upon which to herd our livestock. It was in the summer when we met with our enemy with white skin at a place north of Fort Canby to agree to a treaty. Land was set aside for us. They gave us land that was already ours. What despicable person does that? It is fortunate that they did that.*

The great Peace Leader Ganado Mucho was the second leader to acknowledge land boundaries that had been drawn on the eastern side of the lands the Naabeehó people called their home.

"Neeznáá nááhai yę́ędą́ą́' dóó yówohjį', nihidine'é ha'a'aahjigo kéédahat'ínée bikéyah bąąh yist'įįd. Nihe'anaa'í bilį́į' dahólónígíí shį́į 'éí kéyahígíí yidáahjį' daazlį́į'go biniinaa Naabeehó dine'é kéyah yikáá' kéédahat'ínée dóó yikáá' nida'niłkaad yę́ę bąąh yist'įįd. Nihidine'é kéyah daabíí'ii yę́ę bich'ą́ą́h ídzohgo 'ályaa. 'Éí 'ákót'éego naaltsoos bee 'aha'diit'aah bikáá' yisdzohgo 'ádayiilaa lá ne'. Ch'ééh kéyah bąąh dashiijée'go, da'noh'įįhgo biniinaa kéyah nihąąh yist'įįd nihi'doo'niid. Ch'ééh ńída'jookąąhgo, nihidine'é 'e'e'aahjigo 'adeineeskaad lá ne'. Neeznáá dóó yówohjį' nááhai yę́ędą́ą́' ákóhóót'įįd. Éí naaltsoos bee 'aha'diit'aah bii' shízhi' yisdzoh. Shízhi' bíighahgi 'ałná 'asézoh, shí dó'. Íídą́ą́' kéyah Naabeehó dine'é bá hahoodzooígíí baa náhást'įįd ne'." *Ten or more years ago, our people who lived in the eastern part of our land had their land taken from them. Our enemies who had livestock wanted the land the Navajos occupied. Because of their wishes, the land the Navajo people lived upon and cared for their livestock upon was taken from them. A boundary was drawn to keep the Navajo people from their eastern land. That boundary was declared in a treaty. We tried holding on to the land but they told us the Navajo people had been raiding and stealing and that was the reason the land was taken away. Although the people pleaded with them, they (the military) still chased the people toward the west. That happened over ten years ago. My name is written in that treaty. I placed my X mark near my name. Land boundaries for the Navajo people were declared in that treaty.*

Barboncito declared that he, along with the great Peace Leader Ganado Mucho, the feared War Leader Manuelito, and Delgadito and Armijo were present at the treaty that was negotiated and signed at Fort Fauntleroy in the cold of winter. He recalled that an east to west land boundary was reestablished on the southern border of the land the Naabeehó people occupied. He ended his argument for the return of his people back to the lands the military had identified in earlier treaties by saying,

"Nihinaaltsoos bikáá' yisdzoh áádóó nihizaad k'ehjígo bikáá' yisdzoh. T'áá 'ákónéehee kéyah shiNaabeehó dine'é bá hadahaasdzohígíí naaltsoos bee 'ałha'diit'aah nihá bikáá' ádaohłaa." *The words are written on your paper and it is written in your language. It is fortunate that you declared land boundaries that had been set aside for my Navajo people in that treaty.*

Standing tall and thin, Barboncito raised his leadership stick and when he was acknowledged, he bravely said in soft commanding words,

"T'áá hazhó'ó t'áá nihí nihikéyahgóó t'éí nídanihí'ni'. Kéyah náánáła' bich'į' éí dooda. Éí baa nídanihooshkąąh." *We do not want to go to any other country but our own. Do not send us to another country. I plead with you.*

Members of the Peace Commissioners and the Washington delegation shook their heads as they listened. They were well aware that the Constitution of the United States was considered the supreme law of the land, and that the Constitution of the United States declared that treaties are also considered the supreme law of the land as long as they are made under the authority of the United States. Senator Tappan, who was well aware of the importance of Indian-U.S. Treaties, as discussed in the Constitution of the United States, asked that a telegram be sent to Washington D.C. to research the contents of earlier Navajo-U.S. Treaties. A messenger was sent to Santa Fe to send a telegram. In the meantime, a member of the Peace Commission announced,

"Formal treaty negotiations will commence." A paper prepared by the Peace Commission was brought forth. Thirteen items were slowly read in English and interpreted into Navajo to which the leaders were asked to discuss and agree.

The first article dealt with peace and the Naabeehó people promising to keep and maintain peace. When the second article was read and interpreted, the children were silenced, an intense silence fell upon the Naabeehó people. Their return to their own land between their sacred mountains was under discussion. The women held their collective breaths. When Jesus Arviso mentioned place names that became the boundary of the small reservation, the people smiled when they recognized the names of the places. They nodded as if they were agreeing to stay within that particular boundary. It was all the people could do to remain seated when what they wanted to do was to run, run back to the land they knew as home.

The third and fourth articles named the buildings that would be built at the agency post, which the people assumed was Fort Canby and stipulated that an Indian agent would live among the people to maintain and preserve the peace the leaders promised to keep. The fifth article gave the people permission to obtain land tracts of varying acreages where the people were to cultivate the land. The leaders shrugged their shoulders and the Peace Leaders smiled. They knew their people would each maintain a large dá'ák'eh *cornfield.*

Article six caused the women to grab their children and hold them close. The leaders promised the Peace Commissioners that their people would send their children who were between the ages of six to sixteen to school. The question,

"Ha'át'íísh óolyé naaltsoos bíhoo'aah?" *What does it mean to learn paper?* echoed throughout the parade grounds. The people trusted their leaders who were not speaking loud enough for everyone to hear. They knew their leaders would not commit their children to another experience like becoming prisoners of war. To take the edge off of their feelings of apprehension, the women turned their attention to the possibility they were returning to their land between their beautiful mountains.

Article seven caused the people to snicker. If the seeds the Peace Commission promised in the article was anything like the food the soldiers provided, the Naabeehó people wanted no part of the promise of seeds. The women complained,

"Ei shįį́ hádą́ą́' shįį́ dadííłdzidgo baa dajidlee'. T'áá yee' nihí hádaoht'ínígíí k'éédadohdléeh doo." *They are most likely generous with rotten seeds. You can obtain your own and plant those.* Article eight promised goods not to exceed a minimal value. The type of goods was to be determined by the Indian Agent which could be clothing or blankets until the people could make their own. The ninth article confused the people because it discussed the freedom for the United States to build railroads near their lands. The people had no idea what a railroad was and the purpose for it. A mention of the freedom for the men to hunt brought the people smiles. Their men were expert hunters. The people hugged their empty stomachs as they listened to the promise of the freedom to hunt.

Article ten promised protection of the newly established Reservation from loss of land. The people agreed wholeheartedly to the article. Article eleven required that the Naabeehó people be removed to the newly established Reservation and while en route be provided subsistence and transportation for the ones who were not able to walk. Article twelve promised the distribution of sheep, goats and cattle to the people. The women hoped the promised sheep, goats and cattle would not prove to be the skinniest of animals. The people associated the soldiers with skinny sheep, goats, horses, and cattle. The last and thirteenth article gave the people hope. It required that the Naabeehó people agree to make the reserved lands their permanent home. The people lifted their faces to the sky and breathed a prayer of gratitude to the Creator for their survival and their return to their land between the four sacred mountains.

A second day of discussion took place. In the meantime, the Naabeehó people nervously waited for the messenger to return with word on the land boundaries discussed in earlier treaties. The messenger returned from Santa Fe carrying the response in a telegram. It was confirmed that:

The 1855, Treaty of Laguna Negra specifically set aside land for the Navajo people.

The 1858, Bonneville Treaty defined a new eastern boundary for the Navajo people.

The 1861, Canby Treaty established that land boundaries were acknowledged in the treaty.

In addition, the 1849, Washington Treaty promised that the U.S. government would formally set aside the land the Navajo people already occupied within the four sacred mountains. The land was for settlement, and the treaty further promised to adjust the territorial boundaries. The fact that the Washington Treaty of 1849 had been ratified by the U.S. Senate forced the Peace Commissioners to acknowledge the existence of reserved lands for the Navajo people.

After much discussion, it was unanimously agreed upon that the Navajo people were to be sent back to their original land. Four Navajo-U.S. Treaties prevented the Peace Commission from sending the Navajo people to Indian Territory. After hours of long discussions that delayed the treaty negotiations, the Naabeehó people could be told and reassured they would be returned to their own land.

When the announcement was made by the young Mexican, Jesus Arviso, a soft collective gasp was heard drifting throughout the parade grounds. Hashké Yił Naabaah was being crushed by the embrace of his two sons, Kiizhóní, and his young Mescalero Apache son-in-law. In a hoarse voice, Hashké Yił Naabaah said,

"Ahéhee', shiTaa'. Nihisodizin nihá sidíníts'ą́ą́'. Ahéhee'." *Thank you, my Spiritual Father. You have heard our prayers. Thank you.* His little huddled group agreed saying,

"Aoo'," "Aoo'," "Aoo'," "Aoo'."

Hashké Yił Naabaah raised his head to see the women had fallen against one another and were clinging to one another, softly crying. Some lowered their heads, crying softly, careful to catch their tears in their hands so their tears would not be shed on the land of their enemy. Every once in a while, he heard a woman stop weeping to voice the words,

"Da' t'áásh'aaníí? T'áá nihí nihikéyah bich'į' nihida'íłníih?" *Is it true? They are releasing us to go back to our own land?*

"Baa neiiyéyeelísh?" *Did I dream about it?*

"T'áásh ákót'éego sidéts'ą́ą́'?" *Did I hear it correctly?* After word of their release to their own land was repeated many times, the emotion-filled, collective voice of the women were heard to softly and reverently say,

"Háshinee'. Nihikéyah, naa nániikááh. Ayóó 'át'éego nídahwiilzááh nít'ę́ę́'. Hálâanee'ęę'!" *Dear one. Our land, we are coming back to you. We were greatly missing you. Dear one!* Soft sobs could be heard coming from different groups of women who clung to one another and heaved as one from years of extreme hardship as prisoners of war. Every once in a while, a loud wail would escape the lips of the women who lost a child, a parent, a sibling, an elder relative, a spouse, or all their relatives.

Strong Naabeehó leaders struggled against their pent-up emotions as their chests heaved with an intense feeling of great relief. Hashké Yił Naabaah wanted so much to take his beautiful Nínááníbaa' in his arms and hold her and his daughters close. They had suffered the most. He and his sons had trained themselves to withstand hardship, but his Nínááníbaa' and their daughters were not trained as warriors, but they fought valiantly against hardship. With raw emotion in his voice, he whispered,

"ShiNínááníbaa', shiDédii, shiDzáníbaa', naabaahii 'ílíinii danohłį́. Háshinee'..." *My Nínááníbaa', my Dédii, my Dzáníbaa', you are worthy warriors. Dear ones...*

He looked out across to the opposite side of the parade grounds and in his peripheral vision, he saw his people's shoulders shaking as they cried. He looked in the direction of the Bíís Kamísii and saw that the Senator and several members of the Washington Delegation were blinking back tears that danced in their eyes as they watched his people.

The Naabeehó leaders had to calm their people so the final step in the treaty negotiations could continue. A map was produced that outlined the new Navajo Reservation which was only a fraction of what the Naabeehó people knew as nihikéyah *our land*, still, the naat'áanii *leaders* were happy they were going home.

Although it was difficult for the leaders and their people to concentrate on the messages contained in the proposed treaty, the treaty was accepted by the Naabeehó leaders and approved by the Bíís Kamisii on the morning of June 1st, 1868.

Hashké Yił Naabaah looked up at the sun.

"Dei 'adeez'ą́ąjį' ahoolzhiizhgo 'ałtso. Yízhí 'ádaalne' áádóó nihinaat'áanii naaltsoos Bíís Kamisii yił yee 'ałghada'deest'ánée yidadilchííd." *It has become midmorning and it is completed. Names will be written and our leaders will place their thumbprint on the paper they negotiated with the Peace Commissioners,* he said, still looking at the position of the sun in the sky. The Naabeehó leaders invited Hashké Yił Naabaah to become a member of the Navajo signatory team of twenty-nine leaders but Hashké Yił Naabaah told the leaders,

"Shí 'éí naat'áanii na'abaah bił haz'ą́ąjí yá nidaha'áhígíí 'atah nishłį́. Ániid da'di'níigo dasidiits'ą́ą', ch'éénídaanígíí yaa halne'go. Íídą́ą' naat'áanii 'ídlį́įgi nahgóó nidiní'ąą dóó shahastóí dóó shinaat'áanii, dąą dóó shį́ bii' nahalzhiishgo nihá hoo'áłígíí bikéé' niníyá. 'Atah nihá nahó'á dashidooniidígíí shił nilį́į nidi, nihi'í'óol'įįł bik'ehgo dahinii'náago nihá yá'át'ééh. Dąą dóó shį́ bii' nahalzhiishgo 'atah nahash'áa dooleełígíí doo shá 'ahóót'i' da. Naat'áanii Sání baadaaní, na'abaah bił haz'ą́ąjí yá naat'áanii nilį́į dóó yá naha'áhígíí t'áá'íídą́ą́' nihił 'atah naha'á. Shí 'éí 'éí baa jíínísh'łį́. Ánahat'áagi hayóí. Bíni'dii bí 'atah nihił hoo'ááł." *I am a member of the War Leaders. I placed my leadership aside when we heard the first thunder declaring the recent appearance of the spring season. At that time, I accepted the leadership of our elder and Peace Leader who is our leader during the spring and summer seasons. I respect your request asking me to join you in leadership, but it is better that we live according to our cultural protocol. It is not possible for me to be a leader during the spring and summer seasons. The son-in-law of Narbona is a War Leader (Manuelito), let him be a leader with you. I have confidence in him. He is an able leader. Let him be the one to be a leader among you.* The leaders immediately accepted his decline of their offer because they greatly respected Hashké Yił Naabaah. Holding his walking stick, Hashké Yił Naabaah returned to stand near his elder Peace Leader and his sons and Kiizhóní and his young Mescalero Apache son-in-law. Nínááníbaa' and Dédii and Dzáníbaa' and Tsék'iz Naazbaa' and their adopted children and grandchildren sat nearby. He wanted to be near them to watch the concluding activities of the treaty negotiations.

Hope was etched on the faces of the Naabeehó people as they held their breath when they watched their brave leader, Barboncito grip the pen and place an X between the words "his mark" written near his name. Delgadito was next to place an X on the line next to his name.

Dédii and Dzáníbaa' and their brothers were emotionally touched when they heard Armijo insist that he sign his own name on the Signature Page of the treaty. Armijo picked up the pen held out to him and as he did, he shifted his feet as if to maintain his balance then bent over and slowly wrote his name on the line below Delgadito's name. Dédii and Dzáníbaa' and their brothers held their breath as they witnessed Armijo sign his own name. They noticed Delgadito intently watching Armijo slowly write his name in cursive. Delgadito bravely approached the table upon which the Signature Page neatly lay and raised his leadership stick. He leaned toward Jesus Arviso and told him to ask the Bíís Kamisii if he could be given the chance to write his own name, saying,

"Shooh, t'áá shí shízhi' naaltsoos bikáá' ádeeshłííł nít'ę́ę́'. T'áá shí..." *I should have written my own name on the paper. On my own...* Jesus Arviso told the interpreter what the leader said and waited. There was a discussion between the Peace Commissioners before they both nodded to the scribe. The scribe dipped the pen into the bottle of ink and handed the pen to Delgadito then pointed to the line upon which he wanted the leader to sign his name. Gripping the pen as if he was afraid it would fall out of his hand, Delgadito looked the Signature Page over, then firmly set his hand down on the lined paper. Slowly and deliberately, he wrote his name in the empty space below Armijo's name as the pen wobbled in his hand, after which he stood up straight and squared his shoulders. There was a collective sigh among the Naabeehó people who watched their brave leader sign his own name.
The scribe picked up a pen, dipped it in red ink and using

a ruler he crossed out Delgadito's name that had been written by the scribe. Delgadito's X mark was also struck through with the red pen. The scribe blew on the red line he drew then placed the Signature Page back down on the table and motioned for the next leader to approach the table to write an X between the words "his mark" near his name.

Dédii and Dzáníbaa' admitted Delgadito's brave solitary act was a demonstration of their people's belief who have always stated,

"Táá hó 'ájít'éego t'éiyá..." *It is up to an individual to succeed...* meaning it is up to an individual to summon the desire, courage, and bravery to accomplish what a person sets their mind to. Delgadito's signature represented to the two sisters their people's desire, courage, and bravery to survive four long years of extreme hardship, loneliness, hunger, disappointment, and despair. Tears flowed freely down the faces of many Naabeehó people. Their leaders' simple act of bravery gave them hope.

Dédii and Dzáníbaa' knew the phrase "t'áá shí..." *on my own...* very well. Their father and their mother taught them and their brothers the phrase stood for strength, independence, quality, and self-assurance. They could still hear their parents say,

"T'áá shí... jiníigo 'éí bíneesh'ą́ą́ lą́ą jiníigo 'óolyé." *When you say, "I will do it myself," it means you are saying I am able to do it on my own.*

"Ła' hoodzaa jiníigo 'óolyé." *It means you are saying work has been completed.*

"Doo t'óó 'a'jólíi dago 'óolyé." *It means you are not depending on someone.*

"'Haah, níká 'iishyeed' jiníigo 'óolyé." *It means you are willing to say, 'Here, let me help you'.*

"Doo hoł hóyéé'góó 'éí 't'áá shí' jididooniił." *If you are not lazy, you will say, 'I will do it myself.'*

"Hojíyóigo 'éí 't'áá shí' jiníi dooleeł." *If you are a hard worker, you will say, 'I will do it myself'.*

"Hojíyą́ągo 'éí 't'áá shí' jiníi dooleeł." *If you are wise, you will say, 'I will do it myself'.*

Their parents' list could go on and on, which Dédii and Dzáníbaa' and their brothers had heard throughout their lives. They avoided a lecture from their mother and their father by doing things for themselves.

On the other hand, their parents hated the word, "Shá...", which represents a request in which you are asking someone to, *"Do it for me."* They also hated the word, "Ch'ééh...", which meant *"I tried but I couldn't."* They clearly remember their father telling them,

"T'áadoo 'Shá,' dine'é danohłínígíí. *Don't be people who say, 'Do it for me'.*

"T'áadoo 'Ch'ééh,' dine'é danohłínígíí. *Don't be people who say, 'I can't do it'.*

Remembering the words of Delgadito,

"Táá shí, shízhi' ádeeshłííł nít'ę́ę́'." *I will do it myself... I should have written my own name* made a great impact on Dédii and Dzáníbaa' and their brothers. The two sisters made a promise to one another to teach their sons of the full meaning of the powerful phrases,

"T'áá shí..." *I will do it myself...* and "T'áá hó 'ájít'éego t'éiyá..." *It is up to you if you want to succeed or not...*

****

Not long after the Navajo-U.S. Treaty had been signed, the Peace Commissioners shook hands with one another and left the negotiating table. Later in the day, the Peace Commissioners and the Washington delegation left Fort Sumner in fancy wagons for the the town of Santa Fe.

Dédii and Dzáníbaa' and Nínááníbaa' and Tsék'iz Naazbaa' stopped talking after they heard women talking about a soldier who was recklessly pulling a goat with a rope tied around its neck. Instantly thinking of her goat that saved her life when her daughters were first kidnapped, Nínááníbaa' caught her breath. She spun around to look toward the sound of the goat struggling for air. The goat resisted being pulled into the middle of the parade grounds but was finally yanked to where a wooden stump protruded out of the ground. The goat was tied to the stump with a thick rope.

Leaving the goat struggling to get free and bleating loudly, the soldiers yelled loudly telling the Naabeehó men to wait for their rations before they were free to return with their families to their camping areas. While waiting in a long line, events of the treaty negotiations were discussed among the men. Happy chattering was heard from the women as they waited patiently for their men. In the distance, Hashké Yił Naabaah heard the sound of the bleating of a goat in distress. He anxiously looked for his Nínááníbaa'. He knew his Nínááníbaa' loved the sweet taste of goat's milk, for which she had yearned over the past four years.

The happiness of the Naabeehó people was interrupted when the soldiers ordered them to gather in the parade grounds. Through the interpreters, the soldiers announced they were not sure the Naabeehó people understood the seriousness of signing a treaty with the United States government. In order to make an impact upon the people, the soldiers untied the goat and pulled it to a pole that stood in the middle of the parade grounds. Two soldiers stood nearby holding long bats. A tall mean soldier stepped forward, placed a megaphone next to his mouth and announced,

"This is what will happen to you if you disobey the terms of the Treaty!" Turning to the first interpreter but looking at Jesus Arviso, he yelled,

"Tell these savages so they know they can't return to their old raiding, stealing, robbing, savage ways," he announced loudly then nodded to the two soldiers holding bats.

One soldier grunted loudly as he hit the goat in the stomach with the bat and with great force! Nínááníbaa', along with her Naabeehó people gasped.

"Haash woht'į́?" *What are you doing?* she yelled loudly. "Haash nihilaago...?" *What did it do to you...?* she screamed, before she bolted forward. It took Dédii and Dzáníbaa' and Tsék'iz Naazbaa' to hold their mother back. Willing to risk their lives, the women under their father's leadership surrounded their kind leader's wife to shield her from the evil soldiers and stood shoulder to shoulder and gripped one another's hand tightly. The women were aware of the time Nínááníbaa"s favorite goat saved her life. A woman shoved herself forward and covered Nínááníbaa"s ears while Dédii and Dzáníbaa' and Tsék'iz Naazbaa' held their mother tightly.

Looking up for an instant, Nínááníbaa' noticed the women covered the eyes of their children and tried shielding their own eyes. She pushed her daughters aside and watched as the goat lunged forward in great pain. The loud bleat of the goat was similar to the sound of a scream. Nínááníbaa' cried out in pain,

"K'adí dabidohní!" *Tell them that is enough!* Over the loud wails of the women and children, everyone heard the loud uneven bleating of the goat as it struggled against the rope that held her. Tears ran down the faces of the women and children. The second soldier grasped his bat and hit the goat in the head so hard the people heard either the bat break or the bones in the goat's head break. The severely injured goat still resisted, and tried freeing itself from the rope that held it against the pole. Still not satisfied, the soldiers took turns beating the goat until it was an unrecognizable heap of meat, goat hair, and blood. The ground was saturated with blood, tufts of goat hair and small pieces of red meat.

The blood stopped flowing. The sounds of the struggle for life stopped. Only the sobs of the women and children and the heavy breathing of the soldiers was heard.
The bats were thrown into the midst of the

Naabeehó people gathered in the parade grounds. Blood splattered on the people who stood in the path of the flying bats.

The men were held back at gunpoint from moving toward the parade grounds. Hashké Yił Naabaah stepped forward and five young soldiers pointed their rifles at his head. He stood still and listened to the horrific sounds although he did not see the horrendous act taking place. He heard an older Naabeehó man speak the hateful thoughts of the men when he yelled,

"Ch'į́įdiitahgóó jidookah, t'áá'ájít'é! *They will go to hell, all of them!* The Naabeehó men agreed with the elder, saying,

"Aoo', aoo', aoo'!" *Yes, yes, yes!*

The once happy Naabeehó people stood shocked, unable and afraid to move. Fear entered the hearts of the people. Tears blurred their eyes as they turned away from the horrific sight. The horrific act did indeed place fear in the hearts of the Naabeehó people. Jesus Arviso told the leaders what the first interpreter told him. He hoped the leaders would tell their people what the soldier said. The people did not sleep that night or the nights following.

Soldiers with their rifles drawn chased the Naabeehó men as the men ran toward the parade grounds to look for their families. Hashké Yił Naabaah ran to look for his Nínáánîbaa'. He looked for a large crowd of women. Sure enough! The women stood holding one another's hands as they crowded around their kind leader's wife. Hashké Yił Naabaah spoke in a soft voice when he said,

"Shá dahooł'aah." *Make room for me.* The women recognized his voice and stepped aside to allow their leader through but stepped back into their protective stance. Hashké Yił Naabaah fell to the ground near his beautiful Nínááníbaa' and hoarsely whispered,

"Shiyázhí, shiyázhí, shiyázhí." *My little one, my little one, my little one.* He picked up her slender body and gently lifted her onto his lap. Their daughters fell forward and held their parents and cried loudly. They all held one another. A soldier tried pushing the women aside but their loud scolding kept him back. Resigned, he stood quietly by.

Dédii wondered where her little one's father was. "Why wasn't he here to stop this evil?" she thought. "Did he order this despicable act?" she wondered. "How could he be kind in one place and be a part of an act so incredibly cruel and shameful in another place?" she silently asked her confused mind.

Four young men reached down and gently helped the crying heap to their feet. The young Mescalero Apache man pulled his Dzáníbaa' to her feet and held her close as he led her to the outside of the group. Kiizhóní lifted Dédii up and led her to where the young Mescalero Apache man stood holding Dzáníbaa'. The two sisters embraced and sobbed together. Their mother had told them about the goat that saved her life and about the mean soldiers killing her goat. The impact of their mother's devastating recollection did not affect them until they saw their mother's reaction to the evil that just took place.

Nahat'á Yinaabaah and Tł'ée'go Naabaah came rushing up with all their nephews in tow. They helped their mother and their father to their feet and took turns carrying their mother away from the crowd which still protectively moved with them.

No one spoke on their walk back to their camp. The women could not stop crying. The children cried out every time they heard an unfamiliar sound. Relieved to be back at their camp, the people looked to their kind leaders to help them make sense of the evil soldiers. All the people could say was,

"Yówéé 'ádazhdooníít!" *How could anyone do something like that!*

Dédii sought out her family along with Kiizhóní and gathered them in one place then announced,

"Nihe'anaa'í doo shiyázhí bizhé'é jílįį da. T'óó yówohgo da hajiiséłáá'." *Our enemy is not the father of my little one. I have even more dislike for him.* Nínááníbaa' and Hashké Yił Naabaah lunged forward and embraced their daughter who spoke her deep sorrow. Hashké Yił Naabaah told Dédii,

"Doo t'áá sáhí niyázhí biyaa hwiidííł'aał da, shiyázhí. Bik'éí daniidlį́. Nihiyázhí nilį́. Nihitsóí nilį́. Shicheii yázhí nilį́. Niyázhí doo t'áá sáhí biyaa hwiidííł'aał da, shiyázhí. Bimá sání hólǫ́. Bimá yázhí hólǫ́. Bidá'í hólǫ́. Bicheii hólǫ́. Bik'éí hólǫ́. T'áá'ániit'é biyaa dahwiidiil'aał." *You will not raise your little one alone, my little one. We are his relatives. He is our little one. He is our grandson. He is my little grandson. You will not raise your little one on your own, my little one. He has a maternal grandmother. He has a maternal aunt. He has maternal uncles. He has a maternal grandfather. He has relatives. We will all raise him together.* Dédii nodded and hugged her mother and her father. Her family hugged her, letting her know they knew her pain.

Kiizhóní hugged her and held her longer than any member of her family held her.

"Shí nihaa 'áháshyą́ą doo. 'Éí bee nihoní'ą́ą doo." *I will take care of you all. That is my promise.* In response, Dédii lifted her face and felt her lips brush against Kiizhóní's soft full lips.

Dédii sat alone under the vast starlit sky. Grabbing her chest, she wondered, "How do I get the tall gray-haired one out of my heart? How do I get him out of my mind? It's my memories that will not let me walk away from him." She shook her head and stomped her feet, doing her little dance and thought, "I will make new memories. That is how I will get him out of my heart, my mind, and my memories."

She felt a warm body next to hers. She knew it was Kiizhóní. He was holding her little one who was whimpering. Dédii leaned into Kiizhóní's body and let her mind and body rest.

Dédii and her family never learned the tall gray-haired one and several of his soldiers had left with the Peace Commissioners and the Washington delegation to ensure their safe arrival at Santa Fe.

Chapter Eleven

Taking the First Steps

Women from other camps approached Nínááníbaa' asking if she knew of anyone who had a spare rug dress. The frantic women wore oversized blouses that resembled the shape of a rug dress and skirts that were gathered at the waist, both items of clothing were made of bright calico fabric. Leaving Nínááníbaa''s side, the women ran from one woman to another asking if they had a spare rug dress they could borrow until they reentered their own land between their sacred mountains. An older woman explained their frantic activity in saying,

"Díí yee' nihe'anaa'í k'ehgó 'ééh shiijée'go biniinaa t'óó nihaa yáhásin dóó baa yádaniidzin." *We are embarrassed because we are wearing the clothing of the enemy and we are ashamed of it.*

An older woman who lost her husband two years before and whom Hashké Yił Naabaah brought into their camp, along with two little girls, shamefully approached Nínááníbaa' and her daughters. Nínááníbaa' knew the woman to be a hard worker who helped the women herd the sheep, kept their camping area clean, and who cooked and cared for the elderly Naabeehó who could no longer care for themselves. The woman wore the same dress she wore when she was brought into the camp many months before. She wore a dirty, crudely sewn calico dress that was cut and sewn in the shape of a square dress where two square-shaped pieces of fabric were sewn together at the top with a wide opening for the neck. The sides of the fabric pieces were sewn, leaving an opening for the arms. A long belt made of brittle dried yucca leaves was loosely tied around her waist. Parts of her dress where the bright colors of the calico fabric had worn off left the faded white background of her dress hanging over her breasts, her shoulders, her abdomen, her hips, and her buttocks. Two little girls, the woman called her granddaughters, both wore dresses that were cut and sewn in the same fashion. Their dresses also had spots where the bright colors of the calico fabric had worn off. The woman quietly greeted Nínááníbaa' and her daughters, saying,

"Yá'át'ééh, shideezhí dóó shich'é'é nohłínígíí." *Hello, you who are my younger sister and my daughters.*

"Aoo', yá'át'ééh, shádí," *Yes, my older sister,* Ninááníbaa' answered.

"Yá'át'ééh, shimá yázhí," *Hello, my maternal aunt,* Dzáníbaa' and Dédii politely answered. The woman smoothed her dress and said,

"Biil éé' yee' ła' shóideesht'eeł nisingo biniiyé nihaa níyá. Nihikéyah bich'į' nihéé'doolnih hodoo'niidgo doodagóó baa shił hóózhǫǫd, nidi shibiil éé' ts'ídá t'áá 'óolyéego bii' haashwod, ałtsoh shąąh niníyá. T'óó díí naaka'at'ąhí bee 'éé' ádá 'íishłaago bee naasháago k'ad daats'í ła' náhááh. Nihikéyahgóó nihéé'doolnih hodoo'niidgo shibiil éé' bił haashwod áko hasht'e' niníyįį nít'ęę' t'óó 'ayóo ch'osh ałtso shits'ąą' dayííłchozh lá. T'áá haada yit'éego da háida shaa jiidoobaał nisingo biniiyé nihaa níyá, shideezhí." *I want to obtain a rug dress and that is why I have come to see you. When we were told we were being released to our own lands I became extremely happy. I literally walked right out of my rug dress because I wore it out. I put it away and when I took it out, I realized bugs had eaten my dress. The reason I came to see you, my younger sister, was the hope that someone would have compassion for me.* Filled with compassion, Nínááníbaa' looked over the woman's slender frame, got up, reached for Dzáníbaa's old rug dress, and handed it over to the woman.

"Díí daats'í níighah, shádí." *Maybe this will fit you, my older sister*. The woman looked the worn rug dress over and timidly reached out and said,

"Íishjááshįį, t'áá daats'í shíighah." *We'll see, maybe it will fit me.* Gripping the dress in her thin hands, the woman returned to her camp. Later that afternoon, Nínááníbaa' and her daughters saw a woman approaching them. The woman's hair was brushed and placed in a neat tsiiyééł *hair bun* and her face was relaxed and free of the devastating side effects of her status as a prisoner of war. Nínááníbaa' recognized the biil éé' before she recognized the woman. Amazed at the person who approached them, Nínáánÿbaa' watched the smiling woman come close and gracefully sit down near her. Dédii and Dzáníbaa' both said at the same time,

"Da' niísh ánít'į?" *Is it you?*

"Aoo', t'áá nihí nahalingo hadínísht'é k'ad. Doolá dó' ahéhee'gi 'ádashohłaa da. K'ad, t'áá nihí nihikéyah biih náásdzáago doo naaki nilįįgóó Naabeehó nishłínígíí bee shéé ho'dílzin dooleeł. Doo shi'diił'áhígóó 'atah hooghangóó shitsóóké náásh'ish doo. T'áadoo lé'é nihich'į' kódeeshłíłígíí 'ádin áko nidi t'áá hazhó'ó k'é bee nihénáshniih dooleeł. Ayóo dajiinohba' lá. Nihinaat'áanii, nihizhé'é, 'ayóo jooba' ałdó'. Nihit'áahjį' iikaigo nihikáa'jį' hazlįį'. K'asídąą' shįį dichin nihíighą́ą'." *Yes, I am dressed like you. You have done a thankful thing for me. Now, when I reenter our land, there will be no question that I am known as a Navajo. I will have no worries as I lead my two grandchildren back home. I have nothing to offer you, but I will remember you through kinship. You are all kind, I observed. Our leader, your father, is also very kind. When we joined your group, we survived. We nearly died of starvation.* The woman gracefully got up and offered to help with the food preparation.

Dédii and Dzáníbaa' looked at one another with tears in their eyes. They had taken for granted how closely their people are tied to their land. Dédii and Dzáníbaa' sat up straight, pulled the loose ends of their hair into place and moved closer to their mother to hug her and hold her tight. They held and kissed their mother's soft thin hands. Nínáánîbaa' smiled and thought, "What joy a little compassion can bring a person".

Many times a day since the treaty signing, Dédii and Dzáníbaa' and their mother heard the pitiful request by Naabeehó women who were out looking for a rug dress they could have for when they began their long walk to return to their own land.

A woman with an unusually loud voice explained the frenzy many Naabeehó women felt when she came by pleading for a spare rug dress. She explained,

"Díí yee' t'óó nihaa yáhásin. Nihibiil éé' ałtso nihik'i nidahaazt'óodgo biniinaa kót'éego hadadíníit'é. Shí 'éí shibiil éé' ałtsoh biníkádahoosdząągo bii' sétįį nít'ęę', shimá sání shich'ahóóshkeedgo yii' hashiníiłcháá'. 'Ei yee' bizéé' dahazlį́'ígíí, diné daneeznáníígíí, t'éiyá bi'éé' biníkádahoosdząągo bá 'ájiił'įįh,' shidíiniid, shimá sání. 'Bi'éé' doo bá 'ákójiił'įįhgóogo 'éí jóhonaa'éí bik'íníghalgo 'éí 'ei diné t'óó 'ałhosh lá dínóozįįł, jiní'." *We look so shameful. Our rug dresses wore out on us, that is the reason we are dressed like this. I am dressed like this because my rug dress that I was wearing had many holes in it and my maternal grandmother scolded me because I was wearing a dress with holes and chased me out of my rug dress. 'Only the people who have died can be placed in clothes that have holes in them,' my maternal grandmother told me. 'The sun recognizes them as people who have died when they are wearing clothing that have holes. If you do not poke holes in the clothing of the ones who are deceased, then the sun will look upon them and think they are only sleeping, it is said.'*

Dzáníbaa' wondered how many of her Naabeehó people who died had their clothes prepared that way before the soldiers buried them. Dzáníbaa' looked at her sister. She frowned when their mother left the group and came back with Dédii's old tattered rug dress. The woman caught her breath and gratefully accepted the dress. She put it up against her body to ensure it would fit her thin frame. Without hesitation, the woman dove under a rug blanket that was spread out on the ground and made a few grunts before her calico dress flew out from under the rug blanket and carelessly landed on a dried bush nearby. A few more grunts and the woman slid out from under the rug blanket pulling the hem of the rug dress down past her knees. At first, tears danced in her eyes, which led the woman to fall to her knees, sobbing. She crawled to where Nínááníbaa' sat on the ground and buried her head in her shoulder and cried. Nínááníbaa' hugged her back and softly said,

"K'adí, t'áadoo nichaaí. Nik'ihojisdli'. K'ad nááná ła' da baa jiidííbaał, bíká'adíílwoł. Sáanii náás daazlį́'ígíí da ła' biyéél bá yíłjił dooleeł, hooghangóó nihéé'ílnii'go."
That's enough. Stop crying. You have been blessed. Now you can show kindness to another person, help them. You may show kindness to an older woman by carrying her belongings when we are released to return home.
The woman slowly got up and hugged Dédii and her sister before turning to their people and showing them the rug dress she was given. She left her worn calico dress hanging on the bush. Nínááníbaa' called out to the woman, saying,

"Shooh, ni'éé' bii' háínilwodęę haada niléęh. Doo nínízin da nidi, nik'idéjoolgo yee naa 'áhoosyą́ąd." *Look, do something with the dress you ran out of. Even though you don't want it, it took care of you by providing a covering for you.* The woman sheepishly said,

"Ahéhee', shimá yázhí. T'óó yee shił áhásdįįd. K'ad łą́ą, nihikéyah biih náásdzáago shikéyah shééhodoosįįł." *Thank you, my maternal aunt. I lost my wits. Now I can walk back into our land and it will recognize me.* The woman carried the calico dress to the fire that burned on the south side of their camp and reverently placed the dress in the fire and watched it burn. With tears in her own eyes, Nínááníbaa' responded,

Lą́'ąą'. *You are welcome.*

****

The Naabeehó people were told they could not leave because they were to wait for additional soldiers to help escort the people back to Fort Canby. Although the people were told they would be leaving the Bosque Redondo Indian Reservation, many of the Naabeehó people, especially the older women, agonized over the fact that they would leave their deceased loved ones in their angry enemy's barren land. An elder woman cried,

"Aají nizhé'é yishjool. Yisnááh ánihi'diilyaa yę́ędą́ą' ts'ídá t'áá'awołíbee txi'dahwiisii'nii'. Yéego shitah honiigai yę́ędą́ą' shaa 'áhojilyą́ągo bee náádiisdzá. T'áadoo kót'é 'ílíní t'óó naa'ajíítłizh. Ch'ééh nídidoo'nah t'áá nisingo, t'áá'ákwe'é bíséłdáago be'iina' bii' haalyá. Łą nááhai 'ałhaa 'áhwiilyą́ągo. Háish bich'į' chonáá'iidiil'įįł? Nizhé'é doo bits'á shíni' da nidi nihikéyahgóó 'akéé' ná'iiljił doo." *Your father is buried over there. Even though we were suffering greatly, he took care of me when I got very sick and because of his care, I got well. He fell down without warning. I hoped he would get back up, but his life was taken from him right there. We had taken care of one another for many years. Who will I depend upon now? I don't want to leave your father but we will carry our belongings as we follow our people back to our land.* Many people felt the same about their loved ones who died during the difficult years at Fort Sumner. Men and women who lost their children, their parents, a spouse to disease or starvation did not want to leave their loved one in their enemy's land.

While waiting for word of when they could leave, the Naabeehó people prepared their hearts for the time when they would have to walk away from their loved ones who were buried at the Reservation. Hashké Yił Naabaah encouraged his people when he took time to visit one grieving family after another. His soothing voice and his strong words comforted the people as they prepared for departure for their own lands and leaving a loved one behind. At different times, he spoke words of comfort to his people when he would say,

"Shidine'é, ha'ahóní bee hadadínóht'é." *My people, you are made up of hope.*

"Hada'íínółní, shidine'é." *Take comfort, my people…*

"Saad bee ha'ahónínígíí bee nihada'áłchíní bich'į' háádaohdzih." *Speak words of hope to your children.*

"Nihitxé'ázíní bąąh ádahasdįįdígíí saad bee ha'ahóínígíí bee bich'į' háádaohdzih." *Speak words of hope to your close relatives who have lost a loved one.* To a mother, he said,

"Na'áłchíní bá ha'íínílní." *Comfort yourself for the sake of your children.* To a child wo was orphaned, he said,

"Hágo, shíighahgi nídaah. T'áadoo nichaaí."
Come here, sit down beside me. Don't cry.

Loud sounds of children and women weeping drifted across the Reservation in the evening and long into the night. Although the people were excited about going home, their thoughts and memories of their deceased loved ones crept into their thoughts and dreams.

****

The soldiers announced they requested as many wagons as possible to transport the Navajo people who were old, pregnant, very sick or too weak to walk very far. Every day, the Naabeehó people packed and repacked their few belongings to distribute their things for comfort when carrying their belongings. At Hashké Yił Naabaah's request, the men picked up their packs and carried them around their camps to get their bodies used to carrying a load. The young men searched for straight cottonwood tree branches that could be made into canes for the elderly people and for the ones carrying heavy packs on their backs. The older men eagerly waited for the branches and once they were brought, busied themselves making as many canes as they could. Still others carried heavy rocks to get their arms and backs used to carrying an elderly relative who was sick or would not be able to walk very far. He also told his people to repair their moccasins and for those who did not have moccasins, he asked his warriors to hunt for rabbits to use the skins of the rabbits to place under the soles of their feet and to have meat to eat to strengthen the people. The women repaired their water pots while the men braided ropes using yucca leaves to attach to the pots as handles and to use for tying their bundles to their bodies.

When the Naabeehó people could not wait any longer, several soldiers and the interpreter arrived to tell Hashké Yił Naabaah and his people to arrive at the parade grounds for counting and to obtain their rations. The people asked their elder Peace Leader about the sheep they had cared for the past several months. Hashké Yił Naabaah reminded the people the sheep belonged to their enemy. Not wanting to leave the sheep, the women pulled out what little grass they could find and fed the sheep one last time. Tears were shed for the herd of sheep that gave them hope and comfort when they needed it the most.

The landscape was covered by many groups of Naabeehó people who followed their leaders and migrated to the parade grounds to wait. The women and children avoided the center of the parade grounds remembering the helpless goat that was beaten. The people were ordered to stand near their leaders who held up their leadership sticks.

A herd of donkeys with heavy bags filled with water tied to their backs were led to the dusty wagon road.

Two soldiers followed each donkey to keep them moving forward. Several donkeys refused to move forward which made the soldiers angry. The soldiers who beat the goat earlier approached the donkeys and raised their bats. Just before they brought their bats down on the backs of the donkeys, the high-pitched scream of a woman echoed throughout the parade grounds. The stubborn donkeys turned toward the sound of the woman's scream. The woman screamed again and again. The donkeys moved toward the sound of her screaming, nearly running people over. Water was spilling out of the closely woven bags as the donkeys ran toward the screaming woman. The screaming woman rushed forward. The donkeys and their owner were reunited. The woman cried in high-pitched screams as the donkeys crowded around her, nuzzling her from every side.

Everyone stretched their necks to see what the commotion was about. It was the woman named Asdzą́ą́ Télii Neiniłkaadí *the Woman Who Herds Donkeys,* the one whom Hashké Yił Naabaah invited along with her daughter to join his people at their camp. Hashké Yił Naabaah dropped the pack on his back and rushed forward, followed by his sons and Kiizhóní and the young Mescalero Apache man. The soldiers raised their whips to force the men and donkeys back into the line that was forming. Several soldiers raised their whips to whip the woman to force her to retreat. Hashké Yił Naabaah and his four young warriors stood defiantly in front of the woman. To protect her leader and his sons who were willing to risk their lives, Asdzą́ą́ Télii Neiniłkaadí took several steps backwards. When she did, the donkeys bolted after her with their packs bouncing up and down on their backs. Water sloshed over and spilled on the people standing nearby. The woman whistled then yelled,

"Ádahodołzééh!" *Stop what you are doing!* a command which made the donkeys stop in their tracks and turn to look at her. The soldiers whipped at the donkeys and screamed at the woman but the woman would not retreat further as ordered.

Hashké Yił Naabaah heard his Dédii scream,

"Hágo, hágo nidishní!" *Come here, I said come here!* Then she screamed,

"Shizhé'é!" *My father!* Instead of her father coming to the rescue, Kiizhóní broke through the crowd and came face to face with Dédii. Dédii told him her young Naabeehó 'Ashkii left her side and sped out of the crowd, running toward one of the buildings. Kiizhóní left her side, calmly asking,

"Shá dahooł'aah." *Make room for me.* At his request, people moved aside. They pointed their lips in the direction the young boy was running.

The young Naabeehó 'Ashkii sped up the steps of the officer's building. He banged on the door calling,

"Folton! Folton! Folton!" The door flew open and standing in the doorway was the tall gray-haired one.

"Aren't you supposed to be with Sunflower at the parade grounds, young man?" the tall gray-haired one asked, looking down at the young Naabeehó 'Ashkii.

"My mother..." was all the young Naabeehó 'Ashkii could say. The tall gray-haired one reached down and turned the young boy around then placed his hands firmly on the boy's shoulders and followed him down the steps. The young boy pointed at the confrontation between his maternal grandfather and the angry soldiers. Still holding onto the young boy's shoulders for support, the tall gray-haired one and the boy hurried to the parade grounds.

"What is causing all the commotion? Where is your grandfather's leadership stick? Why isn't he holding it up for his people? Where is Sunflower?" The young Naabeehó 'Ashkii could not keep up with the tall gray-haired one's questions, all he could do was lead the tall gray-haired one toward his maternal grandfather who was in a confrontation with the soldiers. All the young boy could say was,

"Enemy man mad at my leader." The tall gray-haired one called to his soldiers and to the one who was poking Hashké Yił Naabaah in the chest with the handle of his whip, ordering him to leave the control to him. Hashké Yił Naabaah grabbed the whip and yanked it out of the hand of the soldier then threatened to hit him with it. The reaction of the soldier told the Naabeehó people that he was a coward when he ducked and squeaked loudly and held his hands in front of his face for protection. The soldier's reaction brought laughs from the Naabeehó people, which only escalated the anger of the other soldiers.

The tall gray-haired one limped to stand in between the two confrontational groups. In a low voice the tall gray-haired one ordered his soldiers to leave the parade grounds then turned to the young Naabeehó 'Ashkii and Hashké Yił Naabaah. He asked what started the confrontation. The young Naabeehó 'Ashkii pointed at the woman who was reunited with her donkeys then explained that as a leader, his maternal grandfather had to protect anyone under his leadership.

The tall gray-haired one listened to the young Naabeehó 'Ashkii as the boy told the story about the lawless man named Adilohii *Rope Thrower*, who stole the entire herd of donkeys from the woman and even kidnapped her daughter. He also told about the woman reuniting with her daughter and the loss of her husband once he was reunited with their daughter whom they had not seen in years.

Tall gray-haired one looked toward the woman who was surrounded by her donkeys. He stared for a length of time then asked the young Naabeehó 'Ashkii to stay with his grandfather while he talked to the soldiers. Calling for a young skinny soldier, the tall gray-haired one asked the young man to bring his cane, the request to which the young man turned and hurried away.

The tall gray-haired one stayed with Hashké Yił Naabaah and his sons and spoke quietly with the young Naabeehó 'Ashkii. While waiting for his cane, the tall gray-haired one searched the faces of Nahat'á Yinaabaah, Tł'ée'go Naabaah, the young Mescalero Apache man, and Kiizhóní, who had returned. He stared at the young Mescalero Apache man, then asked,

"Didn't you live across the Pecos River with the Mescalero Apache people?" He turned and called for an interpreter. After a conversation with the young Mescalero Apache man, the interpreter confirmed he was but stated he was married to his leader Hashké Yił Naabaah's youngest daughter. After learning more about the young Mescalero Apache man, the tall gray-haired one rhetorically said with a silly grin on his face,

"So, you are a captive heart just like me." Confused, the interpreter whispered the interpretation to the young Mescalero Apache man which brought a puzzled look to the young man's face.

Leaning on his cane, the tall gray-haired one called for his troops to assemble at the parade grounds. Quickly the soldiers stepped into place forming a neat long line then saluted their officer.

"We need the donkeys to transport the water jugs for us. More importantly, we need this woman to stay near her donkeys. The donkeys belonged to her before Kit Carson stole them from her. I understand she was not reunited with her animals until earlier today. We need her to control those stubborn animals. We also need you to be tolerant of the Navajo people. They have suffered at the hands of our military and our government. We do not want any more dying on our watch. Understood?" More instructions were conveyed but Hashké Yił Naabaah returned to his wife and daughters, not wanting to stay and witness the activity.

More Naabeehó people were arriving with their leaders, overwhelming the parade grounds with their numbers. The people kept an eye on the position of the sun as it began its downward slide toward the western horizon. A beautiful sunset greeted the people before darkness overtook the people. The men were comfortable at the parade grounds but the women and children were afraid. They slept very little that night.

Early the next morning, the soldiers placed several long poles across the Pecos River, positioning them side-by-side for the people to cross over the river. The pine logs were flat on the exposed side while the side that faced downward above the river, remained rounded and still covered by bark. The people were forced to cross over the river, marching from the western side of the river and stepping off of the poles onto the eastern side of the river.

When she stepped off of the rickety logs, Dzáníbaa' searched for the place she and her young Mescalero Apache man once called home. She turned to her husband and asked in Navajo where they camped. Laden down with their belongings and their little one, her husband pointed with his lips and nodded toward a large clearing downstream. Dzáníbaa' giggled when she saw her husband's puckered lips. Tears filled her eyes when her mind flitted from one Mescalero Apache person to another. Her mind rested on the kind old woman who spared her life on their beautiful mountain home. She also thought of the young kind Naabeeho woman who came to live with them in their brush arbor and who returned to her Naabeehó people who also lived on the eastern side of the river. Dzáníbaa' also never forgot the kind Naabeehó woman who bathed her in the home of the big white woman.

She remembered the kind young woman whom she called,

"Shinálí." *My paternal grandmother.* The image of the woman standing near the river's edge the night she turned and stepped into the arms of Naabeehó warriors to be reunited with her mother and father that one moonlit night never left her mind. Tears spilled down her face as she breathed,

"Ahéhee', shinálí, yéego shíká 'íínilwod. Nizhónígo shį́į́ nighandi nídíídááł." *Thank you, my paternal grandmother, you have helped me in a great way. May you arrive home safely as you walk home.*

****

The Naabeehó people were quickly separated into large groups according to their leaders. The people were ordered to stay with their leaders. Nínááníbaa' watched the long pieces of fabric fluttering from the leadership sticks that were held high in the air. It was a colorful sight. "The colors of the many pieces of fabric are the colors of nihikéyah *our land*," she thought.

Finally, the next day, on June 18th, 1868 the people were told to remain with their leaders as they took their first steps on their walk home. The long procession consisted of soldiers on horseback, a group of

Naabeehó people, a few wagons provided for the old and sickly people, wagons piled high with supplies, more soldiers on horseback, a row of donkeys, a group of Naabeehó people, soldiers on horseback, wagons for transporting people and another set for supplies, more Naabeehó people, more soldiers on horseback, a row of donkeys, a group of Naabeehó people and more of the same as far as the eye could see. Nínáánííbaa' and her daughters discussed the whereabouts of Asdzą́ą́ Telii Neiniłkaadí *the Woman Who Herds Donkeys.*

To begin the day's activity, the tall gray-haired one rode his horse to the middle of the procession and announced that traveling ten miles a day would be a productive day as long as all the old, pregnant women, handicapped, and extremely sick people rode in the wagons. After his words were interpreted into Navajo, the tall gray-haired one asked the old people to be the first to step forward and get into the wagons that were provided for that purpose.

Nínáánííbaa' and her daughters watched in horror as many Naabeehó people recklessly rushed toward the wagons, wanting to obtain a spot on the wagons so they would not have to walk. The soldiers tried in vain to push back the healthy, younger, and able-bodied Naabeehó people and herd them away from the wagons. Nínáánííbaa' was saddened to see her people who demonstrated such inner strength for the past four years lose their resolve and clamor and claw for a place to sit or stand on the wagon. They hit and shoved anyone who tried to force them out of the wagon. It was of no use. Confusion ensued.

"Haash dajit'į? Doo hanii hoł aadahojooba' da?" *What are they doing? Don't they have any kindness within them?* Nínááníbaa' scolded in disbelief. She was so sad and embarrassed of her people and their behavior. The old, infirmed, pregnant, and handicapped Naabeehó people stepped back and waited patiently while their healthy people lost all sense of ił ahojooba' *kindness.*

Women and children who got separated in the confusion were screaming for one another. There was no order to the crowd. Shots were fired into the air to no avail. In anger and disgust, the tall gray-haired one stepped back and signaled the lead wagons onward toward the west. The horses strained against the great load in the wagons as they took their first cumbersome steps forward. The horses finally were able to pull the wagons forward as a few Naabeehó people still fought for a position on a wagon.

"As discussed, take the water route," the tall gray-haired one hollered. The message was carried from one soldier's mouth to the next soldier until it reached the ears of the drivers that led their cumbersome wagons down the bumpy path. The drivers responded with a wave that was communicated from one soldier's hand to the next to reassure the tall gray-haired one that his message had been delivered and heeded.

Dédii and Dzáníbaa' screamed and grabbed onto their mother's arms when they saw two children fall off of the wagons. They screamed even louder when they saw three more people fall, losing their struggle to hang on to the side rail of the wagon when they tried climbing into it. In their failed efforts to hang on to anything they could grasp, their bodies were shaken loose and thrown under the wagon and into the path of the horses and wagons that followed closely. When wagon wheels ran over a portion of the bumpy dirt wagon trail, a few more people were shaken loose. A mental image of the beaten goat flashed before Nínáánínbaa"s mind as she watched three people's bodies writhe and thrash when they tried in vain to move out of the way of the horses and the wagon wheels' path. A young Naabeehó man reached down and tried to catch a young woman who was jarred loose from the precarious spot she sat upon, but the young man lost his balance and lost his grip on the young woman's wrist and fell out of the wagon. He grabbed her leg, pulling her with him as he tried not to fall off. They both fell into the following wagon's path. The soldiers driving the wagons were either not aware of the unfortunate incidents or were not willing to stop to save the lives of their captives as they kept their eye on the sandy bumpy path before them and urged their horses forward.

The soldiers' voices and orders and the pleas of the Naabeehó leaders faded into the commotion. Dzáníbaa' grabbed her son and Dédii's little ones and held on tight. Their children cried as they held their hands over their eyes to shut out the hideous sight before them as they crowded behind Kiizhóní and the young Mescalero Apache man who came rushing back to shield the children from danger. Nínáánínbaa' could not fathom how a day that was supposed to be such an exciting day could become a nightmare that was initiated by her Naabeehó people

Once the commotion died down and the dust cleared after the first procession moved completely out of sight, Hashké Yił Naabaah and his family saw thousands of Naabeehó people patiently waiting for their leaders to raise their leadership sticks and lead them homeward. Tears danced in the eyes of the people who defiantly faced away from the fort. No one dared to turn around to look at the place, the fort, the reservation that became their source of indescribable pain every day for four solid years.

The soldiers on horseback set the pace for the first long procession of Naabeehó people. The Naabeehó people who never considered riding in a wagon were kind and helpful to one another.

Dédii's mind raced. She wondered, "Where are the leaders of the Naabeehó people who thought only of themselves?" She knew they had spent years encouraging and helping one another to survive during desperate times. "Couldn't they have been patient just a few more days?" she asked herself with disappointment. "Were any of my father's people among the ones who forgot one another as they clambered onto the wagons?" she wondered. She looked around at the people who gathered near their elder Peace Leader who held his maroon leadership stick high in the air. Looking at the stick with the attached maroon fabric fluttering in the wind brought a sense of peace to her heart. "Are all of my father's people here?" she worried. "I don't blame my Naabeehó people because they are tired, sick, hungry, and so exceedingly anxious to get back to their own land and their own homes," she sadly thought. Hashké Yił Naabaah gathered his family together and hugged his Nínáánibaa' and his family close.

"Doo lá dó' doo dahígi 'áhoodzaa da! T'áá 'óolyéego nihaa yáhóósįįd!" *What a horrible happening! We have shamed ourselves!* he declared in a hoarse voice. "Diné bąąh dah nidahaz'ánígíí dóó náás daazlį́'ígíí dóó bich'į' anídahazt'i'ígíí dóó sáanii daoltsánígíí dóó 'ałchíní yázhí t'éiyá tsin nidaalbąąsí yii' naazdáago bi'doogééł dooleeł ha'nínée, hastóí dóó tsíłkéí dóó ch'ikéí doo bąąh daatéeh da yę́ę, jó bí da, 'iihíjée'go biniinaa diné ła' adahineezdee'go bik'i nida'aswod. Doo lá dó' dooda da. Nihe'anaa'í binááł t'óó nihaa yáhóósįįd." *They said only the ones who are sickly and elderly and handicapped and women who are pregnant and little children could ride in the wagons but men and teenage boys and teenage girls and ones who are healthy got into the wagons and because of that, some of our people fell off and were run over. How horrible. We shamed ourselves in the presence of our enemy.*

Nínáánibaa''s shoulders shook from the sobs she cried. Her daughters cried right alongside her. Many women cried, describing what they saw to one another, which started another round of tears and sobs. Hashké Yił Naabaah raised his voice and said to his people,

"Nihi'ílnii' yę́ę la' t'óó bił tsi' nisiikai!" *We were released and yet we ruined it!* he said with much emotion in his voice. Hearing Hashké Yił Naabaah's voice brought his people a sense of peace and order. Noticing that the people had settled down, he continued,

"Baa nídanihooshkąąh, shidine'é, t'áá hó 'ájít'éego dadii'níigo nihina'nitin nilįįgo bee nihikáa'jį' dahazlį́'ígíí baa dayohnééh lágo. Náánà, nihił aahojooba' bee t'áá nihizááká hada'iisiilniidgo bee nihikáa'jį' dahazlį́'. T'áadoo t'áá nihí t'éiyá 'ádaa nitsídaohkeesí, shidine'é. Danihitxé'ázini béédaołniih, nihik'éí béédaołniih, nihada'áłchíní béédaołniih, t'áadoo t'áá 'ádíighahígo 'ádá nitsídaohkeesí, t'ááshǫǫdí, shidine'é, 'éí baa nídanihooshkąąh. Haashílá 'ił hóyéé' nihik'eh dódle' lágo. Dooda!" *I beg of you, my people, don't forget, it was the teaching of, 'It is up to you if you want to succeed,' that has spared our lives. It was also by our sheer kindness for one another that we were comforted, which is what spared our lives. I beg of you, my people, don't only think of yourselves, instead think of your relatives, think of your clan relatives, remember your children, don't only think of yourselves, please, my people, I beg all of you. Don't allow laziness to get the best of you. No!*

"Shą́ą́' ániid nihinaat'áanii naakigo t'áá bí bízhi' naaltsoos yikáá' yik'i 'ashchį́. Doo 'éí shízhi' shá 'ádoolníił níígóó, nidi t'áá nihí nihízhi' ádiilníił níigo yee nihoní'ą́. Nihí dó', nihinaat'áanii binahjį', 'T'áá shí,' ha'nínígíí dóó, 'T'áá hó 'ájít'éego,' ha'nínígíí bik'ida'di'diitį́įł. T'áá nihí nihijáád dóó nihikee' dóó nihízhi' bee hooghandi nídiidááł. T'áadoo nihe'anaa'í bitsin naalbąąsí bada'íiníidlíígóó nihikéyah biih nídiikah." *Remember our two leaders who wrote their own names on the paper. They did not expect someone else to write their names for them, instead, they made a vow to write their own names. We too, because of the actions of our leaders, now let us understand what it means to say, 'I will do it myself,' and 'It is up to me to achieve success.' By means of our own legs, our own feet and our own body, let us return to our homes and not enter our land by means of depending on our enemy's wagon.*

Áadi nidi shįį́ doo ts'íí'áhoot'éégóó nihich'į' nidahwii'náa doo háálá k'ida'dilyéegi biláah ahoolzhiizh. Nihada'áłchíní shą' ha'át'íí adeidiyoołnah? Ha'át'íí shą' yiih naazhjée'go doo dadoodlóoł da, dííghaaí? Nihikéyah nidi shįį́ t'áá nihígi 'át'éego bíni' shaazh silį́į́'. T'óó baa hojoobá'ígo ch'ééh hánihidéez'į́į́, 'Háájísh adajiiskai,' nihó'níigo'." *It will be extremely difficult for us when we get back to our own land because the time for planting has passed. What will our children eat? What will our children wear so they do not freeze this winter? Our land's mind has been bruised in the same way our minds have been bruised. It is pitiful in the way it has been looking for us, wondering where we have gone.*

"T'áá nihí 'ádaniit'éego nihighan nídahodoodleeł, nihilį́į́' náádahódlǫǫ doo, danihizáanii nááda'atł'óo doo dóó dibé dóó tł'ízí bee náádahódlǫǫ doo. Nihahastói ninááđaalzheeh doo dóó nínááda'niłt'į́įh doo dóó béégashii dóó łį́į́' ninááđeiniłkaad doo. Áádóó nihada'áłchíní nínááda'niłkaad doo dóó nidaanée doo. Díí t'áá'át'é baa nitsídeiikees doo ni'. Éí bich'į' nihił chodahoo'į́į doo ni'. Nihe'anaa'í baa nááda'íínídlíi dooleełígíí 'éí ts'ídá dooda, shidine'é.

T'áá nihí 'ádaniit'éego t'éí nihikéyah biih nídiikah dóó nihił náádahójǫ́ǫ dooleeł." *It will be up to us to make our homes once again and have livestock again. Our spouses will weave once again and they will have sheep and goats once again. Our men will hunt and they will plant once again and will have cows and horses and they will herd them once again. And then our children will herd sheep and they will be playing once again. Let us think about these things so we can have a home once again. To depend on our enemy once again is absolutely wrong, my people. It will be up to us to successfully reenter our land and be happy once again.* Hashké Yił Naabaah noticed the tall gray-haired one was politely waiting for him while he was speaking to his people. He stopped talking and turned toward the tall gray-haired one.

The next procession of soldiers, people, wagons, and donkeys had formed once again. Hashké Yił Naabaah searched the faces of the people in the wagons. To his relief he did not see his people perched precariously on the wagons. It was impossible to search all the wagons. The procession was stretched out in a neat line for miles. He was thankful to his people for not being so selfish as to take an older person's spot or the spot of a person in physical need.

Nínááníbaa' could not hold back her pent-up emotions she held back for nearly three years. She cried out loud,

"Ahéhéé', shiTaa'. Nihi'ílnii'ígíí doo ts'íí'át'éégóó baa 'ahééh nisin. T'áá nihí nihikéyahgóó nihéé'ílnii'ígíí 'ałdó' Nich'į' baa 'ahééh nisin. Nizhónígo hooghandi nídiikahígíí baa nánooshkąąh dooleeł, shiTaa'. *Thank you, my Spiritual Father. I am extremely grateful for our release. I am also grateful that we have been released to return to our own land. I plead with you, my Spiritual Father, that we will return to our homes in safety.* The sound of cries echoed back throughout the procession. Nínáánібaa''s family held onto one another as they cried tears of relief.

Hashké Yił Naabaah's people stood bravely in the procession. They looked pitiful. Some were barely able to stand, others leaned heavily on their canes as they carried a weak loved one on their backs, still others tied their few belongings to their backs and leaned forward, waiting to take the first step homeward.

With hope in his heart, Hashké Yił Naabaah led Nínáánібaa' and their children and their grandsons, as well as Kiizhóní and the young Mescalero Apache man forward. His family members lifted their faces toward the horizon that stretched before them as they took their first steps outside of the Fort Sumner Indian Reservation. They all breathed a collective sigh of relief. Behind them were all the suffering of their people, the hunger, illnesses, death, bitter tasting water, stench of dysentery, and their loved ones who were buried in shallow graves.

Before them lay flat land that was interrupted by ditches created by the rain waters that ran from the higher elevations into the Pecos River. Soft whispers of the people encouraging one another were heard in between the sound of hundreds of footsteps falling on the hard ground beneath.

A reporter asked the tall-gray haired one,

"How many Navajo Indians were forced to walk to this God forsaken country, officer?"

"My records are sealed," was the sterile answer.

The tall-gray haired one looked around at the Navajo people who bravely walked, placing one foot in front of the other. Speaking to no one, he said,

"More than eleven thousand Navajos were forced to walk here. But that's only the recorded numbers. Only five thousand are returning to their land in the northwest. Six thousand Navajos died under our watch, but then again, that is only the recorded deaths. Many more have died whose deaths were not recorded. I'm so grateful I did not have to record the death of my beautiful Sunflower."

Forgetting that he was not alone, he spoke to his beautiful Sunflower.

"My beautiful sweet Sunflower, you have... You have

beautiful eyes that drew me in,

a beautifully shaped nose,

a beautiful full smile that revealed white teeth as lovely as a string of pearls,

lovely soft welcoming lips that were cool and pliable under my demanding lips,

a voice that is as soft as the falling petal of a sunflower,

soft round breasts with sweet supple nipples that became taut when I kissed them,

a flat stomach that tightened when I kissed it,

firm thighs that held me close,

a gentle hidden softness that made you draw your breath when I touched you, strong legs covered with soft, flawless browned skin,

feet with beautifully shaped toes,

soft gentle hands that pulled me toward you ever so timidly,

beautifully shaped arms that show no muscle, but ones that have power over me,

and, mmmmmm, your soft hair that lay softly on my skin as we moved as one.

My beautiful Sunflower, my hearty flower of the desert,

I named you rightly, you are as hearty as the sunflower in the desert sun.

My beautiful Sunflower, you are unaware of your beauty, your power over me.

My beautiful Sunflower, come back to me.

Come back to me.

I love you ever so much, Mrs. Charles Arnold Folton. My beautiful wife..."

****

Nearly three days into their slow return to Diné bikéyah *Navajoland*, Hashké Yił Naabaah finally found all his people. They reported that they also watched in horror as selfish people forced their way onto a wagon.

"T'ahdoo nihikéyahdę́ę́' ch'ínihidi'neelkaad yę́ędą́ą́', ił ahojooba' bínanihiníłtingo biniinaa Naabeehó dine'é tsin nidaalbąąsí yich'į' ałk'inaaskaigo t'óó nihił daayéé'go danihiínááł." *Even before we were forced to walk away from our land, you taught us about kindness and that is the reason we just watched in horror as our Navajo people clamored over one another to get to the wagons.*

With tears in their eyes, Hashké Yił Naabaah and the elder Peace Leader thanked their people for not becoming unruly and selfish.

****

Dédii and Dzáníbaa' did not recognize the able-bodied people who were sitting in the wagons. They noticed that the able-bodied people who rode on the wagons were angry, short tempered, and mean to one another but the Naabeehó people who chose to walk were kind to one another and thoughtful of each other. While walking on the sandy wagon road, there were many times when Dédii and Dzáníbaa' pointed out to their mother, different ones who stopped to help the ones who were very weak. In the beginning of the long walk home, they witnessed the younger or stronger men offering to carry the rolled-up bundles of the ones who were elderly, sick, weak, hungry, or in the last trimester of their pregnancy. Although Hashké Yił Naabaah's people needed the canes the men made to stabilize themselves, they offered their precious canes to the ones who were having trouble walking.

Looking at the healthy people in the wagons with disdain, the elderly man Dédii called "shicheii" *my maternal grandfather* refused to leave the side of his family for the chance of riding in a wagon.

"Díí yee' ayóo dinishwo'. T'áá ni' yisháałgo shikéyah bii'jį' dah yiideeshteeł. Doo 'éí shoołjiłígóó, doo 'éí shoołtéłígóó, doo háida shoodzįsígóó, t'áá shí shikee' bee shikéyah biih yah anídeeshtł'ééł. Háadi shįį́ shiyaago shikéyah biih yah anídeeshwoł. Nááná ła' da yishjiłgo nidi bíighah dooleeł," *I am still able to run. While still walking, I will take off running into my land. No one will be carrying me on their back, no one will be carrying me, no one will be dragging me, I will reenter my land running on my own two feet. I will be jumping high in the air as I reenter my land. I will even be able to carry another person on my back,* he said as he skipped several steps toward the western hill.

The soldiers led the procession of horses, wagons, people, donkeys northward. At the end of the long day the wagons stopped, and the people were told to rest for the night.

"Fourteen miles. A good day! These people sure want to go home, don't they?" a soldier reported. Hashké Yił Naabaah and his elder Peace Leader asked the people to lie down and rest for the night.

Chapter Twelve

Taking the Water Route

A soldier announced,

"Tomorrow we take the wagon trail that leads northwest toward Anton Chico. We will be met with supplies there and maybe rest for a couple of days before we head out over some relatively rough terrain. After that, according to these orders, we will follow the streams that lead through Blanco Canyon and past the White Lakes, then join the streams that will lead us through the Tijeras Arroyo and end up at Tijeras Canyon above the town of Albuquerque. There is plenty of water on this route but the Sandia Mountain is steep and the terrain will be rough as we travel through the Tijeras Canyon Pass."

"Taking the mountain route and crossing the Rio Grande won't be easy for our captives...," another soldier quickly commented as he was looking at the map,

"They are not our captives anymore. They are free, the treaty set them free."

"You are right, but as long as they are in my care, your care, they *are* our captives!" the two soldiers argued, both angry that they had to ride horses over many miles to deliver the Navajo people into the hands of soldiers who would be coming from Fort Fauntleroy or Fort Canby.

"We will be free of them on the eastern bank of the Rio Grande River," one soldier said, smiling.

The people rested but could not rest their minds. They asked one another if they were only dreaming, afraid they would wake up still being held to their status as prisoners of war. From dusk until the predawn light, darkness covered the earth.

With the light of dawn illuminating the faint outline of the Sandia Mountains ahead, the Naabeehó leaders pled with their people to walk, instead of rushing to get a place in the wagons.

"Danihahastóí dóó danihizáanii náás daazlį́'ígíí baa dahojoobá'í. 'Éí tsin naalbąąsí bee bi'doogéełgo t'éí beełt'é. Nihí doo nihąąh daatxéhígíí 'éí 'akéé' dayínółyeedgo 'éí bídanoł'ą́. Naabaahii hanii t'óó nidabi'digé. Dooda lą́ą." *The older men and older women need our sympathy. It makes sense for them to be transported by wagon. Those of you who are healthy need to be running alongside us. Warriors are not to be transported. Absolutely not!* the people were told.

The next morning, order was being restored. A few more resisting Naabeehó people were willing to walk instead of fighting for a spot on the wagons, except for a man who climbed into the wagon after helping his pregnant wife obtain a spot in the wagon. Hashké Yił Naabaah saw the man plop himself down in the wagon near his wife and refused to move over for an elderly man who could not walk any further. Hashké Yił Naabaah grabbed a soldier's long whip and deftly raised the long handle in the air and snapped the whip with a loud crack toward the man in the wagon to get the man's attention. The tip of the string slashed a small clean-cut hole in the man's already tattered shirt. The man did not move, instead, he lowered his chin onto his chest and appeared to be asleep. Annoyed at the young men and boys who were able to walk but chose to sit in the wagons, Hashké Yił Naabaah decided to make the man an example for the others. He approached the man and asked bold questions in a loud voice, loud enough for the people to hear.

"Da' niísh ná 'i'niichį?" *Is the baby to be born for you?*

"Aoo', ha'át'íí lá?" *Yes, what is it?* the man answered in a lowered voice. Hashké Yił Naabaah leaned over and faced the man from a short distance and asked in a loud voice,

"Da' niísh ałdó' a'ninałchį?" *Are you also going to have a baby?*

"Nidaga'," *No*, was the answer. Hashké Yił Naabaah then stood tall and yelled,

"Jó 'áko lá 'ii' haniních'į́įdiiínee'! K'eshchosh la' k'adni' ni'niiłhxį! Jó ni da!" *Well then get the hell out of the wagon! You are dying to be treated like a baby whose mother is expecting another child! You, instead of the baby!* Embarrassed and humiliated, all the man could say was,

"Hágoshį́į́." *Okay.* He quietly climbed out of the wagon, grabbed his family's belongings and stood beside the wagon. The elder Peace Leader joined in and further humiliated the man by saying,

"Aají, íighah a'nííłk'aih!" *Waddle alongside over there!* Very agreeable, the man said,

"Kojí, ya'? *Over here, right?* The two leaders both said,

"Aoo'." *Yes.*

The Naabeehó people who overheard the conversation were laughing. Men and boys who had secured a seat in a wagon by bullying others, spilled out of the wagons from fear of being humiliated and being the butt of all the jokes. Throughout the day, the event was retold many times and it kept the Naabeehó people laughing as they walked over rough terrain.

Nínáánníbaa' was proud of her husband, the War Leader. She knew he wanted to chastise the young men who only thought of themselves and no one else, but she knew her husband would not overstep his bounds by reprimanding another naat'áanii *leader's* warrior. When no leader stepped up to put the able-bodied men in their place, her husband took over.

****

After weeks of moving the people and the wagons steadily along the winding rough wagon path and uneven terrain, the procession faced the looming Sandia mountain range from the east. The Naabeehó people looked at the sprawling mountain and wondered how the wagons and their tired people could climb the mountain.

They lifted their faces to the cool breeze that blew off from the mountain which they found inviting after having breathed fine łeezh *dust,* swatting away ts'í'ii *gnats* and ts'í'ii nineezí *mosquitos.* The air smelled different after crushing many ch'osh *bugs* of all kind and k'íneedlíshii *stink bugs* that unsuccessfully ran out of the way of a wagon wheel that rumbled by and horses' hooves that ground the bugs into the ground upon which the soft feet of the Naabeehó people treaded. Tł'ish *snakes* that claimed the floor of the wilderness as their home crawled among the hosh *cacti,* both of which the people said "bá'át'e' dahólǫ́" *some are dangerous.* The people saw rodents, dlǫ́ǫ́' *prairie dogs,* gah and gah tsoh *rabbits and jack rabbits* scurrying in different directions when they heard the heavy sound created by the cumbersome weight of the wagons coming long before they saw the long procession. With the soldiers setting the pace, the people could only lick their lips in the lost hopes of hunting, killing, skinning, and cooking a fat rodent for a meal, further torturing the famished Naabeehó people.

The people were anxious to begin their climb to the summit of the mountain. They knew the farther they ascended up the mountain, the more the mountain offered fresh spring water, ample edible vegetation, deer and elk and other animals that were free of any taboos for hunting and eating. The thought of fresh meat wet their mouths with saliva in anticipation of eating delicious fresh meat. The old men lifted their free hand to their mouths and pretended they were lifting a bone that had been boiled in water and cooled for the purpose of a picnic. The Naabeehó people called the boiled meat "hahaazhbéézh" *boiled meat that is packed for a picnic.* The hungry children watched their grandfathers and followed their action as they lifted the imaginary piece of boiled meat that was still attached to the bone, took a bite of meat and tore the meat off the bone and chewed and chewed the imaginary delicious meat.

"Ayóó 'áhálniih!" *It is very delicious!* the children heard their grandfathers say so they repeated the words. The young boys watched their grandfathers wipe their dusty tired hands on their tattered pant legs and mumbled quiet words as they also said,

"Ayóó 'áhálniih!" in a softer subdued tone of voice. With broken hearts, the grandfathers watched their grandchildren's actions. To keep from crying, Hashké Yił Naabaah said to his grandsons,

"Ei dzééh dóó bįįh dóó jádí doo nidadilna' da. Biyah hozhdiłhxisgo t'áá'íídą́ą́' hats'ąąjį'go dah diilyisgo haz'ą́ą łeh. Éí biniinaa nijilzheehgo doo 'íits'a'ígóó 'adabikéé'góó bikéé' ajoołkah łeh. *Elk and deer and antelope move quickly. If you scare them, you will find they will take off in an instant. That is why you do not make a sound when you are following their tracks when you are hunting.*

The soldiers' call to stop their slow ascent up the mountainside to distribute rations sickened the people. The rations were sparse and consisted of mostly flour, a little pinch of tobacco for the men, water, and rotten meat, but the Naabeehó people knew better than to eat the food offered to them and turned to the land to provide for them by collecting vegetation, digging for roots, and hunting prairie dogs and rabbits, which they shared even if it meant they only had a taste of a little morsel of meat.

The dilemma of hauling water up the uneven rocky slope would have posed a deadly tragedy in the efforts of keeping the Naabeehó people alive, but the soldiers admitted the donkeys and "Donkey Woman" and her daughter were invaluable in transporting water. Transporting water in leaky barrels caused so much waste due to the bumpy wagon trails where the water would slosh out of the barrels. The people thought back to the time when they were chased to Fort Sumner where there was a constant shortage of water. They told stories of how much they suffered because of the scarcity of water. Using the donkeys to haul the waterproof bags of water alleviated their most immediate and grave concern and comforted the people. The donkeys provided a semi-smooth ride for the water with very little waste. Asdzą́ą́ Télii Neiniłkaadí kept busy working with her donkeys. Her daughter followed in the next procession of soldiers on horseback, wagons, Naabeehó people, and donkeys. Asdzą́ą́ Télii Neiniłkaadí and her daughter expertly trained a few of Hashké Yił Naabaah's young warriors to handle the donkeys to make them obey orders. The warriors were interspersed throughout the long processions of Naabeehó people.

Many times Dédii and Dzáníbaa' heard their father and the men say,

"Díí yee' dooda! Tó tsin naalbąąsí bee yigéełgo doo bíighah da doo nít'ęę́'! Tóshjeeh bii'dęę́' tó hahalk'oołgo wónáasii' tó 'áłch'į́įdígo tóshjeeh bii' siziid doo ni'. T'áá 'ákónéehee 'Asdzą́ą́ Télii Neiniłkaadí dóó bich'é'é nihit'áahjį' yisdá'ahi'noolchą́ą́'. T'áá 'óolyéego yisdánihi'éésh. Bik'i hojidlíi doo. T'áá 'Ałtsoní 'Eidii'aahii bik'ijidlíi dooleeł." *This would have been impossible! It would have been impossible to haul water by means of wagons! Water would have sloshed out of the water barrels until only a little water would be left. It is a good thing The Woman Who Herds Donkeys and her daughter sought refuge among us. They are literally saving our lives. They will be blessed. The One Who Gives Us All That We Have Need of (the Creator) will bless them.* Dédii and Dzáníbaa' nodded their heads in agreement as they gave Asdzą́ą́ Télii Neiniłkaadí grateful, gentle glances.

The higher up the mountain, the slow procession of soldiers on horseback, Naabeehó people, horse or mule drawn wagons and donkeys moved, the more narrow and rocky the wagon trail became, causing the already long procession to become even longer, stretching back down the mountain and far across the White Lakes valley. Words of ha'ahóní *hope* and t'áá hó 'ájít'éego t'éiyá *it is up to you to help yourself reach success* were spoken by the Naabeehó leaders to the people under their leadership. Hashké Yił Naabaah heard his elder Peace Leader say,

"Saad bee ha'ahóní la' bee nihe'anaa'í bik'ijį' nideiibaah. Ch'ééh a'didááh dóó dichin dóó jį́įgo naanáhonoogah dóó tł'ée'go hak'az bik'ijį' nideiibaah.

T'áá nihí nihikéyah biih néiikaijí t'éí sih hasin. Nihe'anaa'í bitsį daalgaiígíí t'áá yéeni' nihich'į' ádaanídaast'įįd dóó 'ádádahalchį' yéeni' ádahodiilzee'. Náás nihidi'noolkałígíí bik'ee txi'dahwii'níih nidi tsxį́įłgo t'áá nihí nihikéyah biih nídiikahjį' bich'į' náás deiiyíníilkaal. Saad bee ha'ahóní bee 'ałch'į' háádeiidzihgo tsxį́įłgo danihighan yę́ęgi ninádahidiikah. Éí nihidine'é bee bił náhwiilnihgo t'áá shǫǫ yee bí dó' ak'eh dadidoodleeł." *Our words of comfort that we speak to our people are the weapons we use to fight against our enemy. Fatigue and hunger and heat in the day and the cold at night are what we are also fighting against. We will not have relief until we walk back into our own land. Our enemy with white skin have become less harsh and the anger they had has died down but we are suffering from the way we are being forced to hurry forward but we are set on quickly entering our own land. When we speak words of comfort to one another then we can quickly return to our former homes. Let us tell that to our people. In that way, they will be victorious and overcome our enemies.* Hashké Yił Naabaah agreed, saying.

"Éí lą́ą, shinaat'áanii. Saad bee ha'ahóní 'ayóó 'ábóodziilii 'óolyé." *That will be good, my leader. Encouraging words of hope are extremely powerful.*

The two leaders had the chance to speak to their people when the soldiers announced their horses needed rest and ordered the people to rest as well for the night. No rations were available for the people. They had received their rations three days before. No one complained. The people were content to be far away from the fort and in the safety of the mountains. Although it was cold, the people rested. No one complained. They settled in an area where a narrow stream of water flowed over large boulders to create a soothing sound. The people looked even higher up into the Sandia Mountain. The mountain rose and met filmy white clouds in the blue sky above. The people shuddered when their gaze fell on the immense boulders that precariously hugged the mountainside. A chorus of the word,

"Hatxíhíláane'ęę'!" *How scary!* was repeated as the women looked intently at the boulders, hoping their gaze would hold the boulders in place. The people did not sleep much that night. Thoughts and fear of the boulders dislodging and tumbling down the mountain to crush them kept the Naabeehó people from falling asleep. They listened and waited. Grateful for the thin light of dawn that was cast on the side of the mountain by the faint rays of the eastern sunrise provided the people with a few minutes of rest.

The harsh sound of the bugle blast interrupted the silence and announced that the soldiers were ready to move farther up the side of the mountain. The old people, the pregnant women, the handicapped people and the little children were told they could not ride in the wagons due to the steep incline of the bumpy wagon path. Hashké Yił Naabaah tied a soft worn rope made of yucca around his waist and tied the other end around the waist of the elder man Dédii called shicheii *my maternal grandfather.*

"Shínaaí, díí tł'óół tsá'ászi' bit'ąą' bee yishbizhígíí noozhníí' gónaa be'ashtł'ó 'áádóó díí tł'óół yíníjí'go 'atiingóó neesłóos doo. T'áásh bííníghah?" Dédii heard her maternal grandfather speak his favorite words,

"Hoohéii, shitsilí. 'Ahéhee'gi 'áshidíníniid." *Yes, my younger brother. You have spoken words to me of which I am grateful.* The old man smiled at Dédii with a sparkle in his eye and pulled gently on the rope. Hashké Yił Naabaah turned around and smiled at the old man and looked at Dédii and smiled at her. Dédii turned around to watch her father's young strong warriors tying ropes around an elder in the same manner. There seemed to be no end to the steep mountain slope as she looked higher and higher up the mountain.

Hashké Yił Naabaah looked back at his people who were ready to trudge forward and said,

"Sáanii danohłínígíí, nanise' daadánígíí nihist'e' danilįį dooleełígíí hádasídóo'íį' áádóó nihada'áłchíní dóó danihitsóóké dóó danihinálíké bínidabinołtin. Bíni'dii t'áá bí dabist'e' ádá hádaat'į, yinahjį' náásgóó 'áłahíjį' dabist'e' dahólǫǫ dooleeł dóó náásgóó doo bich'į' anídahazt'i'góó nanise' daadánígíí dabich'iiyą' nilįį dooleeł." *Women, search for edible plants for food and teach your children and your grandchildren about the plants. Let them learn to gather their own edible plants so that in the future they will always have food to eat, and in the future, they will not face hunger when they eat edible plants as their food source.* Pointing to the side of the path, he said,

"Akǫ́ǫ́ tł'oh azihii dóó ch'il awhéhé 'adaaz'á. 'Aají 'éí tsá'ászi' dóó tsá'ászi' niteelí yíl'á. Nihinaagóó ts'ah naazhóód dóó biníi'gi waa' naazkaad. Nihinaagóó 'éí chąąsht'ézhii tsoh bit'ąą' hadaaz'á. Chiiłchin halchin, éí shįį́ 'ałdó' t'óó'ahayóí kǫ́ǫ́ naazkaad. Nihinaagóó 'áda'azįįd bee 'ádoolníłígíí yíl'á. *There's wild tea growing. Over there, there are plenty of yucca and banana yucca plants growing. There are large bushes of sage growing all around us and in the midst of them wild spinach is also growing. Around us you can see the leaves of wild carrots growing out of the ground. The scent of sumac bushes is in the air. There are most likely a lot of them. There are enough edible plants to have a feast.*

"Áko nidi, shooh, shidine'é, t'áá hazhó'ó nihada'áłchíní dóó nihí t'áá 'ádíighahígo nanise' daadánígíí 'ádá 'ádaohłe'. Náasdi t'áá díigi 'át'éego nanise' daadánígíí dził bąąh deiyíl'á. Doo 'éí t'áá kwe'é t'éiyá da. Nihikéédę́ę́' yinéłígíí dichin yik'ee yinééł. Éí bá, ła' ą́ą́dadoohsįįł, t'ááshǫǫdí, baa nídanihooshkąąh, shidine'é. Nihił aadahojooba'go 'áda'dołne'. Atsį' dííłdzidígíí t'éí yikiin yinééł. Bíni'dii bí dó' áda'azįįd ádá 'ádeidoolííł." *My people, only gather enough for yourselves and your children. There is plenty more up ahead on the mountain, this is not the only place the edible plants grow. The ones who are following us are also hungry as they walk. Save some for them, please, I beg of you, my people. Make yourselves mindful of others. They are only eating rotten meat. Let them also make a feast for themselves.* When Hashké Yił Naabaah finished talking, he gently tugged on the end of the rope so he could pull the old man along. The men showed their muscular frames as they strained against the weight of carrying an elder who could no longer walk up the steep side of the mountain. Everyone strained against the steep rocky incline as they anxiously trudged up the side of the mountain.

Talking to the dinééh danilínígíí *young men* and tsíłkéí danilínígíí *teenage boys,* Hashké Yił Naabaah pointed to the various trees that grew near the wagon path.

"Akǫ́ǫ́ gad ni'eełii sikaad. Náasdi 'éí gad naazkaad. Chá'oł adaaz'á 'aají. Tséch'il ałdó' hólǫ́ǫ́ lá, 'ei yigą́ąhgo 'ayóo łikon. Bighą́ą'di shį́į́ k'adę́ę hadeii'nééh, áyaaní da nídíshchíí' níléí wódahdi 'adaaz'á. Bi'iil daats'í danineez. T'óó dził bíikai yę́ędą́ą' éí t'iis bit'ąą' kódaníłtéél léi' naazhóodgo bíighah ch'íniikai." *There are cedar trees growing widely there. Up ahead, there are several large juniper trees growing. Pinon trees grow over there. Oak trees grow here too, when they wither, they make a good fire. It seems that we have nearly climbed up to the summit because pine trees are growing in the high elevation. They possibly have long cones. When we first started ascending up the mountain, we walked past big cottonwood trees that had large leaves.* The Naabeehó men talked about how each tree contributed to Navajo society. The conversation carried them halfway up the mountainside.

The light from the late evening sun reflected in the clouds that skidded across the skies above the high rocky horizon told Hashké Yił Naabaah and Nínáánibaa' and their people they had nearly reached the summit. The light pulled them higher and higher up the side of the mountain. Each time they looked up, Hashké Yił Naabaah loosened his grip on the yucca rope with which he pulled the old man.

Before he released the rope, he made sure someone had grasped the rope, then he turned and grabbed his Nínááníbaa' and led her up the last few steps so they could see the landscape spread out before them together. Their hands shook as they held hands and looked down into the valley before them. They could hear a stream rushing nearby. Soft sobs rose into the air as members of their family joined them. Hashké Yił Naabaah raised one hand and said in a shaky voice,

"Nihidził, Tsoodził la' nizhónígo dah noot'ááł. Nizhónígo bik'i'diidíín. K'os éí bich'ah áyiilaa léi'..." *Our mountain, Mount Taylor is holding its head up. It is beautiful in the sunlight. It made the clouds its hat...* Hashké Yił Naabaah could not speak any longer. A raspy sob exited his lips and echoed across the valley. His children held their father and their mother up to keep them from falling down. As more people joined them on the summit, the cries of the people rose high into the sky. They all pointed to the small image of Tsoodził *Mount Taylor* standing straight and tall. The wind had blown most of the clouds off Mount Taylor, leaving what appeared to be a collar that was draped around the mountain below the snow covered peak. The sun's beautiful colored rays were reflected in the clouds, adding beautiful orange, peach, magenta colors to the mountain's cloudy shawl. The mesmerizing landscape, with the Naabeehó people's sacred mountain as its centerpiece was interrupted when the people heard a loud crashing sound.

The sound was created by a runaway wagon rushing down the winding wagon path that was embedded in the streambed. Echoes of the wagon bouncing off of the rocky and steep incline kept the people's attention as they watched the wagon bounce up in the air, empty its contents, twist, nearly turn over, and finally break up into pieces. The people murmured sounds of relief when they noticed the horses had outrun the wagon, but their sounds of relief was short lived when the people noticed one horse limping. Seeing Tsoodził *Mount Taylor,* their sacred mountain of the south, gave the people the courage to begin their dangerous descent down the winding wagon path.

The tall gray-haired one had sent a soldier to give additional orders to the procession ahead of him. After reading his scribbled message, a soldier announced,

"This is the last of the dangerous parts of the journey, men. Once we reach the base of the mountain we will take these wild Indians to the banks of the Rio Grande and hand them over to soldiers coming from Fort Fauntleroy, then we are to report to Fort Union toward the northeast. Lt. Col. Folton sent orders stating that we are not to rush the Navajo people down the mountain. They are tired, exhausted, hungry, and anxious to get back to their land but let the wagons take the lead just like we have done since we left from Fort Sumner. Come on, boys, let's see how fast these people can run!"

The horses had more sense than the dirty, smelly soldiers. Regardless of the number of times the strings of a whip were laid across their backs, the horses cautiously, picked their way down the mountain path. When the sun slipped behind the flat horizon far away, dusk settled quietly on the Sandia Mountain. When the stars twinkled in the darkened eastern skies, the soldiers called out orders for the people to stop and rest.

The sound of fresh cold water running nearby calmed the people as they filled the waterproof bags in the dark. The filled water bags were hung on the branches of trees to allow the donkeys to rest. Hashké Yił Naabaah and his warriors sat down on the ground and told stories while the women distributed the edible plants they gathered earlier in the day. Feeling refreshed, Hashké Yił Naabaah handed out little thin sticks that he broke off from the full sage brush bushes.

"Díí bee danihiwók'iz nida'ohtsih. Dibé bitsį' ła' joolghal nahalingo danihiwók'iz nida'ohtsih. T'áá shǫǫ da nihizhéé' bee nídadínóohchał. Bikéédóó tó ła' dadohdlį́į́ł dóó da'iidołhosh. Yiskáągo tsin naalbąąsí bikéé' halgaijį' ch'ídii'nééł. *Use this to clean between your teeth. Pretend that you had some mutton to eat. You will at least get full from your saliva. After that, drink some water and go to sleep. Tomorrow we will move behind the wagons down to the flat lands.* That night, the people rested their tired bodies in anticipation for the descent off of the western wall of the Sandia Mountain.

Just as the thin light of dawn stretched its thin rays into the sky above the summit, Hashké Yił Naabaah awoke to a strange sound, the faint sound of bells chiming in the valley below. He turned his head and smiled when he heard the soft sound of his Nínááníbaa' sleeping next to him. His arm ached from the hard earth beneath them and it ached because he had placed his arm under Nínááníbaa''s head as a pillow the night before. He did not want to move but he wanted to see the outline of Tsoodził *Mount Taylor*, their sacred mountain of the south. When Nínááníbaa' stirred in her sleep, he carefully pulled his arm out from under her head then looked toward the west to catch a glimpse of their sacred mountain. The heavy clouds overhead and the light fog hid everything from view except their immediate surrounding. He heard his Nínááníbaa' say in her chiding voice,

"Doo hanii ch'ééshinísíid da lá. Shí dó' Tsoodził dah noot'áałgo dínéesh'į́įł nisin. Níighahgi sézį́įgo Tsoodził dínéesh'į́įł nisin nít'ę́ę́'." *You should have woken me up. I also wanted to see Mount Taylor lifting his head. I wanted to be standing beside you when I looked at Mount Taylor.*

"K'os dóó 'áhí ni' nikeeldoh léi' doo hoot'į́į da. Nihinaagóó t'éí hoot'į́. Dahtoo' bee ni'góó hoditłéé'. Aho'niiłtą́ą daats'í. 'Aho'niiłtą́ągogo 'éí hashtł'ish hodooleeł dóó tsédaatahgóó yídéeltǫ' doo. Tsxį́įłgo dah náádii'náago t'éí. Nihikéédę́ę́' náá'oo'nééł. Háájíshą' o'oolyiz? Shą́ą́' nihe'anaa'í tsxį́įł danilį́įgo danihinoołkał ne'?" *Clouds and fog have covered the ground so it is hard to see. I can only see what's around us. The ground is wet with dew.*

Maybe it will begin to rain. If it rains, it will be muddy and the rocks will be slippery. It is best if we move on soon. People are coming behind us. Where did they all go? Remember, our enemies were so much in a hurry as they chased us? he said while straightening his tattered buckskin shirt. He laughed when Nínáánîbaa' answered,

"Aají shį́į́ bił asdzą́ą́ t'ah nidii bik'i dah nidahaltsaad." *Sleepy Women are probably sitting on them (soldiers)*. Hashké Yił Naabaah reached down and pulled Nínáánîbaa' to her feet and held her close, burying his face in her loose tsiiyééł *hair that was tied in a knot.* Absent from her hair was the sweet scent of the yucca plant. Nínáánîbaa' looked around and saw her own children and grandchildren still on the ground resting. In a low voice, she said,

"Ei shą' ha'át'íí? Niha'áłchíní dóó nihitsóóké dóó nihaadaaní bił asdzą́ą́ dóó bił hastiin, bité'ázíní yił, niha'áłchíní yił da'ałhosh. Nídoohjeeh bidiní." *What about them? Sleepy Woman and Sleepy Man and their relatives are sleeping with our children and our grandchildren and our son-in-law. Tell them to get up.* Hashké Yił Naabaah did not want to leave Nínáánîbaa''s side, instead, he scooped up a handful of pebbles and threw a pebble at each one of his children and his grandchildren and his son-in-law, saying,

"Nídoohjeehéi! Nídoohjeeh! Nídoohjeeh! Bił asdzą́ą́ dóó bił hastiin nahgóó 'adaołgeehgo nídahidoohtxáád. Díí yee' nihe'anaa'í doo hodítxééhgóó da'ałhosh. 'Shooh, Naabeehó dine'é 'ąąhéeshjéé' ádeiilyaa yę́ę nihits'ą́ą́' dah diijéé' dó 'íshłé!' doo nidó' hwiinidzingóó "ts'íkąąd" yiits'a'go da'ałhosh. Nihe'anaa'í t'áá bítséédi nídohjeeh. Nídoohjeehéi! Nihitaa' bich'į' ahééh danohsįįh. *All of you, get up! All of you, get up! All of you, get up! Shove Sleepy Woman and Sleepy Man aside and jump up. Our enemies are all around us sleeping. As they sleep soundly, they don't even think, 'The Navajo people whom we made our captives may have run off!' Get up before our enemies do. All of you, get up! Give thanks to our Spiritual Father.*

The tired Naabeehó people jumped up when they heard the loud yawns of their enemy. The people did not realize they had been freed from their status as prisoners of war earlier in the month when their leaders negotiated with the representatives of the United States and signed or put their "X" on the line of the Signature Page of the Navajo-U.S. Treaty. The people jumped up, splashed fresh cold water on their faces, gathered some edible plants and stuffed them into their mouths, rolled up their belongings, and cleaned up their camping area before they formed a line and waited for orders.

Walking down the side of the Sandia Mountain was not easy. The rocks were slippery from the drops of early morning dew. The men carried their elderly ones in their arms, causing them to lean forward from the weight knowing that the position of their bodies threatened their balance. Without a free hand, the women could not reach out and stabilize their steps on the rocky uneven ground because all the women carried either a child, hugged their few belongings, or held the hand of a toddler or an elder. The coolness of the cold crisp mountain air kept their muscles tight as they slowly picked their way down the side of the mountain.

The familiar sound of Asdzą́ą́ Télii Neiniłkaadí's voice was soothing to the people when she called to her donkeys.

"Hazhóó'ígo. Hazhóó'ígo nidahidoołtaał. Tó nihá deiyínóhheeh. Tó 'ayóó 'áníłdáasgo 'át'é. Hazhóó'ígo. Tó baa hą́ą́h danohsin. Ayóo bídin hóyéé'. Hazhóó'ígo." *Slowly. Step slowly. You are hauling water for us. Water is very heavy. Slowly. Be careful of the water. Water is scarce. Slowly.* When she cracked the whip she borrowed from the tall gray-haired one, no part of the whip ever touched the hide of any of her donkeys. The crack of the whip resounded through the rocky mountainside, as did her gentle raised voice. The Naabeehó people who heard her words, giggled politely. The donkeys seemed to know they were hauling their owner's precious commodity of fresh water.

Nínáánníbaa' smiled and giggled as well. She knew the love Asdzą́ą́ Télii Neiniłkaadí had for her donkeys, she had the same love for her sheep and goats as well. She missed the sheep they had adopted at Fort Sumner, but she especially missed her own herd. Her sheep and goats knew her voice just like the donkeys knew their owner's voice. Tears rolled down her face as Nínáánníbaa' thought of her flock of sheep and goats, especially the goat that saved her life with his funny "Hee, hee, hee," sound he made when he bleated.

A fat soldier with a loud booming voice broke the silence, making the people jump. The soldier was giving orders from the tall gray-haired one in which the soldiers were ordered to split up the procession. Only one set of soldiers on horseback, wagons, Naabeehó people, donkeys, followed by soldiers on horseback could make their way down the steep wagon path to avoid falling rocks caused by the horses and wagons.

"Our supplies have to last five days, men! Those are our orders from Lt. Col. Folton, the old guy. Slow down. No one will be following us until we are far enough down the mountain." When they heard the fat soldier's booming voice, the Naabeehó people looked up at the rocks that sat in precarious positions. When he shouted out the orders, the people were afraid the huge pale green rocks would become dislodged and fall down upon them or fall into the sandy tan path before them. The women nervously whispered,

"Yíiyá. Ha'át'íísh biniiyé 'ayóó 'íits'a'go jidilwosh. Doo hanii 'áhojilyą́ą da. Tsé da ła' adah adoolts'ił. Yíiyá." *Scary. Why is he yelling so loudly? He must be crazy. Some rocks might fall down. Scary.* Walking as fast as they safely could, the people looked up to see uniformly shaped rocks stacked upon one another which appeared to have been deliberately stacked. Dzáníbaa' asked her father,

"Kin Yis'áanii dine'é daats'í 'ei tsé dadik'ánígíí t'oo bił danizhónígo dayiiłts'ą́ 'áádóó 'akót'éego nizhónígo 'ałk'idaastł'ingo dayiiłtsą́ągo yinahjį' tsé nizhónígo dadik'ą́ągo 'ádayiilaa 'áádóó 'ałk'ideistł'ingo bighan yee 'ádayiilaa, ya', shizhé'é?" *Is it possible the Pueblo and Hopi people saw these square rocks all stacked neatly upon each other so they created their walls in the same fashion, my father?"* Hashké Yił Naabaah looked at the rocks Dzáníbaa' was pointing to and smiled and remembered her as his little inquisitive child. He said,

"Ákót'éé shį́į́, shiyázhí." *It is possible it is that way, my little one.* Hashké Yił Naabaah wondered if his people were taking the time to notice their surroundings and the wonder of it. They must, he thought when he noticed his people taking deep, deep breaths of the crisp mountain air. He closed his eyes and breathed in the scent of the tall pine trees. He picked up the scent of crushed green plants underfoot that exuded the scent of a newly torn blade of grass. His puckered lips were a natural reaction to his thought of the extremely sour sumac berries that lined the wagon path, but the remembrance of the sweetness of sumac berry soup made his mouth water. Each time a juniper tree's branches whipped the sides of a wagon rumbling by, it released a pungent scent that reminded him of the cultural importance of the tree. He looked at the earth that was still wet in places which brought thirst close to his lips as he licked his lips. The waste of the horses interrupted the deep breaths he and his people were taking as they took extra steps to avoid stepping on the waste.

Hashké Yił Naabaah noticed that when his group, which included one set of soldiers on horseback, horse drawn wagons, Naabeehó people, donkeys, and more soldiers on horseback began its descent, billowy sheer gray clouds dotted the bright blue sky but when they reached flatter terrain, the clouds became a solid mass of gray. When the people slowly rounded a bend in the wagon path, they drew in their breath. Before them, along the side of the path, several square gray houses made of hewn stone dotted the bottom of the gentle sloping landscape below. The houses resembled the homes of the Kin Yis'áanii *Hopi or Pueblo people.*

The Naabeehó people ignored the scene before them and searched the far-away horizon for the peak of Tsoodził *Mount Taylor,* their sacred mountain that demarcated the southern boundary of their beautiful Naabeehó bikéyah *Navajo land*. They peered into the western horizon before they were led farther down into the sloping valley. The filtered sunrays illuminated the mesas and mountains but clouds kept their sacred mountain hidden.

Sighing a deep sigh, the people searched for edible plants, roots, bark, and flowers to feed themselves before they reached the base of the mountain below. The dew that had settled on the sleeping Naabeehó people in the early morning hours, coupled with the cold mountain air, forced the people to rush toward the warm air they knew blanketed the entire valley. The horses pulling the cumbersome wagons over the rough wagon trail strained their muscles to reach the valley floor where the terrain would be sandy and less rocky. The men driving the horse teams pulled on the reins in attempts to slow the pace of the horses' steps.

The old people, the sickly ones, the pregnant women, and little children who were reloaded into the wagons bounced from side to side and up and down. They wished they were walking but they dared not jump out of the moving wagon, so they sat tight, gritting their teeth.

The soldiers warned the people that they would not hesitate to shoot anyone who tried to steal from the homes they would be forced to rush past on their way to the place where the people would be crossing the great Rio Grande River on rickety rafts. There was no need for the soldiers to voice their warning. Men stood in front of their homes holding up long rifles, ready to shoot an intruder, while the women stared from behind doors that were slightly ajar. Children wrapped in their mothers' full skirts for protection peered at the dirty procession of people rushing down the sloping hill.

Nostrils flared when the Naabeehó people caught the scent of roasted chili and heated corn tortillas. With only nanise' daadánígíí *edible plants* in their tummies, Hashké Yił Naabaah knew his people were craving a meal of mutton or rabbit atoo' *stew,* názhneezkaadí *tortillas,* and ałk'íniilgizh *jerky.* To keep his people's minds off of their surrounding activities, he hollered,

"Nida'doh'a'. Ąąhéeshjéé' daniidlį́įdę́ę́' nihééda'ílnii'. Nida'doh'a'. Háni'dii nihada'áłchíní danihiyiin yee hada'ólniih. Hooghandi náníikaigo baadaaní nishłínígíí nihá ní'dooł'ah. T'áá nihí danohsinjį' atoo' dadoołch'ał." *Sing. We have been released from being prisoners of war. Sing. Let your children comfort themselves with your songs. When we get back to our homes, the man to whom I am a son-in-law, will butcher sheep for us. You will be able to lap up all the stew you want.* The people collectively licked their lips in anticipation of the promised meal. Their parched lips crackled under the wetness of their tongues.

The soothing words of Asdzą́ą́ Télii Neiniłkaadí reminded the people they had a supply of water as she spoke to her donkeys. All they needed was for the soldiers to stop long enough for them to drink fresh mountain spring water.

Ignoring their thirst and hunger, the Naabeehó women stared longingly at the thick rug blankets hanging on the crude fence. They pulled their tattered rug blankets tightly around themselves, lowered their heads and placed one brave foot in front of the other.

The wagon path widened. The horses picked up the pace. The tired Naabeehó people smiled at first, then giggled as they listened to Asdzą́ą́ Télii Neiniłkaadí's words. In a gentle tone, she said,

"Txį', náás." *Let's go, forward.* When the donkeys picked up the pace, she said,

"Txį', txį', txį', txį'...," *Let's go, let's go, let's go, let's go...* Her expression of the words "Txį', txį', txį', txį'..." kept up with the donkeys' steps. The donkeys seemed happy to be running on flat sandy ground, but started galloping to keep up with her words. Asdzą́ą́ Télii Neiniłkaadí interrupted their pace when she said,

"T'áá yee' hazhóó'ígo. T'áadoo dah nidaołgeedí. Tó yee' hahalk'ooł." *Take it slow. Don't buck up and down. Water is spilling out.* When the donkeys slowed down, Asdzą́ą́ Télii Neiniłkaadí said,

"Aoo', akót'éego łą́ą." *Yes, that is the right way.* Remembering her own flock of sheep and goats that listened and obeyed her commands caused tears to roll down Nínááníbaa''s cheeks. Hashké Yił Naabaah heard her sniffle. He knew why she was crying. He placed his arm around her waist and drew her close to him and whispered,

"Shiyázhí, hooghandi nániikaigo dibé yázhí dóó tł'ízí yázhí ła' ná shóideesht'eeł. Nilį́į́' nááhódlǫ́ǫ dooleeł. Dibé bighan nitsaaígíí ná nideesh'ááł. Nilį́į́' nihighan binaagóó yíl'áa doo. T'áá nihí daniidzinįį' nínáda'iil'ah doo. T'áá ni nínízinįį' tł'ízí bibe' náníłbishgo nánídlį́įh doo. 'Ałk'íniilgizh ánídeiil'į́įhgo danihist'e' doo..." *My little one, when we arrive back home, I will obtain lambs and kid goats for you. You will have livestock once again. I will build you a large sheep corral. Your sheep and goats will be wandering around our home in great numbers. We will butcher any time we want. We will prepare jerky and preserve it for our meals...* Nínááníbaa' interrupted her husband, saying,

"K'adíhéíí! T'áadoo bééshiyíłníhí. Díí yee' ach'ą́ shi'niiłhxį́, t'áá 'óolyéego shi'niiłhxį́!" *That's enough! Don't remind me of it. I am dying for the taste of mutton. Literally dying!* Still holding her close, Hashké Yił Naabaah whispered,

"Hahaazhbéézh, atságah dóó 'átsą́ą́' tsíídkáá' sit'éego..." *Boiled mutton, the breast meat, and ribs cooked over the coals...* Nínáánibaa' reached under his rug blanket and poked her finger into a hole in her husband's tattered shirt and pinched him.

"K'adí, t'áadoo shich'į' nahoyíłnání." *Stop, don't make it difficult for me.*

"Ayóo! Shisíníts'ih!" *Ow! You pinched me!*

"Áko lá, t'áadoo nihich'iiyą' bitaa' ííńízhíhí. *Alright then, don't name the foods that we eat.*

"Ayóo! 'Ayóo bik'e'ashch'íi'go shisíníts'ih." *Ow! You really pinched me hard.*

"I 'áá ni 'áníť'į. K'adí t'áadoo baa yáníłti'í." *You did it to yourself. Now, stop, don't talk about it.*

"Hágoshįį́, shiyázhí. Doo 'ánáádideesh'niił da." *Okay, my little one. I won't say it again.* Noticing that he hurt Nínáánibaa''s feelings, he softly whispered,

"Shiyázhí, níni' yiił'a'ígíí baa shíni'. Shaa nídiní'aah, t'ááshǫǫdí." *My little one, I am sorry I hurt your feelings. Forgive me, please.*

"Dibé kǫ́ǫ́ hólǫ́ǫgo 'índa 'akót'éego yá'áti'ígíí beełt'é. K'ad éí dooda. Doochohoo'į́įgóó dichin dóó ch'ééh a'didááh bik'ee txi'hooshnííh, txi'dahwii'nííh. *When the sheep are right here then speech like that is acceptable. Not now. I am suffering severely from hunger and fatigue, we are all suffering.* Nínáánibaa' realized her husband was only trying to comfort her. She felt bad about pinching him and chiding him. She leaned her head against his shoulder and whispered,

"I'íí'ą́ągo, hááʼdeiilyį́į'go nisétsʼih yę́ęgi ná deestsʼǫs, áko neezgai yę́ę dínóokʼeeł." *When the sun sets and when we have rested, I will kiss the place where I pinched you and the spot will stop hurting.* Hashké Yił Naabaah took a few high steps in a circle and sang,

"Hííhííya'! Shígaa'!" *Oh wow! How fortunate for me!* In anticipation, he reached and grabbed his skin where he was pinched, and made a face depicting pain and whimpered,

"Ayóo, ayóo, ayóo, ayóo dóʼ neezgai," *Ow, ow, ow, it really hurts.* He looked out of the corner of his eye to see Nínáánibaa''s reaction, but she ignored him. That night, near the river's edge, Nínáánibaa' kept her promise and moved closer to her husband and slid under his thick rug blanket. She gently rolled him on his side, lifted his tattered shirt, and kissed him gently on the spot where she pinched him earlier. With her lips, she felt a welt that had formed on his skin. She felt so bad. She continued kissing him until her lips found his ticklish spot. Hashké Yił Naabaah rolled over and pulled his beautiful Nínáánibaa' close to him. In the dark of night, the two lovers had to ignore their want of each other, hoping the other would not touch the spot that brought them pleasure, but at the same time, wishing the other was bold enough to touch their erotic spot.

Regretting that their children and grandchildren and their people were nearby, Hashké Yił Naabaah kissed his wife's body through her thick rug dress before he smoothed her dress and her hair down and clutched her sensuous body close to him. In a soft, hoarse whisper, he said

"Nibe' yilzhóólígo shiyid béshjéé'." *Your soft breast is pressed against my chest.* Through her husband's soft worn pants, Nínáánībaa' could feel her husband's soft mound become more insistent. She dared not move. She whispered,

"Hooghandi nániit'áazhgo lą́ą. 'Ádee ní'diildįįł. Íłhosh, shiyázhí. Yiską́ągo, t'óó ha'íí'ánígo, nidine'é nihikéyah bich'į' náás dah náádidíí'ish." *When we get home, we will satisfy one another. Go to sleep, my little one. When the sun comes up tomorrow, you will lead your people forward toward our land.* With soft moist lips, Nínáánībaa' deeply and softly kissed her warrior. Her War Leader kissed her back with the strength of a warrior. She fell asleep in his arms. She awoke when she felt his long drawn out breaths softly blow the loose strands of her hair around her face which tickled her face, but she did not move. She wanted her leader to rest.

The moon exited from behind the thick clouds, illuminating their surroundings. Tears moistened her eyes when she thought of how hard she pinched the man who loved her. "He was only trying to cheer me up with the thought of food," she told herself. With tears still in her eyes, she softly whispered,

"Háshinee', shiyázhí. 'Ayóó'áníínísh'ní..." *Dear one, my little one. I love you...* The Milky Way disappeared from the eastern horizon, but its starry pattern still filtered across the western horizon when Nínáánībaa' fell asleep next to her leader, her warrior, her lover.

Chapter Thirteen

Going Home

The chiming of bells was loud when it echoed through the hills. Before them, the people noticed many houses of different shapes. Most were of a sandy color with holes in the walls. They had seen holes in the walls at the fort where they were held prisoners of war. Their breaths quickened. They were afraid they were being led to another fort where they would suffer for another long length of time. This scared them and made their thoughts wander through many frightening scenarios. Many soldiers lined the streets just like they did at Fort Sumner.

Nínááníbaa' could not believe they were entering another angry enemy's land again.

"Hatxíhíláane'ęę́'. Ąąhéeshjéé' ánáádanihidoodlííłjį' adanihineeskaad. Doo lá dó' dooda da! Haash dahwiilyaago? Díí yee' doo bił hadadólchídígóó nihił hoo'a'." *Scary, they have chased us to another place where we will become prisoners of war again. What a terrible happening!*

What did we do to them? We have nothing with which to protect ourselves. Another wave of fear rushed through her thoughts. Her people. Her daughters. Her sons, the warriors. Her husband, her warrior and War Leader. Her grandsons. Her Naashgálí *Mescalero Apache* son-in-law.

As they marched relentlessly forward, closer to the many rows of square houses, the soldiers raised their rifles and aimed at the procession of exhausted Naabeehó people. The soldiers on horseback raised their arms and placed a flattened hand to their forehead and snapped their hands away from their forehead. The soldiers holding the rifles nodded. Behind the soldiers, standing at attention, were many people wearing colorful clothing. Some yelled angry words. Others just stared.

Onward and forward the Naabeehó people plodded along. The sandy street was hot. Nínáánībaa' wondered if her daughters and her adopted children were suffering from the feeling of fire underneath their feet.

Her grandsons walked close to her just like they did over the long dusty trail from Fort Sumner north to Anton Chico, and onward along the hot dusty wagon trail that led them through the canyon the soldiers called Blanco Canyon. They walked on past the White Lakes which had many streams that flowed nearby, which led to the Tijeras Arroyo where the flow of fresh cool water was abundant, and finally on to the beautiful summit of the Sandia Mountain the soldiers referred to as Tijeras Canyon Pass north of the town of Albuquerque.

Now their future was uncertain. Her grandsons were strong just like her sons were when they were young. They never complained. They preferred to sleep near her and their cheii *maternal grandfather.*

****

The soldiers did not stop until they reached the bank of the great Rio Grande River. The sand had cooled enough for the people to sit down to rest. The sun was disappearing behind the tall trees that lined the river bank.

"Tell them we will proceed with the crossing of the river in the early morning." Using the dried wood from the summit that Hashké Yił Naabaah and his warriors gathered, the people built small fires to keep rodents and insects away. Naabeehó men were assigned to watch and keep the fires going all night long.

Faint shadows dressed in black approached the people then scampered away. All night long, the sounds of large forms approached, then scampered away. The soldiers talked loudly and argued throughout the late hours of the night. Soon, silence reigned. Only a lonely soldier approached every so often throughout the night. The women were afraid of the faint figures that came close then disappeared into the night without a word. The people chased the children to the center of the large gathering of Naabeehó people. The women slept near the children and spoke words of comfort to the fearful children. The men slept on the outside of the large circle of people. Nínáánítbaa' heard a man say,

"Ha'át'íí lá? Ha'át'íísh haohkai?" *What is it? What do you want?* A grumpy Naabeehó man said,

"Kojį', t'áadoo kojį' náádadołwo'í!" *Go away, don't come running over here!* The scolding voices kept the people relatively safe throughout the night. The sound of the river flowing nearby kept the people company, reminding them that they still had a dangerous river to cross before they could rush westward toward their land. The Naabeehó men were anxious for the illuminating light of dawn so they could track the footprints nearby to see what clues the mysterious forms left behind.

The Sandia Mountain looming overhead in the east hid the early morning sun. The filtered light from the sun cast light on the activity of the mysterious forms. On the damp earth lay many large baskets laden with thin, nearly see-through tortillas, slabs of meat that were cooked over hot coals, chili peppers, cut squares of fruits the people had never seen before, cooked squash, jugs of water, clothing for the young and old, thin blankets, and flat shoes for women, men, and children of all ages.

The Naabeehó people stared at the food and supplies. They looked at their kind leader and waited while their mouths watered at the sight of food. Hashké Yił Naabaah lifted his arms and yelled out,

"Háíshą' ch'iiyáán yee nihaa dajoozba'? Doolá dó' ahéhee'gi 'ádanihohłaa da! Nihik'i dahojidlíí le'. T'áadoo nihich'į' bił hadadólchídí da. T'áá hazhó'ó nihizaad t'éiyá. Nihe'ajooba' béédeiilniihgo binahjį' danihighandi ninájhidiikah. Ahéhee'." *Who showed us such kindness in providing food for us? You have done a thankful thing for us. May you all be blessed. We have nothing to give you in return, only our words of gratitude. In remembering your act of kindness, we will be able to return to our respective homes. Thank you.* The women helped Nínáánábaa' tear the slabs of meat apart to make sure everyone received a large piece of meat. They were surprised everyone received a piece of meat and a tortilla. Nínáánábaa' said,

"Da'iilwoshgoósh danihi'déelta', áyaaní da, nizhónígo nihininíłna'." *Were we counted while we slept? It seems so, because there was just enough for us.* The people licked their fingers long after they ate their food. The act of kindness was just what they needed to give them courage to cross the wide, swift flowing Rio Grande River on the rickety rafts.

Unexpectedly, a woman moved out from behind a tall bush. She was dressed in the colorful dresses the Naabeehó people had seen when they walked onto the flat terrain at the base of the Sandia Mountain. Other colorfully dressed women stood up. The first woman greeted the Naabeehó people, saying,

"Yá'át'ééh, shidine'é. Háshinee' dó' ádaoht'į. Nihí ch'iiyáán nihich'į' kódeiilyaa. T'óó nihił nihaa dahojoobá'ígo biniinaa ch'iiyáán dóó 'éé' dóó ké nihich'į' kódeiilyaa. Ahíłká'iijée'go ch'iiyáán ádeiilyaa. Nihí Diné bikéyah bits'ą́ą́dóó yisnááh ádanihi'diilyaaígíí 'ádeiit'į. 'Áádóó danihisnáhígíí Naakai dine'é yich'į' nidanihiisnii'. Naalte' daniidlįį nidi t'áá yá'át'éehgo nihaa 'ádahayą́. Shí sha'áłchíní Naakai yádaashchíín. Ádóone'é nishłínígíí 'éí doo bénáshniih da, háálá t'ah áłchíní yázhí nishłįįgo yisnááh áshi'diilyaa. Díí sáanii t'áá Diné danilį́įgo bił ahínéeshkahgo bits'ą́ą́dóó shizaad nínáádiilá. Háláane'ęę' dó' ádaoht'į́. Haleebee 'ádaoht'į́įgo nihikéyah biih nídohkah." *Greetings, my people. Dear ones. We are the ones who placed the food for you. We had so much compassion for you so we brought forth food and clothing and shoes for you. We helped each other in preparing the food. We were kidnapped from Naabeehó land. The ones who kidnapped us sold us to the Mexican people. Although we are slaves, we are being treated well. My children are born for a Mexican. I don't remember my kinship affiliation because I was kidnapped when I was a little child. In getting together with these women who are Navajo, I have been able to speak my language once again. Dear ones. Be persistent in reentering your land.*

Tears ran down the faces of the Naabeehó people. Before they could respond, soldiers from the western side of the river shouted to the soldiers who escorted the people from Fort Sumner. Following the strict orders of the man operating the ferry, the soldiers from both sides of the river helped pull on the ropes that pulled the raft back and forth across the river. The soldiers shouted orders for crossing the Rio Grande River. Quietly, the women and children stepped onto the raft to be ferried across the swift running river.

Before Nínááníbaa' and her daughters and her grandchildren stepped onto the raft, she took time to greet the river.

"Nihí, shí dóó sha'áłchíní doo shitsóóké, Tó 'Aheedlíinii dine'é daniidlį. Nihaa sínízidgo tsé'naa nihił nida'doo'oł. Shidine'é nihikéé' yinéłígií 'ałdó' shá baa sínízid dooleeł. Ádíláah bąąh ádingo, nizhónígo tsé'naa nidii'nééł." *We, my children and my grandchildren and I, belong to the Water Flows Together people. Be careful of us as we cross the river on the raft. Be careful also of my people who are following us. Without any silliness, we will safely cross the river.* With those words bravely spoken to the river, Nínááníbaa' and Hashké Yił Naabaah stepped onto the swaying raft. Her sons stepped on next and helped her daughters and grandchildren board the raft. The family clung onto one another as the raft shifted and swayed toward the western side of the river. Without incident, the family quickly jumped onto the sandy bank and hugged one another, relieved that the great river separated them from the horrors of their status as prisoners of war at Fort Sumner.

Nínááníbaa' turned back toward the river,

"Ahéhee', nizhónígo tsé'naa nihił ni'ní'éél. Shidine'é nihikéédę́ę́' yinéłígií t'áá 'ákót'éego baa jiidííbaał. Éí 'éí baa nánooshkąąh dooleeł. Nihaa dahojoobá'íyee'." *Thank you, we safely crossed the river on the raft. Be just as kind to my people who are following us, I plead with you. We are in a pitiful state.* With those words, she turned her back on the river and walked up the bank and stepped onto dry, rocky, sandy ground. Women and children who followed on another raft stepped onto the western bank and hugged the ones who had already crossed. Tears streamed down their faces.

Hashké Yił Naabaah and his sons and his young Mescalero Apache son-in-law and Kiizhóní walked up the river to where the river ran wide. Down the river, soldiers threw one end of several ropes across the river. With all the ropes in place, the soldiers walked upriver to where the river ran wide while gripping the ropes tightly. They tied the ropes to sturdy poles that stuck out of the ground and ordered the Naabeehó men and boys huddled on the eastern bank to cross the river by holding tightly onto the ropes. Hashké Yił Naabaah and his sons yelled,

"Tł'óół daołtsóód. Yéego bąąh dah shoojée'go tó bii' dahdidohkah. Tł'óół bidadohchííd lágo!" *Grab the rope. Hold on to it tightly and step into the water. Don't let the rope go!* The men obeyed their kind leader. They placed one hand in front of the other and crossed the river by sheer strength. Men and boys half walked and half swam across the river, shaking their heads from side to side once they hopped onto the western bank of the river. Each one greeted the ones who called out encouraging words as they crossed.

When all of Hashké Yił Naabaah's people had crossed, they huddled together in a large circle. Their elder Peace Leader asked the people to make sure all their family members were accounted for.

The people turned back toward the river when they heard Asdzą́ą́ Télii Neiniłkaadí yell out,

"Ádahodoołzééh." *Settle down.* Children watching the excitement pointed toward the river and said,

"Shooh, télii tó nílínígíí tsé'naa bił da'í'eeł!" *Look, the donkeys are being transported across the river!* Asdzą́ą́ Télii Neinilkaadí rode back across the river to load more donkeys onto the rafts while young warriors stayed with the brave donkeys on the west side. The people smiled each time they heard the familiar,

"Ádahodoołzééh," *Settle down,* when it was shouted out by Asdzą́ą́ Télii Neinilkaadí, which calmed the donkeys and calmed the Naabeehó people.

The last order of business was for the soldiers on the eastern side to pay the man who ran the ferry and to hand over to the soldiers on the western side of the river the papers that contained the orders declaring that the Naabeehó people had been freed from their prisoner of war status as of June 1st, 1868. The orders further declared the Navajo people were to be escorted to Fort Fauntleroy and on to Fort Defiance where they were to stay until they received sheep, goats and supplies that were promised in the treaty. From there, they were to be settled in designated areas on the newly assigned Navajo Reservation.

****

Dédii and Dzáníbaa' and their mother grabbed one another and hugged each other with tears of thankfulness and relief streaming down their faces. The people spoke prayers and sang songs quietly as they turned from the Rio Grande River and faced the western horizon with great hope in their hearts. When they heard the word,

"Forward...!" Hashké Yił Naabaah and his elder Peace Leader both shouted out at the same time,

"Tsołtxį', shidine'é, nihikéyah bich'į' dah nídidiikah," *Let's go, my people, we will begin our return to our land.* Dédii and Dzáníbaa' and their mother heard their precious people breathe a collective sigh of relief. The soldiers on horseback set the pace, but the people wanted to walk faster.

Hashké Yił Naabaah and his elder Peace Leader did not trust the soldiers who met them at the Rio Grande River so they decided to take extra precaution to ensure the safety of their people. At night, Naabeehó men were assigned to keep watch as their people rested.

Hashké Yił Naabaah heard Nínáánibaa' and his daughters whispering to one another long into the night. He listened for a few minutes. They still had not told one another about the entire ordeal each one went through after the kidnapping. Worried they would not get enough rest, he quietly said,

"Sha'áłchíní, yiską́ągo 'ahił nináádahołne' doo. K'ad éí da'awosh." *My children, you can visit tomorrow. Now it's time to sleep.* He was sorry he mentioned it. His Nínáánibaa' hissed,

"Díí yee' bii' tádiikaiígíí bee 'ahił nidahwiilne'go 'éí hane'ígíí nihitsii'áał ánídeiil'įįh." *The stories we are telling one another are about what we went through. We make those stories our pillows.* Hashké Yił Naabaah had been worried about his Nínáánibaa', but now he fully realized her power, her health, her stamina were bound to the presence of her children and grandchildren.

For several days, the soldiers pushed the people forward, covering fifteen miles a day to avoid any raiding by their "captives" among the Pueblo Indian communities that dotted the hills and valleys along their path. Dédii and Dzáníbaa' pointed at the Pueblo people peeking out from behind the rocks on either side of the valley through which they marched. They hoped these people were friendly in spite of their father saying "nihe'anaa'í nihąąh nidaa'na'," *our enemies are spying on us.* All the Naabeehó people had for protection were the soldiers from Fort Fauntleroy and their Naabeehó warriors. However, they were well aware their Naabeehó warriors were forbidden to protect themselves and their families. The people did not know the soldiers were afraid for their own lives, afraid they could be overpowered by the Navajo warriors. Further, the soldiers were afraid the warriors would disappear into the rocky mesas and valleys and once again become a menace in this area.

The Naabeehó people were not concerned about their anaa'í *enemy* who lived in square houses like the Kin Yis'áanii dine'é *Hopi people.* They were looking toward the western horizon hoping to catch a glimpse of Tsoodził *Mount Taylor,* their sacred mountain of the south. Each Naabeehó person wanted to be the first one to set eyes on the mountain. At first, only the very peak of a mountain could be seen. Rounding high, red-colored stone mesas, the people saw a mountain stretching wide at its base, then sloping and rising high into the sky, pulling the clouds down around its pointed peak. The elder Peace Leader wondered,

"Da' eísh Tsoodził át'é? K'os bich'ą́ąh shizhóód. Doo la' t'áá'át'é yit'į́į da." *Is that Mount Taylor? The large clouds are in front of it. The whole mountain cannot be seen.* Looking at the mountain, he continued,

"Shą́ą' tsé daalzhingo dah dadeeshzhahgo binánaazkaad łeh. Tsé doodagóó dadeenıı́í lá ne'. Aadę́ę' nihidi'noolkałgo tsé bikáá' neejée' ne'. Nihidine'é t'óó baa dahojoobá'ígo tsé yikáá' nidahidil'ées ne'. Tsé dah dadeeshzhahígíí nihidine'é dabikee' ałtsoh nidayiishgizh lá ne'. Biléisiikaigo dahakee' łeezh dił bee daditłée'go dahakétł'ááhdę́ę' ninákǫs lá ni'. T'áá 'ákót'ée nidi náás nihidi'noolkał. Shidine'é t'áadoo bich'į' bił hadóshchídíígíí biniinaa doochohoo'į́įgóó bik'ee txi'hwiisénii'." *Remember the large field of protruding black lava rocks that cover the area. The rocks are very sharp. When we were being chased through here, we camped on the rocks. When our poor people stepped on the rocks, the protruding rocks cut our people's feet. When we passed the rocky terrain, the blood and sand mixed and created a hard shell on the sole of the people's feet. In spite of that, we were chased forward. I suffered because I could not provide anything for my people.*

Fast moving clouds attached themselves to the dark clouds that hid Mount Taylor from view. Light filmy clouds settled on top of the dark clouds, further hiding the sacred mountain. Desperate to draw strength from their mountain, the people felt as if the environment had betrayed them. To further tease them, the wind changed the shapes of the clouds to reveal a part of the mountain, then hide it to expose it in another area.

No one spoke as they walked through the petrified lava fields. The only sounds they heard were the squeaking of the wagon wheels, the thump when a wagon wheel hit a hole in the path, the sound of horses stepping on the rocks, the sound of the hem of a calico skirt tearing, the sound of moccasins stepping on the rocks, and the sloshing of water as the donkeys carried the full bags of cool water, the sound of the donkeys breathing hard, and Asdzą́ą́ Télii Neiniłkaadí urging her donkeys forward.

Miniature drops of rain falling on the long procession made it difficult for the people to walk on the uneven rocky path but the sun drifting down toward the western horizon and the clouds that made interesting shapes, pulled the people forward. The dark menacing clouds behind them chased them forward. The people had nearly walked past Mount Taylor without realizing it!

The elder Peace Leader asked his people to focus on the billowy clouds that changed colors with the movement of the sun.

"K'os danółʼį́. Níléí wót'áahdi naanáaldohígíí doo hózhǫ́ łahgo 'ánáá'níił da. Nidi biyaadi k'os naanáájahígíí háíshį́į́ na'ach'ąąh nahalingo k'os łahgo 'ałʼąą 'ánáá'níił. Éí danółʼį́. 'Aají gah léi' dah nahat'e' nahalin. Níléíjí 'éí dibé yázhí ła' yilwoł nahalin." *Look at the clouds. The clouds that are moving high overhead do not change much. But the clouds that move around underneath change shapes as if a person is painting a picture. Look at those. Over there is a rabbit that looks like it is jumping up and down. Over there, it looks like a little lamb is running.* Once he pointed out the shapes, the children became excited about the shapes they found in the clouds. Their parents joined in on the excitement.

The soldiers hurried the Naabeehó people through the dry lava valley. In different areas across the valley, the people saw miniature stalks of corn that had been planted in neat rows. Hashké Yił Naabaah looked longingly at the fertile fields. He yearned to plant in his own dá'ák'eh *cornfield.* He looked for the houses of the people who had planted the corn but the filtered light hid the homes from view.

The Naabeehó people sniffed the air. There was the absence of the scent of níłtsą *rain.* Hashké Yił Naabaah listened to Nahat'á Yinaabaah, his oldest son, and Kiizhóní talking when one of them said,

"Níłtsą halchinée t'óó bił yóó 'íiyol," *The scent of rain has been blown away by the wind.* Hashké Yił Naabaah looked back and saw that the clouds had been lifted off of their sacred mountain. The setting sun illuminated their beautiful mountain as their mountain rose high into the air. Hashké Yił Naabaah heard the gasps of his people when the elder Peace Leader announced,

"K'asídąą' la' Tsoodził biléisiikai. Doo lá dó' dooda da! *We almost walked right past Mount Taylor. What a terrible happening!*

A low moan rose from the front of the procession and rolled toward the back of the procession as each individual turned around and looked at their majestic sacred mountain of the south. In one sweep, Hashké Yił

Naabaah grabbed Nínááníbaa' and each of his children and hugged them so hard the air was being crushed out of their chests. A loud rumbling moan began in their father's abdomen, rose into his chest, through his throat, and out of his mouth it came in a high-pitched cry. Kiizhóní pressed into the crying group. The young Mescalero Apache man held his son and his nephews back to prevent them from being crushed.

Dédii hugged her father tightly. She was shocked at how thin he was. She could feel his rib cage protruding from his thin frame. All the pent-up tears began as dry sobs, then exited out of her body as a loud wail. Dzáníbaa' hugged their mother to stabilize her. Her mother's old tattered rug dress did not hide her mother's severely undernourished body. Dzáníbaa' had not looked at her mother's hair up close, but looking down at her mother's hair, she noticed the bright shine had left her mother's dark graying hair. The strands of hair were uneven and thin. She became so very sad when she admitted her mother had aged in the years since she and her sister were kidnapped from their home.

When their father released his tight hold on his family, Nínááníbaa' became aware of her surroundings. Their Naabeehó people had fallen to the ground and were crying as sobs shook their shoulders uncontrollably. Their eerie cries of relief echoed off of the mountain and the mesas and hills nearby. Cries of,

"Nihikéyah!" *Our land!*

"Nihikéyah!" *Our land!*

"Aháláanee'ee', nihikéyah!" *Dear one, our land!*

"Nihikáa'jį' hazlį́į́'!" *We have been spared!*

"Nihikéyah biih néiikai!" *We have reentered our land!* Cries rose from the huddled groups on the valley floor.

Aware that many Pueblo Indians lived in the area, the soldiers fired their rifles into the air to force the Navajo people forward.

"We cannot allow these savages to raid, kill, or kidnap anyone! It's our orders!" a soldier shouted above the cries of the Naabeehó people. More rifle shots were fired into the air to push the people forward. In vain, the soldiers tried pushing the people forward. The Naabeehó people couldn't move. They kept turning around to look at their mountain.

Dédii and Dzáníbaa' told their mother how seeing their sacred mountain of the south comforted them. The setting sun's golden rays illuminated the gold colored peak of the mountain. Soon the sun cast a dark orange glow on the mountain which later turned to a magenta color and then slowly disappeared into the landscape. The people cried for their mountain when they reluctantly turned westward and started their walk away from their mountain.

The soldiers did not realize that when they were yelling at the people and shooting their rifles, several Navajo men turned back and disappeared into their mountain to collect and gather its healing and restorative bounties.

Nínááníbaa' and Dédii and Dzáníbaa' and the children were placed in the care of the young Mescalero Apache man. Although rations were handed out,

Nínáánībaa' and her daughters did not allow the young Mescalero Apache man to obtain their regular ration of rotten meat. Water dipped from the water bags the donkeys hauled was what sustained Nínáánībaa' and her family.

The Naabeehó people were ready to leave even before the sun rose in the east. Nínáánībaa' was ashamed she had slept through her people's sounds of preparation. She noticed a small fire burned and small pieces of meat were cooking on the hot coals. Her son-in-law had hunted and killed several rabbits for his family and was cooking. Everyone had a substantial taste of the delicate meat. Dzáníbaa''s face gleamed at her husband for providing for her large family. Nínáánībaa' was thankful for their early meal. It sustained them through the twenty miles they were forced to walk.

Even more elderly and sick Naabeehó people were placed in the wagons. The old man Dédii called "Shicheii" finally agreed to a bumpy ride in a wagon. Hashké Yił Naabaah and his sons were gone for another night. On the third night, after the people could not imagine they could walk past the twenty miles they had walked, Hashké Yił Naabaah and his warriors returned, laden with berries, medicinal herbs, sumac branches, wild carrots, flowers, yucca roots and more bounties from their sacred mountain. Hashké Yił Naabaah even brought short branches from pinion trees, pine trees, oak trees, and juniper trees so his Nínáánībaa' could be reminded of the scent of their mountain home on Dziłíjiin *Black Mesa.*

He handed her fat yucca fruit to eat and yucca root with which to wash her hair.

"Díí yee' dzidze' dóó neeshch'íí' dóó hosh bineest'ą' dóó ch'ééh jiyáán dóó naayízí dóó naadą́ą́' łeeh shibézhígíí dóó ch'il ahwéhé dóó k'íneeshbízhii dóó bááh dootł'izhí dóó taa'niil dóó tł'ízí bibe' shibéezhígíí baa neiseeł nít'ę́ę́'. Bee náníichaad gi'át'é." *I was dreaming about juniper berries, pinon nuts, cactus fruit, melons, squash, corn roasted in the ground, Navajo tea, blue ground corn dumplings, blue corn, blue corn mush, boiled goat's milk and such things. I think I got full dreaming about them.* Hashké Yił Naabaah hugged his Nínááníbaa' and whispered,

"Háshinee', shiyázhí, k'asídą́ą́' dichin aníiłna'. Hooghandi nániikaigo 'áda'azįįd ádá 'ádadiilníił." *Dear one, my little one, hunger almost swallowed you up. When we get home, we will make a feast for ourselves.* Nínááníbaa' snuggled up close to her husband, her warrior and fell asleep again to dream about their feast on Dziłíjiin *Black Mesa.*

In the morning, Hashké Yił Naabaah announced,

"Aají, honí'ąąjí, nihe'anaa'í bitsį' daalgaígíí bił haz'ą́. 'Áadi danihi'dótą'go díkwíí jį́ shįį́ 'azlį́į'. Áko̜o̜ daats'í nihidi'noolkał?" *Over there, over the hill is where our enemies with white skin are. We were held there for several days. Maybe that (Fort Fauntleroy) is where we are being chased once again?* At his announcement, the people became afraid and extremely sad. Worried looks crossed their faces.

"T'áadoo nídaołdzidí. Díí yee' t'áá nihí nihikéyah bich'į' nihi'ílnii'. T'áadoo nídaołdzidí. Dziłíjiindi, danihighandi ninähidiikah. Hada'íínółní, shidine'é. Hada'íínółní." *Don't be afraid. We have been released to return to our own land. Don't be afraid. We will go back to our homes at Black Mesa. Have hope, my people. Have hope.*

****

The next day, Hashké Yił Naabaah and his people were forced to walk to Fort Defiance, near the home of their great War Leader, Hastiin Ch'il Haajiní *Manuelito*. Dédii gasped when she saw the fort. She turned away from the scene before her and hid her face in her hands. She was surprised. She remembered the houses were very large, but comparing them to the houses at Fort Sumner, the houses were small in size. She frantically looked in different directions. Tears filled her eyes. Her thoughts were confused. Her little house with the lock on the outside of the door was no longer standing. The house where the tall gray-haired one lived was also falling down. The roof had holes in it. The large square houses made of tall pine logs were crumbling. The windows were cracked. The road to the fort was overgrown with weeds and was narrow, whereas she remembered a wide dirt road on which the wagons traveled to and from the fort. The road her Naabeehó people were forced to walk on as they were forced to walk eastward to Fort Sumner was flat and wide. She gripped her chest and whispered,

"Haash hóót'įįd, kodi? Kin naaznil yę́ę t'óó 'ahiih nídadiłdaas. T'óó la' hook'eego haz'ą́." *What happened here? The square houses that were here are falling apart. It is deserted.* A whirlwind answered her with a howl as it spun past her, picking up leaves in its path and tossing them into the air, then dropping them as it hurriedly spun toward the square houses. The scene before her stirred the love she carried for the tall gray-haired one. Tears spilled out of her eyes. She looked up to the high ridge where the tall gray-haired one took her and kissed her on her lips. She shook her head slightly when she remembered she thought he was hungry and that was why he was kissing her on her lips. Her heart was hurting. With deep, deep sadness, she told herself, "I am no longer in love with him. I am in love with his memory but his memory will not love me back." Trying to rid her mind of his memory, she did her little dance by stomping her feet on the ground.

Her family gathered around her and held her tight. Her mother softly said,

"Nichxǫ', t'áadoo baa nitsíníkeesí." *Don't. Don't think about it.* Dédii wondered whether her mother said, "*Don't think about it" or "Don't think about him?* She stepped away from her family to look at the scene before her again. Sadness filled her heart. "I took great care and cherished my love for him all those years, even after he abandoned me and our child. When I really needed him, when my people really needed him, he abandoned us once again." Her shoulders were shaking from the pain she felt in her heart.

She felt someone at her side. She heard the words,

"Shimá..." *My mother...* A little hand slipped into hers and she held it tight. She looked down to look into the eyes of her son, her little one. Bravely, she told him,

"T'ahdoo ni'dichííhdą́ą́' kwe'é shi'dótą'go díkwííshį́į́ nídeezid. Kwe'é nizhé'é bił ahééhosisząįd." *Before you were born, I was held here for several months. I came to know your father here.* Her son did not ask questions about his father.

Dédii felt someone breathe into her hair. Chills ran down her spine. She quickly turned around to find Kiizhóní standing directly behind her. She sighed deeply. She did not know he stepped forward when he heard her tell her son about meeting his father. Her son placed his other hand in the hand of Kiizhóní. She noticed Kiizhóní held her son's hand tightly. Without a word, she felt Kiizhóní place his arm around her and hold her close. She shook in his embrace. He pulled her even closer. Her family gathered around her once again and her father gently turned her away from the fort and led her away.

Many Naabeehó people were already camped near the fort. Rations were handed out again but the people sulked at the provisions. Thinking of his daughter Dédii, Hashké Yił Naabaah announced,

"Díí yee' dooda. Dabich'iiyą' dííłdzidígíí yee danihidooghą́ą́ł t'éí biniiyé kojį' adanihineeskaad. Nihidine'é da'níłts'ą́ą́'dę́ę́' ch'ídabidi'neeskaad yę́ę, jó kojį' da 'adabidi'noolkaad. Dabikéyahgóó ch'ééh nídabí'ni'. Ádin, t'áadoo baa na'ódza'í da, kodi. T'óó hooghangóó néii'nééłjí nihá yá'át'ééh. T'áá nihí 'ádá há'ádeiit'įįgo t'éí nihá yá'át'ééh. T'óó ch'iiyáán nihich'į' ch'éédít'áahjí bídaneeldin. Dooda łąą! T'áá nihí nihikéyahgóó dah nídiikaijí nihá yá'át'ééh. Da'iighaazhgo hooghangóó yóó 'adadíníit'įįł. Díítł'éé', dah didii'nééł. Dziłíjiingóó nídii'nééł. Hasht'e' áda'díínółzin doo." *This is not right. They just want to kill us with their rotten food and that is the reason they forced us to walk here. Our people who were chased out of their home areas have been forced to walk here. They want to return to their homes. There is nothing useful to do here. It is best for us to return to our homes. It is best that we take care of ourselves and not depend on others. We have become used to having food given to us. Absolutely not! It is best that we leave to go back to our own home. We will secretly leave from here when everyone falls asleep. Tonight, we will leave. We will leave for Black Mesa. Be ready.*

As promised, Hashké Yił Naabaah and his people left Fort Defiance without a sound and without being noticed. They walked up the steep slope behind the fort. Dédii was relieved they had not left when the sun was still up. She knew they would be traveling past the beautiful place where the tall gray-haired one declared his love for her in his soft but demanding kiss.

She wondered what she would do if Kiizhóní kissed her. "Would she keep her eyes open when he kissed her? Would her eyes be crossed again? Would he laugh or would he gently tell her to close her eyes?" she wondered.

"Dooda, t'áá néshch'il dooleeł. Doo she'anaa'í nilį́į da." *No, I will close my eyes. He is not my enemy,* she whispered.

Hashké Yił Naabaah and his people split up according to the home areas they claimed and lived within before they were forced to walk to Fort Sumner. They would travel much faster and be able to hide small groups of people.

Not knowing they had walked past the boundaries of the Reservation outlined in the treaty their leaders signed, Hashké Yił Naabaah and Nínááníbaa' spoke only of the promise their land on Dziłíjiin *Black Me*sa held as they pressed onward.

Every day, they searched the horizon for their sacred mountain of the west, the great Dook'o'oosłííd *San Francisco Peaks*. They were desperate to see their mountain. On their journey, it rained nearly every afternoon. Clouds covered the southwestern horizon, hiding their mountain. Their father told them their mountain of the west always had a hat made of clouds which did not hide the entire mountain.

Traveling only in the early morning hours and after sunset, Hashké Yił Naabaah and his family arrived after dark at their summer home on Dziłíjiin *Black Mesa.* The people breathed deeply, once, once again, and again. The air was inviting, exciting, strong, powerful! Hashké Yił Naabaah announced,

"Nihighandi nániikai!" *We have come back to our home!* They plopped their bundles down and fell down upon them and rested. Sleep placed its restful blanket over their exhausted bodies.

****

The light of the eastern sun rays bursting forth dimly illuminated their home area. Hashké Yił Naabaah and his warriors noticed many tracks crisscrossing their home area. They saw bear tracks, wildcat tracks, horse tracks, small rodent tracks, sheep and goat tracks, and so many more animal tracks. They wondered where the animals came from and where they went. The men hastily made weapons to protect themselves and others.

Their forked stick hogans had been destroyed. The logs that once made the walls of their home lay scattered near the spot where the homes once sat. Nínáánííbaa' pointed and shouted,

"Shooh!" *Look!* Everyone turned to look. The sheep corral was still intact but needed repair. With no sheep or goats, Hashké Yił Naabaah decided to place their efforts into building a new hogan. Nínáánííbaa' was elated that her sheep corral remained intact because it meant her daughter's umbilical cords were still buried near the corral.

Hashké Yił Naabaah was joined by his sons when he left Nínáánííbaa''s side to see if their táchééh *sweat hogan* was still standing. Happily, he reported,

"Nihitáchééh t'áá si'ánéegi 'át'éego si'ą́. T'áadoo táádayooshchxǫ' da." *Our sweat hogan is still standing just the way it was. They did not dismantle it.* He looked up at the sky and said,

"Ahéhee'. Ahéhee', nihik'idíní'įį́'go kodi, nihighandi náníikai. 'Ahéhee', shiTaa'." *Thank you. Thank you, we returned to our home because You watched over us. Thank you, my Spiritual Father.* Once his prayer of gratitude was spoken, Hashké Yił Naabaah walked around the sweat hogan. Yes, his sons' umbilical cords were still buried. The spot was left untouched.

Hashké Yił Naabaah felt an extreme urgency to build sturdy homes to provide protection from predators for his family. To protect themselves from wild animals, the women and children slept on the roof of the chaha'oh *brush arbor* and the men slept on make-shift benches they made. Without going too far, the men collected construction materials they needed to build the hogans for Nínáánībaa' and her daughters and grandchildren.

One cloudless morning, Nínáánībaa' rose early to greet the dawn. She turned toward the southwestern direction to look for their mountain. For the first time since their return, she saw the faint outline of their beautiful Dook'o'oosłííd *San Francisco Peaks.*

Weak and tired, Nínáánībaa' felt her body shaking as she heard a loud, mournful wail leave her body as she shed pent up tears. Even when her people cried at the sight of Mount Taylor, she did not shed tears because she had not yet returned home.

Hashké Yił Naabaah and his children jumped up from the place where they slept. In haste, they ran to the large rock where their mother stood. Hashké Yił Naabaah grabbed his beautiful Nínáánībaa' to keep her from falling and held her close. All she could say was,

"Shooh..." *Look...* Following her gaze, her family saw their sacred mountain of the west, the great Dook'o'oosłííd.

Once again, the family crushed one another with hugs and cried tears of relief. The hot bitter tears they shed were cooled down by the realization that they were home. They had survived four horrifying years at Fort Sumner and now they were home! Their beautiful mountain of the west, the great Dook'o'oosłííd *San Francisco Peaks* was testimony of their return.

Chapter Fourteen

This Is Not Your Home!

After the long cold winter, two men, one a short messenger and the other a tall Naabeehó guide, both on horseback came to their homes. Hashké Yił Naabaah was told by the messenger all Navajo families were ordered to report to Fort Defiance.

"Danihiyéél t'áá nihídaastł'ǫǫgo 'áadi nihidoohkah. T'áadoo 'ádaohdzaagóogo 'éí danihighan nihits'ą́ą́' ałtáádadii'nił," *Come there with your belongings. If you don't obey, your homes will be dismantled,* the messenger demanded. Hashké Yił Naabaah asked,

"Ha'át'íí lá biniiyé? T'áadoo nidó' k'é nihidooniidgóó nahjį', nihidohní." *What for? You did not even greet us first before you told us to leave.*

Fear gripped Nínáánібaa"s heart. Fort Defiance was where her daughter Dédii was taken when the Utes kidnapped her and where she was sold to the tall gray-haired one five years earlier! Dédii clutched her heart. "The fort was a terrible place, it represented pain and suffering just like Fort Sumner," she thought. She begged,

"Dooda, shizhé'é, dooda. Dooda bidiní. Shí doo 'ákǫ́ǫ́ náshí'ni' da!" *No, my father, no. Tell them no. I do not want to go back there!* Upset that their lives were to be uprooted again, Dzáníbaa' stubbornly said,

"Shí dó', doo 'ákǫ́ǫ́ shíni' da! T'áá yee' kwe'é danihighan." *Me too, I do not want to go there! This is where we live.* Ignoring the words of the two daughters, the messenger demanded,

"T'áá k'ad ádaoht'įįgo t'éiyá. T'áadoo nida'áhodoołziidí. Tséhootsoįį' anídohkah. Doo 'éí t'áá nihí t'éiyá nihaa hootah niit'áazh da. Diné kǫ́ǫ́ nihinaagóó kéédahat'ínígíí 'ałdó' baa niit'áazhgo bee bił nahosiilne'." *Start now. Don't take your time. Get back to Fort Defiance. You are not the only ones we have visited. We have gone to see the people who live around you and have told them.* Nínáánibaa' asked,

"Ha'át'íísh biniiyé nihikéyah bits'ąąjį' dah didiikah?" *Why should we walk away from our land?* The messenger interrupted her and shouted,

"Díí doo nihí nihikéyahgóó bikáá' dahosohbį' dóó hooghan nidanoonilgo bii' kéédahoht'į́. Doo 'ákódadohníił da nít'ę́ę́'!" *This is not your land, and yet you cleared it and placed your hogans on it and now live in them. You should not have done that!* Hashké Yił Naabaah boldly asked,

"Da' díísh ninikéyah nít'ę́ę́'go baa saad hosíníłį́į́'?" *Is this your land and that is the reason you are making a fuss about it?*

"Nidaga'," *No,* the messenger answered.

"Díí yee' ánii naasháhęęʼdąąʼ kojįʼ shá ʼíʼdéékidgo binahjįʼ kojįʼ íiyá. ʼAsdzání shaa ʼáhályąągo k'ad naadiin dóó yówohjįʼ náhááh. Hó dóó shí, ʼákwíí náhááh ʼahísiilkéego. Nihaʼáłchíní ʼéí dį́įʼ. Daneeyą. Nihitsóóké dóʼ hólǫ. Doo t'áá ʼáníídídąąʼ kweʼé nihighango hahoolzhiizh da. Díí ʼasdzání, shaʼáłchíní bimá, t'áá kweʼé biyaa hooʼaʼ. Díí yee' kéyah nihaa ʼáhályąągo biniinaa nihí dóʼ kéyah baa ʼádahwiilyą." *When I was young, I asked to become a husband to her and that is the reason I came to live here. My wife has taken care of me for over twenty years. We have been married for that many years. We have four children. They are all grown. We also have grandchildren. It was not just a short time ago that we declared this area our home. This woman, the mother of my children, was raised here as well. This land takes care of us, and that is the reason we take care of this land.* Pointing to Nínááníbaa', Hashké Yił Naabaah continued, "T'áá kweʼé biʼdizhchį. Doo t'áá ʼáníídígo kojįʼ ninii'nááníígíí ʼádaniit'ée da. Doo ʼéí nihí nihikéyah dadii'níigo baa daniichįʼ da ʼałdóʼ." *She was also born here. We did not arrive here a short time ago and declare this land as ours. We do not claim the land as belonging to us and we are not stingy with our land.*

Although the messenger attempted many times to interrupt her, Nínááníbaa' explained their ties to the land, stating,

"Aají dibé bighan siʼą. ʼÁkweʼé ch'éʼátiingi shaʼáłchíní, shich'éʼéké, bits'ééʼ łeeh sinil." *Over here is the sheep corral. There, at the entrance, is where my daughters' umbilical cords are buried.* Pointing to the nearby hill, she continued, "Aají 'éí táchééh si'ą́. 'Áájí dó' she'ashiiké, shiyáázhké, bits'éé' łeeh sinil. Díí kéyahígíí doo yits'ą́ą́' dah didookah da hwiindzingo. Jó nít'ę́ę́' nihe'anaa'í bitsį' daalgaiígíí kéyah baa 'ádahwiilyánée yits'á danihineeshchą́ą́', dadínii'nééł biniiyé. K'asídą́ą́' shį́į́ t'áá'ániit'é nidanihistseed. Iiná doo bił danilį́į da lá." *Over there is the sweat hogan. It is there, that my sons' umbilical cords are buried. We did that so they would not wander away from this land. But our enemy with white skin chased us off of the land that we cared for, just to kill us. They almost killed all of us. They do not value life.* Nínááníbaa' wiped her tears away and continued, "Nihéé'ílnii'go kojį' anéiikai, yá'át'ééh nídadiidleeł hwiinidzingo. Jó nít'ę́ę́' nihí, nihe'anaa'í nahalingo, nihikéyah yę́ę bits'ą́ąjį' kónihoł'į́. Da' t'áadoósh hózhǫ́ yéego txi'dahwiisii'nii' da nohsingo biniinaa, nahjį' dohníigo nihidááhdóó soozį́?" *When we were released, we came back here to heal, to get well again. But, like our enemy, you are pushing us away from our land. Is it because you think we did not suffer enough, and that is the reason you both stand before us and say, 'Get off of this land'?* Hashké Yił Naabaah could not believe his beautiful Nínááníbaa''s resolve. She was not afraid. He was impressed with her warrior attitude.

In a lowered voice, the messenger responded,

"Díí doo nihí nihikéyah át'ée da, 'azhą́ 'ákót'ée nidi hooghan nidanoonil dóó bii' kéédahoht'į́. Doo 'ákódadohníił da nít'ę́ę́'. Shą́ą́' naaltsoos bee 'ałgha'diit'aah hadilyaa yę́ędą́ą́', kéyah nihá haadzoh. Nihinaat'áanii naaltsoos

yidadeeshchid. Éí shįį́ béédaołniih?" *It's not even your land and you cleared it and built homes on it and live in the homes. You should not have done that! You remember, land was set aside for us, it was done when the negotiated paper (treaty) was drawn up. Our leaders touched the paper in agreement. You probably remember that.*
The men pulled out a crumpled paper that showed a map of the Reservation that was set aside for the Naabeehó people. The messenger showed Hashké Yił Naabaah the map. He pointed to a little square on the paper. Pointing to another place on the map, he said,

"Níléí kojí, doo deeghánídi kéédahoht'į́. Kojí, nihá hahoodzoh yę́ę doo deeghánídi biléihsohkai." *Way over here is where you live. You went past the boundary that was drawn.*

Dédii wondered, "Was it the tall gray-haired one who wanted her back?" Dzáníbaa' cried out in fear.

"Dooda, shizhé'é, shí dóó Dédii yee' hojoobá'ígo, kodi nihighan nít'ę́'ę́ędi náníit'áázh." *No, my father, Dédii and I just came back here where we used to live.* Dzáníbaa' and her sister could see the look of fear in their mother's eyes as well. Frantically, they searched Hashké Yił Naabaah's face for understanding. With sadness in his voice, he responded,

"Doo 'ak'eh dahoniil'įįgóó 'éí kéyah ha'a'aahjí yaa nídahalnih yę́ęgóó nihá 'adadidoolnih. Halgai Hóteel hoolyéégóó, nihe'anaa'í łą́ągo kéédahat'ínígóó nihił áda'doolííł. *If we do not obey, they may send us to the land in the eastern direction they used to tell us about.*

They may send us to the place they call Large Prairielands (Indian Territory), to the place where many of our enemies live

"Aoo', aoo', t'áá'aaníígóó háínídzíí', shínaaí," *Yes, yes, you have spoken the truth, my older brother,* the messenger said. With sarcasm, Hashké Yił Naabaah responded,

"Índa la' nihik'éí sínílį́į́'. Háida baa jigháahgo lá 'áłtsé 'ádóone'é 'ídlį́įgi baa ch'íhoji'ááh. Bá naołnishígíí, bitsį' daalgaiígíí nahalingo k'éhígíí doo nihił nilį́į da. T'áadoo hodiwoshígóó 'ałdó'. Nihe'anaa'í shį́į́ nihizadadíízhéé' áyaaní da t'áá 'éí k'ehgo nihich'į' dołwosh. T'áá nihígi 'át'éego hojooba' daniidzingo kojį' anéiikai. Doo ts'íí'át'éégóó txi'dahwiisii'nii'. Danihíni' yéigo shaazh daazlį́į́'. Nihí shį́į́ t'áadoo 'ákǫ́ǫ́ 'atah nanihidi'neeskaad da, áyaaní da, nihe'anaa'í yádaałti' k'ehgo nihich'į' dołwosh. Doo Naabeehó dine'é nohłį́į da lá', háálá t'áá nihí nihidine'é doo nihił nilį́į da." *You have finally claimed you have relatives. When you go to visit someone, the first thing you do is tell about your kinship affiliation. You don't respect kinship just like the ones you work for, the ones with white skin. There is also no need to yell. Our enemies must have spit into your mouths, you speak to us in the same manner they spoke to us. Just like you, we have come back here looking for kindness. We have suffered extremely. Our minds have been greatly bruised. You probably were never chased there (to Fort Sumner) because you yell at us the way our enemies yelled at us. You are not Navajo people because you do not respect your own Navajo people.*

"Tséhootsohjį' oonáago 'éí ch'iiyáán dóó dibé t'áałá'ígo dóó tł'ízí t'áałá'ígo dóó dá'ák'ehgi bee na'anishí bee danihik'ihojidlíi dooleeł, jiní. 'Éí naaltsoos hadilyaa yę́ę bikáá' yisdzohgo biniinaa 'ákót'éego yee hadahaasdzíí'. Áádóó 'ałdó', shooh, doodį́łígíí doo 'éí t'áá nihí háda'dołts'i' da doo. Kǫ́ǫ́ 'éí doo sohodoobéézhgóó naanish biih noodee'. Áadi 'éí t'áá 'íłdingo haz'ą́," *When you move back to Fort Defiance, you will receive one sheep and one goat and you will also be blessed with tools with which to work in your cornfields, it is said. It is written in the treaty, that is the reason they have declared that. And also you will no longer have to work at providing food for yourselves. Here, you have fallen into work that is very difficult in order to provide for yourselves. There (at Fort Defiance, formerly known as Fort Canby), you will be provided with everything you need,* the messenger replied.

Hashké Yił Naabaah looked into the hills and said,

"Aadę́ę́' nihinaabaahii nídeiyíkááh. Nihik'iidoojah dóó Kin Yis'áanii dine'é bikéyahdi nihida'doołnih. Doo ts'íí'ádaat'ée da. Nílááh, yówohjį'. T'áadoo shidine'é bich'į' nahwiiyoołnání." *Our warriors are coming back. They will fight with you and leave you in the land of the Hopi people. They are treacherous warriors. Go on, go. Don't make it difficult for my people.*

Hashké Yił Naabaah visited all the families under his leadership and told them to get their belongings together so they could go as one group to Fort Defiance. Within eight days, Hashké Yił Naabaah and his people left the homes they worked hard to rebuild and walked toward the eastern direction.

Dédii and Dzáníbaa' walked over the hill toward their former home and walked on past. They both shuddered when they saw the place where they had been kidnapped and when they saw the arroyo where their enemy had run with them. The two sisters talked about the kindness of their father who decided they would begin their new lives in an area where his two daughters would not have to be reminded of their horrible kidnapping. The high hill near their current home hid the entire valley where their ordeal began. Hashké Yił Naabaah glanced at his daughters and announced,

"Kodi nídiikahgo 'át'é, sha'áłchíní. Kǫ́ǫ́ yee' danihighan. Díí kéyah nihaa nídoot'áałgo 'át'é. 'Azhą́ shį́į́ nihidá'ák'eh bii' k'ida'sidiilya' nidi, nizhónígo da'neest'ą́ągo kodi nídiikah. Eí biná nihimá binoo' áyiilaayę́ę hayiiznil. Éí shį́į́ bikiin áadi nahísíitą́ą dooleeł. Díízhíní shį́į́ tsídii dóó naaldlooshii yázhí dá'ák'ehgi 'áda'azį́įd ádeidoolíił. T'áá'áko, bí hanii doo baa dahojoobá'í da." *We will come back here, my children. We live here. This land will be given back to us. Although we planted in our cornfield, we will come back just in time for the harvest. In the meantime, your mother has taken out the items she stored away. That's probably what we will be eating while we are there. The birds and rodents will have a feast this summer in the cornfield. That's okay, they need compassion as well.*

"Shí 'éí sha'áłchíní dóó shitsóóké shił baa dahojoobá'ígo biniinaa 'ákǫ́ǫ́ nániikaigo t'éí nihá yá'át'ééh. Ákǫ́ǫ́ náníikaigo nihe'anaa'í niha'áłchíní dóó nihitsóóké doo 'atxídeidoolíił da. T'óó yee' shił yéé' hazlį́į́'.

Shą́ą́' t'ahdoo nihi'ílníih yę́ędą́ą́', hastóí naakigo tł'ízí ts'ídá yéego néineeshxaal ne'. Doo 'ak'eh dahonoł'į́įgóó 'éí kónihi'di'doolníił, shą́ą́' ní. Nihe'anaa'í ts'ídá doo 'ádahalyą́ą da. Shí 'éí 'ei doo nihá nisin da. Nihá hwíínį́'į́įgo 'ákǫ́ǫ nikéé' yiikah doo," *I have compassion for my children and my grandsons, and for that reason, it is best if we go back (to Fort Defiance). If we go there, our enemy will not torture our children and our grandchildren. I became very fearful. Remember the two men who beat the goat just before we were released? They told us we would receive the same treatment if we did not obey the terms of the treaty. Our enemies are not sane. I do not want that for us. Be our guide as we follow you,* Nínáánínbaa' announced. The next day, Nínáánínbaa' looked back at their hastily built hogans. Unwillingly, she said,

"Txį'ínee'." *Let's go then,* which was all she could say as she leaned into the brisk breeze and walked eastward following her husband and her family. Each one of the men carried a bundle that contained their rug blankets, the food Nínáánínbaa' had hidden away in her secret place, and the few weapons they made since they had come back to their home. She reminded her children of the benefits, if she could call it benefits, of returning to Fort Canby when she said,

"Bił ałhéédahosiilzį́įd yę́ę da shą' háí 'áadi ninéheeskai doo? K'adę́ę la' bił nída'ahiistséęh. T'áá hazhó'ó nihe'anaa'í bitsį' daalgaiígíí ts'ídá t'áadoo ła' náánéiłtsą́ągóó shił hózhǫ́ǫ doo. T'óó shį́į́ 'ahojíyói doo. Jó niidlą'í da, níléídę́ę' nániikai," *I wonder who of all the people we have come to know will have come back there? If I never see another one of our enemies with white skin, I will be happy. There will probably be a lot of people. There were many of us who returned from that distant place.* Hashké Yił Naabaah smiled at her. He could not believe his Nínáánibaa' was anxious to return to the fort where their daughter was held, just so she could see her many acquaintances from Fort Sumner.

Childhood thoughts visited Dédii as she wished her father could carry her once again. Instead, she straightened her shoulders and walked beside her mother and her sister. Hashké Yił Naabaah was their guide as they walked eastward, past many different rock formations and landscapes that changed color many times. Their father named places as they walked, telling them stories of the many War Leadership meetings he and his sons attended.

Once at Fort Defiance, after nearly nine days of walking eastward, Nínáánibaa' and her daughters caught their breath at the same time.

"Yáadi shą' díidí! Díí yee' doodago haz'ą́," *What a sight this is! This place is horrible!* Nínáánibaa' quietly said. They saw campsites for miles in every direction. As they walked through the campsites, they searched the faces of the people. A woman jumped up and ran to Nínáánibaa'. Her children watched her hug the woman real tight and they both started crying. Their shoulders shook in unison. Nínáánibaa' heard Dédii's young son ask with tears in his eyes and his voice shaking,

"Shimá, da' t'óó bahoo'iih yę́ęgóósh t'áá ni' nídeekai?" *My mother, are we going on foot back to that awful place (Fort Sumner)?*

"Dooda, shiyázhí, díí yee' nihidine'é bił ąąhéeshjéé' daniidlínée 'ádaat'į́. Nimá sání dóó níléí 'asdzą́ą́ doo 'ahoot'į́įgóó díkwíishį́į nídeezid. Ałhíhoosa' nít'ę́ę́', éí biniinaa nimá sání yichah, shiyázhí." *No, my little one, these people are the ones with whom we were prisoners of war. Your maternal grandmother and that woman have not seen one another for several months. They missed one another and that is why your grandmother is crying, my little one.*

"Haashį́į nízahjį' t'áá kǫ́ǫ́ danihi'dótą' doo, hóla," *It is uncertain how long we will be kept here, I don't know,* Hashké Yił Naabaah announced to his family. Worried, Nínááníbaa' answered,

"Nihinaadą́ą́' dootł'izhí yik'ánígíí shį́į haanízahjį' nihidínóołnah. T'áá doozhǫǫgo 'ádeiilyaa. Nanise' daadánígíí 'ałdó' łą́ągo nídaheedláa'go nihist'e' ádeiilyaa. 'Éí dó' baa dasiitxi'go t'áá nízaadgóó deiidą́ą nidi bíighah." *It is uncertain how long our supply of blue corn flour will last. We made quite a bit. We also gathered a lot of edible plants for our food source. We need to be careful with our supply which can last us quite a long time.* Sarcastically, Hashké Yił Naabaah stated,

"Shą́ą́' hastóí bik'éí 'ádinée 'ání, nihe'anaa'í nihanída'ałtso' doo níine'..." *Remember the two men (the two messengers) who have no relatives told us our enemy would feed us...* Dédii and Dzáníbaa' interrupted their father and cried out,

"Dooda, shizhé'é! Nihe'anaa'í bich'iiyą' t'óó baa'iihígi 'áhálniih." *No, my father. Our enemy's food tastes horrible.* With her hand around her throat, Dédii stated,

"Ch'ééh iishneeh łeh." *I have a difficult time swallowing it.* Dzáníbaa' was very unhappy when she said,

"Niłchxongo tsík'eh, tóó 'iiłkóoh łeh." *It's worse when it smells bad, it's nauseating.* Hiding behind their mothers, the children all said in unison,

"Dooda, shicheii." *No, my maternal grandfather.* The young Naabeehó 'Ashkii said,

"Hooghangóó nídiikah, t'áá k'ad. Ákǫ́ǫ nánihidí'éésh, shicheii. T'áá kǫ́ǫgo 'éí t'óó náhádzid. Nídeiildzid, shicheii." *Let's go home, right now. Take us home, my maternal grandfather. It is frightening here. We are scared, my maternal grandfather.* Hashké Yił Naabaah looked into the eyes of each one of his adopted children and his grandchildren and sadly told them,

"Dooda, shitsóóké dóó sha'áłchíní danohłínígíí. T'áá kǫ́ǫ dahoniidlǫ́ǫgo t'éí nihá yá'át'ééh. Naaltsoos nihinaat'áanii 'atah hadeidiilaa yę́ę 'ákót'éego bikáá'. Kéyah ahodiyooyázhígo nihá haadzoh lá, 'áko nihí 'éí hahoodzoígíí tł'óó'jígo kéédahwiit'į́į lá. 'Íishją́ąshį́į, ha'át'íí daaníí dooleeł. Díí yee' índa niikai. Shí dó' nihighangóó náshí'ni'. Nihimá sání dó' ákǫ́ǫ nábí'ni'. T'áá'ániiltsoh ákǫ́ǫ nídanihí'ni'. Níléígóó nihidine'é bitah dadíínóh'į́į'. Bí shį́į 'ałdó' hooghangóó nídabí'ni' nidi kǫ́ǫ naazdá. Hada'íínółní, sha'áłchíní dóó shicheii yázhí, hada'íínółní. Danihighangóó nídiikahgo 'át'é. 'Ádahodoołzééh. Nihaa 'ádahwiilyą́ą doo."

No, those of you who are my children. It's best we stay here. The paper our leaders agreed to is written in that way. They set aside a little tiny piece of land for us, but we were living outside of that land. Let's wait and see what they say. We just got here. I also want to go back to our home. Your maternal grandmother also wants to go back there. We all want to go back there. Look among your people. They probably want to go back to their own homes but they are sitting here. Have hope, my children and my grandsons, have hope. We will go back to our homes. Stop fretting. We will take care of you.

"Nihidine'é ła' t'áá'íídą́ą́' kodi yíkai lá. 'Éí bíighahgi nihá nídahodii'ą́ą́ lá. Tsołtxį', ákǫ́ǫ́ nááná." *Some of our people are already here. They have saved a place for us. Let's go over there.* Still carrying their bundles on their backs, Hashké Yił Naabaah and his family left to settle near his people of whom he was the leader. His people had selected a spot under many pinon and juniper trees which provided shade for the warming weather.

Dédii followed without looking toward the fort where she was kept for many months. Her mother and her father stayed right by her side to protect their precious daughter.

Dédii regretted not having buried her son's umbilical cord at their home on Dziłíjiin *Black Mesa*. She wanted to wait until her permanent hogan had been built. She forced herself to believe in the words her father spoke to the children,

"Danihighangóó nídiikahgo 'át'é." *We will return to our homes.* Softly she said to herself,

"Shizhé'é bizaad bee ha'ííníshníi dooleeł. Sha'álchíní bá ha'ííníshníi dooleeł." *I will have hope in my father's words. I will have hope for my children.*

Chapter Fifteen
"I Will Learn Paper"

Hashké Yił Naabaah was asked to attend a meeting with Naabeehó leaders and the Indian Agent. Worried, Dédii and Dzáníbaa' watched their mother brush their father's long graying hair and fold it into an elongated bun then tie it in the middle with a long coarse woolen yarn. With every brush Nínááníbaa' gave her husband a piece of advice, starting with,

"Nihá honíyą́ą dooleeł." *Be wise on our behalf.*

"Niha'áłchíní bá honíyą́ą dooleeł." *Be wise for our children's sake.*

"Hódzą' bee nihá nahó'áa dooleeł." *Make plans regarding our future with wisdom.*

"Nihitsóóké dóó niha'áłchíní nihá baa nitsíníkees doo." *You must think of our grandchildren and our children.*

"T'áadoo t'óó 'akéé' ninánílwo'í dooleeł, hazhó'ó baa nitsáházkéezgo 'índa kót'é didíiniił." *Don't just agree on things discussed, instead, think first before you make a decision.* On and on Nínááníbaa' went. Dédii and Dzáníbaa' wondered if other leaders were given advice just as their father was given. They smiled, watching the scene before them. Their father looked at them, pointed to their mother, and smiled, saying,

"Nihimá 'ayóó'áshó'ní. Bidine'é 'ałdó' ayóó'áyó'ní..." *Your mother loves me. She also loves her people.*

Nínááníbaa' interrupted him, saying,

"Shooh, kéédahwiit'ínéegóó nihéé'doolnihígíí bee sínííltxee' dooleeł, ííshjąąh. Niha'áłchíní 'áadi bits'éé' łeeh naaztą. 'Éí béénílniih dooleeł. T'áá nihí danihighanígóó nídeiyíníikáah dooleełígíí bee sínííltxee' doo." *Listen, be adamant about our return to our homeland. Our children's umbilical cords are buried there. Remember that. Stay firm on the return of all of us (Naabeehó people) to our own lands.*

Hashké Yił Naabaah kissed his Nínááníbaa' and stood up straight and tall. Chills ran down Nínááníbaa''s spine as she watched her husband place his hand on each one of his grown children's heads, then on the heads of his grandchildren and his adopted children as if to remind himself of his responsibility to all the children whose families were camped there at the fort.

Nínááníbaa' knew her husband needed to look his best because he was one of the War Leaders who was an advisor to the great War Leader Manuelito and the wise Peace Leader Barboncito. Her beautiful husband took his walking cane in his hand and disappeared into the midst of the large gathering of Naabeehó people.

Everyone in Hashké Yił Naabaah's family was happy to see him return to their crudely made lean-to. When he entered, his children saw the worried look on his face. He looked around at each of the young children and sadly announced,

"Áłchíní hastą́ą́ dóó níléí hastą́'áadahjį' béédááhaiígíí nihe'anaa'í bizaad naaltsoos bikáá' daasdzohígíí yídahwiidooł'ááł biniiyé da'íídóołta, nihi'doo'niid. Naaltsoos bee 'ałgha'diit'aah hadilyaa yę́ę t'áá 'ákót'éego bikáá' yisdzoh, áko nihinaat'áanii danilínígíí yee lą́ da'asłį́į'go naaltsoos yidadeeshchid. Éí t'áá'ániit'é danihíínááł." *Children between the ages of six and sixteen are to learn the words of the enemy that are written on the paper and for that reason they have to go to school, they told us. The paper that was negotiated was written in that way and our leaders agreed to it when they touched the paper (Treaty). We all witnessed that.* Nínááníbaa' and Dédii and Dzáníbaa' frantically looked around at their children and automatically felt a heightened sense of anxiety. Each one of the women thought of the age of their children. Nínááníbaa' and Hashké Yił Naabaah's adopted children were within that age limit. Dédii's son and her five adopted sons were of school age and Dzáníbaa''s son was also of school age.

Hashké Yił Naabaah further stated,

"Áłchíní tádiin yilt'éego 'áajį' nidadoohnił, nihi'doo'niid. Niha'áłchíní naaltsoos dayółta' dooleeł biniiyé 'áajį' nidanii'nilgo 'índa ch'iiyáán nihich'į' ch'ídidoot'ááł, jiní. Naabeehó dine'é t'áadoo bada'áłchíní 'áajį' nideiznilgóogo 'éí díighaaí yéego bich'į' nidahwii'náa doo. T'áadoo dayóyą'í da doo." *They told us to send thirty children to school. It was told that once we send thirty children to school then our people will have their rations. If we do not put thirty children in school then our people will be facing hunger this winter and will experience hardship. They will have nothing to eat.*

"Naat'áanii bił ahíishkaiígíí 'ádaaníigo 'éí nihí, naat'áanii daniidlínígíí t'éiyá, nihada'áłchíní t'áálá'ígo 'áajį' nidadiiltééł, naaltsoos yídahwiidooł'ááł biniiyé. 'Áłchíní tádiin yilt'éego nihá bíighah nádleeh dooleeł háálá łą́ niilt'é. T'áá hazhó'ó t'áá'ákwíí jį́ 'áłchíní tádiin yilt'éego nída'óltah doo, danihi'doo'niid." *We leaders decided we would be the only ones to put one of our children in school to learn paper. There will be thirty children in school and that will be enough because there are many of us (who have children).*

"Áádóó 'ánáádadii'níigo 'éí nihada'áłchíní doo bąąh daatxéhígíí 'éí bíni'dii t'áá hooghangi 'áká 'anídaalwo'go 'ádeiyíníilzin doo. Nihada'áłchíní kanidaakaiígíí t'éiyá 'ólta'jį' nidadii'nił, dadii'níigo binidahosiit'ą́. T'áá hazhó'ó t'áá'ákwííjį 'áłchíní tádiin yilt'éego da'ółta'go 'ádeiyíníilzingogo 'éí nihidine'é doo dichin yik'ee dadínóonéeł da." *We also said, our children who are healthy will stay at home to help us. We will send only our children who are sickly to school. That is what we said as we planned it. As long as we keep thirty children in school to learn paper, our people will not die of hunger.*

Nínááníbaa' placed her hand over her mouth and said, "Nihitsóóké t'áá'áłah doo bąąh txéeh da.

Bíighahí yii' tádíí'áázh lágo 'índa nihit'áahjį' yisdá'ahi'noolchą́ą́'. Hojoobá'ígo yee' índa bił ałhééhosiilzįįd. Niha'áłchíní 'íil'ínígíí nidi nihit'áahjį' adahineezhchą́ą'go bikáa'jį' dahazlį́į́'. Dédii ba'áłchíní 'ííł'ínígíí nidi bit'áahjį' adahineezhchą́ą'go, bí dó' bikáa'jį' dahazlį́į́'. Ei yee' nihe'anaa'í nihá nidaha'áhígíí 'át'é. K'asídą́ą́' yee' ałtso nidanihistsxeed. Shí 'éí doodají bee sézį́ doolееł. T'áadoo nidó', nihí nida'shiilchínígíí kót'é danihidooniidgóó t'óó bee lą́ da'soołį́į́'. Yówéé' át'éego doo nihił da'niidlį́ da doo!" *Our two grandsons are healthy. They went through so much when they finally came running to us to find safety. We finally got to know them. Even our children whom we have adopted came running to us for safety after suffering such hardship. Dédii's children also ran to her for safety and in that way, they were spared. You are telling us what the enemy has planned for us. They nearly killed all of us. I am standing to say no. You agreed to this and did not even ask those of us who bore the children. What a way to show us that we do not matter to you!* Hashké Yił Naabaah felt torn at Ninááníbaa''s words. He knew he should have discussed it with her first before dictating to her the collective decision of the leaders. He thought, "At the time we were discussing it, all we were thinking of was that our people will have food to eat when we send thirty children to school. It is true, we were not thinking of our women who bore the children for us. The children are their immediate responsibility. We, men, help in feeding our children, we provide a home for our children, we teach our children, and we are a spiritual leader for our children, but the future planning for our children is a responsibility that lies in the lap of our women, our spouses."

Hashké Yił Naabaah was extremely upset, he had allowed their enemy to dictate how their children should be raised and educated. He shrugged his shoulders and told Nínáánìbaa',

"Jó nihidine'é t'áá'át'é baa nitsídeiikeesgo biniinaa 'ákót'éego nidahosiit'ą́. Doo dichin yiih dínóodah da hwiinidzingo." *Well, we were thinking of our people and that is the reason we planned it that way. We did not want them to fall into hunger.*

Before any one could say anything else, Dédii's first adopted son, Naabeehó Ashkii, stood up and said,

"Shí łą́ą, naaltsoos bíhwiideesh'ááł. Shidine'é bá naaltsoos bíhwiideesh'ááł áko doo dichin yiih dínóodah da." *I will, I will learn paper. I will learn paper for my people so they won't fall into hunger.* He did not want his mother or his siblings or his family to suffer from hunger again. His uncles, and Kiizhóní and the young Mescalero Apache man promised the young Naabeehó 'Ashkii they would do their part to hunt every day for small game so he could have a good meal.

Dédii jumped up and spoke a name no one had heard before.

"ShiNa'niłkaadí Ts'ósí, háshinee', nidine'é baa sínízidgo biniinaa, 'Shí naaltsoos bíhwiideesh'ááł,' dínínìid." *My Thin Sheep Herder, you are mindful of your people and that is why you stood up and offered to learn paper.* Naabeehó 'Ashkii was the only name her oldest adopted son was known as.

Hashké Yił Naabaah promised,

"Shí 'ákǫ́ǫ́ nił ałnánásht'ash dooleeł áádóó t'áá 'ákwe'é niba' naashą́ą doo, 'ałtsojį'." *I will be the one who will walk with you (to the school) and I will wait there for you until you are finished.* Hashké Yił Naabaah stopped talking and turned around and asked,

"Háíshą' óolyé, Na'niłkaadii Ts'ósí?" *Who is the one who is called Thin Sheep Herder?* Laughing, Dédii responded,

"Jó shiyáázh, aláąjį' naagháhígíí 'óolyé." *My son, the oldest one, is the one who is called by that name.* She told her family about her adopted son who spared her life after the tall gray-haired one abandoned her.

The entire family sat in the lean-to, eating berries and rabbit stew with dried baked corn while they discussed the topic of their young Naabeehó 'Ashkii going to school.

****

On the day the children were to arrive at the fort for the first day of school, it was cloudy. The young Naabeehó 'Ashkii looked up into the clouds and wished he was a cloud that was free to drift from one place to another. He watched a cloud bump against another, then drift away to look for another cloud to bump into. His grandfather had to tell him,

"T'áadoo deigo t'éí díní'į́į'go yínáłí. Chą́ą́h didíígoh da. Diné 'akǫ́ǫ́ naazdá." *Don't just look up into the sky as you walk. You might trip. There are people here who are sitting on the ground.*

The young Naabeehó 'Ashkii slowly followed his grandfather to the fort. He was shocked at what he saw. The soldiers shouted and pushed the Naabeehó children into small groups. The brave little children sat in little groups crying. Naabeehó 'Ashkii was afraid but the presence of his grandfather made him brave.

The Naabeehó families who brought their children, received rations.

"Leave your children here!" a soldier shouted as he raised a whip high in the air.

"No, you can't follow your child into the school!" another soldier shouted in the midst of the commotion caused by shouting, yelling, crying, and confusion.

Worried, Naabeehó 'Ashkii said,

"Shicheii, naaltsoos bíhoo'aah la' ił aahojooba' bąąh ádin. T'óó 'áłchíní bił daayée'go 'ádayósin. Hojooba' ádeinízingo kwe'é niheeskai yéę t'óó bił daayéé'. Shimá dóó shizhé'é 'ada'diyoołnah danízinée, haash dajił'į?" *My grandfather, there is no kindness in the learning of paper. They are making the children very scared. The children came here hoping to help their people but they are scared. They thought they would be able to feed their mothers and their fathers, but what are (the soldiers) doing to them?* His grandfather answered,

"T'áadoo hanii bee hwiih dajizlįį' da? Txi'danihijiyoołníihgo dįį' nááhai! 'Éí hanii doo 'ílįį da? T'óó yee' ahonii'yói 'ádanihi'disdįįd. Yáadilá bich'į' anidíí'ąą dó', shicheii yázhí? 'Azhą shįį 'ákódaat'įį nidi, t'áadoo bééníldzidí. Nídaaldzidgo biniinaa 'ákódaat'į. T'áá kwe'é, tł'óo'gi niba' sédáa dooleeł. Doo háágóó da nits'ąą' dah dideesháał da. Ha'íínílní, shicheii yázhí. Nidine'é bá 'ánít'į."

Didn't they get enough? They tortured us for four years! Doesn't that mean something to them? Too many of us perished. What did I give you over to, my little grandson? Even though they act like that, don't be afraid of them. They act like that because they are afraid. I will wait for you right here, outside. I will not wander away from you. Have hope, my little grandson.

Hearing his grandfather's words of hope, the voices of the soldiers trailed off as they continued shouting at the Naabeehó people, yelling,

"Where are all the filthy Navajo children? There have to be more! Look for them! Tell the families they will not receive their rations unless they send their children to school!" The young Naabeehó' Ashkii shuddered when he saw soldiers running in pairs in different directions to harass more Naabeehó people.

Hashké Yił Naabaah sat beside his grandson and thought back to the time when the leaders gathered to discuss "learning paper". "When school was first announced, my Naabeehó leaders devised a plan that would satisfy the soldiers and still allow the children to be at home to learn about their traditions, their culture, and their lifestyle." The leaders decided that each family would rotate sending their children to school to learn paper. After all, they understood that thirty children were required to attend school every day. The children who were not healthy were the ones who were chosen to attend school. "I don't have a grandchild or a child who is not well, so I did not have to choose who would go," he thought.

He remembered the soldiers identified the days of the week by the type of ration or event that would take place. "Before this, I had never heard of the words naaltsoos wólta' *reading paper* or naaltsoos baa 'ólta' *learning about paper.* Even the words sound funny," he thought as he snickered and spoke them. "We were told the day when seeds for planting are distributed would be the first day (Monday) of learning paper." Waving away a cloud of dust, he thought in disgust, "I don't know why they will give us seeds for planting when the time for planting is far past and worse yet, we have nowhere to plant! I don't need harmful seeds my enemy wants to give me. My seeds are stored away in Nínááníbaa"s secret storage area."

He looked up into the sky and thought, "The second day (Tuesday) is when our angry enemy will give my people small parcels of meat that smell just like our enemies after they have been out in the sun for a whole day." Counting on his fingers, he thought, "The third day (Wednesday) is when my people are given ak'áán *flour* that feels like greasy dirt and gohwééh *coffee*, little black round things that look like berries, berries that make the water very bitter and black."

"On the fourth day (Thursday), my people will be given hay. How do people eat hay?" he snorted in contempt. "Our enemy with white skin took all of our livestock away from us and now they stupidly give us hay for livestock we don't have. Do they see what we cannot see? Our livestock? They promised us livestock but I have not seen one Naabeehó person receive one sheep, goat, cow, or horse. Can't they see? The hay will go to waste. I will use the hay they give me to make the ground where my Nínáánívbaa' sleeps a little softer and warmer, where my daughters' sleep too."

"The fifth day (Friday) is when our enemy will give us dried fruit. Mmmm, I like the dried fruit our Kin Yis'áanii *Hopi* neighbors used to give us. Didzétsoh yázhí *apricot,* when it is dried is so tasty." His mouth watered thinking of the sweet taste of dried apricots. "That will be my favorite day," he thought, smiling. He made a fist and squeezed it tight, hoping apricots would be the dried fruit they would receive. "The sixth day, (Saturday) our enemy told us we could gather in the parade grounds and race our horses across the valley." He looked around him, "What horses?" he thought with indignation. "They, the enemy, took all our horses from us so we would not escape from that horrible place of death (Fort Sumner). All of our beautiful horses that were so well trained, the soldiers confiscated from us! But, the day they told us we could race our horses is the day the place where the children learn paper is closed. The next day, the seventh day (Sunday) is when our enemy have to learn their paper prayer books, whatever that is. I hope it helps them become more kind and thoughtful!"

Still deep in his thoughts, he remembered the second decision the leaders made. They felt one day a month was enough for a child to be sitting in school to learn paper so they identified the families whose children would attend school on the day the seeds were distributed. A different set of thirty children was selected to attend school on the day the disgusting parcels of meat were distributed. A whole new set of thirty children were to attend on the day flour and coffee were given to the people who sent their children to school. On the day hay was distributed, the families who lived farther from the fort would bring thirty children. On the day dried fruit was given, the families who lived even farther from the fort would bring their children.

"I am proud of my leaders," he thought as he nodded with pride. The leaders were proud of their decision to comply with Article Six in the Treaty, but they were never told the same thirty children were to attend school every day for many, many months.

Hashké Yił Naabaah noticed the commotion had died down and more Naabeehó leaders had gathered. Barboncito stood in the middle of the crowd. Hashké Yił Naabaah looked at the large group of Naabeehó people, then looked toward the large number of soldiers who stood in one place guarding the Navajo people who gathered together. The peace and quiet that reigned around his people was amazing to him. His people acted as if they were still prisoners of war. They were making the best of their leaders' decision. The soldiers were boisterous, loud, angry, and annoying. He was glad he was a member of the best of the two groups.

Barboncito was given a metal box to stand on to address the Indian Agent and the soldiers. Raising his voice so all could hear, he said,

"Aají 'áłtsé 'ádahodoołzééh." *You all, over there, be quiet.* The soldiers were asked to be quiet and listen. Once the message was translated, he continued,

"Kwe'é nihikéyah biih néikaiígíí doo ts'íí'át'éégóó baa 'ahééh ilį́. Naaltsoos bidadeelchid yę́ę bida'diilnííł, nihada'áłchíní naaltsoos yídahwiidooł'ááł. Áko nidi, díí 'éí nihá baa 'ákodanohsin doo, baa nídanihooshkąąh, shidiné'e. Nihada'áłchíní hooghandi, t'áá nihí nihighandi, yídahwiidooł'áałii dahólǫ́. Dííghaaí, haigo baa dahane'ígíí dayíists'ą́ą'go bá yá'át'ééh. Nááná ła' éí dá'ák'ehgi na'anish biniiyé hastóí doo 'ashiiké bee na'anishí hasht'éé deidle', dąągo choidoot'įįł biniiyé. Ch'éénídąąhgo naanish nitsaaígíí bínínéiikah. Dá'ák'ehgi dahwiilbį'go dóó k'i'dilyé biniiyé hasht'eh hodi'néehgi dóó k'i'dilyéejį' doo ts'íí'át'éégóó naanish nitsaaígíí bínínéiikah. 'Ei T'ą́ą́ Chil dóó níléí Bii' Anit'ą́ą́ Tsoh ahalzhishjį' dá'ák'ehgi na'anish łeh. Éí bikéédóó 'índa dá'ák'ehgi na'anishígíí ni' kónídeiil'įįh. Doo 'éí t'óó hooghangi nisiidáa da. Díí baa hweeshne'ígíí niha'áłchíní nihits'ą́ądóó yídahwiidooł'ááł biniiyé bíni'dii t'áá nihighandi naháazt'ąągo yá'át'ééh." *We are very grateful to have reentered our own lands. We will abide by the paper we touched, our children will learn paper. But, be aware of this on our behalf, I plead with you, my people, our children have things to learn at our homes. This winter they need to hear stories that are told in the winter. It is good for them. The men and boys need to repair the items they will use during the spring season when they are planting in the cornfield. We encumber ourselves with a great amount of work. We clear the cornfield, prepare for the planting of corn, and then the actual planting process begins which is an extreme amount of work. From the month of Miniature Leaves (April) through the month of the Big Harvest (September) we work in the cornfields. After that, we place our work in the cornfield aside. We do not just sit at home. Our children need to learn about what I told you and that is why they need to be at home.*

"Hastóí dóó sáanii, náás daazlį́'ígíí, níléí da'ni'néédę́ę́' hojoobá'ígo ninádahaaskai. Nihada'áłchíní náás daazlį́'ígíí hooghandi yaa 'ádahalyą́ągo náás daazlį́'ígíí yá'át'ééh nídadoodleeł. Nihada'áłchíní náás daazlį́'įgíí yits'ą́ądóó na'nitin nídeididooléél. Yinahjį nihi'í'óol'įįł bił béédahózin doo. Nihe'iina' bee 'ádeiil'ínígíí bił béédahózin doo. Bik'ehgo dahonii'nánígíí bił béédahózin doo. Naabeehó 'ídlįįgi bił béédahózin doo. Dį́į' nááhaijį' da'ni'né yínáskai, dichin yínáskai, txi'hoo'nííh yínáskai, ts'ídá t'áá'ałtsoní t'óó dabaa'iihígíí t'éí yínáskai. 'Éí 'éí nihada'áłchíní doo bá daniidzin da." *In their own homes, our children are needed to care for their older male relatives and their older female relatives, who barely made it home from the place of death (Fort Sumner). Our children can help our elders recover. The children can pick up valuable teaching from their elder relatives, in that way, they will know about our culture, they will know about our lifestyle, they will know about our traditions, and they will know how to be Navajo. For four years they were immersed in death and dying, they were immersed in extreme hunger, they were immersed in torture and suffering, they were immersed in so many awful things. We do not want that for our children.*

"Nihada'áłchíní Naabeehó danilį́į dooleeł biniiyé danihighangóó nídaníhí'ni'. Áko nidi, naaltsoos bidadeelchid yę́ędą́ą' bee nidahosiit'ánéé bida'diilníił. Nihada'áłchíní da'íidóołtah. Nihá baa dajiinohba' dooleeł. Baa dahojoobá'íyee'." *We yearn to return to our homes so that our children may be Navajo. But, we will keep the promise we made when we touched the paper (the Treaty). Our children will go to school. Be kind to them for us. They deserve your sympathy.* Hashké Yił Naabaah wondered if the Indian Agent heard and understood the message of the great Peace Leader

Hashké Yił Naabaah agreed with the great Peace Leader Barboncito, but he wished the Peace Leader would have also included the work of the women. "He only spoke of the responsibilities of the men," he sadly thought as he observed the number of little girls sitting in the many groups that had been formed at the orders of the soldiers.

After leaving the little children to sit in the hot sun for many hours, the Indian Agent finally came out to the parade grounds to announce the teacher for the school had not arrived yet, so the school would not open.

"You children and parents are free to go. Do not leave the fort. We will tell you when the teacher arrives." With great relief, the Naabeehó parents listened to the translated message. The words,

"Txį'ínee'," *Let's go then,* were heard many times over.

****

Throughout the summer season, the Indian Agent promised the Naabeehó people the teacher would arrive soon. While the mothers and fathers waited for the school to be opened, they were happy because it meant their children would be at their temporary home where they were safe. The summer passed, Hashké Yił Naabaah and his family were glad the teacher never arrived; however, they were saddened that the summer season had passed without their gardening tools touching the fertile soil at their home at Dziłíjiin *Black Mesa.* Daily, Nínáánībaa' reminded her children of how difficult the winters can be without the availability of corn. She worried about her sons and her adopted grandsons who were not learning the art of planting the corn.

****

With the arrival of the fall season, the Indian Agent announced to the Naabeehó people the teacher had arrived and the school would be opened on the first of October. The people had mixed emotions. They learned the teacher was not happy with the large crude building made of sod and logs. Ignorant of the meager leanto each Naabeehó family lived in while they waited for her presence in the extreme cold days and nights that threatened their lives, she demanded a new building suited to her taste be constructed before she commenced her teaching duties.

Once again, the Naabeehó mothers and fathers were glad their children were free to be at home. The first frost that announces the beginning of winter had come early that year and brought with it a great cold air that hovered over the people for many, many days. Hashké Yił Naabaah was honored to accept the responsibility of being a leader to his people once again.

Regardless of the cold, the fathers and grandfathers were anxious to tell their children and grandchildren the stories limited to the winter season, stories which are laden with many cultural teachings. The entire family joined in and taught the young ones winter games that kept each member close. The closeness kept the people relatively warm on the cold winter nights. But, the cold air seeped in through the holes in the lean-to.

Hashké Yił Naabaah noticed his Nínáánībaa' was not as spry as she used to be. Whenever he asked her, she would respond,

"Shighan yee' bídin sélį́į́'." *I miss my home.* He wanted to go home as well but they had made a promise in the Treaty and they had to keep it, otherwise they would face the soldiers who disregarded life, the ones who beat the helpless goat to death. There was the threat they may be sent to Halgai Hótéél *the place of Wide Prairies* or Anaa' Łání bikéyah *The Land of Many Enemies (Indian Territory, Oklahoma)*.

Hashké Yił Naabaah held his Nínáánībaa' close at night, shielding her thin body from the cold with his own thin body, but she started coughing just like many of their Naabeehó people. Hashké Yił Naabaah asked his entire family to move into their lean-to to make it warm for Nínáánībaa'. The crowded home made Nínáánībaa' feel better and stronger but she still missed her home. Many nights, she said,

"T'áá 'ákónéehee shibeedí noo' íishłaa lá." *It is a good thing I hid my utensils in my secret place.* Thinking about her children and grandchildren and her home gave her hope. Her thoughts kept her company on long cold nights when she could not sleep because of her coughing. Many times a night, she asked Hashké Yił Naabaah,

"Shine'dę́ę́' shá náníkad. Yéego! Yéego!" *Slap me on the back. Harder! Harder!* Various family members would speak up on her behalf asking Hashké Yił Naabaah not to slap their mother or grandmother so hard on the back. Not long after, she would cough up the mucus that made her cough. Hashké Yił Naabaah felt helpless. He missed his horses, his beautiful horses, the ones who made it possible for him to race out and obtain whatever his Nínáánibaa' needed. He knew the plant she needed to regain her health but it only grew on Dziłíjiin *Black Mesa.*

One day the family wondered where Kiizhóní and Tł'ée'go Naabaah had disappeared to. "Was it possible they were working on the school building?" they wondered. Two nights later, the two men returned, laden with medicinal plants. Navajo tea, roots, parched corn they traded with a lone Kin Yis'áanii *Hopi* family, butchered rabbits, prairie dogs, and whatever they thought would be useful.

The most healing, the most useful, the most gratifying news they brought was that Nínáánibaa''s father had returned with a new wife to reclaim their old home site. For nearly six years, Nínáánibaa' had worried about her father. He was the one who helped the young warriors pick the most potent and most effective of the medicinal plants for his daughter.

Hashké Yił Naabaah held his Nínáánídbaa'. Her shoulders shook as she cried tears of relief. All she could voice was,

"Ahéhee', shiTaa'," *Thank you, my Spiritual Father,* many times over. As expected, Nínáánídbaa' slowly recovered. She never knew her body had been fighting pneumonia, the deadly disease that took the lives of so many of her people that early winter.

Later, the family learned Tł'ée'go Naabaah and Kiizhóní had stolen two horses from the soldiers late one moonless night. They wondered if the horses had belonged to their father or one of his warriors because the horses knew which direction to run and helped them find their home in the early morning hours. They knew Hashké Yił Naabaah trained his horses well and had trained them to fight and race in the dark of night. Reluctantly, they returned the horses to the corral but not before they spoke a word of gratitude to the horses, which the horses seemed to understand.

****

The soldiers and the Naabeehó men spent the next two months constructing a new school building that would satisfy the new teacher. The school did not open until the first of Níłch'ih Tsoh *Big Winds, the month of December,* when it was extremely cold.

The new teacher's name was Charity Gaston. The Presbyterian Church, a Protestant Missions group, had finally found her to be suitable and willing to teach among the Navajo Indians.

The young Naabeehó 'Ashkii was taken to the school by his grandfather. Hashké Yił Naabaah was told to leave his grandson there but the fear that gripped their hearts was almost too much to bear. Naabeehó 'Ashkii remembered the words of his mother who did not want her son in school but allowed him to go to keep his people from starvation. Dédii wanted her oldest son to learn the characteristics that created great leaders.

That morning, she fed him berries and sumac juice, and told him,

"Shiyázhí, Naabeehó nílínígíí baa yóónééh lágo."
My little one, don't forget you are Navajo. His mother spoke many other words to him but his jumbled mind could not focus on the other words. He thought, "...don't forget, these are the people who tried to change you just like they did to us at the place of death. ...don't eat their food, your body does not know their food. They are very mean people and they will try to make you mean by forgetting who you are and who your relatives are." With his mother's words coming back to him, Naabeehó 'Ashkii looked at his grandfather's big hand and placed his thin hands in his grandfather's hand, then lifted his grandfather's hand and placed it near his cheek to warm his cold face and his fearful heart.

Naabeehó 'Ashkii bravely entered the little school building. Close to thirty children walked into the dark room surrounded by brown adobe walls. Several rows of rough wooden benches sat on the floor. Their teacher was a skinny woman who wore an embroidered starched white blouse with long sleeves and a long gray woolen skirt that covered her ankles and black boots. Naabeehó 'Ashkii thought, "Her hair is the color of the early sunset." Her voice was kind when she spoke her first words. He did not know the people with white skin could be kind. "Her voice is soft just like my mother's," he thought, but immediately he felt guilty of the thought. "She is our enemy," he reminded himself.

Naabeehó 'Ashkii and the children sat and stared at the woman with hair the color of the early sunset and a kind voice. She was young.

Little did the children know their fathers or grandfathers stood right outside the school house to make sure the teacher did not kidnap their children. Naabeehó 'Ashkii was confident that his grandfather stood straight and tall right outside the door. The Naabeehó men made sure there was no other opening through which the teacher could escape with their children and grandchildren.

Naabeehó 'Ashkii stared at the teacher's mouth. All the other people with white skin yelled and shouted but the teacher smiled and spoke softly. He could not get over the difference. "Should I tell my mother about this lady who does not shout or yell or hit us?" he thought. This was his first day. He was already confused.

Although the children did not understand her even when the interpreter translated her words, the teacher said,

"Hello, children. My name is Miss Charity Gaston. You must call me Miss Gaston when you want to get my attention or when you want me to speak to you." Naabeehó 'Ashkii noticed the teacher wore something green that covered her hands. He did not know they were called gloves. She moved her hands around a lot. Up and down, side to side, around in a circle, in a circle the other direction, pointed at the wall and pointed at the children a lot. Naabeehó 'Ashkii wondered if something was wrong with her hands. He hoped she would not get close enough to him because he was afraid of what was on her hands. Without realizing it, he softly said,

"Yíiyá. Bíla' shį́į́' łóód. T'áadoo bídílchidí." *Scary. Her hands probably have sores on them. Don't touch her.* His ears started ringing when he saw the teacher approach each student then point to them with a stick that had a sharp tip. He wondered if that sharp stick was her weapon.

The teacher walked from one student to the next, asking the interpreter,

"Ask him what his name is. Ask her what her name is."

"Haash yinílyé, ní?" *She said, what's your name?* the interpreter asked each child in a mean voice. Soon, Naabeehó 'Ashkii's ears were really ringing. The teacher and the interpreter were standing in front of him.

"Ask him what his name is," she asked in her gentle voice.

"Haash yinílyé, ní?" *She said, what's your name?* the interpreter asked. Naabeehó 'Ashkii moved to the side because the teacher's green hand was right in front of his face, holding her pointed weapon.

"Naabeehó 'Ashkii dashijiní," *They call me Navajo Boy,* he replied. The interpreter turned to the teacher and said,

"He said his name is Navajo boy."

"Well, that is unacceptable," the teacher responded. "We will call him Joe. What is his father's name?"

"Nizhé'é shą' haa wolyé?" *What's your father's name?* the interpreter asked.

"Hóla. Shizhé'é 'ałk'idą́ą́' ádin. Nihe'anaa'í dabiishxį́. Áko nidi, shicheii 'éí Hashké Yił Naabaah wolyé." *I don't know. My father died a long time ago. Our enemy killed him. But, my grandfather's name is The One Who Goes to War Scolding.* No one had ever asked Naabeehó 'Ashkii about his father's name before, which puzzled him and scared him at the same time but the sharp object the teacher was pointing at him with her green hands made him give all that information.

"His father died too long when he was baby. His grandfather is Hashké Yił Naabaah," the interpreter said.

"What is his grandfather's name?" the teacher asked still pointing at Naabeehó 'Ashkii.

"Hashké Yił Naabaah."

"Naba is all I heard. His name will be Joe Naba," she reported to the interpreter. Facing Naabeehó 'Ashkii she said, pointing to another bench,

"Joe, you sit over there." Pointing at the bench again she said,

"Over there. Over there, I said. Go,"

"Níléíjí dah nídaah, ní," *She said, sit over there,*

the interpreter ordered. Naabeehó 'Ashkii was glad to move. He was afraid of the teacher's green hands and her pointed weapon. He glanced up to see the teacher using the sharp weapon, which was a pencil to mark on a wide flat board she held in her arm.

"These poor little things cannot speak a word of English," she said, moving her hands all over again. She looked at the interpreter and asked,

"How do you say children in Naavaho?" The interpreter clearly responded, saying,

"Áłchíní." *Children.*

"What?"

"Áłchíní." *Children.*

"Say it again? What are you doing to your tongue when you say it?" she asked, moving close to the interpreter and staring at his mouth.

"Áłchíní." *Children.*

"Alteeny?" she asked. The interpreter shook his head and said,

"Áłchíní." *Children.*

"All-chin-ee, when I say this word, you answer me. The word is All-chin-ee." Naabeehó 'Ashkii watched her tap her sharp weapon on the board she held in her green hand. Once again, she said,

"All-chin-ee"

"All-chin-ee, look up here. This is an a. It is the first letter of the alphabet."

"All-chin-ee, look up here. These are the first five letters of the alphabet. a b c d e." She held up her green fingers when she said the word "five". The teacher forgot about the interpreter.

"All-chin-ee, look at my mouth when I say the letter a."

"All-chin-ee, now look at my mouth when I say the letter b."

"All-chin-ee, look up here. Look at my mouth when I say the letter c."

"All-chin-ee, look at my mouth when I say the letter d."

"All-chin-ee, look at my mouth when I say the letter e."

"All-chin-ee, say it with me." Helplessly she looked at the interpreter and asked, "Why don't they listen when I call them?"

"You are not saying children..." She interrupted the interpreter and asked,

"What am I saying then? You told me to say it that way and when I said it, you did not correct me. Now, how do I say children? Slowly now. Slowly. This is my first day learning this."

"Ał chí ní," the interpreter slowly spoke the word.

"Are you saying it slowly? Once again," she said, staring into the interpreter's mouth. The children watched intently, their heads turned from the interpreter's mouth to the teacher's mouth and back to the interpreter's and back again. Naabeehó 'Ashkii smiled, thinking about the crows that sit and watch his family's activities from the branches of the trees near their little lean-to.

"Ał chí ní," the interpreter repeated.

"All-chin-ee," she continued with the same pronunciation she learned earlier which she thought was correct. She clapped her green hands to get the children's attention and assigned more names to the children.

Naabeehó 'Ashkii noticed the teacher reached into her pocket and brought out a round flat object. She looked at it, shook her head and quickly turned around, saying,

"Maybe if I write it down on this hard board, the children will learn to speak and write at the same time. How clever!" she said clapping her hands. Turning back to the large board against the wall, the teacher wrote an "a" on the hard board fastened to the wall.

"All-chin-ee, look up here. This is an a. It is the first letter of the alphabet."

"Aadi, "a" dadohní." *Go on, say a,* the interpreter ordered.

"Ei" *That.*

Nááná shą'. *Again,* the interpreter repeated.

"Ei." *That.*

"Nááná." *Again.*

"Ei." *That.*

Aoo'." *Yes.*

The lesson continued through the letter "e". All of a sudden, the teacher looked at the interpreter and frantically said,

"I need to go to the..." then started to ask,

"Where is the...? Without waiting for an answer, she ran to the back of the room, flung the door open, and ran out the door, waving her green hands.

The children sat quietly, without moving. Only their eyes moved from one strange item in the room to another, which were a globe, a dictionary, and a Bible. The interpreter sat looking down at his hands.

The students heard the teacher walking. Her black boots announced her approach. She came racing back into the school, picked up the board she held in her arm earlier, and asked,

"Where is Joe Naba? He is quite smart. Not clean, but smart."

"Smart?" asked the interpreter. She smiled at him and said,

"Yes, he is the only one who gave full answers when we asked questions about his name and his father. That is smart."

"Joe Naba? Who is Joe Naba? Who did I assign the name Joe Naba to, all-chin-ee?" she asked. When no one answered, she said,

"Dear Lord, help me teach these little savages something. It's probably because they were not baptized when they were babies and that is the reason they are rather dumb."

Naabeehó 'Ashkii did not let the teacher know he understood many of the things she said. He thought, "She is not like the tall gray-haired one who was quiet, thoughtful, and slow to speak. She is more like the soldiers who did things before thinking about their actions, the ones the tall gray-haired one was always scolding."

The teacher reached into her pocket and took out the round flat object again and looked at it. She told the children to put their hands together and close their eyes. When the interpreter translated her request, the children did as they were told. The teacher spoke a short prayer and told the children they could open their eyes.

"School is over for the first day, All-chin-ee," she said smiling. She looked at the interpreter and asked if she gave the children a "body break" or a lunch break. He slowly shook his head.

"Oh, dear Lord, they have been here for six hours and didn't say a word?"

"You did not ask children," the interpreter replied, then slowly said,

"Tsołtxį', kéédahoht'ínígóó nídeiyínółyeed," *Let's go, run back to where you all live,* and walked out the door, stretching his arms. The children followed him out the door and ran for the nearest hill to find a bush to hide behind so they could relieve themselves.

As promised, Hashké Yił Naabaah was waiting at the door for his grandson.

"Da' naaltsoos bíhwiinił'ą́ą́', shicheii," *Did you learn paper, my grandson?* he asked. Naabeehó 'Ashkii smiled. He knew he would not be returning to the school for another three weeks. He felt sorry for the teacher who really wanted to teach the children how to speak and read her language. Hashké Yił Naabaah walked his grandson back to their lean-to, then left after a quiet word with Nínáánībaa'.

He returned to tell the family he met with the Naabeehó leaders to let them know he needed to take his Nínáánibaa' home to fully recover. The leaders understood. They had lost too many of their members to the dreaded disease that came on the cold winds of winter. They counted the number of days when Hashké Yił Naabaah's grandson was to come back to the school. He could not wait until darkness settled on the earth so they could take his beautiful Nínáánibaa' back to their home to see her father.

In the filtered light of the moon the family picked up their bundles and walked up the long steep trail. Dédii kept her eye on the horizon not wanting to look around, knowing they were following the path the tall gray-haired one followed when he first kissed her in the beautiful pasture with many flowers. When they reached the top, their bodies felt stiff from the cold. They fell to the ground when they heard the sound of shuffling feet. Everyone held their breath while their heartbeat resounded in their ears. No one spoke a word.

Hashké Yił Naabaah whispered,

"Háí lá 'át'į? *Who is it?* A woman's voice responded, saying,

"Shí dóó shich'é'é, nihí 'íit'į." *It's me and my daughter.* Immediately, Hashké Yił Naabaah knew who they were. It was Asdząą Télii Neiniłkaadí *The Woman Who Herds Donkeys* and her daughter.

"K'asídąą' yee' yéé' bee nihíínígháą'," *You almost killed us with fear,* Hashké Yił Naabaah said quietly.

"Ha'át'íísh haohkai, kodi? Kǫ́ǫ́ doo naagháhí da." *What are you doing up here? There is no one here,* she questioned.

"Hooghangóó yee' nikééniikai. Yóó 'adaneet'įį́'." *We are leaving to return home. We have escaped,* Hashké Yił Naabaah answered.

"Háísh ádaoht'į́?" *Who are you?* she asked.

"Shí Hashké Yił Naabaah dashijinínígíí 'ásht'į́. Sha'áłchíní hooghangóó nídé'eezh." *I am the one they call One Who Goes to War with Scolding. I am leading my children home.*

"Yáadilá 'óolyé. Nihí yisdánihííní'eezh yę́ę 'íit'į́." *What a thing to say. We are the ones whose lives you spared.*

"Aoo', yá'át'ééh, shitsi'," *Yes, hello, my daughter,* he greeted.

"Yá'át'ééh, shizhé'é yázhí," *Hello, my paternal uncle,* she answered.

"Doo deeghánígóó yee' t'áá ni' nikéénohkai. Doo hanii télii nídanihoogéeł da? Ayóo dahayóí dóó bee nidahaldoh. Łą́ądi Diné dabiníghanígóó ninádashiit'eezh." *You have a long way to go to get home. Why don't you ride the donkeys? They are hardy and run fast. Many times we have taken many Navajo people back to their homes.*

"Dooísh nihikéé' oołkahí da łeh?" *Does anyone track you?* Hashké Yił Naabah asked

"Diné bikéyah bikáa'gi naaldlooshii t'óó'ahayóí yílą́ąd lá. Nidabikéé'góó doo 'ééhózin da. T'óó 'ałná'adabikéé'. Ei náshdóí dóó jádí lá, dóó bįįh dóó tł'ízí da'ałchiní dóó dibé da'ałchiní dóó gah dóó gałbáhí dóó ma'ii tsoh dóó jaanéèz da'ałchiní dóó ma'ii dóó dlǫ́ǫ́' dóó dóolaa da'ałchiní dóó ma'ii dootł'izhí da, dóó dasání dóó náshdóí tsoh dóó łį́į́' da'ałchiní dóó níléí hazéísts'ósíįį', t'óó 'ahayóigo naanáásééł. T'áá bíni'ídii haníít'ą́ą́ lá. Nichxǫ', t'áá ni'go 'éí dooda. T'áá'íídą́ą́' ła' danihíí'aal doo ni'." *There is an overgrowth of animals on Navajo land. There is no telling from one track to another. Their tracks are everywhere. There are wildcats, antelope, deer, wild goats, wild sheep, rabbits and cottontail rabbits, wolves, wild mules, coyotes, prairie dogs, wild bulls, foxes, porcupines, mountain lions, wild horses, and down to chipmunks, all are running free in great numbers. They were free to breed. No, it is too dangerous on foot. The animals will eat you,* the Women Who Herds Donkeys warned. Surprised, Hashké Yił Naabaah responded,

"Yáadilá 'óolyéé dó'. Naakidi t'áá ni' ninásiikai. 'Áłtsé 'éí nihighangóó ninásiikai, 'áádóó 'áádę́ę́' hadanihineeshcháá' yę́ędą́ą́', áádę́ę́' nánii'ná, t'áá ni'." *What a thing to say. We traveled on foot twice. First, to return to our home and when we were chased out, we came back on foot.*

"Nihidine'é t'óó'ahayóí yóó 'adahineest'į́į́', kodóó. Ts'ídá t'áá'ákwíí tł'éé' yóó 'adahinit'įįh. Eí shį́į́ naaldlooshii nahgóó hadeinilkaadgo halgaigi naanáásééł k'ad." *There are many of our people who have escaped from here. Every night, more escape. They probably chase the wild animals out and the animals run to the lower elevations and run wild there now.*

"Hágoshį́į́, shitsi'. 'Idéená biniiyé t'áadoo nich'į' bił hadóshchídí da." *OK, my daughter. I don't have anything to give you in exchange.*

"T'áá yee' íídą́ą́' nihinahjį' aniicháą'go bee nihikáa'jį' hazlį́į́'. T'áadoo 'ákǫ́ǫ́ nitsíníkeesí, shizhé'é yázhí. Kwe'é nihíká'ahi'niilchą́ą'go 'ayóó 'át'éego baa nihił hózhǫ́ǫ doo. Tsołtxį'." *You have already spared our lives once before. Don't think that, my paternal uncle. To have helped, you will make us very happy. Let's go,* she said.

Nínááníbaa' was wrapped in several rug blankets as she lay against her husband while they rode a donkey. They were surprised at the smooth ride the donkey gave them. In the light of morning, they saw what Asdzą́ą́ Télii Neiniłkaadí *Woman Who Herds Donkeys* was telling them about. There were hundreds of tracks that were made by many animals. During the night, whenever they heard wild animals come near, Asdzą́ą́ Télii Neiniłkaadí told her donkeys to bray and jump up and down. Hashké Yił Naabaah and his people smiled, then laughed when they heard the wild animals swiftly run away in fear. Nínááníbaa' shuddered at the thought of being a wild animal's breakfast.

By midmorning they arrived at Nínááníbaa''s father's home. Father and daughter fell into each other's arms and cried bitter tears that would not stop. Their bodies crumpled to the floor and still, they cried. Nínááníbaa' cried tears because of her mother whom she never saw again, and cried over the lost years. Afterwards, family members crashed into one another and hugged and cried. Berries and roots and edible plants were quickly gathered and served to Asdzą́ą́ Télii Neiniłkaadí and her people who helped.

Nínááníbaa"s father told stories that were testimony of the danger of all the wild animals that ran free and bred freely for over four years. Hashké Yił Naabaah and his sons and Kiizhóní and the young Mescalero Apache man realized many animals needed to be killed for them to live in safety. They spent days making arrows and repairing their bows that were stored in Nínááníbaa"s secret spot. The younger children were kept inside at all times.

Naabeehó 'Ashkii did not miss school. He followed his grandfather and the men when they went to hunt wild animals. He was learning the ways of his people. He did not want to learn the ways of the mean, strange people who tortured many of his people to death. He yearned for kindness. In his mother's home and in the home of his maternal grandmother, he felt kindness all around.

****

After four months of school, Naabeehó 'Ashkii had been to school only five times. Fewer and fewer students were arriving on time at the school on their assigned days. When Naabeehó 'Ashkii arrived at the school one day, the teacher was nice but she seemed to get discouraged easily when the students did not respond to her. He tried his best to respond to her in English, which brought a much-needed smile to the tired teacher's lips. It was the beginning of the spring season and Naabeehó 'Ashkii felt bad that he did not know how to read or write but he was proud of his speech.

He heard the teacher standing in the back talking to herself, or so he thought. She said,

"Dear Lord, I can't teach these children anything. From day to day, I don't recognize them. They don't remember one letter from one day to the next. Dear Lord, You told us in Your Word to go into all the world and preach the gospel. I chose to come here, but I am not getting anywhere. Please send me a helper. In Your Name..."

Naabeehó 'Ashkii smiled when the teacher raised her hand to her face to brush aside a stray strand of hair. She was wearing black colored gloves. She has green and dark blue and dark red and dark gray hands. "What is wrong with her hands?" he wondered.

"Bíla' shįį́ łóód bąąh," *She probably has sores on her hand,* he whispered to himself.

Two Naabeehó men opened the door and entered without knocking, counted the children, and hastily left the school house. A few minutes later, the teacher's writing lesson was interrupted by a loud commotion at the door. The two men, who entered earlier, shoved several crying children through the door and sat them down on a bench with a loud thud, then turned around and stood quietly near the door. The teacher frowned. She asked the interpreter if he had seen the children before. He nodded his head and named the children. She shrugged her thin shoulders and continued teaching. Satisfied that they had kept their promise, the two Naabeehó leaders left the school house to take their place outside the school to keep watch over the children. The Naabeehó leaders were never told they were supposed to send the *same* thirty children to school every day.

The day was much like the other five days, except for the crying children who were shoved into their seats, but Naabeehó 'Ashkii was glad it was over. Just as his maternal grandfather had promised, Hashké Yił Naabaah stood near the door waiting for his grandson to exit the school. The young boy was anxious to get home and listen to his maternal grandfather's wise words.

****

A few more times, Naabeehó 'Ashkii and his grandfather returned to the school with a few warriors who protected their leader and his grandson from the wild animals. The lessons were similar to the first lessons. The gloves the teacher wore were always a different color.

His grandfather kept his promise to stay right outside the school until his grandson exited the building. Other Naabeehó leaders did the same. They found the school was a great place to renew friendships, plan for their people, and visit.

One day, when Naabeehó 'Ashkii and his grandfather Hashké Yił Naabaah arrived at the school, after having traveled from Dziłíjiin *Black Mesa,* they found the school house locked. They learned Miss Gaston had married a young missionary preacher and that they left the fort to live among the Pueblo Indians. This meant no more school! Naabeehó 'Ashkii was elated. He never understood the reason he had to sit in one place all day and stare at the little pictures the teacher was drawing on a large flat board.

Hashké Yił Naabaah and his grandson stayed at the fort a few days longer than the two days they usually allowed themselves. Hashké Yił Naabaah and other Naabeehó leaders met and decided they kept their promise to send their children to school but the federal government had not kept its promise. The school had been shut down. The leaders decided their people needed to return to their own homes to protect their lands from white settlers, other Indian groups who were looking for additional land, and all the wild animals which still ran in great numbers.

Naabeehó 'Ashkii listened to the great Peace Leader Barboncito tell the many Naabeehó people who still resided at the fort,

"Danihikéyahgóó 'anídahidiikah. Áadi bik'ehgo dahinii'nánée, bee danihidi'neelzánée bee nída'diildįįł. Nihe'í'óol'įįł bee nída'diildįįł." *Let's return to our own lands. There, let us immerse ourselves in the traditions with which we were raised. Let us immerse ourselves in our culture.* He paused and continued,

"Łą́ nídiidleeł. T'óó'ahonii'yóí 'ádanihi'disdįįd. Hastóí danohłínígíí, niha'áłchíní bik'i nidaołdzil. T'áadoo bich'į' nidahwiiyołnání. Hojoobá'ígo dahazlį́'ígíí 'ádaat'į. Yéego txi'dahooznii'ígíí 'ádaat'į." *Our population will grow again. Many of us have been killed. Those of you who are men, work to provide for your children. Don't make life difficult for them. They are ones who barely survived. They are ones who experienced extreme suffering.*
He paused again before he continued, saying,

"Danihizáanii bik'i nidaołdzil, t'áadoo nihik'ee nidanichéhí. Yéego txi'dahooznii'. Áłchíní nihá nidayiishchį́." *Work to provide for your wives, don't ever make them run for safety because of your actions. They have suffered greatly. They have borne your children.* Looking at the men, he said,

"Doo 'éí nihe'anaa'í k'ehgo dahinii'náa da doo. 'Ahíłká 'anídaohjah, t'áadoo t'óó nigháíjí dziil dadiits'a'í, áká 'adoołwoł." *Let us never live like our enemy. Help one another, don't just listen as someone exerts strength in another area. Help one another.*

"T'áadoo kéyah ałch'į' baa danohchxį'í. K'asídą́ą́' yee' t'áadoo baa néiidzáa da! Nihe'anaa'í nihikéyah yidáahjį' daazlį́į́'go biniinaa nahgóó, da'ni'néégóó, 'adanihineeskaad. Áadi txi'dahwii'níihgo, kodi nihikéyah yę́ę t'óó bíni' si'ą́ągo biniinaa naaldlooshii da'ałchiní yikáa'gi yíląąd ha'ní. Nihikéyah ałch'į' baa danohchxį'gogo 'éí 'ákónááhodoo'nííł." *Don't be greedy with your land. We almost did not come back to it! Our enemy coveted our land and that is the reason they chased us away to the place of death (Fort Sumner). There, we suffered while our land stood idle, and for that reason our land has been overrun with wild animals, it is said. If you are greedy with your land, it will happen again.*

"Kéyah binidaołnish. Dá'ák'eh naazhóodgo 'ádeiyínósin. Sáanii danohłínígíí, nááda'ohtł'óogo nihá yá'át'ééh." *Work the land. Maintain large cornfields. Those of you who are women, weave once again, it is good for you.* Blinking back tears, he continued,

"Shooh, shidine'é, baa nídanihooshkąąh. Díí saad béédaołniih dooleeł dóó bik'ehgo dahinohnáa doo. Díí saad béédaołniihgo ts'ídá doo nihik'idínóochéeł da. Nihich'ááh nidaabaah dooleeł ahwííyéel'áágóó:" *Listen, my people, I beg of you. Remember these words and live by them. When you remember these words, they will never forsake you. They will enter warfare on your behalf, long into the future;*

"K'é lá. *There is kinship.*

"Ił ídlį́ lá. *There is respect.*

"Ił aahojooba' lá. *There is kindness.*

"Ayóó'ó'ó'ni' lá. *There is love.*

"Sodizin lá. *There is prayer.*

"Hayiin hólǫ́ǫgo lá. *One should always have a song to sing.*

"Ił hada'íínółní. *Have patience with one another.*

"Hada'íínółní." *Have hope.*

"Díí dó' shooh. Díí saad béédaołniihgo ts'ídá doo nihik'eh hodeesdlį́į'go haz'ą́ą da doo. 'Áádóó 'ałdó' béédaołniihgo dóó bee 'ałch'į' háádaohdzihgo, nihada'áłchíní bee bich'į' háádaohdzihgo ts'ídá doo nihik'idínóochéeł da.

T'áá hó 'ájít'éego t'éiyá..."

This too, listen. Remember these words, they will never leave you defeated. And also, if you remember these words and speak them to one another, and speak them to your children, these words will never forsake you:

"It is up to you if you want to succeed...

Chapter Sixteen

New Life!

The white light of dawn danced on the eastern horizon when Hashké Yił Naabaah woke his grandson. They placed their few belongings on their backs and turned their faces toward the long steep western slope behind the fort.

On top of the high hill, they saw the camp of the Asdzą́ą́ Télii Neiniłkaadí *Woman Who Herds Donkeys.* She saw them approaching and wanted to speak to Hashké Yił Naabaah. Behind her on the ground, sat a young woman whose face was badly bruised and who was crying.

"Díí 'asdzání háíshį́į́ hainitá. Nihe'anaa'í bitsį' daalgai bidiníníigíí 'atxídabiilaa lá. *This young woman is looking for someone. The ones you call our enemies with white skin are the ones who hurt her.* Turning to the young woman she asked,

"Haa lá 'éí wolyé, diníi ne'?" *What did you say was the name?*

"Dzáníbaa'. Hastiin yił iiná 'íił'ínígíí 'éí Naashgálí dine'é nilį." *Dzáníbaa'. The man with whom she makes her life is a Mescalero Apache man.*

"Éí daats'í bééhonísin? T'áadoo jidóya'ígóó da, jiní. T'óó t'áákáa da bína'ídídéeshkił, jiníí nít'ę́ę́' doo yildiní ła' hassiłgo dah hodiidzį́į́z lá, 'áko nidi yéego shį́į́ bił ahijoogą́ą'go 'índa hodíichid, jiní." *Maybe you know them. She has no where to go, it is said. She wanted to ask around, but the awful ones grabbed her and dragged her off, she fought fiercely against them and they released her, it is said.*

The young woman told Hashké Yił Naabaah how she met the woman named Dzáníbaa' and their lengthy stay on the eastern side of the Pecos River when they were held as prisoners of war at Fort Sumner. Hashké Yił Naabaah listened and assumed the woman was from the western side of Diné bikéyah *Navajo land* based on her pronunciation of many Naabeehó words.

"Kéédahwiit'ínéegóó nihikéé' náádáał doo ch'ééh bidííniid nidi, 'áłtsé 'ei 'asdzání jíízhi'ígíí hadínéeshtaał jiníigo biniinaa kwe'é haba' nahísíitą́." *I asked her to come home with us but she wanted to look for the young woman she named and that is the reason we are waiting here for her.* Hashké Yił Naabaah remembered his Dzáníbaa' had told him about a Naabeehó woman who lived with her and helped her deliver her son, so he asked,

"Ei 'asdzání Dzáníbaa' biyázhí yishchíníígíísh ashkii 'éí doodai' at'ééd?" *The young woman Dzáníbaa', the little one she birthed, was it a boy or a girl?*

"Ashkii yishchį. Éí 'áádóó bádí yił ná'ahiiltsąągo, bádí bá baa 'áháshyąą nít'ęę'. Dzáníbaa' bádí bizhé'é biyiin yidiizts'ąą'go yiniiłt'aa bité'ázini kéédahat'ínígóó 'íiná." *She delivered a boy. After that, she reunited with her older sister and I cared for her older sister. Dzáníbaa''s older sister heard the song of her father and by means of the song, they returned to their relatives.* Hashké Yił Naabaah was speechless. He told the young woman,

"Shitsi' Dzáníbaa' wolyé. Hanítáhígíí 'éí shitsi'." *My daughter's name is Dzáníbaa'. The one you are searching for is my daughter.* The young woman whimpered softly while Asdzą́ą́ Télii Neiniłkaadí comforted her.

"Áko lá, txį', hooghangóó ni." *Okay, let's go home,* Hashké Yił Naabaah declared. Both women screamed as they scrambled, trying to get up off of the ground. Asdzą́ą́ Télii Neiniłkaadí ordered her young helpers to grab the reins of four donkeys. She grabbed the reins out of the hands of the young men and pushed them into Hashké Yił Naabaah's hand, saying,

Nihí nihidine'é ła' níléí Tó Haach'í'ígóó télii bee nídadeegį, sáanii t'áá yéego náás daazlį́į' léi', áádóó 'éí t'áá nihí, shich'é'e dóó shí, nihikéyahgóó nídee'ná. 'Ei télii ts'ídá t'áá 'ałtsogóó dahoo'į. Hooghandi nánohkaigo bidadidíichił. Ei t'áá łáhígi 'ádaat'įįgo kéédahwiit'ínídi nídookah. Ayóo bił béédahózin. Shooh, bich'į' hodiwoshgo t'éí. Doo bich'į' jidilwoshgóó 'éí t'óó hach'į' be'ádadíláah łeh. Ayóo 'ak'ehdahółʼį. Dei 'oo'ááł. Nizhónígo shį́į hooghandi nídohkah. Ahéhee', shizhé'é yázhí, nit'áahjį' aniicháą'go bee nihikáa'jį' hazlį́į́'. Ayóo 'aajiiníba'go naa 'ákonisin." *We are transporting some of our people back to Tohatchi, some elderly women and men. After that, me and my daughter will move back to our own land. Those donkeys have been everywhere. When you get home, release them. Without stopping, they will return to our home. They are very knowledgeable. Listen, you need to scold them. If you don't scold them they will act silly toward you. They are very obedient. The sun is rising. May you return home nicely. Thank you, my paternal uncle, you spared our lives when we ran to you for protection. I know you are a very kind man.*

"Ahéhee', shitsi', nihí dó', nizhónígo hooghandi nídoohkah. Dziłíjiinjį' dishoo'áazhgogo, nihaa ji'ash. Áadi nihik'éí hóló̜." *Thank you, my daughter, you also, may you return home nicely. When you come to Black Mesa, come to us. There, you have relatives.* With those parting words, Hashké Yił Naabaah placed the young woman on a donkey, climbed on a donkey, yelled at the donkeys to get them going, and led the group homeward.

He was anxious to see his beautiful Nínááníbaa'. He knew she was worried.

****

Nínááníbaa' was steadily regaining her strength. She was worried about Hashké Yił Naabaah and Naabeehó 'Ashkii and Kiizhóní and the two warriors who accompanied them. They were not back from taking her grandson to attend his one day of school. She knew Dédii was also wondering where they were. With every breath she took, she listened for the sound of horses' hooves on the soft earth. She caught her breath, no, she thought, they are on foot.

"Sha'áłchíní bizhé'é dóó shitsóí dóó Kiizhóní nizhónígo kodi tsxį́įłgo nídookah, t'áadoo nidabiníłtł'aaígóó," *Bring the father of my children and my grandson and Kiizhóní home safely and quickly without anything slowing them down,* she prayed. Her worries were getting the best of her when she heard the sound of animals running into their valley. "The men are out hunting wild animals, only the young boys are here who can help us protect ourselves," she thought. "I used it once before to protect myself, I will use it again," she vowed as she grabbed her spindle and held it tight as she stood near the door of her hogan.

The sound of hooves became louder. Just when she stood firm on her feet with her spindle tightly grasped overhead, she heard,

"Shiyázhí... Shiyázhí..." *My little one... My little one...* She dropped her spindle and raced out the door and into the arms of Hashké Yił Naabaah. The two lovers' lips met, oblivious of the four donkeys who patiently stood nearby waiting for orders. One donkey still held its rider, the young woman.

Hashké Yił Naabaah called his daughter Dzáníbaa'. His daughter, hearing his voice quickly exited her make-shift home, looked at the young woman, smiled weakly at her, and stood at her father's side. Her father said,

"Díí 'asdzání íkanitá. Níléídęę' bił nániikai." *This woman is looking for you. We brought her back with us.* Dzáníbaa' reached out to the woman. The woman started crying and could not talk. Tears mixed with dried blood flowed down her face.

"T'áá shizááká íkanishtáago 'aadęę' akéé' shi'deegį. Doo nidi shįį́ shéénílniih da." *By sheer desire, I have been looking for you. I was brought here. You probably don't remember me.*

"Shinálí, da' niísh áníťį?" *My maternal grandmother (by clan), is it you?* replied Dzáníbaa' in a compassionate voice.

"Aoo', shí 'áshťį, shinálí. T'óó shaa'iih." *Yes, it's me, my granddaughter. I look awful.* Hashké Yił Naabaah bolted forward to catch the woman who lost her balance while sitting on the donkey. Held securely in his arms, he took her to Dzáníbaa''s make-shift home.
Loud cries were heard. It was the voice of Dzáníbaa' telling the woman,

"Nighandi néínídzá, shinálí. Háshinee'. T'áá kǫ́ǫ́ nighan áhodíílííł." *You have come back to your home. Dear one. Make your home here.* Later, Dzáníbaa' asked her brothers to build the woman she called, "Shinálí", a temporary hogan, which they promised they would.

Hashké Yił Naabaah called his family together to inform them of them of the events that took place at Fort Defiance and the decisions that were made by the Naabeehó leaders. The family cheered when they heard the young Naaabeehó 'Ashkii would not have to return to

Fort Defiance with his maternal grandfather and Kiizhóní. Hashké Yił Naabaah proudly announced,

"Díí, shicheii yázhí Naabeehó 'Ashkii dabidii'ní. Doo 'éí 'ei bízhi' da doo. K'ad éí 'Ach'ą́ąh Naabaah wolyée dooleeł, háálá hadine' ch'iiyáán bich'į' ch'éédadit'áah dooleeł biniiyé, t'áá kónízáhíjį' nidi, naaltsoos yíhooł'ą́ą́'. Bił aahojooba' lá. K'ad łą́ą 'ałtįį' ła' bá 'ádoolnííł dóó k'aa' ła' ádá 'íidoolííł." *We call my young grandson Navajo Boy. That will not be his name anymore. He will be called One Who Goes to War Protecting Others, because, even for a short time, he learned paper just so his people could be given food. He is kind. Now a bow will be made for him and he will make his own arrows.* 'Ach'ą́ąh Naabaah looked at his mother and smiled so sweetly.

Hashké Yił Naabaah told his warriors,

"Naaldlooshii da'ałchiní łą́ągo t'ah nidabikéé'. Éí 'ałtso nidadooltsxił, ákogo 'índa nihada'ałchíní t'áá bí danízinjį' tł'óo'di nidaanée doo. Naaldlooshii báádahadzidii doo nihit'áahjį' nídadikah da daazlį́į'go 'índa nihimá bidibé dóó bitł'ízí dóó nihilį́į' níléígóó nihicheii nihá 'iineeskaad yę́ę kojį' anídadíníilkał. Áko sáanii náá da'atł'óo doo. Nihí 'éí ninéádeiilzheeh doo dóó dá'ák'ehdi ninéádeiilnish dooleeł. Naabeehó dine'é daniidlį́! Haa'íshą', t'áá dahinii'nánéegi 'át'éego dahinii'náa doo." *There are still many tracks of wild animals. We will hunt them, once we do, our children will be able to play outside all they want. When the dangerous animals no longer come near our homes, we will bring home the livestock your maternal grandfather took to an uncertain place for us. The women will weave once again.*

We will hunt and we will work in our cornfields once again. We are Navajo! Let us live the way we used to live.

Hashké Yił Naabaah's warriors cheered. They were ready to perfect their hunting skills once again.

****

The young Naabeehó woman Nínáánícbaa' and Hashké Yił Naabaah renamed Akéé' Naazbaa' *One Who Followed in Warfare*, brought with her sad news. She reported that the tall gray-haired one was killed when his horse bucked him off when the fifth procession of Naabeehó people were escorted by the soldiers through the rocky wagon road that ran near one of the Pueblo villages.

"Łį́į́' adah abíí łgo'go tsé yíneesnih. T'áá 'ákwe'é haa'ígishį́į́ yá hadahwiisgeedgo 'ákwe'é yishjoolgo 'ádayiilaa. T'áá 'ákwe'é bínaháaltą́ągo yaa 'a'deez'ą́. Shą́ą́', éí hastiin na'nilhod dóó bigish hólǫ́ǫ́ dóó bináá' t'óó bé'áshjéé'. Naashgálí dine'é bitahgi nihighan yę́ędą́ą́' nihitah ałnáhanádáah ne'. Doo 'ayóo bináhashch'ííʼ da nít'ę́ę́'." *The horse bucked him off and he hit his head on a rock. They dug a grave for him there. We stayed nearby until late afternoon. He was the man who came around when we lived among the Mescalero Apache people. Remember, he limped and used a cane and had a patch over his eye? He was not mean.*

When Dédii heard the news, she jumped up and ran from the group, running wildly toward her maternal grandfather's home. Hashké Yił Naabaah and Kiizhóní ran after her. They found her amidst the sagebrush bushes where she had fallen. Her father knelt beside her and consoled her with gentle words only he could speak to begin to heal her broken heart.

"Ních'aad, shiyázhí. T'áadoo nihe'anaa'í baa nichaaí. Hastiin, niyáázh bá shíníłchínígíí baa nichago 'éí t'áá'áko. 'Éí hastiin biniiłt'aa nihiyázhí hólǫ́. Nihiyázhí, shicheii yázhí, 'ayóó'ádeiyí'níi'ní." *Don't cry, my little one. Do not cry over our enemy. It is alright for you to cry over the man for whom you bore your child. It is through him that we have a little one. We love our little one very much. My little grandson.* The reason Hashké Yił Naabaah spoke those words was because he remembered his Dédii had announced the tall gray-haired one was not the father of her son because he had never acknowledged his son nor did he greet his son, and in addition, she felt he had abandoned her and her people once again when the two men killed the goat at the parade grounds at Fort Sumner.

"Éí hastiin doo shił naaki nilį́įgóó 'ayóó'íiní'níigo łą́ nááhai. Bí dó' ayóó'ánó'níí nít'ę́ę́'. Niyázhí t'áadoo k'é yidííniid daígíí biniinaa t'áadoo baa néínídzáa da. Doo bił ahidini'ts'a'góó biniinaa t'áadoo hazhó'ó bił ahił nahosínílne' da. K'ad t'áadoo baa níni'í. Niyázhí bik'éí t'óó'ahayóí. Bik'éí yiníi'gi bighan." *Without a doubt, I know you loved that man. You did not return to him because he did not greet his son. It was because you did not speak the same language that you never were able to discuss it with him. Now don't feel bad about it. Your little one has many relatives. He lives among his relatives.* Dédii crawled into her father's arms and cried tears that had been hidden deep in her heart for many years. Layers and years of hurt came spilling out of her as raw emotion shook her thin body.

"ShiDédii, t'óó naahojoobá'ígo nichah, nik'éí 'ádin nahalingo nichah. Shiyázhí, t'óó shił naahojoobá'í. Éí hastiin Tsé Hootsohdi yisdáníídzį́į́z. 'Aoo', aoo', ayóó'ííní'níí nít'ęę́', shiyázhí, aoo', aoo'... Ních'aad, shiyázhí, ních'aad..." *My Dédii, you cry so pitifully, you cry as if you have no relatives. I have such sympathy for you. That man saved your life at Fort Defiance. Yes, yes, you loved him very much, my little one, yes, yes... Don't cry, my little one, don't cry...* was all Hashké Yił Naabaah could say as he held and consoled his daughter, stroking her hair and wiping away her tears. When Dédii's pitiful cries became whimpers, Hashké Yił Naabaah asked Kiizhóní to help them up.

In one swoop Kiizhóní picked up Dédii and waited for Hashké Yił Naabaah to get up. Without a word, father, daughter, and friend walked home.

"Kojí yah aniłteeh, bimá shį́į́ yich'į' bíni'," *Bring her in here, she most likely wants to see her mother.* Kiizhóní carried Dédii in and gently placed her in her mother's lap. Fresh cries shook Dédii's frail body while her mother gently spoke kind loving words to her. Nínáánībaa' wiped her daughter's face with a soft wet cloth. Nínáánībaa' could hear Kiizhóní clearing his throat as he stood near the entrance of the hogan. When Dédii's cries became a whimper, Kiizhóní walked out of the hogan.

The cries stopped. With her head in her mother's lap, Dédii lay still with her head next to her mother's abdomen. She felt a gentle poke and another one. Dédii sat up, the stray strands of her hair standing straight up. She excitedly screamed,

"Shimá, da' niiísh...?" *My mother, are you...?* pointing to her mother's abdomen. Embarrassed, her mother said,

"Aoo', nitsilí 'éí doodai' nideezhí haleeh." *Yes, you are going to have a younger brother or a younger sister.* Forgetting her sadness, Dédii screamed,

"Záanii, Záanii, hágo!" Záanii, Záanii, *come here!*

"Ge' shooh, t'áadoo t'óó 'ayóo baa nahołne'é. 'Amá sání sélį́į́'go, t'óó 'ayóo kónísht'é. Nihí yee' nida'iiyołchííhgo beełt'é. Yáadilá, 'ałdó'!" *Now listen, don't tell others about it. I have become a grandmother and I am like this. It is more appropriate for you all to birth babies. What a happening!* Dzáníbaa' came rushing in thinking something happened to her sister. Seeing her sister's wild-looking hair, she became even more concerned. Stepping closer to her sister to smooth her hair down, Dzáníbaa' cried,

"Haash yinidzaa?" *What happened to you?*

"Díí yee' nihitsilí 'éí doodai' nihideezhí shinii'jį' náshineeztáál!" *Our younger brother or our younger sister kicked me in the face!* Dédii cried. Confused, Dzáníbaa' cried,

"Háí? Hádą́ą́'? Háadi? Ha'át'íísh baa yáníłti'?" *Who? When? Where? What are you talking about?* she demanded to know.

"Ániid, shimá bitsék'ee nésh'ą́ą́ nít'ę́ę́' awéé' shiniijį' náshineeztáál." *I had my head on my mother's lap and a baby kicked me in the face.* Still confused, Dzáníbaa' turned toward her mother and asked,

"Shimá, ha'át'íísh yaa yáłti'?" *My mother, what is she talking about?* Noticing their mother's embarrassed grin, Dzáníbaa' noticed her mother placed her hands over her abdomen. Dzáníbaa' looked down. Finally the realization crept over her face.

"Shimá, da' ni?" *My mother, you?* Nínááníbaa' smiled sheepishly and said,

"Aoo', k'adí t'áadoo baa nahołne'é." *Yes, now stop, don't tell anyone.* Dzáníbaa' looked at her sister and started laughing, saying,

"Nitsii' t'óó nił dah deeshzhah! Awéé chí'í shįį́ biyah hodíníłhxizgo biniinaa nánineeztáál!" *Your hair is standing up all over! You probably scared the fetus and that is why he/she kicked you!* Dédii and Dzáníbaa' started giggling as they hugged their mother real close. Nínááníbaa' told her daughter,

"Tó ła' ná nídiishkaah. Nitsii' ná táádiigis. Ninitsékees hastiin nahgóó bąąh anił'eeł." *I'm going to get you some water. We will wash your hair. Wash the memories of that man off of your mind.* Nínááníbaa' stepped outside to find her sons, Kiizhóní, Hashké Yił Naabaah, Tsék'iz Naazbaa', Akéé' Naazbaa' and all the children standing right outside her door. As if she was yanked back inside by a rope, Nínááníbaa' disappeared back inside her hogan. She was so embarrassed.

"T'óó 'ayóo diné ch'é'átiingi 'ałk'idabinii'. *People's faces are piled on top of one another outside (there is a large crowd outside).* She sat down on her rolled up rug blanket and buried her head in her hands and did not want to face anyone. Dzáníbaa' stepped outside and gestured to her father to let him know his presence was needed inside. Hashké Yił Naabaah nearly jumped over his children to get to his Nínááníbaa' who sat red-faced on her rug blanket. He knelt down beside her and spoke in quiet words to his wife. She asked in a whisper if the people outside heard the news of her pregnancy. Hashké Yił Naabaah smiled the biggest smile she had ever seen.

"Díí yee' baa hózhóonii, baa 'ahééh ílíinii nihich'į' áhoodzaa. Nihiyázhí ła' nááhádleeh. Naabaahii yázhí 'éí doodai' atł'óhí yázhí nihee haleeh. Hahgo da, t'áá sáhí háágóó da diit'ash. Áadii ninááł naashgeed doo biniiyé." *This is a beautiful happening, a grateful event has happened to us. We are going to have another little one. We are going to have either a little warrior or a little weaver. Sometime, we need to go somewhere, just by ourselves. I want to show off there in front of you.* Nínááníbaa' laughed and interrupted him,

"Tł'ízí chǫǫh haniih. Shą́ą́' éí tázhdígishgo naanáalwoł łeh áádóó naalgeedgo bitsii' yiłmaz łeh." *You're not a billy goat. Remember when you shear it, it runs around and bucks all over the place while it shakes its head back and forth.* Hashké Yił Naabaah laughed and added,

"K'ad nidi, k'adni' kodóó ch'íníshgeed, háálá nihich'į' áhoodzaaígíí doo chohoo'íį́góó baa shił hózhǫ́." *Even now, I want to go out and jump up and down because I am so excited about what has happened to us.* Soon, Nínááníbaa' was smiling and wondered,

"Háájí 'i'iisdee'?" *Where did everyone go?*

"Dabighanígóó shį́į́ 'anáákai. Nihaa bił dahózhǫ́ǫgo. NihiDédii 'éí bii' hááhwiisdoh." *They probably went back to their own homes. They are happy about us. Our Dédii feels better.* Hearing his words, Nínáánîbaa' told her husband how Dédii learned she was pregnant, recalling Dédii's accusation that the fetus kicked her. Hashké Yił Naabaah laughed so hard. Tears danced in Nínáánîbaa''s eyes. She had not heard her husband laugh so loud and so hard in over five years. Her husband pulled her into his arms, kissed her passionately and deeply and held her ever so closely. When he heard footsteps approaching, he reluctantly let his wife go and walked out to meet the person who came to visit. Watching her husband leave their home, Nínáánîbaa' placed her hands over her abdomen and breathed,

"Ahéhee', shiyázhí." *Thank you, my little one.*

Tsék'iz Naazbaa' entered Nínáánîbaa''s hogan wanting to speak to her. She started crying and could not speak. Finally, she told her mother-in-law,

"Shí dó' yistsą́ą gi'áté." *I think I am pregnant also.* Nínáánîbaa' asked a few questions and determined her daughter-in-law was indeed pregnant. The two women embraced. Nínáánîbaa' asked Tsék'iz Naazbaa',

"Shiyáázhísh t'áá'íídą́ą́' bił hwíínílne'?" *Did you tell my son already?*

"Nidaga', t'ah dooda. Hazhó'ó bínanídééłkidgo 'índa nisingo ch'ééh aadę́ę́' nich'į' dah yisháah nít'ę́ę́'." *No, not yet. I wanted to ask you questions about it first. I have been wanting to come over and see you.*

Nínááníbaa' was so excited. She hugged Tsék'iz Naazbaa' and whispered,

"Ahéhee', awée'. Shinálí yázhí haleeh. Shiyáázh doo ts'íí'át'éégóó yaa bił hózhǫ́ǫ doo." *Thank you, baby. I am going to have a little grandchild through my son. My son will be extremely happy about it.*

****

After her daughter-in-law left, Nínááníbaa' thought back to the night her little one was conceived. It was a clear night, a night when all her adopted children were invited to stay with her daughters and their sons.

She remembered the way the fire in the center of her make-shift hogan cast a beautiful peach glow on the log walls of her home. She was sharing a cup of wild tea with her husband while they discussed their deep gratitude for their release as prisoners of war and that their family had remained intact throughout the process.

Time passed without either saying a word. Nínááníbaa' smiled to herself. She had secretly wondered how their time alone would be made possible. She had also wondered how they would express their love for one another. She had missed her husband.

Hashké Yił Naabaah whispered sweet amorous words to her, melting her heart. She knew he spoke the truth in that he had proven his love for her since the day they married so many years ago. She remembered at that time they discussed how they had not made love to one another in nearly six years. He told her how much he missed her even though she was right by his side nearly every night in that many years.

Her husband reached up and loosened her hair tie and watched her hair unfold slowly down her back. He picked up her loosened hair, lifted it to his face and buried his face in her hair, whispering,

"Mmmmmm." He lay back on their rug blanket and gently pulled her back to lay near him. With his strong hands, he touched her face, her neck, her arms, her lips, then followed his touch with kisses. Nínáánábaa' watched him kiss her fingers with his soft supple lips, then her wrists, then moved closer to her to overwhelm her senses by whispering words of love in her ear. His sensuous low whispers were as soft as her own sighs of wanting. His fingers found holes in her rug dress, through which he felt her soft skin and moaned a soft moan as he touched her in places he had forbidden himself to touch.

She opened her eyes to notice the peach glow from the fire had disappeared and had left a soft muted glow in its place. Her husband pressed his insistent mound against her thigh and begged her to remove her tattered rug dress.

"Ni biil éé' nits'ą́ą́' adeesǫ́ǫ́s sha'shin. Hadiigeeh, shiyázhí." *I may tear your rug dress. Take it off, my little one.* In one swoop of her arms, Nínáánábaa' had her rug dress off. They both giggled at how quickly it flew off. In the dim light, her husband lifted himself up on one elbow and said,

"Áłtsé, t'óó ninésh'į́." *Wait, let me look at you.* He slowly shook his head and said, "Doo lá dó', ayóó 'áníínílnin da." *You are so beautiful.* Nínáánábaa' blinked her eyes and said,

"Ni shą'? Ni'éé'?" *What about you? Your clothes?* Hashké Yił Naabaah stuttered, saying,

"Wah! Ádeiisis'nah lá. Haa'íyee', hait'éego tsxįįłgo ádaa'di'deeshjih. *Oops! I forgot about myself. Let's see how fast I can take my clothes off.* Laughing, he rolled onto his back and pulled off his tattered shirt and kicked his loose pants off. In the dim light of the fire, Nínáánibaa' looked at her husband's beautiful naked body. She could not believe she had starved herself for so many years by not allowing herself to see and touch his beautiful body. She gently pulled him close to kiss his full supple lips that were cool to her own lips. He breathed on her face ever so gently and she felt life coming back into her own body. His impassioned kiss brought back a deep longing she had missed as she drew his sweet tongue into her mouth. They held hands as they kissed deeply.

Nínáánibaa''s hunger for her husband grew deeper in their deep passionate kisses. Slowly, she guided his hand over her naked body wanting him to touch her in places that were coming alive. As he touched another part of her body, she heard him whisper over and over again,

"Nídin sélįį' nít'ęę́', shiyázhí..." *I missed you, my little one.* Nínáánibaa' turned her back to him to feel him with her entire body. Her body moved with every kiss he left on her back, her neck, her earlobes, her waist, as his hands explored her thin sensuous body, bringing her heightened pleasure. With each of his kisses, she guided his hand to a different part of her body, urging him to touch her softly. When she could no longer wait for him to claim her, she turned to lay on her back and whispered,

"Ha'át'íishą' biba'? Hágo..." *What are you waiting for? Come here...* She gently reached under him and opened her warm wanting body to him. She felt his mound enter her wanting body, making her gasp with pleasure, and matched his movements with passion. She felt wet drops falling on her face. Thinking it was his sweat, she gently wiped his drops of sweat off of her face with his shirt. She was going to wipe his face when she realized her husband was crying. He had starved himself of their love too. She answered his body by claiming it and clung on to him as tightly as she could as she answered his every move. Hungrily and passionately, they made love to one another in the soft light of the moon that filtered in through the open smoke hole.

Sensuous sounds of love burst forth as they let each other know of their satisfaction. Hashké Yił Naabaah kissed her glistening body to slow his heartbeat. His beautiful Nínáánībaa' had led him through an unrestrained lavish night of lovemaking. When the white light of dawn spread a dim light over the sky, Hashké Yił Naabaah gently made love to his beautiful wife again, guiding her movements with his stimulating words that he spoke in his low sensuous voice.

****

Several weeks later, Dédii had just finished sweeping her hogan floor when she stopped to hear someone yelling in the distance. Fear gripped her heart. Her mind flew back to a few seasons ago when they heard men yelling.

Frantically, she searched the nearby hill for her children. She saw them hiding behind what was once their large sheep corral her father and the men were rebuilding. Some children were hiding behind a pile of logs. Her heart was beating so loud and hard she could not hear what the man was yelling. She braced herself against the two poles that stood at the entryway of her home and listened. The man was talking to someone. She stretched her neck to see, and became even more afraid. The man was speaking to her mother. She listened even more intently. Her heart settled just a bit when she heard the man tell her mother of his clan.

"Tł'ááshchí'í dine'é nishłį́į dóó... Hane' yish'áałgo 'ásht'į́..." *I am of the Red Bottom people... I am bringing a message...*

Dédii straightened her back and forced herself to walk out the door to walk toward her mother to protect her. She did not recognize the man. She noticed he was dressed differently. "He could be sent by the soldiers to lure them out so they could be captured again because they had stepped out of the boundary that was set forth in the Treaty," she thought. Her mind would not rest. Many fearful scenarios flipped though her mind.

"Oh good, my mother has her spindle in her hand and she is grasping it tightly," she thought with a faint sense of relief. "Where is my father? Where are my brothers? Where is Kiizhóní?" she wondered, frantically looking around.

She watched her mother nod her head without speaking a word. The stranger pointed toward the northwestern direction. She held her breath when she saw the stranger extend his hand out to her mother. Her mother reached for his hand. Dédii walked to where her mother stood and cleared her throat. Her mother jumped back.

"Shí 'ásht'į́, shimá. T'óó yee' níighah yideesįįł nisingo biniiyé 'aadę́ę́' níyá." *It's me, my mother. I just wanted to stand here next to you, that's why I came here.* Her mother smiled.

"Ei dinééh hane' nei'áá léi' yiniiyé kodi hootaagháá lá. Naat'áanii Hashké Neiniih deiłnínígíí bidine'é yił 'aadę́ę́' nihich'į' deeznáá lá. 'Áda'azįįd nihá 'ádei'niilaa..." *That man brought us a message to tell us the leader named One Who Hands Out Scolding is coming here with his people. They are going to prepare a feast...* With those words, Nínáánībaa' started crying and grabbed her daughter and held her tight.

"Díí yee' t'áá 'óolyéego 'ach'ą́ shi'niiłhxį́. Dibé bitsį' tsíídkáá' sit'éhígíí séłįhgo náádideeshdááł. Atoo' ła' yishdlą́ą'go náádideeshdááł. Átsą́ą' bídeesht'ą́ą'go náádideeshdááł..." *I am literally dying for the taste of mutton. When I taste mutton that has been cooked over hot coals, I will regain my health. When I drink lamb stew, I will regain my health. When I tear meat off of a mutton rib, I will regain my health...* Dédii could not stand it any longer, she interrupted her mother, saying,

"K'adí, shimá, k'adí. T'áadoo bitaa 'íínízhíhí. Shí dó' ach'ą́ shi'niiłhxįįgo 'át'é." T*hat's enough, my mother, that's enough. Don't name them. I am also dying for the* *taste of mutton as well.* Mother and daughter stumbled back into Nínááníbaa"s home and collapsed on the bare floor.

"Ashdla' yiskąągo nihaa 'íldééh, jiní. Jáád da baa ni'dooldah dóó 'ahaahoniné 'ałdó', jiní." *It is said they will be here in five days. There will be races and games as well, it is said.* Dzáníbaa' and Tsék'iz Naazbaa' heard the happy screams from the two women and were curious about the reason.

Nínááníbaa' and her daughters learned Hashké Yił Naabaah and the men had visited several leaders in the area. The leaders were worried about the elders who had not recovered, had no homes, or who had been left to fend for themselves. Hashké Yił Naabaah announced each family would be required to adopt an elder who was alone, as well as adopt children who were left orphaned. The leaders also wanted their people to ensure the children were happy and cared for. He wanted the people to resume their way of life before it was needlessly and carelessly interrupted. He pleaded,

"Áłchíní nidaanéé dóó yádaałti' dóó 'anídaadloh
yiits'a'go bee yá'át'ééh nídadiidleeł.
"Áłchíní sin nideidi'a' yiits'a'go bee
yá'át'ééh nídadiidleeł.
"Áłchíní k'i'dilyéegi 'áká 'anídaalwo'go dóó
nida'niłkaadgo bee yá'át'ééh nídadiidleeł."
When we hear the children playing and talking and
laughing, we will get better.
When we hear the children singing songs,

we will get better.

When we see the children helping in the cornfield and herding sheep, we will get better.

"Shooh, doo 'éí 'áłchíní t'éiyá da. 'Acheii dasoolį́'ígií dóó 'amá sání danohłíngíí dóó 'análí danohłínígíí 'ałdó' nidaohnéego dóó da'ohk'áago dóó yádaołti'go dóó da'ohtł'óogo dóó sin bee nida'doh'a'go dóó nida'nołkaadgo dóó k'ééda'dohdléehgo dóó 'anídaohdloh yiits'a'go, bee yá'át'ééh nídadiidleeł dóó nihikéyah bikáá'góó yá'áhoot'ééh náhodoodleeł. *Listen, this is not only in regards to our children. Those of you who are maternal grandfathers and those of you who are maternal grandmothers and those of you who are paternal grandparents also, when we hear you play and grind corn and talk and weave and sing and herd sheep and plant corn and laugh, we will all get better and it will heal our land.*

"Nihikéyah doo ts'íí'át'éégóó nihíhoosa'go 'át'é. T'áá'ániit'é nihits'ą́ądóó hodiits'a'go t'áá'ałtsoní yá'át'ééh nídadoodleełgo 'át'é. Háda'íísíníilts'ą́ą' doo." *Our land desperately missed us. If we can all be heard from, all things will get better. Let's all listen for the sounds.*

****

The day of the gathering was a day filled with Naabeehó people renewing acquaintances. When elders saw one another, wails of relief of survival were heard throughout the day. The elders worried about having so many of their people gathered in one place at one time. They scolded the leaders for the gathering, reminding them that each time the people gathered for the counting of the people at Fort Sumner, many Naabeehó people lost their lives. For that reason, the elders remained outside of the happy gathering, visiting among themselves. The elders told their people the Naabeehó people were to be scattered throughout the land they called Diné bikéyah *Navajo land* and not in little villages like their enemies. They wanted their people to scatter past the small Reservation that was set aside for the Naabeehó people in the Treaty. There was plenty of land between the four sacred mountains, the mountains that would remain their boundary.

The elders warned.

"T'ááláhígi 'ałk'íikah. Doo bá nidanitł'aaígóó nihe'anaa'í dah danihidínóołkał. Níhíláah danihighanígóó 'anídahoohkááh," *We are closely gathered in one place. It will not be difficult for our enemy to chase us off. Go, back to your own homes,* they urged. The leaders consoled the elders but the look of fear was still etched into the faces and eyes of the elders.

****

A feast of mutton broiled over hot coals near the large fire pit was the event most talked about. The children's eyes nearly popped out of their sockets when they saw over one hundred sheep in the makeshift corral that was built for the gathering. They wondered who the sheep belonged to.

Nínááníbaa' told the children the sheep belong to the leader named Hashké Neiniih *One Who Hands Out*

Scolding. He and his people were never forced to walk many miles to the east. They hid in canyons beyond Naatsis'áán *Navajo Mountain*. He is a great leader. He took good care of his people. He is the one who planned this gathering.

Beyond the sheep corral was another corral where nearly twenty beautiful horses were kept. Pointing to the horses, she told the children the horses belonged to the great leader Hashké Neiniih. The children were in awe of the great leader.

Dédii and Dzáníbaa' and Tsék'iz Naazbaa', and the new arrival, Akéé' Naazbaa' stepped away from the crowd. They looked through the crowd of young men who were braiding whips from fresh yucca leaves and weaving bridles from the tanned hides which were placed before them. Dédii and Dzáníbaa' saw their father standing tall among the leaders as he sliced through the hides to make strips for the whip making contest. Their brothers were braiding whips, competing to see who could make the most handsome whip for their father.

The four women turned to watch a group of women butchering two sheep for the feast. It was unheard of! The women usually had to be coaxed into killing a sheep. They looked at the faces of the women standing over the sheep. Tears were flowing down the faces of the women. They treasured the memory of having a full corral of sheep. Dédii and Dzáníbaa' tried to remember the last time when they heard the sound of a sheep being butchered. The women shouted friendly orders to one another, other women were grunting together,

"Wóó'małaa!" *(Sound of strength being exerted).*

"Aadi, 'aadi!" *Help, help!*

"Tsxį́įłgo, tsxį́įłgo!" *Hurry, hurry!*

"Aadóó yiiłtsóód." *Get a hold of it from there.*

"Kojígo yiisił!" *Get a hold of it from this side!* Soon all that was left were the skins of the two sheep. The skins were carefully and quickly stretched and pinned to the ground with sharp sticks. The meat was prepared for roasting over the hot coals by another group of women. Dédii and Dzáníbaa' felt guilty for standing by and watching the activity but the older women insisted they wanted to have the honor of butchering the sheep and preparing the meat, an activity they had missed for six long years.

Dédii and Dzáníbaa' saw their mother sitting on the ground with other women. Their mother's rug dress was tattered and worn but she sat proudly with the women. They were making blue corn crepes for the elders and for the children who waited impatiently. Instinctively, the two sisters closed their eyes and breathed deeply. They could smell the faint scent of browned blue corn. Their mouths watered and tears danced in their eyes.

Everyone let out a cheer when the great leader Hashké Neiniih announced,

"Da'oosą́ąooo. Da'óhsą́. Da'ohsą́!" *Eat. All of you, eat. All of you, eat!* The group sat down to a meal they had only dreamed of for six long years. The only sound heard was the sound of people breathing. Contentment hovered above the heads of the starved Naabeehó people.

After the tasty meal and after a short time of resting and visiting, the great leader, Hashké Neiniih asked the young men to join a foot race to win prizes. Two of the prizes were the skin of the two sheep that were butchered.

Dédii and Dzáníbaa' watched with eagerness as their two brothers bravely entered the race. With dust rising at their feet, Nahat'á Yinaabaa and Tł'ée'go Naabaah disappeared over the southern horizon. At the end of the day, they saw Nahat'á Yinaabaah running among the sagebrush. He was the first runner to return. With his face dripping with sweat, he collapsed at his wife's feet. He was pleased at his win because it meant he won one of the sheepskins. He had already decided he would give the soft sheepskin to his mother so she could have a thick, soft sheepskin upon which she could sleep.

When Nahat'á Yinaabaah was presented with the sheep skin, he turned and gave it to his mother. With tears in her eyes, Nínáánibaa' gently ran her fingers over the thick woolen fibers. Dédii and Dzáníbaa' hurriedly helped their mother stretch out the skin and pin it to the ground to dry. That night, Nínáánibaa' dreamed of the night when she could lie down on the soft sheepskin to be surrounded by its soft warmth. She had a restful night thinking of her new gift. She was grateful for her gift.

The next day, the meat left over from the day before was prepared in a dumpling stew for the people. While the stew was boiling over an open fire, the great leader Hashké Neiniih called together the women who had recently returned from Fort Sumner. The leader asked his young men to give each woman two sheep. The women gasped! Tears flowed freely down each woman's face. Nínáánibaa''s hands shook. The yucca ropes the young men made the day before were used to lead the sheep to their new owners. Nínáánibaa' could not believe ten sheep were led to her and her daughters and Tsék'iz Naazbaa' and Akéé' Naazbaa'. The sheep were yearlings, fat, and so beautiful.

"K'ad náá'ítł'óo dooleeł, shimá," *Now you will be weaving again, my mother,* Dzáníbaa' said softly.

"Aoo, aoo'," *Yes, yes,* was her mother's reply.

An unwilling young ram was pulled to the center of the gathering and led to Nínáánibaa'. Everyone laughed because the ram lowered his horns and tried to ram a few children. Secretly, Nínáánibaa' named the ram "Doo Bá 'Ats'ídí" *One who is not happy.*

The people were puzzled when young men brought large bags, the kind of bags used by the soldiers at the fort. The men struggled with the bags. They placed the bags at the feet of the women. Nínáánibaa' peeked into her bag through a hole and squealed, a sound her family had never heard come from her. The women peeked into their bags to find their bag fully stuffed with soft, clean, washed wool. They laughed because the young men fooled them, acting as if the bags they carried were extremely heavy.

Once again, Nínáánibaa''s hands shook. She poked her hand through the hole and pulled out a tuft of wool, brought it to her nose and breathed in deeply, then rolled the tuft of wool between her fingers and brought the tuft of wool to her nose again to breathe deeply once again. Her teardrops hit the little tuft of wool making it shake and spring right back up again. Designs she would weave were already forming in her mind. Her weaving tools were safely stored away in her secret spot, ready to be put to use.

Nínááníbaa' looked up when she heard people breathe collectively,

"Yáa!" The great leader led a beautiful brown horse with its colt out of the make-shift horse corral and handed the reins of both horses to Hashké Yił Naabaah. Hashké Yił Naabaah picked up the reins, looked at the great leader then looked at his people gathered before him, but he could not speak. He stood in their midst blinking back tears. The great leader asked Nahat'á Yinaabaah and Tł'ée'go Naabaah and Kiizhóní and the young Mescalero Apache man to select a horse for themselves from the horses in the corral, which they did while voicing words of gratitude. War Leaders and Peace Leaders in training under Hashké Yił Naabaah and the elder Peace Leader's guidance were invited to select a horse from the corral as well.

The great leader announced to the people his group raised sheep and horses in anticipation of the time when Hashké Yił Naabaah and his people were released from their status as prisoners of war.

"Yéego nihich'į' anídahazt'i' dooleełígíí nidasiidlíí'. Nihééda'ílnii' hodoo'niidgo ch'ééh aadę́ę́' nídadíit'įįh. T'óó doo 'áhoot'éhí da. Nihahastói, Hashké Yił Naabaah yaadaaní nilínígíí, 'aadę́ę́' dah diiná, ch'ééh t'áá kǫ́ǫ́ nahísóotą́ dabidii'níi nidi nihits'ą́ą́' iiná. 'Éí baa nidadíníitaał dadii'níigo 'aadę́ę́' bikéé' nii'ná. T'áá 'ákónéehee 'ádeiidzaa lá. Jó nihikáa'jį' dahazlį́į'go nihikéyah baa nánohkai. 'Éí doo ts'íí'át'éégóó baa nihił dahózhǫ́." *We anticipated that you would have encountered much hardship. When we heard you were set free, we kept looking this way. There was no activity. The man who is the father-in-law to your leader Hashké Yił Naabaah, left our area to move back here. We tried telling him to stay near us but he moved away. We wanted to check on him so we followed him here. It is good we did. You are all here. We are so very happy that you have come back here to your land.*

****

Since Dédii learned of the death of the tall gray-haired one, she spent many evenings sitting on a rock facing the southwestern direction. She looked at her mountain of the west, Dook'o'oosłííd *San Francisco Peaks.* She did not miss the tall gray-haired one personally, but she mourned the memory of him that she lovingly nurtured through the years. Many times she asked herself, "Will I ever love again? Will I ever be loved again? Will I ever feel love the way the tall gray-haired one loved me so many years ago? Will my sons ever have a father, one they can call shizhé'é?" she wondered. Many nights she cried until the sun announced the beginning of a new day.

Her son and her adopted sons heard her crying many times. One day, her son was so concerned for his mother, he approached his mentor Kiizhóní.

"Shimá tł'ée'go yichah łeh. T'óó shił baahojoobá'íyee'. Da' hastiin sání, nihe'anaa'í nilínéeésh yaa náchah? Shą́ą́' łį́į́' biishxį́ ha'nínée?" *My mother cries at night. I feel so sorry for her. Does she cry over the old man who was our enemy? The one who was killed by a horse?*

"Aoo', nimá 'éí hastiin ayóó'áyó'níí nít'ę́ę́' dóó 'éí hastiinígíí nimá 'ayóó'áyó'níí nít'ę́ę́'." *Yes, your mother loved that man very much and that man loved your mother.*

"Háida shimá 'ayóó'áyó'níi doo ch'ééh nisin," *I have been wanting for someone to love my mother,* the young boy replied. Kiizhóní wanted so much to tell the young boy that he loved his mother since he laid eyes on her so many years ago. On another occasion, Ach'ą́ą́h Naabaah, the one they used to call Naabeehó 'Ashkii, came to see Kiizhóní.

"Hastiin Fólton wolyéhę́ę 'ádin silį́į́' dóó wóshdę́ę́' nihimá 'áłahjį' tł'ée'go yichah łeh. Łah da t'óó deiyísíníilts'ą́ą'go nihí dó' deichah łeh. Shimá t'áá sáhí ch'éétłizh. Ni dó' t'ah t'áá sáhí naniná. Doo hanii t'óó shimá bił síníkée da? T'áá yee' íídą́ą́' nihizhé'é nílį́ nahalingo naa nitsídeikees. Nihízhé'é nílį́ nahalingo nihaa 'áhólyą́ągo k'ad łą́ náhááh." *Since the time the one they called Folton died, our mother cries a lot at night. Sometimes we listen to her and we also cry. My mother came out alone. You are also alone. Why don't you make a home with her? We already think of you as our father. You have taken care of us as a father would for many years.* Kiizhóní knew he was a strong, valued warrior but he felt he was a weak man. On many occasions, he had asked Dédii to be his wife but she always told him, "She'awéé' bizhé'é hólǫ́,"

My baby has a father, and he respected her wishes. She had remained faithful to a man who never claimed his son.

Since the conversations with Dédii's sons, Kiizhóní rode swiftly into the mountains of Dziłíjiin *Black Mesa* to practice his speech for when he approached his leader and Nínáánībaa' to ask them if he could take their Dédii under his care and love her and her children. He wanted to ask Dédii again but she had turned him down so many times he felt he needed allies to help change her mind.

He noticed Dédii was smiling again although he sensed sadness in her voice on many occasions. He consulted his best friend, Nahat'á Yinaabaah and received a resounding "Aoo!" *Yes!* just as in the many, many times before. His best friend never gave up.

"Haalá 'áhánééh, shik'is! Nizhóní doo!" *What a happening, my brother! It will be good!* With one vote of confidence behind him, Kiizhóní made many attempts to see Hashké Yił Naabaah and Nínáánībaa' but each time, the topic of the conversation was dictated by his leader and his wife. The day arrived when Kiizhóní was sure if he never asked, he would never get the chance to do so again.

He wondered what the protocol was in asking for a woman. All he knew was the language for working hard and being a valued warrior. He approached his kind leader and Nínáánībaa' after a day of taming horses. He clumsily blurted out his desire to care for their Dédii.

"T'óó shééldizgo naashá. T'áadoo nihich'į' bił hadóshchídí da. T'áá hazhó'ó nihiDédii nizhónígo nihá baa 'áháshyą́ą dooleełgi t'éí nihináál bee nihoní'ą́ą doo." *I have nothing to give you as a dowry. All I have is the promise I make in your presence to take care of your Dédii.*

His leader jumped up and hugged him and said,

"T'áá yee' íídą́ą' iisínílbą́. Dédii baa 'áhólyą́ągo łą́ náá hai. Ba'áłchíní ná nidahaazhchį nahalingo bik'i díní'į́į'go kǫ́ǫ́ hoolzhish. Bicheii dó' baa 'áhólyą́ągo łą́ nááh. Háish dó' ákódooníił? Hooghan bá nidíí'ááł. Dinééh ílíinii nílį́įgo naa nitsíikees." *You have already earned her. You have cared for Dédii many years. You have watched over her children as if they were born for you. You have also cared for her maternal grandfather for many years. Who would do that? You will build her a hogan. We believe you are a man of value.*

Kiizhóní left Nínáánibaa"s hogan to walk back to his lean-to but he could not walk in a straight line. He saw Dédii gathering firewood. He did not even think to ask her first before he approached her parents. Afraid he would lose his courage, he marched up to her and stated,

"Siikée doo, jiní." *We will live together, it is said.* Dédii looked at him and said in a soft voice,

"Hágoshį́į́." *Alright.* Kiizhóní nearly fell over. He left her holding an armful of firewood and blindly walked back to the lean-to he shared with Dédii's youngest brother and the old man.

****

Dédii and Kiizhóní honored the four days of abstinence to observe the sacredness of their wedding. They stayed in Dédii's hogan alone, without any physical contact. Dédii had not realized her new husband was actually her best friend and she knew in the conversations they had that she was also his best friend. They laughed more in the four days than they had in the six or more years they had known one another. The first night, Dédii wished him a restful night by saying,

"Aají hatł'a'iinił'á. *You rest over there with your butt up in the air.* Kiizhóní answered,

"Háǫoshį́į́." *Alright.* They could not stop laughing at Dédii's command. The dark circles that appeared under her eyes began to disappear. She lovingly spread out her wedding gift from Kiizhóní which was the soft thick sheep skin he won in the footrace that was held when the great leader came with his people to visit.

After their four days of observance, Kiizhóní took Dédii into his arms and gently kissed her tears away. At times, tears of relief rolled down his face too. His rug blanket which they used as a pillow was left with a wet spot where their tears found a place to land.

"Ních'aad, shiyázhí, t'óó naahojoobá'íyee'. Ayóó'ánííních'ní," *Don't cry, my little one. I have so much sympathy for you. I love you,* he repeated many times. They never made love that night. Instead, they endured two more nights of tears before Dédii's tears dried up and acceptance of her new lover took their place.

"Hágo, shiyázhí, kwe'é shíighahgi níteeh. Ádíníínishtą'go 'iidiilwosh," *Come here, my little one, lie down beside me. We will go to sleep while I hold you,* Kiizhóní said as he offered an open arm.

"Iidiilwosh is! Náshiníts'ǫs dooleełgo ga'!" *What do you mean, sleep! You should be kissing me!* she scolded with a smile, then softened her tone when she said, "Shí dó' náninists'ǫs doo." *I will also kiss you.*

"Hágoshį́į́, 'aadi náshiníts'ǫs." *Okay, kiss me.* He said with his lips pursed.

"Ni 'áłtsé! Náshiníts'ǫs," *You first! Kiss me,* Dédii scolded.

"Hágoshį́į́..." *Okay.* Kiizhóní made kissing sounds, saying, "Ts'ǫ́ǫ́s, ts'ǫ́ǫ́s, ts'ǫ́ǫ́s..."

"Táadoo t'óó 'ayóo t'áá'áni'di'nínígi 'ánít'éhí!" *Don't be so obedient!* she scolded, while Kiizhóní had a difficult time composing himself.

"Hágoshíínee'." *Okay then,* he said smiling. Dédii had to admit she had never laughed so much since her kidnapping. She felt her burdens drop off of her shoulders. Kiizhóní was what she needed for so long.

After a long day of tedious work, Dédii took her time washing her body with a soft cloth then washed her hair before Kiizhóní came home. The scents that drifted around her home calmed her to where she could concentrate on herself instead of her six children and their many needs as well as the man she called "shicheii" *my maternal grandfather.* She tied her hair back and let her hair cascade down her back as it hung thickly below her knees.

With the scent of yucca root soap drifting about the room, she roasted lamb jerky over the hot coals and prepared thin blue corn crepes, her favorite meal. She loved seeing Kiizhóní freely enter her home. He made it a practice to stomp his feet right outside, then clear his throat to announce his presence. The young couple enjoyed their meal while Kiizhóní discussed the day's happenings.

Kiizhóní told her he wanted to wipe his body off and wash his hair. His hair had grown to hang down below his waist, thick and very black. In the dim light of the fire, Dédii watched him take his shirt off. His muscles strained against his beautiful tight brown skin. Dédii offered to wash his hair. The scent of yucca root soap permeated the air and drifted around the two lovers. She braided his hair so he could wash his body. The coals became embers, but the faint light drifted on to his body to illuminate his high, tight buttocks and lean long legs covered with soft brown skin. Dédii shook her sheepskin, laid it on the floor and sat down to brush her hair to braid it.

Kiizhóní sat down behind her on her soft sheepskin, pulled her hair to the side and kissed her neck softly. When she tilted her head to the side, he felt welcome to kiss her more. The soft scent of yucca soap lingered on her skin,

"Nizhóní dó' honílchin. Tsá'ászi' ániid bąąh heestxi'ígíí honílchin." *You smell so good. You smell like a newly broken off yucca plant.* Dédii tilted her head to the other side to invite more of his kisses.

"Nikágí yilzhóólíyee', shiyázhí," *Your skin is soft, my little one,* he said in his soft gentle voice. She felt him gently lick her skin, then breathe a soft breath on her moistened skin. His breath accentuated the moistness of his kiss, leaving Dédii wanting to remove her rug dress. He read her mind.

"Nigaan deh kóníléêh. Ni'éé' naadiishheeh. *Lift your arms. I'm going to take your dress off.* Without any coaxing, Dédii lifted her dress to her waist and sat down. She lifted her arms high in the air and felt her dress slip over her head while Kiizhóní lifted her heavy rug dress off with one arm, with the other, he held her arms high in the air. With her dress carelessly thrown, Kiizhóní leaned against her, reached around her and gently caressed her breasts with his free hand. Sounds of satisfaction left Dédii's lips. He placed her arms around his neck and with both hands caressed her body while he kissed her softly on the arms, neck and upper back. He cupped her breasts with his hands and gently caressed her nipples. Dédii felt weak under his caresses.

He pulled her onto his lap. With their legs extended, he wrapped his long legs around her legs and pulled her legs apart and caught his breath when he reached down and felt her warmth.

With his strong arms, he lifted her up with very little effort and turned her to face him. He took her legs, and gently spread her legs to straddle him. His kisses became more intense as he held her arching back. Dédii fell forward against him and weakly kissed his face, his neck, his chest and stopped. She felt his chest.

"Díísh ha'át'íí?" *What is this?* She desperately wanted to see his chest in the light. She felt his chest with her hands. Her hands became buried in a thin pelt of chest hair. For a second, she thought of her first lover, shook her head and shook her body. Kiizhóní giggled in her ear, and said,

"Ge'." *Pay attention.* With his strong hands around her waist, he pressed her body down against him. She felt him. He loosened his grip on her, slightly moved his legs apart and pressed his mound against her softness. A soft moan escaped Dédii's lips. When he felt her body demanding satisfaction, he asked,

"K'adísh? *Now?*

"Aoo'," *Yes,* was all she could say. Without warning Kiizhóní lifted her off of him and slid her body off of his lap and laid her down on the soft sheepskin. She gently pulled him down on her and their bodies moved as one. "He is my warrior. He is protecting me with his body, I am not protecting him," she thought as she met his every movement with her body. His chest hairs tickled her nose but she kept moving with him, wanting to feel the satisfaction her body craved. He started kissing her.

"K'adę́ę, k'adę́ę..." *Almost, almost...* he pleaded, then softly asked, "Nishą'?" *What about you?* Dédii felt her body burst forth. She had never imagined how sensuous making love in Navajo was. She wanted to hear more of his words of love. She wanted to feel more of his love, his body, his words...

He lay down near her, his breaths still uneven. He turned toward her and drew her into his arms and kissed the little beads of sweat that glistened on her body. Weakly she begged,

"Ádíshiiłtsóód." *Hold me close.* He wrapped his arms around her tightly, leaving kisses on her weak body.

"Shíí'ii nílínígíí 'ayóo nashiiłná, shiyázhí. K'ad ts'ídá doo ha'át'íhí da bídin nishłíní da. T'áá hazhó'ó ni t'éiyá." *I am moved that you belong to me, my little one. I have no need of anything else. I only need you,* he whispered,

"Shí dó' t'áá'ákót'éego naa nitséskees. Ahéhee' niháíníyáhígíí." *I feel the same way about you. Thank you for coming to us,* she whispered.

"Ééh nínídááh, shiyázhí. Ha'íí'ą́ągo niha'áłchíní 'aadę́ę́' yah adoojah. 'Shimá, shimá,' daaníigo. K'ad shitah yá'ánááhoot'éeh dooleeł. Shitah hwiinéi dooleeł, shiyázhí." *You better get dressed. Our children will come running in when the sun comes up, saying, 'My mother, my mother'. Now I will feel healthy again. I will have a lot of energy, my little one.*

Dédii could not wait until daylight to catch a glimpse of her Kiizhóní's chest. She found it to be very sensuous. "Love in Navajo is so sensuous and fulfilling," she thought.

After several days, she forgot how sensuous love with Kiizhóní was. She was so sick to her stomach. She told her mother and her mother laughed a gleeful laugh and said,

"Ayázhí shį́į́ bíká nahohłáá nít'ę́ę́'. *You two probably performed ceremoniously to conceive a little one.*
Dédii could not wait to tell Kiizhóní. She knew he would

never be the same. She knew he loved children. Her six children he claimed as his own were testimony of that.

****

The young Naashgálí *Mescalero Apache* man had a difficult time adjusting to life among the Naabeehó people. It was possibly due to the closeness the Naabeehó people were forced to live in, first at Fort Sumner then on their forced walk back to Fort Defiance where once again the people lived within arm's length of one another. He was used to living on his beautiful mountains where he did not see another person for days.

It was not until Dzáníbaa' and her people returned to their home on Dziłíjiin *Black Mesa* that he was able to begin to feel he belonged with Dzáníbaa''s people, but his adjustment was short lived when the family was forced to return to Fort Defiance in their efforts to abide by the Treaty and remain within the Treaty Reservation. When Hashké Yił Naabaah returned his family to Dziłíjiin, the young Mescalero Apache man began to accept living among Záanii's (the name he preferred to call her after Dzáníbaa' told him her sister called her Záanii) people.

Even after coming back to Záanii's home the second time, the young Mescalero Apache man experienced displacement and homesickness. Each time he felt that way, he reminded himself of the courage his wife displayed when she was alone with him, far away from home, and with a different group of people she had never seen before or understood. Besides that, he reminded himself, she was forced to walk alone with his people to

Fort Sumner and she was forced to defend herself against the advances of the dirty soldiers. Unlike Záanii he never had to leave a family behind. His only family was the old woman who nursed his Záanii back to life. With those thoughts fresh in his mind, he joined in family activities.

He did have to admit he missed his beautiful mountains that towered above the flat lands and the plains. Toward the east of his majestic mountains was where many of his people's enemies lived and hunted and where land that was flat went on for days. To the south of his mountains was the wide desert covered with fine white sandy hills made of fine granules of white sand. Each time the wind blew, the sand shifted to create a new landscape. Toward the west was where other Apache warrior groups lived, hunted, and entered into warfare. The northern direction was where more of his beautiful majestic mountains rose and towered above the land of many trees. His land was lush and very green, whereas Dziłíjiin *Black Mesa* had trees but the sandy ground was abundant, which he was not used to.

Surprisingly, it was Záanii's maternal grandfather and the old man Dédii called "shicheii" who helped the young Mescalero Apache man adjust and become a part of the family. The two men needed short logs to build a táchééh *sweat hogan* and needed strong arms to obtain the materials and to chop the logs to a specified length. The young Mescalero Apache man's help was solicited and he gladly offered to help.

When Dzáníbaa' and Dédii took food to the young Mescalero Apache man and their maternal grandfathers, they could hear the resounding laughter of the three men. At other times of the day, the two sisters could hear the men singing, and other times the older men were quietly teaching the young man Navajo. The táchééh was beautiful and their next project was building a sturdy chaha'oh *brush arbor* for each of Dzáníbaa''s extended family members.

Dzáníbaa' noticed her husband's beautiful full smile returned. She had not acknowledged the fact that she and her husband had traded places, where he was the visitor. One morning, her husband announced,

"Nihicheii bich'į' déyá. Bíká 'anáshwo'." *I am going to see our maternal grandfathers. I help them.* Záanii was tickled. Her husband was communicating with her! "It is a tradeoff," she thought, "he is learning my language and my culture, but he is away from my home for long lengths of time during the day. I miss his presence," she sighed as she looked toward the hill that hid her maternal grandfather's home.

Her husband had worn the same clothes since his people fled Fort Sumner. His clothes were torn and ragged. She spent their evenings repairing the newly ripped areas in his deerskin clothes and cleaning and stretching them so they would not stiffen or lose their shape.

Wanting to share a tender moment with his wife, the young Mescalero Apache man scattered the burning logs in the center of their home so as to dim the light from the fire. Touching Záanii's shoulder he whispered,

"Hágo." *Come here.*

"Áłtsé ni'éé' bé'áshjoł," *Wait, let me wipe your clothes to clean them,* she answered, sitting with her back to her husband who was covered with his thinning buffalo hide blanket. Still used to sleeping away from him or sleeping near her sister or her mother since their days as prisoners of war, Záanii was reluctant to submit to her husband's request. Once again, he whispered,

"Hágo, kojí..." *Come here, over here...* Záanii's heartbeat sped up. She was afraid of her own emotions, having been separated from him for many years. "He is trying to communicate with me," she thought, feeling a twinge of sympathy and a slight sense of excitement at being close to him. Slowly, she got up, fastened the rug that hung in the doorway to the doorposts and sat down near her husband. He lifted the buffalo hide covering him and patted the soft rug blanket underneath him. He whispered again,

"Hágo." Záanii moved closer and caught a glimpse of his beautiful copper colored skin. She had not seen him unclothed in many years. Slowly she moved closer to him. He whispered,

"Díí shá yíníta̧'." *Hold this for me.* Záanii moved away from him so fast, and questioned,

"Ha'át'íísh diní?" *What are you saying?* Flustered, he helplessly looked at her.

"Hágo," *Come here,* he pleaded. "Yíníshta̧'." *I am holding it.* Helpless herself, Záanii laid back down next to her husband. Hesitantly, she extended her arms to embrace him and said,

"Níínísht̨ą'." *Let me hold you.* He buried his face in her shoulder and said in a muffled voice,

"Aoo', aoo', aoo'." *Yes, yes, yes.* The warmth from the glowing embers warmed her back. The warmth of her husband's body warmed her as he held her close. Slowly they kissed. Záanii noticed his lips were trembling which brought her to tears. He kissed her tears away murmuring soft words to her in his own beautiful sounding language, a language he felt free to make love to her. Záanii explored his body with her hands and fingers, but her lover was bold. He explored her body with his cool lips and his soft tongue. Záanii felt his warm mound press against her hand. Giggling, she said,

"Yíníshtą'." *I am holding it.* He answered,

"Aoo', aoo', yíníshtą'." *Yes, yes, I am holding it.* They both giggled and kissed one another's bodies. Sweetly and gently he led her through their love making, which at times became intense and swift, then returned to where their bodies slowly moved as one. They held each other tightly as their bodies demanded satisfaction.

Listening to the soft rain drops that softly landed on their home, the two lovers held hands and listened to the cold rain drops settle on the hot coals, sizzle and dim the glow of the once glowing coals. Safely in the arms of her young Mescalero Apache husband, Záanii fell fast asleep.

She was awakened when she heard the men's footsteps pounding against the moist earth as they ran toward the east. She heard her father yelling,

"Dadołwosh, dadołwosh..." *Yell, yell...* The deep

sound of the men lifting their voices into the air echoed in the predawn air and was followed by the high-pitched voices of her son and her nephews as they followed the men. Under the warmth of the buffalo robe, Záanii fell back asleep and was jolted awake when she heard her father yelling,

"K'ad nikídadoł'is, nikídadoł'is. Aoo', akót'éego. 'Akódaoht'įįgo nihikéyah bikáá'góó yá'át'ééh náhodoodleeł." *Press your feet into the ground by shuffling your feet. When you do that, our land will become healthier.* The young Mescalero Apache man's son was running back to his mother's hogan after spending the night with his cousins when his father grabbed him and swung him around playfully. The young Mescalero Apache man remembered his beautiful wife slept beside him with nothing between their bodies except their even breaths of sleep. He sent his son running for firewood to give himself time to wake his sleeping wife. He entered to find Záanii frantically getting dressed. He pulled her into his arms and kissed her deeply, hoping the approaching day would speed by so he could be near his beautiful Záanii again. After their previous night of love, their code word for wanting to spend intimate time together was,

"Yíníshtą'." *I am holding it.*

Záanii told her mother she had been feeling sick for nearly two weeks. Her mother smiled at her and asked,

"Da' nihíísh ałdó' awéé' bíká nahohłá?" *Are you two ceremoniously performing to conceive a little one?* Záanii smiled weakly, but her morning sickness hid her excitement. After hearing of his little one, the young Mescalero Apache man could not do anything right. He was so distracted by the wonderful news. His male in-laws would smile at his antics and say, away from the hearing of the women,

"Ei bá 'a'niichį́." *A little one is to be born for him.* The men knew if the women heard them, they would be lectured. It was their happy secret. The men were relieved to see the young Mescalero Apache man smiling so easily again, showing his perfect rows of white teeth.

****

Nínááníbaa' noticed the attraction between her youngest son and Akéé' Naazbaa'. She discussed it with her husband. He told her he would discuss it with their elder Peace Leader since their son had decided to begin his training as a Peace Leader at the elder leader's residence during the spring and summer seasons. Hashké Yił Naabaah told his son the spring and summer seasons would be very busy and hectic for the young man. In addition to training for leadership, he would be required to maintain a dá'ák'eh *cornfield* near his family's residence.

Plans were hastily put in place for the 'a'niiłts'ee' *wedding* due to the anticipated rainy month the new moon predicted.

Hashké Yił Naabaah watched over his family making preparations for the upcoming eating of the blue corn mush for his son and Akéé' Naazbaa'. His gaze moved from one family member to the next. He realized, as a respected War Leader, his family was expanding in unusual ways.

His oldest son married a woman he and his Nínáánібaa' had found hiding in the crevice of the rocky cliffs when they were returning home from a War Leadership meeting. His youngest son was to marry a woman from an area near Dziłabéí *Grey Mountain*, near their sacred mountain of the west, and who had come to them hoping to find a home amongst them. His Dédii had married a member of the enemy, but now was married to one of his trusted warriors who would enter training to become a War Leader like his oldest son. His Dzáníbaa' married a young Mescalero Apache man who spared her life, and was now a trusted member of his family.

In his travels among the people of whom he was the leader, he found other families who had also taken in orphans and adults, and ones who had lost all their relatives during the long walk to Fort Sumner and back. He was proud of the generous hearts of his people. They were living what he had taught them, but he never stopped to think that in taking in people who were lost, he set an example for his people as well, and was living according to what he taught his people. He admired his beautiful Nínáánібaa' for setting an example for her people as well.

He thanked the Creator many times for each member of his family while waiting for the sun to go down so he could help his youngest son begin a new life with Akéé' Naazbaa'. She was the woman who helped his Dzáníbaa' birth her son. Tonight, he was especially thankful for his Nínáánібaa'. She opened her heart to a new member of their family to welcome her in. His eyes filled with tears when he thought of how hard his youngest son Tł'ée'go Naabaah would have to work to build a hogan for Akéé' Naazbaa'. "When did he fall in love with her?" he wondered. He shook his head when he remembered his son's expression when he asked him if he loved the young woman. His son could not hide his happiness. "They work well together. She is a good helper to him. She is generous too," he thought.

"This wedding will not be a traditional one. Akéé' Naazbaa' does not have a family to provide her with sheep and goats. We will have a feast my family has prepared. My family is very different culturally," he thought as he walked into Akéé' Naazbaa''s make-shift home to take his place next to his youngest son and Nínááníbaa'.

They watched the doorway for Akéé' Naazbaa''s entrance. She clutched the tattered rug blanket draped over her shoulders while at the same time she precariously held onto a wedding basket filled with delicious blue corn mush. She was ushered in by the man Dédii called "shicheii." With the disappearance of the sun behind the western horizon, the wedding commenced.

****

To manage her intense labor pains, Nínááníbaa' clung to the sash belt that hung from the ceiling of her hogan. Helpless from her pain, she looked into the eyes of her husband who sat near the door. Tears were streaming down his face. No one told him he was not supposed to witness his child's birth. His daughters and daughters-in-law were gathered around Nínááníbaa' listening intently to Akéé' Naazbaa''s every word of instruction. Akéé' Naazbaa' had proven herself to be an excellent midwife when she helped deliver Dzáníbaa''s son at Fort Sumner.

Nínááníbaa' wanted to release the scream that she hoped would release the pain, but she chose to demonstrate that self control is essential in childbirth. She closed her mouth and moaned softly. After pushing until she ran out of breath several times, the newborn's head easily slid out into Akéé' Naazbaa''s outstretched hands while Dédii and Dzáníbaa' and Tsék'iz Naazbaa' watched intently with tears pouring down their faces.

Akéé' Naazbaa' caught the infant's slippery body. She wrapped the infant in a soft lamb's skin and waited for the afterbirth to slide out. Catching the afterbirth, she noticed Nínááníbaa' was very weak. She raced across the room to place the newborn in Hashké Yił Naabaah's left arm and said,

"Niyázhí, niye', k'é bidiní." *Greet your little one, your son.*

Nínááníbaa' could not release her hold on the sash belt. She felt intense pain in her midsection.

"Haash nisht'é?" *What is wrong with me?* she stuttered. Akéé' Naazbaa' rubbed Nínááníbaa''s abdomen to see if the afterbirth had been severed. Gently pushing on Nínááníbaa''s abdomen she said,

"Sis łíchí'í t'áá bąąh dah sínítį! Ła' náábi'niniłchį." *Keep holding on to the sash belt. You are going to birth a second one.* Nínáánídbaa' could hear her husband softly greeting her newborn son.

"Háshinee', she'awéé'. Tó' Aheedlíinii dine'é nílį."

Dear one, my baby. You belong to the Water Flows Together people... He stopped his greeting. His Nínáánídbaa' was struggling and was in great pain. He saw her grit her teeth and push with all the strength she had as a labor pain attacked her body again. He felt helpless. He felt torn. He was holding his little newborn but his wife was fighting for her life.

"Díí yee' dooda..." *This is too much...* Nínáánídbaa' whispered, hoping her daughters did not hear. They were expecting little ones... Before she could complete her thought, she felt a wild pain which took her breath away.

"K'ad yéego bił anildzííł! *Now push hard,* Akéé' Naazbaa' yelled. "Náána shą', náána shą', náána."

Once more, again, again. With the last breath left within her, Nínáánídbaa' weakly pushed and felt a surge leave her body. Her daughters screamed. A baby's weak cry filled the air and Nínáánídbaa' collapsed on the soft sheepskin. Akéé' Naazbaa' grabbed Hashké Yił Naabaah's spare shirt and wrapped it around the second little one and waited for the afterbirth to slip into her hands. She ran with the little one and placed the infant in Hashké Yił Naabaah's right arm and demanded,

"Niyázhí, nitsi' bine'dę́ę́' bídílnih. Bídílnih, nidishní!"

Rub your little one's, your daughter's back. Rub her, I said! she demanded. The two sisters raced to their father and held their newborn brother while he rubbed his newborn daughter's back. In the faint light, he could see his infant daughter struggling. From across the room, Akéé' Naazbaa' told him to turn the little one face down and rub which he did. The little one coughed out liquid and started wailing a weak cry.

Akéé' Naazbaa' raced back across the room and rubbed the infant's back rather vigorously until she heard a loud wail that split the hushed air. She placed the infant back in Hashké Yił Naabaah's right arm and demanded,

"Niyázhí, nitsi'ísh k'é bidíníniid? K'é bidiní. Bimá baa nídooltéél." *Did you greet your little one, your daughter? Greet her. She will be given back to her mother,* she ordered. Hashké Yił Naabaah, one not used to taking orders, did as he was told. Akéé' Naazbaa' pulled Nínááníbaa''s rug dress off and covered her with a soft rug blanket, grabbed the little infant girl out of Hashké Yił Naabaah's hand when she heard him complete his greeting, and placed the little one in Nínááníbaa''s right arm and said in a soft gentle voice,

"Niyázhí bi'iyíłt'o'. Bi'iiyíłt'o'go k'é bidiní." *Breastfeed your little one. While you are breastfeeding her, greet her.* Looking at Hashké Yił Naabaah who was still holding his infant son, she told him to sit behind Nínááníbaa' to support her. Hashké Yił Naabaah sat down behind his Nínááníbaa' and placed his hand on his infant daughter and said with a steady stream of tears flowing down his face,

"Háshinee', sha'áłchíní yázhí. Háádę́ę́' da shą' ahi'noołchéełgo nihaa 'ahi'noołchą́ą́'. Hait'éego da shą' nihaa tsísidookéezgo nihaa 'ahi'noołchą́ą́'. Ayóó'ánihíínii'ní, nihimá dóó shí. Tó 'Aheedlíinii dine'é nohłį́. Ma'ii Deeshgiizhnii dine'é bá shółchíín. Náániá Táchii'nii dine'é nihicheii danilį́, 'áádóó Tó Dích'íi'nii dine'é 'éí nihinálí danilį́. 'Ákót'éego nihiyázhí nohłį́. K'ad dóó kodóó nihiyázhí nohłį́į dooleeł. K'ad dóó kodóó she'awéé', shiyázhí nihidishníi doo. Nihimá 'éí shiyázhí nihiłníi doo. Ayóó'anihíínii'ní. Nizhónígo nihiyaa hwiidiil'aał. Nizhónígo nihaa 'áhwiilyą́ą dooleeł." *Dear ones, my little children. I wonder which direction you came running from to find us. I wonder how you came to think of us as you came running to us. Your mother and I, we love you. You belong to the Water Flows Together people. You are born for the Coyote Pass people. And the Red Running into the Water people are your maternal grandfathers. The Bitter Water people are your paternal grandfathers. In this way, you are our little ones. Now and from now on, I will call you my babies and your mother will call you her little ones. We love you. We will raise you well. We will take good care of you.* Hashké Yił Naabaah picked up his infant daughter in his right arm and carried his little ones outside and bellowed,

"Awééchí'í be'iinéé' diists'ą́ą́'! Háshinee' dó 'ájít'į́! Nihik'ihojisdli'! T'áá 'óolyéego nihik'ihojisdli'! Ahéhee', shiTaa'. Nihik'ijiisínídli'. *The cry of little infants has been heard! Dear ones for doing that! We have been blessed! We have been truly blessed! Thank you, my Spiritual Father. You have blessed us.* His sons and his sons-in-law hollered out cheers before he walked back into Nínáánníbaa''s home and hugged and kissed Nínááníbaa'. He turned to Akéé' Naazbaa' and hugged her, telling her,

"Ahéhee', yéego nihíká'íínílwod. T'áá 'ákónéehee niháíníyáá lá." *Thank you so much for helping us. It is good that you came to us.*

He sat down near Nínááníbaa' who had been cleaned up. He handed her their newborn son to feed. He watched the ceremonious feeding, grateful his little ones were delivered safely. He was truly grateful that his wife was doing well.

"Naakiií shá shíníłchį́. Naabaahii dóó 'atł'óhí. Ahéhee', shiyázhí. Ayóó'ánííníish'níí dóó ayóó 'át'éego naa 'ahééh nisin, shiyázhí. Háánílyį́įh k'ad." *You have borne me twins. A warrior and a weaver. Thank you, my little one. I love you and I am very thankful for you, my little one. Rest now.*

With plenty of help, Nínááníbaa' recovered quickly. She needed several naps throughout the day to help her get through her busy days.

****

Three women of the Tó 'Aheedlíinii *Water Flows Together* people stood at the doorway of their homes. They looked toward the eastern direction where the bright sun burst forth on the horizon.

Nínááníbaa' watched a dew drop form on a thin twig that was wedged in the mixture of mud, leaves, and twigs that formed the domed roof of her make-shift hogan. The dew drop slowly expanded in the warming morning air. Nínááníbaa' wondered when it would drop off the twig due to its weight but it clung tightly to the twig. When the sun's bright rays fully burst into the sky, Nínááníbaa' looked into the dewdrop and saw the tiniest rainbow she had ever seen appear in the dewdrop. In a subdued voice, so as not to disturb the beauty before her, Nínááníbaa' called,

"Shooh, Dédii, Dzáníbaa', hágo. Díí nół'į." *Look, Dédii, Dzáníbaa', come here. Look at this.* Dédii waddled to her mother's hogan but when she got close, her mother held up her open palm to warn of a fast appearance. Dédii took deliberate steps and stepped close. Dzáníbaa' followed close behind with her hands bracing her arched back.

"Ha'át'íí lá, shimá?" *What is it, my mother?* the two sisters asked simultaneously.

"Díí nół'į. Dah too' yee' dah yiiye'go, dah nímazgo dahidélch'ą́ął. T'áá nésh'į́įgo ha'íí'ą. 'Áádóó t'áá nésh'į́įgo, náá'ts'íílid yázhí léi' bii'jį' yiiłtsą. Éí yee' t'ahdoo ni'diilch'ąąłdą́ą' dínóoł'įįł nisingo wóshdę́ę' nihidííniid." *Look at this. This dewdrop became round as it hung here. The sun came up while I was still watching it, then I noticed a tiny rainbow appeared in the dewdrop. I wanted you to see it before it dropped off, that's why I asked you to come over.* Tsék'iz Naazbaa' stuck her neck out of her hogan when she heard the soft sounds of "Yáa" *surprise* coming from her mother-in-law's home. She grabbed Akéé' Naazbaa' so they could also see what wonderment created the sounds of adoration. Just when they cast their eyes on the fragile dispersion of the colors of the rainbow made by the sun's frail rays, the drop of dew released its tenuous hold on the twig and splashed onto the ground below. No one breathed.

Tears rushed to the eyes of the three women of the Tó 'Aheedlíinii *Water Flows Together* people. Tsék'iz Naazbaa' and Akéé' Naazbaa' knew the meaning and the importance of water for their mother-in-law and their sisters-in-law.

Nínáánbaa' brought out a pot of hot ch'il ahwéhé *wild tea* and beautiful blue corn crepes she made and asked her daughters and daughters-in-law to sit down on the moist earth to hear her story.

When Nínáánbaa' was a little girl, her father's nickname for her was "Shiyishch'ą́łii" *My little drop.* He frequently told her her name represented power. When a drop of water falls, it cleans the surface of the object it fell upon. The object becomes cleaner and clearer, and yet the object is left just as it was. "That is where your power is," he told her many times.

During the times when her father needed her to be strong, he reminded her when many drops combine to make rain or when they combine to create a flood, that is where her power is also. Many drops can alter the land. "My little one, you need to know when to be a drop and when to be a flood," he would tell her, she remembered.

Nínáánbaa' loved it when her father gave both of her daughters the same nickname when they were born. He also told them about the power within a drop of water and the combined power of many drops, encouraging them to know when to know the difference and when they could call upon their power.

The women glanced toward the hill, behind which their father and grandfather lived. They could not wait to see him. Quickly, Nínáánbaa' ran back into her hogan, wrapped her two little ones in her mother's soft rug blanket and walked out the door to join her daughters and her daughters-in-law whose faces were turned toward the eastern morning sun.

Blinded by the bright sunlight, Nínáánîbaa' stepped into her father's dark hogan and walked to the spot where she knew her father would be sitting opposite the door. She handed him first her infant daughter and placed her in his right arm, then she placed her infant son in her father's left arm.

Addressing his granddaughter, he tenderly said,

"Yáa, háshinee', Shiyishch'ą́łii yázhí. Náníbaa' yinílyéé lá. 'Ayóo shį́į́ nimá bíká 'anáníłwo' dooleeł. T'óó la' nízhóní, Shiyishch'ą́łii yázhí." *Dear one, my Little Drop. Your name is Woman Warrior Who Came Home. You will most likely be a good helper to your mother. You are so pretty, my Little Drop.*

Looking down at his grandson, he cooed,

"Díí shą', háshinee', shicheii yázhí. 'Akéé' Naabaah yinílyéego sáanii t'éí binii'gi sínídá. Tł'óo'di yee nida'abaah, wóne'é 'éí dooda. Ch'éénídzííd, shicheii yázhí, dighádílyeed. Dílwoshgo yílwoł," *What about this one, dear one, my little grandson. Your name is One Who Follows into War, and yet, you sit here among women. War is made outside, not inside. Wake up, my little grandson, run toward the east. Yell, as you run,* then he laughed at his words.

The three women of the Water Flows Together people smiled at one another with tears flowing down their faces. Their nickname that represented strength was given to their newest female member of the Water Flows Together people.

They were home. Their father, their maternal grandfather was home. Their men were coming home from their morning run toward the eastern direction. Two more babies would be joining them soon, as well as a third and hopefully a fourth, they said happily.

Chapter Seventeen

We Are Home...

Since their return, Dédii and Dzáníbaa' made it a practice, after their morning run, to face their beautiful mountain of the west. Each morning, the outline of the majestic Dook'o'oosłííd *San Francisco Peaks* interrupted the light blue skyline of the southwestern sky. One clear cloudless day, they decided to express their gratitude to their mountain when they told their mountain,

"Doo niit'į́įgóó 'ashdla' dóó yówohjį' nááhai. 'Azhą́ shį́į́ yéego txi'dahwii'níih nít'ę́ę' nidi nídanihiidiiltséél daniidzingo niniiłt'aa hada'iisiilniid. Nizhónígo dó' dah nííť'ááł. Nizhónígo nihidine'é bá dah nííť'ááł." *We have not seen you in over five years. Even though we were suffering horribly, our want to see you again gave us hope. You beautifully stand tall. You beautifully stand tall for our people.*

The evenings were also their favorite time of the day to visit their mountain. They watched the setting sun light up the sky with beautiful bright vibrant colors that accentuated their mountain, Dook'o'oosłííd. At first their mountain would appear blue against the bright yellow sunset. Soon, the mountain turned a darker blue as light behind the mountain shone a peach colored glow. A bright orange color would burst forth next, then red which would be reflected in the clouds above, and the last color the sun crowned their mountain with was purple. As the colors changed, the near black silhouette of their mountain became more pronounced. Watching the disappearing light, Dédii and Dzáníbaa' would hug each other and declare,

"Doo lá dó' ayóó'ánoolnin da! *It is so very beautiful!* There was no more need for words.

****

After they spent part of the day hunting wild animals that became a menace to the people who had already suffered enough, Hashké Yił Naabaah and his sons and Kiizhóní and the young Mescalero Apache man visited a different family every day to chop down trees to obtain logs to repair homes that had been burned or destroyed. Nínááníbaa' and her daughters and Akéé' Naazbaa' and Tsék'iz Naazbaa', along with her young siblings were kept busy gathering edible plants and berries, some of which they shared with elders and families with young children or they stored away their treasures for the coming long winter.

"Díí nihinoo' ádadiilnííł," *This will be our buried treasure,* Nínááníbaa' would announce when they had plenty for themselves. It was too late for Hashké Yił Naabaah and his sons and Kiizhóní and the young Mescalero Apache man to plant corn. The month of Ya'iishjáásh Tsoh *July* was nearly behind them.

Nínáánībaa' was not worried about their shortage of corn, instead she looked in the direction where she stored away their extra supply of corn in a large burrow they hollowed out in the side of the nearby hill before they were forced to leave their homes six years earlier. She knew they would also survive on the abundance their land had to offer.

She closed her eyes to name the bounties of the land, her mouth watered as her mind feasted on the thought of the sweetness of the ripe, purple juniper berries. Her mind then jumped to the softness of the pinon nuts when they were roasted then crushed by a wide flat rock on the metate to crush the shells, leaving only the meat rolling off of the metate. What about the many rich, sweet seeds that spout out of the round red cactus fruit when it is slightly squeezed which is harvested throughout the summer and early fall. Her mind then flew to the tan starchy root that cleaned your teeth when you ate it raw, the one that resembled the potatoes they were given at Fort Sumner. What about the wide juicy, plump cactus leaves that she cooked over the hot coals all year round.

"Mmmmm," she murmured when she thought of the rough salty jerky she prepared whenever her husband and her sons hunted for rabbits, prairie dogs, or deer. "Oh, the sweet juice of the little red flowers that appear on the hills near my home," she thought as her mouth filled with a burst of her saliva. She looked around and listened, "There are the locusts that make a lot of noise, letting my Naabeehó people know they were available as a food source. I remember the bright reddish-orange berries of the sumac plant that is made into a thick cool soup on warm evenings, but on cool evenings, the soup is warmed up." She looked around her and lifted her chin to the hill where an abundance of wild spinach grew which she harvested and boiled in the sweet water from the cool spring water. She looked into the distant hills to concentrate upon the berries that are gathered from different plants, each plant clutching leaves that matched a color of the rainbow. "There is also my favorite, the yucca fruit which is so filling," she thought.

"Nániichaad la', t'óó nanise' daadánígíí baa nitséskeesgo. Nihinaagóó dadoodį́łígíí łą́ągo dahólǫ́. Doo yee' dichin biih jókáhígi 'áhoot'ée da, kodi," *I got full thinking about edible plants. There is an abundance of food around us. We will never walk into hunger here,* she said softly while looking at the clouds that drifted overhead. She rubbed her abdomen. She was hungry and yet she realized she felt full from thinking of all their land had to offer.

"Dzidze' *juniper berries,*
Neeshch'íí' *pinon nuts,*
Hosh bineest'ą' *cactus fruit,*
Chąąsht'ézhii tsoh *wild carrot,*
Hosh niteelí bit'ąą' *wide cactus leaves,*
Ałk'íniilgizh *jerky,*

Ch'ilátah hózhóón łichí'ígíí bitoo' *sweet juice of the little red flowers,*

Wóneeshch'įįdii *locusts,*

Chiiłchin *sumac berries,*

Waa' *wild spinach,*

Tsá'ászi' bineest'ąą' *yucca fruit.*

Aneest'ą' ał'ąą 'ádaat'éhígíí." *Different kinds of berries.*

"Díí 'aak'eego dóó dííghaaí dóó níléí ch'éénídąąjį' doodį́łígíí doo bídin hóyée' da doo. T'óó 'ayóo nihinaagóó nanise' daadánígíí łą́ągo yíl'á. Nihikéyah nihaa ná'áłtso'go bikiin dąąjį' anáhodoolzhish. 'Ahéhee', shiTaa', nihikéyah biih néiikai." *There will not be a shortage of things to eat this fall and winter and through the spring season. There are edible plants around us in abundance. Our land will take care of us. Thank you, my Spiritual Father, we have come back into our land.*

One evening, Nínáánîbaa' asked Hashké Yił Naabaah,

"Níléígóó shił dí'aash." *Go with me to a place over there.* Hashké Yił Naabaah was tired from hunting and helping families get settled, but he agreed to go with his Nínáánîbaa'.

"Txį', t'ahdoo yéego hiłiijį́įhdą́ą'." *Let's go, before it gets too dark.* They talked about the day's activities and reached a nearby hill. Hashké Yił Naabaah helped Nínáánîbaa' remove large rocks from the side of the hill. They scooped damp earth away to expose sticks and dried branches that camouflaged an opening into a cool storage area. Hashké Yił Naabaah asked,

"Háidíígíí lá? *Which one?*

"Yisdisígíí łą́ą. 'Éí shá habí'íłtséé h." *The one that is wrapped. Use a stick to poke at it to bring it out.*

"Ha'át'íísh bii'? Ayóo dó' nidaaz. Wóó'małaa..." *What is in it? It is really heavy.* Hashké Yił Naabaah made the sound of putting forth great effort. He was finally able to dislodge the woven bag and pull it forward. He shook the bag, loosened the yucca rope tied around it and opened it. The bag contained many dried ears of corn that Nínáánibaa' baked in an earthen oven before they were forced to leave their home. Her favorite grinding stones were also in it, which added to the weight of the bag.

"Nihighan táádayooshchxǫ' yę́ę binaagóó díí nitsédaashjéé' dóó nitsédaashchíín ch'ééh hanétą́ą́'. Sháhanii háida nee yineez'į́į' lá ni. 'Akóne' nooh shíníłchį́į́ léi' t'áadoo nits'á'nídéel da, shiyázhí. T'áá 'ákónéehee 'íinidzaa lá." *I tried in vain to look for these grinding stones around our home that was destroyed. I thought someone had stolen them from you. You did not lose them because you placed them in your secret hiding space, my little one. It is a good thing you did that.*

"Eidíga', *I know,* was all Nínáánibaa' could say in answer to her husband's compliments. Hashké Yił Naabaah brought out the many-colored ears of corn. In the dim light of the evening, he placed the identical colored ears of corn in neat stacks. He deeply admired his Nínáánibaa' for the effort she put into their survival in anticipation of times of hardship and difficulty.

"Níníłt'ánée łeeh dashołbéézh dóó shą́ą'jį' ninínil, dadoogą́ął biniiyé, 'áádóó shinoo' íishłaa. Nihich'į' náhodiyii'náa'go nihich'iiyą' nilį́į doo nisingo, nít'ę́ę' niik'ehę́ę nihich'į' ákóhoodzaa." *Those are part of your harvest that you all baked in an earthen oven. I dried them in the sun and hid them away in my secret place. It was in preparation for the difficult times I thought we might face, which is what truly happened to us.*

"Honíyóí lá, shiyázhí, *You are a hard worker, my little one,* was all Hashké Yił Naabaah could say in a hoarse whisper. He pulled Nínáánîbaa' close to him and embraced her tightly. After replacing the sticks and branches over the entrance to Nínáánîbaa''s storage area, they scooped fresh earth back on top and placed the heavy rocks on top to completely hide the storage pit.

"Ádínáasjį' nitsísíníkéezgo binahjį' doo dichin biih díníidah da. Ahéhee'. Asdzání 'ílíinii nílį́. Kónááhoot'éhí naadą́ą' dóó naayízí dóó ch'ééh jiyáán dóó nímasii dóó naa'ółí nihidá'ák'eh bii' yíl'áa dooleeł. T'áá ni nínízinjį' nánídį́įh doo. *Because of your thoughtfulness, we will not fall into hunger. Thank you. You are a respected woman. Next year at this time, we will have corn and squash and melons and potatoes and beans in abundance in our cornfield.* Hashké Yił Naabaah picked up the heavy bag and placed it on his back then placed one arm around Nínáánîbaa' and led her to their brush arbor. He gently placed the bag on the floor, knowing the grinding stones were sacred to his Nínáánîbaa'. He sat down and wobbled over on the floor.

Their children jumped up to see the contents of the bag when Nínáánídbaa' brought them out one by one. Dzáníbaa' ran her fingers over the smooth face of the grinding stones. Tears pooled in her eyes. She wondered if she could still grind corn evenly, the way her mother strictly taught her. "Could I sing the Corn Grinding Song my mother taught me?" she wondered. In a whisper, she promised,

"Yiskáągo bááh dootł'izhí shimá dóó shizhé'é dóó niha'áłchíní bá 'ádeeshłííł. Dabíni' shaazh daazlį́'ę́ę nídadoodzih biniiyé. Dabits'íís txídadidzaa yę́ę nídadoodzih biniiyé. T'áá nihí nihich'iiyą' deidooyį́įł. Dichin nihits'ádooldoh, éí biniiyé yiskáągo ch'iiyáán ádeeshłííł." *Tomorrow, I will make some blue corn bread for my mother and my father and for our children. Their minds which have been bruised will heal. Their bodies which were tortured will heal. They will eat our own food. Hunger will move away from us, that is the reason I will prepare food tomorrow.*

The next morning, long before the sun's rays punctured the eastern horizon, Dzáníbaa' woke up to begin her day of food preparation. She asked her husband to get Kiizhóní and her brothers to join him in hunting for cottontail rabbits.

"Chizh dó' ła' nídadohjih," *Bring some firewood also,* she said, pointing to the firewood that was depleted.

"Tó 'ałdó' ła' nihá 'ádííłííł," *Also, obtain some water for us,* she said pointing to her husband's tin cans he used to get water when they lived among his people at Fort Sumner.

"Áádóó díí dó' ła' shá nídííjih," *And bring some of these back for me,* she said pointing to cedar branches. "Didoodlił dóó choideesh'įįł." *I will burn it and use the ashes,* she said pointing to cedar branches. Her husband smiled at her and nodded at each one of her requests. In his low sensuous voice, he said,

"Hágoshį́į́," *Okay,* before he left their brush arbor. Dzáníbaa' brushed her long black hair and tied it in a tsiiyéél *hair bun* and washed her face before she left to go to her mother's brush arbor. She heard her father holler,

"Sha'áłchíní, dighádóhjeeh. Deiyínółyeedgo dadołwosh. Háni'dii nihiTaa' nihidiits'į́įh. Bich'į' ahééh danohsįįh. Áłchíní, nihí dó' nídohjeeh. Nikídadoł'is. Áádóó ch'éédasoodzidgo shikéé' deiyínółyeedgo dighádidiijah." *My children, run toward the east. As you run, yell. Let our Spiritual Father hear you. Give thanks to Him. Children, you too, get up. Shuffle your feet in one place. Once you wake up, run after me as we run toward the east.* Nínááníbaa' smiled with tears running down her face. She knew her husband had missed his early morning ritual which included running and yelling and praying to their Creator. She had missed hearing her husband encouraging his sons to run with him. She watched her grandsons and her young adopted children shuffle their feet to let the earth know of their presence. She heard her little ones yelling high pitched yells as they ran after their maternal grandfather.

"Háshinee', shiyázhí danohłínígíí, *Dear ones, those of you who are my little ones,* she said as she held her thoughts of them close to her heart. To Hashké Yił Naabaah, she said,

"Háshinee', hastiin ílíinii nílį́." *Dear one, you are a man who is respected.*

****

Dzáníbaa' greeted her mother with a gentle hug then opened the thick woven bag and took out several ears of blue corn. Kneeling down on the soft dirt floor, she rubbed two ears of corn against the other to remove all the corn kernels. She placed the faded blue corn kernels on the smooth surface of her mother's large grinding stone. She picked up the narrow thin, flat rock and placed it at the top of the grinding stone. A neat pile of blue corn kernels lay before her, ready to be ground into blue corn meal.

She thought of the words to the Corn Grinding Song her mother sang whenever she ground corn.

"Ajik'áago díí sin bee nizhdi'a'go doo ch'ééh a'didáah da. *When a person sings this song, she will not tire easily,* she whispered as she reverently crushed the corn kernels between the two grinding stones. Several times Dzáníbaa' paused her singing. With tears rolling down her face she gave her mother a helpless look.

"Ha'di'deesh'áłę́ę saad beesénah, shimá. Hastą́ą́ nááhai yę́ędą́ą́' t'áá niyiin sidéts'ą́ą́' nít'ę́ę́'. Shá ha'dí'aah áko nikék'ehgóó ni'dish'a' doo." *I want to sing, but I forgot the words, my mother. It has been six years since I heard your song. Start singing the song for me and I will sing along with you.*

"T'óó shił naahojoobá'íyee', shiyázhí," *I have much compassion for you, my little one,* her mother answered.

With tears in her eyes, Nínááníbaa' led her daughter in singing the Corn Grinding Song. With a big smile on her face, Dzáníbaa' placed the neat pile of soft ground blue corn flour before her mother and announced,

"Shimá, k'ad bááh dootł'izhí ła' ná 'ádeeshłííł." *Now my mother, I will make you some blue corn bread.* Tears were streaming down Nínááníbaa''s face. She loved her daughters so much. With sobs choking her, all Nínááníbaa' could say was,

"Ahéhee', shiyázhí. *Thank you, my little one.* Mother and daughter gazed into each other's eyes as tears spilled over. Nínááníbaa' finally added,

"Bááh dootł'izhí doo ts'íí'át'éégóó bídin sélįį' nít'ęę́'. Ná didishjeeh. Aadęę́' gad bits'áoz'a' didoodlił biniiyé nihich'į' yigééł." *I have desperately missed the taste of blue corn bread. I will build a fire for you. They are bringing cedar branches to burn.*

"I will make the best blue corn bread for my mother. My mother will continue to heal," Dzáníbaa' promised herself.

Hashké Yił Naabaah and Dzáníbaa''s husband stepped into the brush arbor carrying twelve prairie dogs wrapped in juniper branches. Hashké Yił Naabaah heard Nínááníbaa' and Dzáníbaa' singing.

"Nihiyiin bee nida'doh'a'go nihikéyah yididoots'į́įł, áko ayóó 'át'éego bił yá'át'éeh doo. Bii' hááhwiildóóh shįį nahalinígi 'át'įįh. Doo kǫ́ǫ nideiikaigóó hastą́ą nááhai. Nihikéyah yéego nihíhoosa'. Nihiyiin dóó nihisodizin yididoots'į́łęę, yíhásáahgo bí dó' t'áá nihígi 'át'éego bíni' shaazh silį́į́'. Díí łid nidi yiłchin. Yaa bił hózhǫ́. Nihikéyah iiná biih náályá. K'ad bidziil nídoodleeł. *When you sing your songs, our land will hear it, and greatly appreciates it. Our land is beginning to feel relief. We were not here for six years. Our land greatly missed us. It missed our songs and our prayers and when it did not hear them, just like us, its mind became bruised. The land even smells the smoke from the fire. It is glad. Life has been placed back into our land. Now it will become strong once again.*

Dzáníbaa' jumped up and ran to her father. She was so excited to see that each member of the family would have one prairie dog to eat. She was so relieved knowing she did not have to eat the food of the enemy any more. Her father hugged her back and said,

"Nihił dahózhǫ́ǫ le'. Dlǫ́ǫ́' dóó gah dóó bįįh łą́ągo nidaajeeh. Kéyah bide'ádzaa nít'ę́ę́' lá. Nihilį́į́' náhodoodleełgo 'át'é. Dibé bitsį' hólǫ́ǫ doo, nihimá tł'ízí bibe' néídlį́įh doo..." *Be glad. There are a lot of prairie dogs and rabbits and deer running about. They overpopulated the land. We will have livestock once again. We will have mutton, your mother will drink goat's milk...* Not wanting her family to become dependent on meat the way many of her people were at Fort Sumner, Nínááníbaa' interrupted her husband because she wanted her young grandsons and her young adopted children to learn to live off of the land.

"Doo dichin nihidooghą́ął da. Nihinaagóó nanise' daadánígíí t'óó'ahayóí yíl'á. 'Éí dó' nihich'iiyą' ádaat'é." *We will not starve. We are surrounded by an abundance of edible plants. Those will be our food as well.*

After the prairie dogs had been cleaned, singed and placed in the hot earth under a large fire, Dzáníbaa' pulled soft clusters of leaves off of the cedar branches the men brought home. She burned the leaves over a wide flat stone. When the soft ash fell onto the stone, she gently brushed them aside to be cleaned, sifted and mixed with water, a mixture that would be added to the soft ground blue corn to make beautiful round, tasty blue bread for her family. While the prairie dogs were baking and the blue bread was being prepared, Nínáánibaa' and her daughter-in-law Tsék'iz Naazbaa' went to collect cactus fruit, yucca fruit, wild spinach, and wild carrots and prepared them to add to their feast.

It was midmorning when the family was called to gather at Nínáánibaa''s brush arbor. Hashké Yił Naabaah was dizzy with excitement when he said,

"Áda'azįįd la'! Da' baa neiiseełísh?" *There is a feast! Am I dreaming?* to which Nínáánibaa' softly said,

"Dinohbįįh, sha'áłchíní." *Sit down, my children.* She glanced at Hashké Yił Naabaah to let him know it was time to say a prayer of gratitude for their tasty provision. His prayer was long and contained so much emotion which left every family member in tears.

The children all waited for Nínáánibaa' to announce,

"Da'ohsą́," *All of you, eat,* before they attacked their fat delicious prairie dog. With fat from the meat, running down their wrists and arms, the children ate without speaking a word. Nínáánibaa' listened to the sound of each family member smacking their lips. It was a beautiful sound to her ears. When the family had consumed their meal, Dzáníbaa' brought forth her soft round blue corn bread. All Hashké Yił Naabaah could say was,

"Doo lá dó' nizhóní da." *It is beautiful.* He took a perfectly round, flat blue corn bread. Everyone reverently placed the bread before them and waited for Nínáánîbaa' to take the first taste. They laughed when she said,

"Doo 'a'jółtsódígi 'áhálniih. Ayóó 'áhálniih, shiyázhí. Ahéhee', nihaa jiisíníba'." *It is so delicious I do not want to share it with anyone. It is delicious, my little one. Thank you for blessing us.* Smiling and looking at Dédii, she said,

"Dédii 'éí bíla' néidiłi'go bideezhí bááh yá náyiyooniłgo yee 'áká'eelwod." *Dédii helped but she burned her fingers each time she turned the bread over.* Dédii smiled and held up her ash-darkened hand. The family giggled at her. Hashké Yił Naabaah looked at Nínáánîbaa' and his family and quietly said,

"Ahéhee', ayóó 'áhálniihgo nihits'ą́ą́' íiyą́ą́', sha'áłchíní, *Thank you, you fed me a delicious meal, my children.* Turning to the little ones, he said,

"Shooh, sha'áłchíní, nihí dó', kódaohnééh. *Look, my children, you do the same.* He rubbed his hands together then rubbed his hands on his legs, calves, and ankles and said,

"K'ad lą́ą, ayóo dinishwo' dooleeł. Ayóo honishyóí dooleeł." *Now, I will run real fast. I will be useful.* Nínáánîbaa' was tickled at her grandsons who were mimicking her husband's words and actions. She wiped away a tear and breathed a silent prayer of gratitude to the Creator.

****

The next day, led by Hashké Yił Naabaah, the men left their brush arbors long before the sun appeared over the eastern horizon. Each man carried a sharp hatchet they had made. They would not have to go far to obtain cedar logs for the four large hogans they planned to build. The trees were in plentiful supply all around. The chore was very tedious. Long heavy logs were brought back to the cleared area where their brush arbors stood. Their former homes that were destroyed were on the other side of the high hill.

With all the logs stacked high near the places where Nínáánibaa', her daughters, and her daughters-in-law selected for their hogans to be built, the men and boys busied themselves, carefully constructing each hogan, beginning with Nínáánibaa"s home first. Just as their culture dictated, each home was built in one day. The men worked hard from when the sun pierced the eastern horizon to when the sun nearly touched the western horizon at the end of the day.

Hashké Yił Naabaah was pleased that his plan worked. In taking his sons and his grandsons along with him when he went to reconstruct his people's homes, they were learning the craft of building a hogan. In repairing and constructing new homes, he wanted his sons and grandsons to become proficient in constructing a hogan before they built their own homes. Under the watchful eye and strict instructions of Haské Yił Naabaah and the old man, the four hogans the boys and young men built were breathtakingly beautiful. Nínáánibaa' and her daughters took their meager belongings into their respective hogans after their homes were blessed.

Dédii clasped her hands to her chest when she placed her few belongings on the dirt floor of her hooghan *home*. Just for a minute, her thoughts turned to the tall gray-haired one. She shook her head, danced her little dance by stomping her feet, then walked outside to send thoughts of him away from her home.

That night with her son and all her adopted children sleeping on the floor of her new home, Dédii felt richly blessed. The old man took over her brush arbor along with Tł'ée'go Naabaah, her youngest brother.

Dédii took a deep breath, then another, and another... She closed her eyes tightly and took another deep breath. She thought back to the few previous evenings when she watched Kiizhóní braiding a large rectangular mat using yucca leaves. The family teased him whenever they watched him braid and weave the thick mat.

"Doósh t'áá ni'góó nániilkáah da?" *Don't you sleep on the ground?* they teased. Kiizhóní would smile and continue weaving and braiding more yucca leaves into the mat.

The hogans were built with new logs and fresh earth. The fresh scent of newly cut cedar logs, stripped of their bark, and the fertile scent of moist fresh clean earth mixed with dry weeds made Dédii dizzy with happiness. She could smell the sensuous scent of yucca when she breathed in again. She remembered she was so surprised and pleased when Kiizhóní hung the yucca leaf mat he had been weaving and braiding over her doorway. She smiled when she glanced toward the doorway. She felt safe in her new home with Kiizhóní and her children. The promise of a bright future met her nostrils every time she breathed in the scent of cedar logs and yucca roots. She took a deep breath just before she closed her eyes to go to sleep.

****

Dzáníbaa' loved to listen to her father's stories. The men were still sitting around a fire outside, telling stories. Her husband was learning her language very quickly. She could hear his low sensuous voice rise and fall as he told short stories about his people. She listened to her favorite sounds, that of her husband's voice and the sound of her little one sleeping soundly near her. The fire her husband built for her, before he went to join the men, crackled and lit the interior of her beautiful hogan.

Her home was cozy. From the firelight, she could see the beautiful geometrical shapes the cedar logs created, resulting from the way they were placed to create the domed roof. Longer logs were strategically placed on the walls of the hogan to serve as the base for the domed roof. The shape of the domed roof was created by placing shorter logs on top of the longer logs until only short stout logs could be seen at the top of the dome with an opening for the smoke to exit the hogan.

The sweet smell of the cedar logs relaxed her and invited her to drift off to sleep. She loosened her tsiitł'óół *hair tie* and caught the scent of yucca root when she shook her hair loose. She placed her hand where her husband sleeps and drifted off into a deep sleep.

The sound of her husband's sensuous voice woke her when he softly said,

"Hágo, Záanii." *Come here.* He pulled her close to him and wrapped his arms around her. She heard him softly say,

"Ummmmmm," when she pressed her body against his muscular body. He spoke soft words to her in his beautiful Mescalero Apache language.

****

Nínáánibaa' admired the handiwork of her husband. Her hogan was more beautiful and larger than the one he built for her days before they married. She heard him laughing. He was outside sitting with his sons, Kiizhóní, his Mescalero Apache son-in-law and the old man they all called "shicheii". They sat around a large fire. The fire illuminated their faces. Nínáánibaa' loved the sound of Hashké Yił Naabaah's laughter.

She looked around her home. She could not wait to shear their sheep so she could weave large rugs again. She counted on her fingers the number of years that had passed since she last wove. It was nearly six years. When Hashké Yił Naabaah was collecting cedar logs for her hogan, he also obtained a log with beautiful reddish-brown hues that appeared in graceful lines on the flat surface of the wood. He told her he was going to use the wood to make her a loom and various tools required for weaving. She was always amazed at her husband's talents and his meticulous workmanship. She rubbed her hands together. She could not wait to feel the woolen yarns sliding through her fingers. She could picture the design she wanted to place in the next rug she would weave.

She heard her husband approaching. He brought in a hot pot of newly boiled goat's milk. In his other hand, he held out a perfectly round blue corn bread her daughters made.

"Na', shiyázhí. Tł'ízí bibe' ła' ná shéłbéézh dóó díí bááh dootł'izhí ná 'ąąsésiid. Háánílyįįh. Hodíínáá'ígo nił yah anídeeshdááł. Iidiilwosh." *Here, my little one. I boiled some goat's milk for you and I saved this blue corn bread for you. Rest. I will come back in a little while. We will go to sleep.*

Nínááníbaa' sat by the fire, warming herself. She took her time sipping the delicious hot goat's milk. She could hear the soft sounds of the sheep and goats in their corral. Feeling relaxed and satisfied, she prepared their rug blankets, placing them side by side.

"Doo lá dó' shí da. 'Ahéhee', shiTaa'," *How blesed I am. Thank you my Spiritual Father,* she whispered when she untied her hair and watched it fall around her. She felt sleep creeping up on her. Taking a deep breath filled with the scent of cedar and yucca, she whispered,

"Hodéezyéél... Hodéezyéel la'..." *Peace. It is peaceful.* She knew her daughters Dédii and Dzáníbaa' and her daughters-in-law Tsék'iz Naazbaa' and Akéé' Naazbaa' were feeling the same emotions, that of contentment and peace and safety.

"Hooghandi nániikai," *We have come home,* she whispered just before she fell asleep. She heard her Hashké Yił Naabaah whisper,

"Aoo', hooghandi nániikai." *Yes, we have come home.* She turned to him and asked,

"Ádíshiiłtsóód." *Hold me.* Her husband took her in his arms and offered his arm as her pillow. She heard him whisper,

"Háshinee'," *Dear one,* just before he drifted off to sleep.

****

The light of day was only a sliver above the eastern horizon when Hashké Yił Naabaah called his sons and grandsons, asking them to join him in their morning run toward the east. She listened to the sound of their footsteps as they bravely ran. Nínáánībaa' thought, "The land felt the feet of my husband and my sons and my grandsons, as well as the feet of my sons-in-law, pressing into it as they ran toward the east to greet the dawn this morning." She knew her land would hear her husband saying,

"Nikídadoł'is. Nikídadoł'is. Nikídadoł'isgo nihikéyah nihaa 'áhoniizįįh." *Shuffle your feet. Shuffle your feet. When you shuffle your feet, our land becomes aware of our presence.*

"Háshinee'," *Dear ones,* she whispered.

A little later that morning, she heard her father and the old man, the one Dédii calls "shicheii", singing and voicing prayers to the Creator once again. She listened.

She knew it was the sounds her land yearned to hear for four long years.

"Háshinee'," *Dear ones,* she whispered.

After feeding her little ones at her breast, she kissed them softly and put them down to sleep. She turned to her loom. She loved the beautiful design she was weaving into the beautiful leader's blanket she was weaving for her husband. She lifted the rug blanket that covered the entrance into her home, she wanted her land to hear the sound of her weaving comb beating down on the thin yarns of wool as she wove. She also wanted her daughters and daughters-in-law to hear the distinct sound. It was an invitation for them to weave. She listened, she could hear her daughters and daughters-in-law weaving.

"Háshinee'," *Dear ones,* she whispered.

After returning from their morning run, Nínááníbaa' heard her husband teaching her sons and grandsons the art of making bows and arrows. In testing their creation, she heard arrows leaving the taut bow as the young ones practiced the art of hunting. She knew her husband and sons would go hunting later that day. Their beautiful land would hear the arrows split away from the taut bows and race toward the heart of an animal the men killed for food. She licked her lips. In hunting, they are preserving my sheep and goats, she whispered.

"Háshinee'," *Dear ones,* she whispered.

In the early spring, Nínááníbaa' reminded her husband who had been working in his dá'ák'eh *cornfield* with his sons, "Our land felt the tools that you and your sons pressed into the ground when you were preparing the dá'ák'eh *cornfield* for the planting of the corn," she remembered

"Háshinee' dó' ádaoht'į́. Nihikéyah nihaa 'ákoniizį́į́'." *Dear ones as you do that. Our land has become aware of your presence.*

When her grandchildren and her daughters-in-law took their sheep and goats out of the corral and led them to the nearby hill, she heard the bleating of their flock.

"Méééeeee', Méeee', Mé'é'é'é'é."

"Háshinee'," *Dear ones,* she whispered with a smile on her lips.

Nínááníbaa' heard her babies crying. She picked them up and carried them to the doorway to expose them to the sun. With their little tongues quivering, they cried loud hungry cries. She soothed them through the words she spoke. They quieted and listened.

"Wohchago, nihikéyah nihidiits'a'." *When you cry, our land hears you.* She kissed her babies and whispered,

"Háshinee', shiyázhí nohłíinii. Ayóó'ánihíínísh'ní." *Dear ones, you who are my little ones. I love you.*

"All these sounds and activities are strengthening our land. Our land has welcomed us home. It is the faithfulness of us, the elders in teaching the Naabeehó youth their culture, their traditions and lifestyle that is helping our land between our four sacred mountains recognize us as Naabeehó people. Our land will become productive again. Just as we are no longer suffering, our land is no longer suffering because it is hearing the sounds of our children laughing, eating, crying, and sleeping."

"Háshinee'," *Dear one,* she whispered as her eyes swept across the landscape before her.

Chapter Eighteen

Healing

The Naabeehó people valued their children. It was the cries and pitiful pleas of the children that forced strength into the hearts of the Naabeehó men who were stripped of their traditional roles when they became prisoners of war. The men were free to restore their role of being the protector of family and land, the hunter, the provider, the planter of corn, the spiritual leader, the bearer of songs and prayers, the sustainer of life, the keeper of winter stories, the keeper of laughter, and the keeper of culture.

It was the heartbreaking cries and pitiful pleas of the babies, children, and elders that forced strength into the hearts of the Naabeehó women who were also stripped of their traditional roles when they became prisoners of war. The women anxiously began to restore their role as that of the bearer of life, insulator of the family, the weaver, the protector of cultural protocol, the gatherer of food, the provider of comfort and courage, the giver of language, the keeper of sheep and goats, the keeper of fire, and the keeper of the home.

****

All these sounds and activities strengthened the land as it lifted its weary head when it heard the sounds of its people. More importantly, the land heard the Naabeehó language being spoken by the children, adults, and the elders.

With open arms the land gladly welcomed its Naabeehó people home. When the Naabeehó people entered their beloved land, they knew they had walked back into life. The land made a promise to its people that it would lovingly protect them for generations to come.

Acknowledgements

Shité’ázíní My close relatives

I thank the Lord daily for placing me in the home of my mother and my father. My mother was from Crownpoint, New Mexico and my father was from Hardrock, Arizona. Their generous recollection of historical events presented me with a rich rendition of Navajo history.

My father encouraged me to search for the truth of our history among my people. I remember his words well when he told me,

"Nidine’é náás daazlį́’ígíí nákéé’ náháne’ ayóo bił béédahózin. Nákéé’ náháne’ yínáskai, yii’ naaskai, ’éí beego nákéé’ náháne’ yee nił dahalne’ígíí ba’íínílí." Your elders know their history very well. They were immersed in it, they walked in it, therefore, trust their stories. My father also made sure I expanded my knowledge of my Navajo culture which placed me in an advantageous position for when I taught Navajo History, Navajo Language and Culture classes at Northern Arizona University. Now I present the last of the four novels in the Her Land, Her Love series, which are based upon Navajo history and Navajo culture and told partly through the Navajo language.

I thank the Lord daily for my wonderful precious children and my granddaughter. Although they never met their maternal grandfather, and my two youngest children never met both of their maternal grandparents, it is through these stories which appear on the pages of these novels that my children have met their maternal grandparents as well as their maternal great grandmother and my granddaughter has met her great maternal grandparents and great, great maternal grandmother.

I so appreciate my daughter, Naomi, who took time out of her busy schedule to edit several versions of my story. Her valuable suggestions enriched my story and additions were made to make it more appealing to the younger generation.

Shíká'íijé'ígíí Those who helped me.

Although the subject of the Navajo Long Walk was a painful memory, I had the special privilege of having relatives who were generous in sharing information with me. I was always excited to find a historical document that reiterated the telling of historical events shared with me by my father, my mother, my maternal grandmother, and my relatives. The documents confirmed I could trust Navajo oral history.

The list of my relatives include:

My precious aunt Rose Claw, my precious cousins Jane Horseson Benally, and the late Marilyn Nez whose. mothers were immediate family members to my father. They remained a source of wisdom, knowledge, encouragement, and support from the beginning.

These precious elders offered wisdom, where I heard my father's stories in their words:

My brother Clarence Blackrock, Sr. (Cactus Valley) and my sister Maxine Kescoli (Forest Lake) and my cousin Bahe Manybeads (Rocky Ridge) confirmed my father regarding the oral history of the Navajo Long Walk.

My dear sister, my cousin Bessie Morris from Mexican Springs, New Mexico confirmed my mother's stories and was a gentle source of encouragement.

Shik'is dóó bił ałhéédahonisziníģíí My dear friends and people I know:

Dr. Margaret Speas was the first person to read my novel when it was first written. She encouraged me to submit it for publishing.

My sister, Lydia Lowe offered to help me drive over six thousand miles during the times when we traveled to conduct research to visit places of significance that were written about in these stories and these novels. Lydia remained a source of strength and kindness during the writing process.

My sister Ruth Van Otten was a source of kind words, graceful strength and encouragement.

Mr. Joe Kee Jr., also one of my first readers, offered a resounding word of support for these novels. "The young Navajos need to know what our people went through," he said.

Dr. Laura Tohe and Luci Tapahonso inspire me with their work.

My Native Harvest Christian Church family and our faithful pastor Rev. Dennis Benale offered support through their prayers and words of encouragement.

Many of my former students of Navajo have offered kind words regarding my written work.

Nearly twenty five years ago I first met Dr. Robert Young at Tsaile on the Navajo Nation. At the time, I was working on my doctoral dissertation and Dr. Young asked me what my areas of research were besides the topic of reasons for language loss. Upon learning I was planning to write a novel (Navajo and English) on the Navajo Long Walk, he clapped his hands and smiled his friendly smile and said, "I'm glad a Navajo is writing the story and it is going to be a bilingual story." He was even more excited to learn my immediate and primary sources were my father and my maternal grandmother and Navajo elders. He inspired me with his reaction and his kind words of encouragement.

Ahéhee' Thank you to the many Naabeehó elders who just happened to talk about an incident regarding the Long Walk of their people or who spoke one word which became a topic upon which the framework for a chapter was built within these novels.

Shinaaltsoos hadilnéehgi shíká 'íįjé'ígíí Ones who made my novels possible

I am so grateful to Salina Bookshelf, Inc. for believing in my work where my manuscript was brought to fruition as not only one novel but four novels. Mr. Eric Lockard (publisher) and Dr. Louise Lockard and Corey Begay (Art Director) handled my written work and the stories of my Navajo elders with great care, integrity and respect.

Eric Lockard

In publishing this novel titled Their Land, Their Love The Return Home within the Her Land, Her Love series, Eric has increased his level of commitment and contribution to the Naabeehó people in helping to maintain and preserve the Navajo language and culture and to protect Navajo history. Eric truly is a loyal friend to our elder, the Navajo language.

Corey Begay

Corey spent endless hours formatting my manuscript to place it in the form of a novel. He was meticulous in his formatting and worked tediously to produce this novel that brings honor to our Naabeehó elders.

Dr. Louise Lockard

Dr. Lockard read and edited my novel which made the editing process meaningful and enjoyable.

LaFrenda Frank

As an editor for Salina Bookshelf, Inc., LaFrenda decided the manuscript I submitted should actually be divided into four stories, four novels. She and I identified the main characters to whom each novel would be dedicated and that led to Her Land, Her Love and Her Enemy, Her Love and Her Captive, Her Love and finally Their Land, Their Love The Return Home. I deeply appreciate LaFrenda's role in this decision.

Scott Smith

Scott Smith who was formerly employed as a Park Ranger at Fort Sumner took time out of his busy day each time I visited the State Park to show me various points of interest and to answer my many questions with ease. I know Scott as a prolific writer and researcher as well as a knowledgeable source of valuable information that I could trust. I always felt safe with his responses regarding the Navajo Long Walk and the conditions of the imprisonment of my Navajo people of old.

Doug Eury

Doug Eury is a retired Superintendent of the National Park Service and formerly from Tijeras, New Mexico. Doug was extremely helpful in identifying the "Water Route" the Navajo people of old traveled through on their return to Diné bikéyah Navajo land from Fort Sumner. The road to his home in Tijeras from Albuquerque gave me insight to the treacherous but beautiful terrain my people of old traveled through.

Naabeehó Youth

I wrote these novels to share with Navajo youth the truth about their history as told by their Navajo elders. I wanted also to inform them about the strength of their ancestors and their Navajo teaching. These novels present the painful history of our people in the form of a love story to illustrate the strength of love in the survival of an individual, a family, and a people. My goal was also to instill within Navajo youth and Navajos of all ages pride for their people, knowing they come from strong stock.

Naabeehó Sáanii Navajo women and girls

Elder Navajo women exemplify elegance, grace, and strength. It is also because of Navajo women that I decided to present a historical romance novel. After all, it was the strength of Navajo women that helped our ancestors survive such desperate and destitute times during their status as prisoners of war at Fort Sumner.